Mr. Drake and My Lady Silver
Tales of Aylfenhame, Book 4

Charlotte E. English

Copyright © 2018 Charlotte E. English

Cover art © 2018 Elsa Kroese

Illustrations © 2018 by the PicSees

All rights reserved.

ISBN: **9492824000**
ISBN-13: **978-9492824004**

CHAPTER ONE

Woah there, hold yer horses! Literal-like, I ain't using a figure o' speech. There, thas better, now we can have a comfortable coze for a minute or two. I won't invite ye t' get out o' yer carriage, not in weather like this! Has it been snowin' all yer journey through? Yer brave, t' make it all the way t' Tilby in this muck. Oh yes, I do live under the bridge. All the way under! Aye, I thank ye, it's cosier than ye might expect. Mayhap I'll show it to you, sometime.

Seein' as the weather's so foul, I won't charge me usual toll t' pass the bridge. Nay, don't thank me. I may look fearsome, but there's nowt t' fear from this old troll. Ask anybody in these parts, they'll tell you right enough. Old Mister Balligumph, ye've no cause t' be scared-like o' him.

I do talk on a bit, though, no denyin' that. But what's better than a tale t' liven up a chilly winter's afternoon? Comin' from Lincoln-way, are ye? I know a fine tale from them parts. Took place not so long ago, in point o' fact. Care t' hear it? It won't take long, an' with just a little magic — there! — ye'll find yer carriage plenty warm an' snug fer the duration. Nay, don't thank me.

All right, then. This tale is about a young chap wi' the fine name of Phineas Drake. He worked in his father's bakery-shop, and 'twas on a day rather like this one tha' some strange events came t' pass. Come to think of it, 'twas Winter Solstice, an' very almost Christmas…

***

The cathedral bells chimed the fourth hour of the morning, and before the ringing sound had died away, Phineas Drake was out of bed and shivering in the piercing cold. He washed with haste, breaking the ice which coated the surface of his wash-basin to reach the frigid water beneath, and dressed as quickly as he could with fingers that shook with cold.

He crept onto the landing and down the stairs, mindful not to incur his father's wrath by waking him at such an hour, and hastened into the kitchens at the rear of the building. Everything was already laid out for him: bags of flour, pungent yeast, great basins to mix the dough in, and ewers of water. He had only to begin, and this he did with all possible dispatch, for while the shop would not open for a few hours yet, he would need every minute of that time to prepare the day's wares.

He set the great stone ovens afire first and stoked them well, for one long counter-top was crowded with wads of dough left to rise overnight, and ready now to be shaped and baked. These would make the morning meal for many of the workers of Lincoln, whose labours brought them out of bed at an early hour, and whose morning could be a little brightened by a fresh loaf.

Two hours flew by as Phineas formed loaves and rolls, mixed dough and ferried bread into the ovens. Then came the difficult part. While the final batch of the morning's wares was in the oven, he would have to leave the bakery in order to make his first deliveries: sugared plum-cakes and mince pies for those already living in happy anticipation of the season's festivities, and inclined to begin a little early. Phineas spared a thought to wish, as he frantically packed cakes and pies into boxes, that his father might spare the coin to hire a delivery boy. Phineas might then be able to resign the freezing duty, and properly tend to the ovens instead. Wishes proving as futile as ever, he abandoned the dream and set out into the snow.

Darkness still shrouded the city, and few were yet stirring abroad; he had a quiet, cold walk up to the top of the hill and into the Bail. The black skies were empty of snow, but a great deal had fallen overnight. It soon saturated the thick leather of his boots, and the wet cold seeped through to his toes.

Quite the largest plum cake he had ever made went to the Porters' household on Newport, and three boxes of mince-pies to smaller houses along the way. By the time he had retraced his steps and passed back towards the Cathedral, he had only one box left: a meagre parcel with a small cake, two pies and a fresh loaf for the

Trent sisters on Pottergate. Miss Trent would be waiting to accept it in person, however early the hour, and Phineas hastened along, mindful both of Miss Trent's eager anticipation and of the bread still baking at home. The cathedral loomed to his left, dark and silent, its spires glinting with the soft light of a moon not quite set. There was no sound save the crunching of fresh snow underfoot and therefore, Phineas was doubly surprised to discover that he was not, after all, alone.

A woman hurried through the darkness some little way ahead of him. She was almost running, splendidly oblivious to the inclement weather, except to keep pushing her wind-tossed hair out of her pale face. That hair was beautiful, but strange: a tangled cloud, too pallid for her apparent youth, for her frame was lithe and her movements sprightly; this was no elderly lady. She wore only a thin gown of some gauzy substance, its style not at all after the fashions of the day, and an airy cloak which streamed uselessly from her shoulders. How she had not already frozen to death was the thought uppermost in Phineas's mind, until she swept past him — without seeming to notice him — and he saw that her ears were curled at their tips.

'Wait!' she called.

'I—' said Phineas, but she had not been addressing him, for she ran on, heedless.

'Please, wait!' she cried again.

Phineas wondered if he had, perhaps, fallen asleep over the warmth of the ovens and merely dreamed his expedition abroad; it would not be the first time if he had. He opened the lid of the Misses Trents' box of cakes and inhaled, filling his nose with the scents of brandy-soaked fruit, and sugar, and bread. Too rich to be dreamt, all that, and oh dear, that meant the lady was real, too, however peculiar her ears, or her attire, or for that matter her conduct. 'Madam?' he blurted, and set off after her. 'M'lady? Pray, pay some heed to the weather! You will catch your death of cold!' He was half-frozen himself in spite of his sturdier garments, and his lips were numb; the words emerged in stammers, half-garbled, and the winds perhaps stole whatever coherence was left, for the lady did not stop.

Clutching his box to his chest, Phineas followed, uncertain how he was to help but unable to abandon her to the merciless cold. She flitted through the silent streets, always ahead of him no matter how fast he moved, and darted into the sloping mouth of the Greestone

Stairs.

By the time Phineas arrived at the top of the hill, she was already halfway down it, almost beyond his sight. He frowned, bemused, for there came a flicker of movement which did not seem to belong to the lady, and even in the pale moonlight he could discern traces of richer colours which made no part of her attire: crimson, perhaps, or purple. It was a mantle of some sort, he would have said, worn by a man of stooped posture, for he was remarkably small. But it could not be another person, for the shape abruptly vanished, as though the mantle and its wearer had turned a corner, or passed through a door.

The street was lined on either side by impassable walls, and there were no doors there.

'M'lady?' he called again, desperate now, for a light snow was once again drifting serenely out of the leaden skies and her arms were bare from elbow to wrist. Had she come, perhaps, from some dinner engagement, and forgotten to collect her warm cloak and bonnet as she left? 'If you are in need of aid, please consider me your servant!'

And, at last, she heard him, for she came to an abrupt halt upon the hill and turned. She stared at Phineas, eyes wide and surprised, as though it were he and not she whose behaviour might be considered bizarre.

'I am sure I can help,' he said, approaching more slowly, for her manner held something of the startled deer, and he did not wish to frighten her. 'Perhaps I might offer you my—'

He broke off, for though her gaze had met his for a mesmerising instant, and held, she had not spoken so much as a syllable in reply. She had turned her back on him again, and taken a step, and… she was gone, just like that, as though she, too, had stepped through a door.

Phineas approached with caution, step by step, until he stood in the very spot the lady had occupied moments before. There was no sign of her, and no apparent means of exit; the icy slope rose behind him and fell away ahead, empty. Naught remained of her save a set of small, narrow footprints in the snow… and something else. There came a glitter near his right boot, and a blush of soft colour.

Phineas stooped, and found a rose in full bloom, defying winter with the same insouciance as its mistress. Its petals were lavenderish, though so thickly crusted with frost that little of the hue showed.

It was only after Phineas had made his belated delivery to the Trents, and retraced his steps home, that he discovered just how unusual the rose was. For, when left safely upon the windowsill in his own small room — a chamber by no means warm, but much milder in temperature than the freezing winter outside — it lost none of its coating of frost. It glittered on, white and crystalline; and when, wondering, he picked it up again, a faint, sweet fragrance teased his senses.

'Sugar?' he breathed, unbelieving. But this surmise he discarded, for when he touched the tip of his tongue to one delicate petal, the frost was icily cold, and the flavour that filled his mouth was not sugar at all.

He set the rose carefully down and stood a moment in thought, as though a prolonged scrutiny of the mysterious flower might persuade it to surrender its secrets. But no answer could he find to the puzzle of the vanishing lady, or to the frosted rose, or to the door that wasn't there.

CHAPTER TWO

If ye've heard any of me tales afore — or, for that matter, even if ye haven't — ye might have a guess as t' where that lady came from, or went to. An Aylir out of Aylfenhame! Though what one o' the Aylf-folk was doin' roamin' the streets o' Lincoln at that hour, wi' snow all about and not a hat t' her name, well… listen on, an' I'll tell ye.

Despite the delay, Phineas returned in time to save the batch of loaves he had left in the oven. They were a fraction browner on the top than was typically considered ideal, but they were not burned. They would do.

He was mixing up a great bowl of fruit and meat for more pies when his father emerged, at last, from slumber. Phineas was adding spices, his favourite part of the process, for the aromas of nutmeg and cloves and mace filled the room, exotic and warming, and he had already the smells of citrus peel and apples and brandy to enjoy…

'You are adding too much,' said Samuel Drake, shattering Phineas's culinary reverie by appearing suddenly at the door. 'I should make you keep the books, Phineas. If you knew the price of nutmeg, perhaps you would not waste it.' He took a mouthful of fresh bread, one of those Phineas had just baked, and added with a sigh, 'You have burnt these.'

Phineas knew better than to hazard any answer, much less a defence of his conduct. He waited in silence, eyes lowered, as his father made a perfunctory effort to neaten his sleep-disordered hair, straightened his shirt and apron, and went forward to open the shop.

Once the kitchen was empty again save only for himself, Phineas quietly stored away the spices and went to work on the pastry. He heard his fathers' voice greeting the first of the day's customers; gruff and sour moments before, now it was raised in jovial good cheer. Samuel Drake had a reputation for a certain glib charm; it was one reason why their little shop had never yet failed.

The forceful accents of Mrs. Batts followed; as always, Phineas heard every word. '... that fine son of yours?' she was saying. 'You're a fine family, Mr. Drake. I fancy the young ladies would welcome a glimpse o' young Phineas a bit more often. And you'll want every advantage you can get what with — thank you, yes, *one* plum-cake, and just the two mince pies — what with that fine, new place openin' any day now.'

'One cake and the pies, then, Mrs. Batts, and a good white loaf — just taken out of the oven with my own hands!' There came the clink of coin, and only then did Samuel say, with studied casualness, 'What place might that be?'

'Why, fancy you not knowin'! There's to be a new pastry-shop up in the Bail. I had it from my sister's girl, whose young man is hired as baker's boy, soon as it opens. It's to be a grand place, so they say, though not so grand that folk like me ain't lookin' forward to a peep. We all like a little bit of the best now an' then, don't we? Thank you, Mr. Drake, that'll be all for now. Wishin' you good day.'

Mrs. Batts' voice faded, and it was some half an hour before the rush of customers ebbed enough to liberate the elder Mr. Drake from the shop. Phineas was amusing himself shaping roses from pastry, to adorn the new pies, but he hastily abandoned this at his father's reappearance, and returned to rolling out tops.

'Mind the shop,' Samuel said gruffly, and tore off his apron. This he threw in Phineas's general direction, and left the kitchen in three quick strides.

The shop door slammed behind him.

Phineas did not suppose that he had been promoted to the shop floor on Mrs. Batts' advice. More likely, his father had gone after news of the pastry-shop. Was it too much to hope that the report might be mere gossip alone, to be relied upon with as much confidence as the majority of Mrs. Batts' news? Alas, no. her authority appeared to be too sound to be dismissed, and it was not the sort of nonsense tale that usually got about.

A whisker of fear uncurled within, and Phineas shuddered. The Drake family bakery had withstood troubles enough; what would such daunting competition do to their business now?

And what might the prospect do to his father's temper?

Phineas tidied his own hair, donned a cleaner apron, and dusted the flour from his shirt. He tried his best to put the matter out of his mind, for the calls from the shop-floor indicated that he was in for a busy morning.

The morning wore away, and the light faded, until by the stroke of four it was dark once again. Phineas lit the lamps in the shop, and turned them low; his father said this made for a cosy, welcoming atmosphere, or at least that was what he said to the customers. But Phineas knew that it had more to do with the price of oil. For the kitchens and Phineas's own room there were only candles, all made from cheap, stinking tallow.

He was not obliged to remain in the shop all the day through, for those who went out to buy plum-cakes at the dawn of the day went home to enjoy them in the afternoon. He spent the quieter hours in the back, turning out pies; and, when he grew wearied of that, tending to the little frosted rose.

He had brought it into the kitchens with him early in the day, for he loved to look upon it, and it seemed wrong to him to leave so rare and lovely a thing alone and unappreciated upstairs. But it had begun to alter as the hours slipped by. The blush of lavender dimmed, and the glitter faded from its petals. He thought, fancifully, that perhaps it hated the dull glow and reeking stench of tallow-light as much as he did, but when he carried it into the shop it remained as it was; the purer, cleaner light of the oil-lamps could not restore its lustre.

It ought to be revived, he thought. He had no means of restoring that odd layer of chill frost, at least not by any lasting method. He did have sugar, however.

And the colour…

Phineas remembered, then, another such day at the end of autumn, when his father had been gone from the bakery for three days together. With a supply of sugar near at hand, an array of vegetables new-harvested which had been meant for his father's supper, and a head full of ideas, Phineas had made a joyous mess of the kitchen as he strove to invent a coarse, glittering sugar with colour enough to adorn some delicate piece of confectionery... he had hidden the results behind the flour-jars in the storeroom, lest his father should discover it and pronounce his efforts as Waste. There the little bags had lain ever since, mere cloth scraps tied tightly with string. The shop was empty and the street was quiet; Phineas hastened down into the cellar.

The colour had bled a little through the cloth, and the passage of a few weeks had inevitably faded the tints; his vibrant red had become an insipid pink, and his delicate purple a dull, washed-out grey; the latter he instantly threw away. But the blue, though dimmed, retained brilliance enough to please and he seized it, filled with a happy purpose, and returned to the kitchen.

He did not seek to dip every inch of the rose in the sugar, for he had not enough to coat it all over. The tips only he treated, and when he had finished he carried the rose forward once more to admire it in the lamplight.

He was pleased with the effect, for the mix of glittering-blue and dusty lavender now appeared elegant rather than lifeless; perhaps even a little magical, once again. Phineas left the rose on the windowsill, where he could see it, and took up his station behind the shop's counter in much better spirits.

He wondered whether his father would notice the flower upon his eventual return, and half-hoped, half-feared that he might. But when Samuel at last came home, it was after dark upon the following day, and very late; the shop was closed, and all the lamps were out. He did not greet Phineas, but went in heavy silence into his own bedchamber whereupon he slammed the door, his passage leaving the tiny landing reeking, fleetingly, of stale alcohol.

Phineas did not dare ask after the news; not then, and not the following morning when his father awoke, and lumbered down into the kitchen. Samuel barely spoke to his son at all, and took no note of his busy labours; his thoughts were elsewhere, and unpleasant they were, judging from the heavy frown which darkened his brow.

Phineas did not feel comfortable again for some time.

The eve before Christmas dawned, and still the rose lay untouched upon its chilly windowsill. It had not withered, to Phineas's interest, nor had it deteriorated any further at all. An intriguing puzzle, but Phineas had little time to think of it — or of the lady who had dropped it — for his father had driven him through a host of tasks with unusual urgency. He spent a whole afternoon cutting sprigs of holly and ivy, branches of laurel and hawthorn, and delicate boughs of evergreen; these he dispersed artfully about the bakery-shop until it looked properly festive. It took him another two hours in the freezing wind to find a sprig of mistletoe with which to fashion a kissing-bough, and by the time all these preparations were complete he was blue with cold. He had still, then, to stack the windows with sugared cakes — which, unusually, his father had permitted him to decorate as intricately as he chose; to set the wassail-bowl in pride-of-place, with bowls of apples to float in the punch come Christmas Day; to wrap plum-puddings in cloth, and prepare the great basins of water to cook them in.

Samuel Drake surveyed all this with a critical eye late in the evening, and by the light of the flickering lamps. Phineas expected some comment upon his profligacy, as might be usual. Instead, his father said, upon a moment's thought: 'It must be more inviting, Phineas. More...'

'More...?' Phineas ventured, when his father did not complete the sentence.

'I want no one to pass the door without coming inside.'

Phineas looked at everything he had done, and wondered. The room bristled with festive greenery; it was packed with sumptuous food, with decorations, with gaieties implied; it had not looked so delightful in years. 'How?' he said. 'What more can be done?'

'You have your mother's way with such things,' said Samuel simply.

Phineas did not try to point out that everything had been different in his mother's time. There had been both money and merriment, more than enough of both to fit the demands of the season. He merely went into the spice-jars, and took precious nutmegs and cinnamon sticks to add to the array — carefully, leaving them intact, so that they might later be reclaimed for use. He fetched his old, red shirt, the cloth worn but sound, that he had intended to wear through the days of Christmas, and cut it up for ribbons. And, heart heavy with regret, he pawned his mother's silver ring and used the money to buy an array of fine, beeswax candles, with which to deck the windows.

When all was done, Phineas fell exhausted into bed and slept the night away, his dreams a confused flurry of kissing-boughs and wine, cold sleet and wind, and his mother's reproachful face when she learned what he had done with her ring.

The rose lay forgotten, half-hidden beneath a spray of evergreen.

CHAPTER THREE

Phineas's work achieved its desired effects, at least for a time. The new candles blazed cheerfully in the windows, their bright flames beckoning chilled passers-by inside during the cold, dark hours; the vibrant greens, the crimson berries and ribbons, and the glimpse of the apple-laden wassail bowl performed the same work during the daylight hours, and Phineas knew that the heady aromas upon entry — the scents of bread and fruit, of meat and wine, and the spices he had hung all about — would keep his father's customers spellbound until they had partaken of some one or other of his wares.

Only, there were not enough of them. Whether it were the desultory flurries of snow that drifted at intervals out of the cold, grey skies, or merely the warmth and companionship to be found at home, something kept the revellers of Lincoln off the streets, and away from the bakery. Not even the prospect of an extra sugared cake, or the need for a new, last-minute batch of mince-pies, could draw them in.

In better years, the Drakes, too, would have been too busy enjoying the season to keep open the shop. But such times were long gone, and Phineas kept his station by the counter all the long, empty day through, surrounded by the semblance of high good cheer yet feeling none of it himself.

About three o' clock, in walked Mrs. Batts.

'Phineas,' she said, surveying first the room in all its splendour, and then him in all his gloom. 'Your mother would have been proud, wouldn't she? Where is your father?' She was wearing a green gown, and had sprigs of holly tucked into her stout pelisse. Positioned before the doorway, with her cold-reddened cheeks and dark hair, she looked almost a part of the decorations herself.

'I do not know,' answered Phineas, a little glumly, and wished Mrs. Batts the joys of the season by way of changing the subject.

These she returned, but she was not to be distracted. 'I come with an invitation,' said she. 'There's me and my daughter sittin' at home with more than enough to share, and you and your father…' She paused, and went on: 'Well, I've a good fire, and there's to be bob-apple later, and a game of Hoodman Blind, and I know not what else. Just with one or two of our neighbours — pleasant folk, you'll like them. You're welcome to join us, Phineas, and your father, too.'

Phineas had no power but to thank her sincerely and explain that his father gave no thought to festivities nowadays, even if he could be found — which, just at present, he could not.

'He's worritin' himself about that pastry-shop, is that it? I never would ha' mentioned it, only I thought as he must've heard on it already.'

Phineas tried to convince her that his father had no such concerns, and hoped that the bright array in the shop might serve to give weight to his argument, and preserve the Drake family's dignity. But his words sounded weak even to him, and Mrs. Batts raised a sceptical brow.

'Well,' she said, when he had exhausted his stock of lies and fallen silent. 'Remember my invitation, Phineas. You're welcome to join us at any time today, or tomorrow, or the day after.'

After which she went away, leaving Phineas to wish, secretly, that he might accept. Miss Batts was a merry girl, and her mother good-hearted; he would like to join them. But there was no one save himself to mind the shop.

Later, when darkness once again shrouded the streets and he had lit all his cheerful candles afresh, he had reason to feel glad that he had declined, and stayed where he was. For the door opened, and in swept a flurry of wind and snow and cold air — and in its midst, the lady of the rose.

She stood framed in the doorway for some time, her eyes eagerly scanning the contents of the room. Those eyes were odd, Phineas noted with dazed interest: hazy silver shaded with grey. Her dress was purple today; some draped velvet confection with a great deal in the way of skirt and sleeve, but not much in the way of warmth. She did not look cold, however, even though snowflakes glittered in the pale mass of her hair. She looked a little flushed, heightened colour blooming in her cheeks. Had she been running again, or was it the eager way in which she surveyed all of Phineas's decorations that brought the pink glow to her face?

She was beautiful. The word flitted uselessly across Phineas's thoughts, insufficient to describe the perfect coils of her pale hair; the exquisite features of her pale, perfect face; and those eyes… A glow seemed to hang about her, an air of vibrancy, of energy, of — of — Phineas could not describe it.

He thought, briefly, of the girls he had previously considered comely. Lizzie Batts, and little Jenny Worther… they withered in his imagination, mere weeds to this woman's glory. Phineas stood with weakened knees, words fleeing from his lips as quickly as he strove to muster them, and said nothing.

Did he flatter himself that she looked upon him with approval? No. Her hopeful air faded, dashing Phineas's private, half-felt wish that she might find something in his work, or in himself, to admire.

'I do not understand,' she announced in a clear, ringing voice, advancing further into the room. 'Who are you?'

'My name is Phineas Drake, ma'am,' he managed to answer. 'You — you may remember that we met, a few days ago? After — after a fashion, that is.'

She looked at him strangely, head tilted, as though he were some manner of creature she had never before encountered, and was not certain that she liked.

She didn't remember.

One long stride (for she was tall) carried her to the window, and she snatched the rose from beneath its evergreen bough and brandished it at Phineas. 'Where did you get this, Phineas Drake?'

He gaped. 'You dropped it. A few mornings ago, on the Greestone Stairs, when you — when you, um.' He wanted to say "vanished", but could not make the word come out of his mouth; not when she stood there, so undeniably solid before him.

Realisation dawned in her, and with it came dismay. She gave a great, weary sigh, and drifted listlessly in the direction of the counter, towards Phineas himself. 'You were the boy who was chasing me.'

Phineas did not much relish the word "boy", for he was three-

and-twenty, and had therefore been a man for some years already. But he let this pass, instead saying apologetically, 'I did not mean to chase you. I was only afraid that you would catch cold.'

'Catch cold?' she repeated, and her odd eyes smiled upon him in some amusement. 'Do I appear as though that is likely?'

'It — well, no,' he admitted, though he did not at all see how it was possible that she should be immune to the inclement weather.

'What would you have done, had you caught me?' She was intrigued, surveying Phineas with a thoughtful air that he could not help but find a trifle intimidating. He felt that there was some expected answer, and that he could very well offer a wrong one.

'I might have given you my coat,' he offered, 'or — or brought you here, for it is always warm in the kitchens...' He said no more, for her attention had wandered back to the rose, which she had set upon the counter before herself, and she was frowning at it.

'How kind of you,' she murmured abstractedly, and touched a finger to the tip of one blue-frosted petal.

Phineas's spirits sank at once. 'I am sorry,' he said, seeing dissatisfaction in the crease of her brow. 'I ought not to have taken such a liberty with your rose, only I hated to see the colour fade so, and I thought—'

'*You* did this?' She said the words sharply, and since the question was attended by a narrow-eyed, searching look, Phineas felt very uncomfortable indeed.

Then again, she did not appear to be angry.

'Yes,' he whispered.

'How?'

So Phineas tried to explain, but he had not got much farther than the part about the cabbages and the sugar before he visibly lost her interest.

'Cabbages!' she repeated in disgust.

Conscious that he had displeased her, but unsure how, Phineas was silent.

The lady's lips tightened, and she drummed her fingers impatiently upon the counter. 'I did not drop this flower,' she said crisply. 'I was following the person who did, but I did not catch him. Again, I could not catch him! When I saw the rose in your window, I thought... but you know nothing of this, your expression proclaims it.'

Phineas could only give her a wide-eyed stare which said, quite clearly, *no*.

'You do not know Wodebean?' she said suddenly. 'You are quite certain?'

'I know no one of so strange a name.'

'Strange, do you call it?' That won him a curious look, but she was not long to be diverted from her purpose. 'Who is the owner of this establishment?'

'My father.'

'Ah! And he is, perhaps, four feet tall? More, if he would not stoop so dreadfully! With an unlovely countenance, and an eccentric mode of dress?'

'No,' said Phineas, bewildered.

'You would call him by some other name, naturally, but his friends might call him Bean. Or perhaps by some other jauntily abbreviated epithet?'

'No!' said Phineas again. 'My father's name is Samuel Drake, he is taller than me, and I don't think that Mrs. Batts would say he is at all unlovely. She thinks him quite handsome.'

'I do not know who this Mrs. Batts may be, but since no creature alive could imagine Wodebean to be at all handsome, it is quite evident that we are not speaking of the same person.' She paused, and her eyes lit up again. 'Unless, perhaps, he has acquired some manner of Glamour! He has made a human of himself, and set up as a baker in this charming establishment! Indeed, I do not know why he would do anything of the kind, but it is perfectly...' She looked keenly at Phineas, and added, 'Only, I do not see how *you* would fit in.'

'I found the rose,' said Phineas steadily. 'I brought it here, since I did not like to leave it to die in the snow. I made it blue when the colour ebbed—'

'With cabbages,' said the lady, with a hint of scorn.

'With cabbages. And I left it on the sill. That is all I've had to do with it.'

The lady gave up her hopes in a sad rush, and drooped before Phineas's eyes. 'It would not matter so, if only it were not so important,' she said, suddenly forlorn, and Phineas's feelings of mild indignation melted away.

'I would help you, if I could,' he said, quite in earnest.

She looked at him steadily. 'Would you, Phineas Drake?'

Phineas swallowed, for under the weight of that stare her words seemed to gather some unspoken but palpable meaning.

'Er,' he said. 'Yes, of course.'

She smiled. It was the first time he had seen her do so, and it transformed her slightly severe features with bright sunshine. 'I will remember your name,' she said, and these words, too, rang with something Phineas could not identify.

Sweeping up the rose, she turned to leave. She had made it to the door before Phineas managed to blurt, 'May I know yours?'

She turned back to regard him, and her smile flickered again. 'That is fair, is it not?'

She seemed to require an answer, so Phineas nodded.

'My name is… it is Ilsevel.' And with a graceful inclination of her head, she passed through the door, and was gone into the night.

Only then did Phineas realise that the door had stood wide open throughout the odd interview, and he was half-perished with cold.

CHAPTER FOUR

T'ain't so very odd t' see Aylfenhame folk wanderin' the streets of England on the Solstice days, in the usual way o' things. Thas when the borders weaken, an' the gates fly open, an' anybody may pass back an' forth quite easy-like, if they happen t' know the way.

But Ilsevel, she ain't quite yer usual visitor. Ain't yer usual anythin', come t' that. There's her clothes, fer a start. Nowt but the best on her — silks, jewels, everythin' fine — an' she's trampin' about in 'em in the snow? An' the style! Fashions like that, well, I've seen nothin' like it in Aylfenhame fer twenty year at least — an' never in England at all.

What, thought I, is such a woman doin' in England? Especially since she didn't go back Aylf-side when th' Solstice was over. Oh, no. Stayed in the city, day after day, always askin' after this "Wodebean" fellow. Well, now. Thas a name I hadn't heard in more'n twenty years either...

Mrs. Yardley's boarding house was not, Ilsevel soon found, in an especially salubrious part of the city. In fact, the neighbourhood was rather dreary. Narrow, cramped streets, characterless houses, and, at times, a medley of unsavoury aromas. What with the cheerless weather casting a pall of gloom over everything, she soon began to wish herself back home in Aylfenhame.

But little was left there to welcome her; and Wodebean's trail had, for some reason, led her to this grey little city. What the elusive wretch could want with such a place she could not imagine, and on this point — as, indeed, on every other — nobody could help her.

No one had even heard of Wodebean. She asked everybody she met, from Mrs. Yardley herself ('Mr. Wodebean? I am not acquainted with anybody of that name, dear. It's to be a bit of mutton for supper, and a bite of apple tart. Shall you be wanting any? And *do* put a proper gown on. What will people think?') to Mrs. Yardley's household brownie, Pettivree ('Wodebean? No such person in these parts, miss,) to the odd boy at the bakery (a blank, gaping stare, and some rambling tale about his father). Wodebean must be calling himself by some other name, she supposed, but after three days in Lincoln she was no nearer to discovering what it might be, or where he might be hiding himself either.

And now they were all caught up with their winter festivals, and everything was Christmas this, Christmas that... Mrs. Yardley could no longer be drawn upon any subject save for mistletoe, and bob-apple, and negus, whatever those things were, and Ilsevel herself was forever being pressed to participate in some noisy festivity with her landlady, and her fellow boarders.

The latter did not much regret Ilsevel's absence, at any rate. Lacking Mrs. Yardley's motive for tolerating Ilsevel's eccentricity of dress, her ignorance of social customs or her lack of respectable connections (that being monied folk; the good landlady was clearly hard-up;) the boarders made their feelings clear with their chilly, reluctant greetings and their habit of giving her a wide berth whenever they should happen to meet her in the hallway, or over the supper-table.

Ilsevel barely noticed these incivilities. They could not, or would not, help her upon the only point that mattered; and therefore, she had no use for their friendship. And Mrs. Trott snored so loudly at night, Ilsevel could hear her through the wall.

The day after Ilsevel's disappointment at the bakery, she rose early, well before the sun showed its weak winter rays to the world, and sat awhile in bed, thinking. No fire brightened the empty grate — the scant stock of comforts at Mrs. Yardley's establishment did not include such luxuries as warmth in the mornings. Candles were in short supply, too, and since Ilsevel could not muster any interest in finding her way to a chandler's shop and haggling with the proprietor over a purchase, she simply bore with the darkness.

At least her clothes contrived to ward away the cold; they might, some of them, have got a little moth-eaten down the years, but their enchantments had hardly faded at all.

The Greestone Stairs. That was where she had last seen Wodebean — disappearing, so she had thought, through a Solstice-Gate, and back into Aylfenhame. But when she had gone through herself, he had been nowhere in evidence. Invisible? Or had he, somehow, contrived to go somewhere else altogether? The rose had not been a typical example of his arts; it was too delicate, too pretty, and above all, too useless. She did not see that there was much chance of a market for such a frippery, or not one that would much interest Wodebean. He did not deal in trifles.

So: why had he been carrying it about with him?

She got out of bed and lit her sole candle, but its wan glow did not afford her any glimpse of the odd rose in any part of her room. The flower proved to be absent from her chest-of-drawers, and her closet too. Where—

Oh. It darted into her head, then: a memory of the rose, lying on the counter in the baker's shop, and of herself, walking away without it.

'Fool!' she cried. The one link she had with Wodebean, and she had left it with that blank-faced baker's boy? Who knew what he might have found to do with it by now?

'Cabbages and sugar,' she muttered with a sigh, discarding her nightgown — *ouch*, the sudden bite of the cold ate at her perishing flesh before she contrived to don her undergarments, and her favourite carmine gown. Half-boots! And today, a hat, for perhaps she ought to make some small concession to appearances once in a while. Away she went into the dark early morn, the sky snowless by some small blessing, though a brisk wind did its best to carry her hat away again.

'Come now!' she protested, clutching her bonnet as she hurried through the empty streets. 'Propriety dictates that I must have a hat! You would not wish to expose me to still more censure, surely?'

The wind, being an uncaring sort of fellow, did not lessen its importunity one whit.

No lights shone in the bakery, yet, and Ilsevel was reduced to pacing impatiently outside. She could dimly discern, by the light of a pallid, sinking moon, that the rose was not on the windowsill where she had seen it before. But the rest of the shop was sunk in impenetrable gloom, and she could not determine whether the flower still lay on the counter.

Then came the rattle of locks turning back their tumblers, and with a soft clatter, the boy came issuing from a side-door.

'Good morning!' said Ilsevel briskly, and stepped forward to meet him.

The boy — Phineas, that was it, Phineas Drake — blinked at her, silent, and dropped a box into the icy street. He stooped at once and scrambled to collect the contents spilling out onto the cobbles. 'G-good morning,' he said while thus engaged, and without meeting her eye.

Ilsevel went to help, but his nimble fingers had everything retrieved and tidied in a trice, and she was not required. 'I've come about my rose!' she said, before he could drop anything else.

Phineas regarded her properly, and after a moment's pause — dismayed, perhaps? — he said: 'Oh, I... I thought you said it was not yours.'

'I said that I did not drop it.'

A faint glimmer attracted her gaze: moonlight glinting off frost and sugar. He was wearing the rose in one of the button-holes of his overcoat. 'Oh,' he said again.

He had fallen in love with the pretty thing, of course. They all did, these starry-eyed human-folk, the moment anything magical came in their way. She suppressed a sigh and said, as kindly as she could: 'By rights, I suppose, it is yours indeed, for 'twas you who found it. But I have great need of it. Will you perhaps lend it to me?'

Phineas shifted his burden of boxes to one hand; with the other, he tenderly plucked the rose from his button-hole and gave it to her. 'No,' he said incongruously, and then to Ilsevel's surprise he added: 'It is yours. Take it.'

Not a trace of resentment was there in his words or his manner; nor of reluctance, either. He adored the absurd thing, but gave it freely nonetheless.

She remembered his odd solicitude about her attire, some days before. Would he really have given her his coat?

'Thank you,' she said.

He ducked his head, apparently incapable of further speech, and made to pass her. The boxes, she supposed, had to be distributed somewhere.

'Wait,' she said.

He stopped.

Why had she said it? The word had emerged from somewhere within her; she could not have said where. She thought quickly. 'Do you know this city well?'

He nodded. 'Yes, milady. I have lived all my life here.'

'Suppose I might like to buy some illicit goods. Where ought I to go? Will you take me there?'

Phineas gazed at her. 'Illicit goods…?'

'Poisons and cursed trinkets,' Ilsevel elaborated. 'Elf-bolts and changeling-stocks. Grass stolen from a faerie throne. A convincing replica of the rosewater-strung Lyre of Maldriggan.' She thought a moment, and amended her speech. 'No, I retract that last one. Wodebean does not deal in fakery. If he purports to be selling the rosewater-strung Lyre of Maldriggan then it is the real one.'

Phineas was still gazing at her.

'No?' she prompted. 'There must be somewhere like that around here.'

'The…' began Phineas, and stopped. 'Elf-bolts and faerie thrones? You are… quite well, milady, are not you?'

'Does your household have no brownie?' she answered, a trifle impatiently. 'You cannot be entirely oblivious to the ways of Aylfenhame, surely?'

'My — m-my father drove him off,' mumbled Phineas, blinking, and then said, as though the idea came as a surprise, 'You are of Aylfenhame.'

'Naturally I am.'

'That does explain one or two little matters,' he said, and actually contrived to smile at her. His gaze flicked to the soft, velvet folds of her gown, so different from the drab fabrics he was himself swathed in.

Ilsevel smoothed a hand over her bodice. 'I will not be here for long, therefore it is not at all necessary to blend in.'

'I quite see that, ma'am.'

'I wish you will cease calling me by that title, for it is not quite correct.'

The boy blushed. 'I am sorry. What had you rather I called you?'

Ilsevel opened her mouth, and her true title hovered for a moment on the tip of her tongue. But one or two lucky recollections saved her from making what must be an unwise revelation, and she bit back the words. 'You had better call me Ilsevel,' she ordered. 'It is a serviceable enough name, is it not?'

'It is a beautiful name.'

'Very well. Now then, the elf-bolts? Not that I wish to *procure* any such wares, you understand. I merely need to question the proprietor.'

'I am but a baker,' said Phineas. 'I know nothing of faerie thrones or magic lyres.'

Ilsevel looked him up and down, taking in the scuffed hem and cuffs of his threadbare overcoat and the worn, obviously beloved cap crowning his head. 'I suppose you would not, at that. But tell me, Phineas the Baker: if you wanted to buy something questionable, where would you go?'

'I... have never thought about it before.' He hesitated as he spoke, and there was a look to his face that told her he was not telling the truth.

Ilsevel, exasperated, made him a tiny curtsey and turned away.

'But,' he added. 'I— I— if I wanted something such, I might go to one of the pawn shops.'

Ilsevel turned back. 'Pawn shop? What is that?'

'If I was short of money I might take something valuable — a watch, say, or a piece of jewellery — to the pawnbroker and he would give me something for it, and then sell it in his shop. It's sometimes said that pawnbrokers are not too particular about where the items come from.'

'Stolen goods?' Ilsevel pondered that. 'It is not Wodebean's trade, but perhaps such a person may know more. Let us go to one of these pawnbrokers.'

Phineas looked down at the pile of boxes he carried, nonplussed.

'After we have delivered your confectionery,' she amended.

'We?'

'Shall you object to my company?'

'N-no, ma'am — um, I could have no objection.'

'And since my hands are free I shall also carry a box.'

Phineas blinked, and offered her the stack of boxes almost reverently. Ilsevel selected two from the top, and tucked them under her arm. 'Shall we hurry?' she suggested. 'It is rather cold.'

'You don't look like you feel it,' said he, setting off up the street.

'No, not in the least. But you do.'

Phineas threw her a startled look, as though he were not at all used to having his comfort considered. His nose was already blue with cold; and the fool boy had been planning to give *her* his coat?

Ilsevel received a curious stare at the first house they stopped at. At the second, an outright disapproving one. Quickly realising that her accompaniment of Phineas might set tongues to wagging, and perhaps to his detriment, she took to waiting in the street while he went up to the doors, her back turned.

And then it was off to the peculiar establishments he had called pawn shops, where she took an instant dislike to the pawnbrokers.

'But it is Queen Amaldria's ring!' she protested for the benefit of a stout, florid man who had, by the scent of his breath, been busy at the port already. 'She is a legend in Aylfenhame! And it is real emeralds, not glass. I will need much more for it.'

The pawnbroker, whose cramped little establishment in an insalubrious part of town had at first raised her hopes, eyed the ring again. 'It's real emeralds, all right,' he agreed. 'But if it's the property of some queen, how did you come by it?'

Ilsevel, quite prepared for this question, launched into a rather involved tale. She had amended some of the truth, and presented a story wherein, she strongly implied, she had appropriated the article for herself under questionable circumstances.

Phineas, more practical than she, allotted some thirty seconds to this narrative, and then said crisply: 'It isn't necessary to ask too many questions about that, is it sir?'

The stout man snorted, and handed back the ring. 'What would your father say, Phineas Drake, if he knew you were consorting with thieves?'

It would depend upon the thief, Phineas thought involuntarily.

So much for the florid man.

Phineas took her to two more such shops, with similar results. In *one*, she surmised, he was not only known, but had actually made use of its services — and recently, too. Hard up, was he? He ought not to be, not with such a fine little shop under his stewardship. Frowning, she tucked that information away — and tucked a sapphire ring from her left little finger into his coat pocket, too, when he was not attending to her.

The fourth pawn shop proved, to her relief, more useful.

Unusually (as she was beginning to learn) the proprietor of this dusty little place was a woman, and a sharp-eyed, shrewd sort. She examined Queen Amaldria's ring with efficient professionalism, pronounced it acceptable, and took it without question, even when Phineas had made clear its questionable provenance.

The money she offered for it was insultingly low, but that was all right. She would not be keeping the ring for long.

She was a shade insolent, too. Eyeing Ilsevel's very handsome dress, she said: 'T'ain't wise, walking about in stolen dresses. Sell 'em to me, and I'll replace 'em with something less eye-catching.'

With dignity, Ilsevel declined. It was bad enough to part with Amaldria's ring, however temporarily. To sell her gowns! Unthinkable! And the *idea* that they were stolen! Forgetting, briefly, their masquerade, she advanced upon the pawnbroker, her mind agreeably full of wretched and painful things to do to her.

Phineas quietly intervened. 'Pardon me, ma'am,' he said to the pawnbroker, with far more courtesy than she deserved. 'Have you perhaps encountered anyone by the name of Wodebean?'

The woman shook her head. 'What manner of name is that?'

'He would not use such a name in these parts, I am persuaded,' said Ilsevel. 'Only I do not know how he may be known instead.'

'Forgive me,' said Phineas gravely to her, and gently plucked the glittering rose out of her hat. He presented this to the pawnbroker. 'Have you seen anything like this, anywhere abouts?'

The woman's eyes lit up. Ilsevel recognised the same starry admiration she had seen in Phineas's face, when he had looked at the absurd flower. 'I've been trying to get me hands on one of them,' said the pawnbroker fervently. 'Last night, yonder by the river, there was some manner of gathering going on. Typical Christmas gaieties, o' course, only them flowers was going around and I ain't never seen the likes o' *them* before. I never did get one, nor would anyone sell me theirs. I'll give you a fine price for yours, sir, if'n you'll let me have it.'

'This one is not for sale,' said Phineas quickly, handing it back to Ilsevel. 'But if you will direct us to the site of this gathering, we'll do our best to find the source.'

The pawnbroker sighed, and furnished Phineas with a garbled batch of directions of which Ilsevel could make no sense whatsoever. Phineas, however, accepted them as if they were perfectly comprehensible, and tipped his hat to the woman. 'Our thanks.'

Ilsevel smiled warmly into the woman's eyes, and exerted herself just a trifle. 'My ring, ma'am, if you please?' said she silkily.

The pawnbroker blinked, and dreamily handed Queen Amaldria's emerald ring back to Ilsevel. 'Of course, milady,' she muttered. 'What was I thinking?'

'What, indeed?' murmured Ilsevel. She dropped the insultingly small pile of coins onto the pawnbroker's counter and sailed out of the shop, Phineas hurrying in her wake.

'How did you do that?' he asked, once they were back on the street.

'Such a woman recognises when she has overstepped herself,' was all that Ilsevel would reply.

Phineas frowned, and said nothing.

'This gathering,' she said a moment later, hurrying to keep pace with Phineas's quick steps. 'Why was there not news of it further up the hill?' For they had steadily moved farther and farther downhill with their visits to the pawn shops, and had now left the great slope entirely behind them.

'Given the type of pawnbroker *she* is, it's my guess the gathering was not for the law-abiding types,' answered Phineas.

'That would be Wodebean's audience, certainly,' Ilsevel agreed. 'It makes a great deal of sense! I am persuaded we shall find him there.'

Phineas drew her a little closer to himself, looking warily about as he strode quickly on. 'Keep close,' he instructed. 'It is not quite safe in this part of town, especially in the dark.'

The street did not look so very terrible to Ilsevel. The buildings were a little shabby, perhaps, but what matter that? She could smell the river-water on the wind, and judged they were not far from it. 'You need not strive to protect me,' she offered by way of reassurance. 'I am well able to take care of myself, I assure you. And of you, too.'

This wounded his pride, she immediately discerned, for he was quick to frown, and said stiffly: 'It is my duty to make sure you are safe.'

With an inward sigh, Ilsevel merely said: 'How kind.'

Phineas led her to an unlovely spot by a dark pool, the water crowded with boats and flanked by great, hulking buildings without beauty or character. Loath though she would be to admit it, she could not be unconscious of an air of something... faintly unpromising about the place, and she was not too sorry to keep close to Phineas. If there was trouble, he might need *her* to preserve *him* from it.

That there had been revelry of some sort afoot was evident, for she was obliged to step over some one or two supine celebrants as she walked along. Mercifully, the sun was just high enough by then for her to discern an occasional dark shape before she stepped on it. There were few of them, however, and when Phineas attempted to question them he received little response save a groan of protest and a curse or two.

'I see no roses, do you?' said Phineas after a time.

'None,' said Ilsevel, 'but they would hardly be left lying in the street, would they? Would you leave yours in such a position?'

'No.'

Another shadowy human shape loomed. Ilsevel paused before it, leaned down, and grabbed it by the shoulder. With a violent shake of the recumbent drunkard she said, loudly and firmly, "Wodebean, my good man! Where is he to be found?'

She was answered, after a fashion. The wan dawn rays glinted off the silvery blade of something sharp, which was presented dangerously close to her face. 'Unhand me, lady,' growled a low voice.

With a short sigh, Ilsevel took the grimy hand in a tight grip and pinched in one or two precise, sensitive spots. The knife fell with a clatter. 'There is no need for that,' she admonished. 'I merely require information. Wodebean. A shortish fellow, rounded in the shoulder, probably swathed in some unnecessarily colourful mantle. He was here last night, indulging in a *quite* uncharacteristic display of largesse — unless he was selling the roses, which would be much more like him. You have been here for some time, I conclude by your state; have you seen him?'

The shape surged to its feet and stood there, swaying slightly. A face was pushed unnecessarily close to hers, and she was treated to the scrutiny of a pair of dark, bloodshot eyes. 'Who are you, lady?'

'My name is Ilsevel, and if you would be so kind as to answer my questions I assure you, my companion and I will be...' She paused, being suddenly aware that Phineas was not with her. 'Happy to leave you in peace,' she finished, dismissing the problem of Phineas from her mind for the moment.

'Them roses,' said the man, for it proved to be a person of the male persuasion. 'Fellow like that was around, handin' them things out like they was mince pies or sommat. Though he said right enough, there was a price on 'em. Folk seemed happy t' pay it.' He belched, and held a hand to his head.

'What was the price?'

'Do I look like the type as wants a spangly flower?'

'My good man, everyone wants Wodebean's wares. That is the nature of the wretch. He has a way of making things... irresistible.'

The man shrugged. 'I resisted 'em just fine.'

'Intriguing.' Ilsevel looked him over thoughtfully, but received no real clues as to his probable nature. He wore a long coat like Phineas's, very nearly as threadbare, though this man's was solid black. Stout boots covered his feet, and his dark hair was in a state of disorder. 'Where did Wodebean go?'

'No idea,' said the man shortly.

Ilsevel sighed in frustration, and turned away. 'My thanks.'

'If it's that important to you, lady, there's another shindig tonight. Mayhap he'll be about again with his fancy nothings.'

'Excellent!' Ilsevel turned back, with a broad smile for the suddenly helpful fellow. 'It is to be held here?'

'Aye. And it's market night.'

'Market night?'

She detected the faint glimmer of whitish teeth in the dim light: a grin. 'There's a market at times fer the sale of... unusual goods, shall we say? Ain't usually frequented by the likes of *you*, o' course. Always held at night, 'cause that's when the law-folk are least lively. And,' he added clinically, 'can most easily be bribed to stay indoors wi' their fires.'

'The perfect environment for Wodebean,' Ilsevel declared. 'What is your name, my good fellow? I am quite pleased with you.'

But the man made no answer, being apparently distracted by the approach of Phineas. Who, she noted, was holding a second frosted rose. 'Phineas Drake,' said her new friend. 'Yer father'll not be pleased to hear of this.'

'My father is rarely pleased,' said Phineas. He gave the rose to Ilsevel. 'I got this off a, er, lady as has spent the night by the water. Said she picked it up off the floor last night.'

'And she just gave it to you?'

Phineas said nothing. She could not quite tell in the darkness, but were his cheeks a trifle flushed?

'No matter,' she murmured.

'Maybe you won't tell my father, Gabriel,' suggested Phineas.

Ilsevel's helpful new friend, Gabriel, eyed Phineas with some scepticism. 'Happen I might not, provided you ain't in trouble.'

'No trouble, I promise.'

Gabriel threw a meaning look in Ilsevel's direction. 'And this fancy article?'

Phineas was definitely blushing now. 'She is a respectable woman,' he said firmly. 'Whom I have chosen to help.'

'That is the truth,' put in Ilsevel helpfully. 'On both points.'

Gabriel grunted. He cast about in the street for a moment, and then stooped. When he straightened, he was carrying a dark, slightly dented hat, which he restored to his head. 'If you'll excuse me,' he said gravely, 'I'll take my leave.' He made them a brief, slightly pained bow, judging from the grimacing twist to his lips, and walked away.

'Does everyone know you, in these parts?' said Ilsevel.

Phineas sighed, though she could not imagine what troubled him. 'My father,' he said shortly.

Abandoning the subject, she beamed at him. 'Well, but Phineas! Our venture has borne fruit. There is another round of revelry taking place tonight, with a market for all manner of questionable things, and I shall attend! For surely Wodebean will be here.'

'Ilsevel.' Phineas took a step closer, his face very grave. 'You cannot attend such an event.'

'Whyever not?'

'I... I think you do not precisely understand the nature of the entertainments.'

'I understand them perfectly.'

He looked helplessly at her. 'Can I not persuade you? There must be some other occasion, some other way that Wodebean may be discovered.'

'None have presented themselves, and I *must* talk to Wodebean, Phineas. It is of paramount importance.'

Phineas gave a short sigh. 'Very well,' he conceded. 'Come to the bakery at midnight. I shall be waiting for you, and we'll go together.'

'I need no guardian.'

'Then I'll come here alone, and find you here.' He gave her the set-jaw look of a young man who will not be dissuaded from carrying out his absurd plan.

She capitulated with a smile, for all things considered, he *was* a useful person to have around. Without his help, she might never have found this wonderful thieves' market. 'We will have a fine time,' she promised.

Phineas muttered something inaudible.

'What was that?'

'Nothing.'

CHAPTER FIVE

At midnight upon the following evening, Phineas escorted Ilsevel back to the waterfront — only to find that the night's entertainments were not to be held in quite the same spot. There were few people present, but an inviting route had been marked out on the ground in paint that shimmered oddly in the moonlight.

Phineas eyed the coiling arrows with misgiving. 'Why do they shine like that?'

Ilsevel did not hesitate, but followed the arrow-path with sprightly step and, apparently, high good humour. 'This is most interesting!' she called back to Phineas. 'I had no notion that the thieves of England and Aylfenhame were so closely associated.'

'The what? You cannot mean— Ilsevel, please, consider a moment—'

Ilsevel did not pause to consider, but turned the corner around a looming warehouse. When Phineas caught up, she was nowhere in sight.

'Ilsevel?' He took a hesitant step forward, and another— and, with a strangled cry, fell into empty space.

The tumbling sensation lasted only for a second or two. Then he was upright again, his feet braced upon solid ground, only the dark silence of the waterfront was gone. He stood instead in a mossy glade alive with music and merriment. The dark boughs of shadowy trees hung overhead, liberally decked with holly and mistletoe and pale hellebores, and the thick moss underfoot felt like the most luxurious carpet. He smelled spices and wine and roasting meat. Clear lights danced among the leaves, and there were people everywhere.

'What did I tell you?' came a deep, disapproving voice, and Gabriel appeared out of the crowd.

'Is my father here?' said Phineas.

'Ain't seen him.' Gabriel had a meat pie in one hand and a clay tankard in the other. He handed the latter to Phineas. 'May as well have some of that, since yer here. But keep yer eyes open. Anything can happen at a gathering like this.'

Phineas hastily handed back the tankard, though it *did* smell enticingly of apples. 'I had better keep my wits about me, hadn't I? Have you seen Ilsevel?'

'Yer ladyfriend? Went thataways.' Gabriel pointed.

Following his pointing finger, Phineas thanked him distractedly and plunged into the crowd.

He found Ilsevel intent upon an array of stalls set up at the rear of the clearing. They were thickly clustered about with all manner of paraphernalia, for which Phineas scarcely spared a glance. 'Ilsevel, we shouldn't linger.'

Ilsevel scooped up something from a stall with a green awning, and gave a glad cry. 'Lady Galdrin's shoe-buckle!' she proclaimed, and then swooped upon something else. '*And* a Herald's Harp! I would know them anywhere.'

The proprietor, a short fellow with a dark cap over his shock of pale hair and a bright cloak around his shoulders, smiled proudly at Ilsevel. 'From Mirramay itself, the harp.'

'The palace,' said Ilsevel, and stuffed the harp into Phineas's hands. It was smaller than he might have expected, and pure gold. He received the shoe-buckle next, a frothy object that looked made from sea-spray and dew. 'Keep those safe, Phineas,' she directed him. 'They are not for the likes of this fellow.'

The proprietor's eyes narrowed. 'Oh, are they not?'

'What do you want for them?' said Ilsevel crisply, unmoved.

The stallholder turned crafty, and pointed a thin finger at Ilsevel's left shoulder. 'That pretty brooch would be a fine price.'

'Outrageous,' Ilsevel snapped, laying one involuntary hand over the shimmering pearlescent brooch she wore pinned into her bodice. 'For stolen property? I shan't pay you anything of the kind!'

Phineas rather lost track of the conversation after that, for upon attempting to fit the shoe-rose and the tiny Harp into his pocket without damaging them he discovered something else at the bottom: a sapphire ring, which sparked with an odd fire under the moonlight. He'd seen Ilsevel wearing it the day before.

He thought briefly of Gabriel. To be sure, the man was more in favour of highway robbery than petty pilfering, but how had the ring come to be in Phineas's own pocket if someone hadn't first taken it from Ilsevel's finger? And who else might have done that, if not Gabriel? Perhaps he had robbed her, and then thought better of it once he understood her to be in Phineas's care.

But that made little real sense. Perhaps it was simply an accident.

'Yours, I think,' said Phineas, offering her the ring.

She gave it only the briefest of glances. 'Once mine, now yours.'

'You put it in my pocket?'

'How else would it have got there?'

Phineas had little to say to that, and Ilsevel returned to her argument.

'I cannot let you give me your jewellery,' said Phineas awkwardly to her back.

Ilsevel snatched up the ring and all but hurled it at the stallholder. 'Then *he* may have it, and we shall take the shoe-rose and the Harp.' So saying, she turned her back upon the stall and marched away, leaving Phineas to hasten after her.

Thankfully, the market-man did not seem disposed to pursue them, or to argue about the price. 'Why should the shoe-rose and the Harp matter so much to you?' asked Phineas.

'Lady Galdrin was a friend.'

'Oh.'

'And the Harp has sentimental value.'

'I see.' Phineas did not at all see, but he chose not to pursue it.

'Since you will not accept jewellery, you may keep the Harp,' Ilsevel decided next. 'Those pawnbrokers of yours will find it highly interesting, I have no doubt.'

'But the sentimental value...?'

'I will get over it.'

'Ilsevel, I am not in need.'

'Oh!' she stopped walking, and looked at him in surprise. 'But you have been selling things to the pawnbrokers recently, have you not?'

Phineas began to feel a headache forming. 'Yes, but that was for a specific purpose—'

'Then you keep the Harp.' She dismissed the matter from her notice on the spot, and launched after a gaggle of household brownies who were wandering from stall to stall, stuffing pies into their mouths. 'You!' she called. 'Stop!'

Phineas did not at all understand what had attracted her notice — until they stopped and turned, and he realised that the glitter in their hair came from bunches of violets all aglow with frost. 'Milady?' said one of the brownies.

'Wodebean made those,' she said, levelling a finger at the flowers. 'Did he not?'

To Phineas's surprise, all of the brownies dissolved into laughter. 'Never met Wodebean, have you?' said one, choking on mirth.

Ilsevel's eyes narrowed. 'Oh, I know him all right. And it is not his style, to be sure. But he had such a thing recently; I'd swear to that.'

'Then he's been at the thieves' market afore now. Hardly surprising, is it?'

'Why do you say that?'

'Why, he's the one as runs it. 'Tis his market, and nobody sells here without his say-so.'

'So he's here!'

The talkative brownie shrugged. 'Might be. Might not be.' Visibly giving up on Ilsevel and her questions, the brownies drifted away. Ilsevel let them. She seemed lost in thought, though her bright eyes scanned the crowd with an eagerness Phineas found vaguely disturbing.

'Ilsevel?' he said, after a moment.

She transferred her piercing gaze to his face, which did little to restore his comfort, and raised one brow.

'Um. Why are you so eager to talk to Wodebean?'

He thought she might not answer. Nor did she, in any fashion he might have expected. Her lips twisted in a wry, perhaps bitter smile, and she tore off the bonnet that covered her hair and threw it carelessly into the moss. Then she turned on the spot in a smooth circle, and to Phineas's amazement rose swiftly into the air.

When she spoke, her voice was impossibly amplified, and boomed across the glade.

'I seek Wodebean!' she proclaimed. 'That filthy, swindling cheat *tricked* me some years ago, and he shall answer to me for it! A Queen's ransom to anyone who finds him!'

Her announcement halted the revelry at once, and the music cut off with a squawk. The thieves of England and Aylfenhame stared in awe at the vision of Ilsevel floating some way above their heads, her pale hair drifting upon an unfelt breeze and a glimmer of magic and rage wreathing her velvet-clad form.

'It is a matter of some moment to me,' she added in a somewhat softened tone. 'For if I can just get my hands on him, much harm may be mended.'

Neither this entreaty, nor her handsome bribe, drew the desired response from her audience. One by one they turned away, muttering excuses. The music struck up again — Phineas could not, now he came to think of it, see any kind of an orchestra anywhere; the music seemed to emanate from the great oak trees themselves. Brownies and hobs, trows and goblins, Ayliri and humans alike returned to their eating and drinking, their dancing and laughing, leaving Ilsevel in solitary and disappointed splendour.

The glow faded from her, and she gave a great sigh, sinking a few feet towards the ground in the process. So grieved did she appear that Phineas's heart gave a wrench. Queen's ransom or no, he would have presented Wodebean to her in an instant had he that power.

'My Lady?' said a tentative voice, and Ilsevel's head whipped round.

A pixie stood nearby, almost concealed behind the broad trunk of an ancient oak. She wore a crumpled leaf for a hat, and a necklace of cobwebs strung with dew hung around her thin neck. 'I know you,' she whispered. 'You are—'

'Ilsevel,' interrupted she. 'That is how I am known.'

Cautiously, the pixie emerged from behind the tree. To Phineas's surprise, she made Ilsevel so deep a curtsey it was almost obeisance. 'As you wish,' she said, barely audible. She glanced around rather fearfully, and inched closer to Ilsevel. 'None know where to find Wodebean,' she said. 'He is grown ever more aloof, and none now know where he dwells. But he was here, two nights ago, seeking flowers like that one you wear.' She pointed one tiny finger at the rose in Ilsevel's hair. How it had got there from her discarded bonnet, Phineas could not have said.

'Seeking them?' said Ilsevel in surprise, lightly touching the petals of her rose. 'He was not selling them, or giving them out?'

The pixie shook her head. 'He took up a great armful of them, one at least of every variety. He was angry. I thought perhaps they were being sold without his permission.'

'And then what did he do?'

The pixie shrugged. 'He vanished. I do not think anyone knows where he went.'

'Vanished.' Ilsevel thought.

Phineas experienced a flash of insight. 'You were following Wodebean, weren't you?' he said to Ilsevel. 'When I first saw you. There was someone— he disappeared—'

'Yes, yes,' said Ilsevel with a sigh. 'He has an irritating way of *vanishing*, quite without warning, and I do not know how it is achieved.'

Coming from the woman who had just raised herself some eight feet in the air with no apparent difficulty, and who still hovered some way off the ground, this was a remarkable comment.

'But you vanished, too,' said Phineas in confusion.

'Oh, no! I merely returned into Aylfenhame, but he was not there when I arrived. He vanished into someplace *else*, and it is getting *quite* tiresome.' To the pixie she said, 'Have you further information for me? Where were those flowers coming from, if not from Wodebean?'

'There was a woman handing them about. She asked nothing for them, not a single coin.'

'What did she look like?'

'Golden hair, blue eyes…' The pixie made a helpless gesture, as though further description was beyond her. 'She was a great beauty.'

Ilsevel, for some reason, froze, her eyes widening. 'A statuesque sort of person, improbably perfect, with an air of determination and an irritating penchant for coquetry?'

The pixie blinked. 'Well, yes—'

'You did not catch her name, I suppose?'

'No, Lady.'

Dismissing the pixie, Ilsevel plucked the rose from her hair and examined it thoughtfully.

'What is it?' Phineas said. 'I don't understand. First we hear that Wodebean is the source of the flowers, and then he is not?'

'I think both are true,' said Ilsevel. 'This one comes from Wodebean, which means it is both special and rather dangerous. The ones being passed around *here* were counterfeits. Sticks, most likely, glamoured to resemble blossoms.'

Phineas saw many examples of just such flowers, adorning the hair and the clothes of the revellers around him. Sticks? 'How can you know that?'

'Because my sister made them, and she never did have a scrap of talent at crafting. Glamour, on the other hand...' Ilsevel shrugged.

'Your sist— never mind,' sighed Phineas, abandoning all hope of understanding her.

'It appears that she is trying to get Wodebean's attention, too,' Ilsevel mused. 'I wonder if she has had any luck?'

CHAPTER SIX

I'd been askin' around about Wodebean. Used to be, his name was a byword fer hard-to-get goods, mayhap veerin' in the illegal direction. But that was years ago. Seein' as I hadn't heard a word o' news about him in such a long time, imagine my surprise to find he was still about — an' not far from my own Tilby, either! Keeps hisself to hisself, that's fer sure. What brought him out o' hidin' all on a sudden, that's what I wanted to know.

As fer Ilsevel, I was gettin' some suspicions as to her nature. If I was right, well... her and her sister in the same place was goin' t' kick up a fine ruckus, no doubt about that.

I decided it was mebbe time fer me to pay a visit t' the city meself...

At some indeterminate hour upon the following day, when Phineas had been so long closeted in the bakery kitchens he had long lost track of the time, he was disturbed in his endless labours by the abrupt slamming open of the door that led into the shop.

His father stood there, wild-eyed.

'Phineas,' he said, and stopped. His lips moved, but no further sound emerged.

Phineas stood, arms buried up to the elbows in half-mixed dough, and waited.

'Someone's asking for you,' said his father at last.

'Ah,' said Phineas quietly, unperturbed. It must be Ilsevel. Perhaps she had levitated again, or some such thing; that would explain the look in his father's eyes. His stomach clenched at thought of her dazzling beauty, and he took a deep, steadying breath.

He took the time to clean his skin thoroughly of all the dough, and when he had rolled down the sleeves of his shirt and removed his apron — trying to remain oblivious, the while, of his father's impatient gestures — he stepped into the shop.

It was not Ilsevel.

'Afternoon,' said the visitor, and tipped the brim of an enormous hat to Phineas.

Frozen in the doorway, his mouth hanging open and his eyes as wide as his father's, Phineas wondered distractedly how his visitor had contrived to fit into the shop at all. His head very nearly brushed the ceiling; he must have bent half-double to get through the door. Huge and bulky, with massive arms and shoulders and an alarming pair of tusks, he was not quite an ordinary customer.

'Troll,' croaked Phineas.

For all his intimidating bulk, this troll appeared congenial enough, for a friendly smile spread across his blue-skinned countenance. He took no exception to Phineas's involuntary rudeness, merely regarding him with a twinkle in his eyes. 'That I am,' he agreed comfortably. 'Name of Balligumph.'

Phineas recollected himself, and hurriedly stepped up to the counter. 'Good afternoon, Mr. Balligumph,' he said. 'How may I help you?'

'I'll take one o' them pies,' said the troll, and pointed a thick finger at an inviting pile of pastries Phineas had taken from the oven only an hour ago. 'Mebbe three, at that,' he amended with a grin. 'One's a mere bite fer the likes o' me, no?'

Phineas tried a smile, and failed. Nervously, he packed three pies into paper and handed them to the troll.

There was no sign of his father.

'Anything else?' he enquired.

Mr. Balligumph carefully counted coins into one vast palm, and then handed them over. 'Nowt t' eat, but I am after a mite of information, if ye have it.'

'I thought it must be something like that,' said Phineas.

The troll grinned. 'Aye. It's about Ilsevel.'

Phineas had expected as much, but could not repress a flicker of suspicion. He eyed his enormous visitor warily, and said: 'What of her?'

'I can't find her,' said Mr. Balligumph bluntly. 'I was hopin' ye could help me.'

The suspicion grew. Painfully aware of the absurdity, Phineas nonetheless drew himself up as tall as he could, and said with an attempt at firmness: 'Forgive me sir, but if you mean her any harm—'

'Size and bad intentions don't necessarily correlate.'

'I beg your pardon?'

The twinkle was back in Balligumph's eyes. 'Big I may be, but I ain't plannin' t' hurt her. On the contrary, I was fixin' t' help her.'

'What with?'

Balligumph shrugged. 'I'd have t' talk to the lady, before I can answer that.'

Phineas mulled it over. Balligumph made for an alarming sight, no question there. But a number of things softened the general unpromising impression that he made. That smile, for one, even if it did make his long tusks twitch. The patience with which he bore with Phineas's distrust. And then he was wearing a patchwork waistcoat, slightly threadbare, that looked as though it had been made for him with love, and long cherished thereafter.

'She once mentioned a boarding house,' Phineas offered. 'The owner is a Mrs... Yardley, I think?'

But the troll shook his head. 'Been there. Ilsevel ain't been seen since last night.'

That was curious, considering that Phineas had escorted her most of the way there himself. She had made a point of leaving him somewhat before they had arrived at her door, this was true, but she had also sworn that she was going straight home.

'She has not been here today,' said Phineas. 'But I saw her yesterday.' He told the troll the tale of the thieves' market by the water, and of the subsequent one in Aylfenhame. He mentioned the roses, and Wodebean, and Ilsevel's sister, and all the while the troll nodded knowledgeably along.

'I have folk who keep me informed,' he said when Phineas had finished. 'Particularly of anythin' goin' on in the county that seems t' come out of Aylfenhame. 'Tis this very tale that's brought me t' see Ilsevel. Ye don't know where she might ha' got to today?'

'I couldn't guess,' Phineas said apologetically.

'No matter, no matter.' Balligumph stood a moment in thought, his gaze resting on Phineas. 'Ye've been seen more than once in

Ilsevel's company,' he said then. 'Will ye tell me the rest?'

So Phineas went back to the beginning, when he had followed Ilsevel through the snow and watched her disappear.

This did not have quite the effect upon Balligumph that he might have expected.

'*Ye* saw Wodebean?' said the troll, suddenly alert.

'I... I saw a dark figure in a mantle, and only a glimpse at that. It was night. I cannot say who it was.'

'But Ilsevel was certain. Where was it that he vanished? Think, lad, this is important. I must know where it was exactly.'

'I can show you, sir, if you wish.'

'What an obligin' fellow ye are.'

And so Phineas found himself abroad in the streets of Lincoln, just as dusk was falling, with a troll ambling along in his wake.

'Yer neighbours'll have a deal t' talk about,' chuckled Balligumph.

They would indeed. Phineas saw three people he knew before they had arrived at the top of the hill — and there was Mrs. Batts bustling across the square, and pausing to stare.

He thought back, a trifle wistfully, to the week before, when he had been only Phineas Drake, the baker, and a person no one ever thought it worthwhile to gossip about. And what more was he to expect out of Aylfenhame, now he had become tangled up in Ilsevel's business? Was it to be ogres next? Goblins? Witches coming to curse his modest little shop?

'I am already missing the quiet life,' he muttered, and pulled down the brim of his cap. It would not conceal his identity from anyone who knew him, but it made him feel better.

The troll chuckled. 'Was it really so satisfyin' a life?'

Phineas was obliged to pause, and think. 'No,' he allowed with a sigh. 'Not so very satisfying as all that.'

A great hand patted his shoulder, a gesture which almost drove him to his knees. 'Life has funny ways of doin' ye a good turn.'

'I don't know what that means, sir.'

'Ye will soon enough.'

The distance from the bakery to the Stairs where Ilsevel had vanished was not great, and soon Phineas stood with Balligumph halfway down the slope, on the very spot where he had caught a glimpse of Wodebean. 'This is the place,' he said, and stood with his feet exactly where he had found the rose, or as near as he could manage.

'Ah!' The troll stood stock-still, his face alight, looking up and down the Stairs as though some profound realisation had occurred to him. 'Ah!' he said again. 'Interestin'! Very interestin' indeed!'

'Sir?' Phineas knew not how to interpret this response, and stood watching with a frown.

A great, triumphant grin split Balligumph's face, and his tusks jutted forward. 'Ye're a treasure, lad,' he said to Phineas. 'What a fortunate day it was when ye caught sight o' Ilsevel! An' bless yer kind heart, that ye thought it best t' follow!' He began striding up and down, and around and around, circling the spot in which Phineas stood. 'Clever, clever,' he muttered. 'Wily Wodebean. But clumsy just a touch, weren't ye? Then again! 'Tis not every day yer pursued by a great lady, an' a baker's lad.'

Phineas began to lose his patience. 'Who is Ilsevel, sir? And who are *you*, and why is everyone so anxious to find Wodebean?'

Balligumph regarded him seriously. 'Thas an old tale, lad, an' I haven't time t' tell it all t' ye just now. But there was once a queen, an' a deal o' trouble which were never quite rightly mended. Wodebean... was involved wi' the business, though as t' *how* exactly, thas a matter of opinion. Tis certainly true that sommat went awry, and Ilsevel is tryin' t' mend it now.'

'That does not make much more sense, sir.'

'It will. An' now! Look at this.' Balligumph gently moved Phineas aside, and placed his own great, booted feet over Phineas's footprints. 'This spot's special. See that stone?' He pointed to an aged, moss-grown stone set into the floor directly between his feet. 'If I were t' scrape away all the frilly green stuff thas growin' on it, ye'd see that it's an odd colour. Thas because it's made out of somethin' special — somethin' out of Aylfenhame. We call it Sagestone, fer it knows a great deal more than it seems. It's here t' mark a spot — an' t' guard a door.'

'A door?' said Phineas, more out of politeness than any real hope of receiving a meaningful response.

'It's hollow.' He grinned again, delightedly. 'I have long held suspicions about this city, an' I think I was right. The entire hill's Hollow!' He said the closing word with a peculiar emphasis, and looked ready to dance with delight. 'Though I suspect as it's dormant, an' not many thas left know the truth of the place now. Not many besides Wodebean. He's had the run of it fer enough years, I think.' Balligumph winked at Phineas. 'What do ye think, lad? Goin' t' help me find a way inside?'

'Inside the *hill?*'

'It's not rightly a normal hill, or only on the top parts. 'Tis part o' the Hollow Hills, them bits as lies somewhere between England an' Aylfenhame, not precisely belongin' t' either. Odd little bits of spaces, they are. Pockets o' this an' that, could be anythin'. An' lawless, which is why it appeals t' Wodebean I suppose.'

Phineas swallowed. It was one thing to offer his aid to Ilsevel; strange though she was in some respects, she was obviously a fine lady adrift and confused in his city, and that called for the kind of assistance Phineas was well able to provide. But lending his efforts to a troll, who rambled about Hollow Hills and proposed to take Phineas somewhere out of England entirely?

'Why me, sir?' he said bluntly, that being the question that rose chiefly to his mind. 'Surely there are others better suited.'

'Ye know this city well. Ye're one of only two people I know has actually seen Wodebean lately, an' I can't find the other one. Further, I suspect ye're t' be involved in this business anyhow, an' I may as well keep ye close if that's t' be the case. Ilsevel'll find ye again at some time, an' she'll find me in the process.'

Phineas merely stared at him.

'Besides, we ain't in Aylfenhame now. Ye've a human's way o' lookin' at things, an' this is *your* territory, not mine. If my fae friends had much notion o' what's goin' on around here, I'd have heard of it by now.'

'My father is unlikely to spare me, sir.'

'Thas no excuse, now,' said Balligumph, gently enough. 'Yer a grown man, not a child, an' yer father can manage the shop without ye for a day or two. What's yer real worry?'

Chastened, Phineas looked away. 'This is beyond my… my skill, my knowledge, my abilities.'

'Aye!' Balligumph tossed his hat in the air with sudden exuberance, caught it again, and threw it back onto his head with a flourish. 'Yer right there! Probably it is beyond mine, too, which is why I need yer help. Anyroad,' he said with a tusky grin, 'When yer way beyond yer depth an' don't know what yer doin', thas when it gets fun.'

Phineas could not help smiling a little at this display of enthusiasm; it was infectious. 'Very well, sir,' he agreed, trying to ignore the way his heart sank as he said it. 'What can I do?'

'Well, now,' said the troll. 'First, ye may agree t' call me Balligumph. Yer makin' me feel old an' stuffy wi' yer *sir* this an' *sir* that.'

'I... um, if you wish.'

'Good. An' fer the rest... listen now, an' I'll tell ye.'

CHAPTER SEVEN

Ilsevel suffered a stab of mild remorse about deceiving poor Phineas. He meant well, and his determination to help her could not but touch her heart, even if she struggled to account for it. But he could have little idea how incapable he was of protecting her from anything that she might genuinely consider a threat. He was much more likely to fall into trouble himself, than to shield her from it, and she was beginning to like him. It would not do to get him cursed, or killed, or — worst of all — turned into something small and slimy, like a frog.

So she let him believe she was going back to the boarding house, and thence to sleep. But as soon as his dark, shabby figure had trodden away into the night and disappeared from sight, she altered her course and went somewhere else instead.

She went back down the hill to the mossy glade beyond the river, where the thieves' market was still being held.

It was not England, this odd little place. Those great, arching boughs belonged to trees too ancient to have survived in a human city, under the development of growing industry. There was a quality to the moonlight that spoke of deep magic, an air of timelessness to the forest and the moss and the music; no, this was certainly not England.

But was it Aylfenhame? Never had she heard of humans mingling so freely, so openly, with the Ayliri and the fae, as they did here. That was partly because the means to cross the borders between those two realms were not widely available. There were some who could come and go as they pleased, but they were few indeed. To the rest, free passage back and forth was the province of the Solstice days, and that was all.

How, then, were so many people crossing from the waterfront into this pocket of a glade, when the Winter Solstice had passed days ago? It could not be Aylfenhame.

But if it was not England and it was not Aylfenhame, then what was it? *Where* was it?

She must discover the answers to these questions, and without delay, for if it lay within Wodebean's power to work such a marvel then he was far more formidable than she knew.

Having arrived before with the intention of attracting some notice, the opposite was now her goal. She hovered on the edges of the clearing, watching covertly as knots of revellers drank and danced and made deals with one another; bought trinkets and heirlooms, ate sweetmeats and pies, drank mead and wine and generally behaved as though they were entirely at home in their peculiar environment. Clearly, this thieves' market was a regular occurrence.

And just as clearly, few of them realised how remarkable it was.

It occurred to her as she watched that the confines of the glade were well defined, though by no obvious means. No one strayed much beyond the warm circle of light cast by the low-hanging lanterns; no one slipped behind the stalls, or ventured very far into the trees. What lay beyond? Why did nobody seem disposed to find out?

Ilsevel was disposed.

She set off, making her way through clusters of Ayliri in dazzling velvet gowns — where *were* they getting those clothes? She had never seen the like — and then through a knot of giggling hobgoblins playing some complicated game with a trio of human women all rosy-cheeked with mead; but just as she was on the point of stepping into the trees, her way was blocked by a forbidding figure in a dark coat. His head was bare of hat, his cheeks unshaven, and his neck cloth tumbling down. The arms-folded posture he adopted before her made his disapproval clear, as did the frown with which he beheld her.

Ilsevel returned look for look, drawing herself up. 'Gabriel, was it not?'

'That it was,' said he. 'But I have a fancy to be called Mr. Winters by *you*.'

Ilsevel gave him a cool look. 'In that case, you may address me as My Lady Silver.'

'Oh? And why is that?'

'Because it is my name. Or,' she allowed, 'one of them.'

Gabriel Winters abandoned this point. 'What are you doing with Phineas?' he demanded. 'Getting the lad into trouble, I'll be bound.'

'You are protective of him.'

'Aye. Someone ought to be.'

'He has a father, has he not?'

'His father is an old friend of mine, and I won't willingly speak ill of him. But he's no manner of guardian to young Phineas. Not now.'

'Oh?' said Ilsevel politely. 'And was he ever before?'

'Some years gone, when Phineas's mother were still alive. Now the lad only has me to look after him, and I mean to do it. I ain't happy to see him frequenting thieves' gatherings, My Lady Silver, and I can see as it's you as has brought him to it.'

'Not exactly,' said Ilsevel distantly. 'He invited himself.'

'That he would, if he thought you needed help. My Lady Silver you may or may not be, but *he* has a heart of gold, and he'll pay dearly fer that if you get him into mischief.'

Ilsevel began to feel impatient. 'I applaud you for your concern, Mr. Winters. Phineas quite deserves your kind offices, I am sure. But since I have gone to some trouble to leave him behind to-night, and precisely in order to avoid dragging him into difficulties, I hope you will excuse me of callousness. And you will excuse me altogether, in fact, for I have urgent business in these parts.'

She detected a slight softening of the man's forbidding posture. 'And what might that be?'

'I told you before, did I not? I seek Wodebean. And also, now, my sister. And I am more than a little curious as to the nature of this peculiar place.'

'Yer sister? There's two of you about?'

'So I understand. She was handing out unusual flowers.'

'Ah.' Winters nodded. 'Gold-haired wench. Eyes full of sky. And wickedness.'

'A most apt description. Did you chance to see which way she went?'

'No.'

Ilsevel sighed. 'Then pray stand aside.'

Winters did so, and made Ilsevel a tiny, only slightly mocking bow. 'She is My Lady Gold, I suppose?' he said.

'No, that was my other sister.' Ilsevel gathered her skirts and marched off into the trees, and only belatedly became aware that Winters had fallen into step behind her.

She stopped.

'I do not quite understand how it is that I continue to attract human followers,' she said with as much exasperation as asperity.

'Oh, I am not following you.'

She blinked. 'You are not?'

He grinned lazily. 'I've long had a fancy to see what's beyond the glade, and shan't be sorry to find out tonight.'

Her eyes narrowed. 'And you have chanced to choose this very moment to explore.'

'Happen you might've put me in mind of the idea.'

Ilsevel chose to ignore that, and to ignore him, too. She set off again; let him trail after her if he would.

He did not. She chose a winding path into the shadowy trees, summoning a mote of wisp-light to guide her steps. Winters veered off in quite another direction, and soon disappeared from sight.

Excellent.

The woods beyond the glade were fairly extensive, she soon concluded, and disappointingly featureless. She trod carefully, for the ground was littered with twisting tree roots poking up out of the earth, poised to catch an unwary foot. Patches of moss grew here and there, black and dark, and occasional clusters of mushrooms and ferns. The trees only seemed to grow vaster, darker and older as she progressed, and she felt beset by shadows; they flickered and twisted and loomed out of nowhere, as though taunting her.

She began to regret, just a little, that she had not brought Phineas with her after all.

'Stout heart,' she scolded herself, and pressed on. What could do the boy do for her here, save provide company? She needed no company, for she was accustomed to solitude.

There came a twinkle in the night, and then another, and more; and then came into view a tree greater and older than all the rest, set in regal splendour in the midst of a wide clearing. Its boughs were hung all about with wisp-lights, like Ilsevel's own. Pale and clear, they glittered among the shadows, and Ilsevel could not decide if they were more eerie or welcoming.

Faint strains of music reached her ears. Someone was singing.

Ilsevel rolled her eyes.

A door was carved into the great, craggy trunk of the ancient tree, and it creaked slightly open as she marched up to it, a line of golden light limning its edges.

Ilsevel kicked it open.

'Really?' she called. 'A haunting voice drifting through the night? A dark tree in the depths of the woods? Will you never give up this absurd siren business, sister dear?'

The singing stopped.

A passageway opened out beyond the door, leading off into the darkness. It did not appear to be concerning itself much with the reasonable confines of the tree's admittedly broad trunk.

Following it, Ilsevel found that it twisted and curled in improbable contortions before opening out into a surprisingly cosy parlour.

Seated in an enormous armchair before a slow-burning fire was the gold-haired wench with the eyes full of sky. Those eyes were turned upon Ilsevel with an expression of stark amazement.

Ilsevel felt an odd flutter somewhere in her heart, a sensation composed half of joy and half of fury.

'Ilse?' said the wench.

'Tylla.'

'You're still alive.'

'So are you.'

The perfect mouth hardened. 'And where have you been all these years?'

'It's a long story.'

'I have time.'

Ilsevel gathered her composure, and fanned the flames of her rage. With Tylla, it was always better to be angry than sentimental, for the latter made one vulnerable. 'Actually, you don't,' she said crisply. 'Anthelaena's still transformed, did you know that? I cannot find Wodebean, I thought you were dead — *why* are you wearing this absurd Glamour? Is your own face not good enough?'

Tyllanthine, My Lady Pearl, fixed her sister with an ugly glower. 'It is not precisely a matter of choice.'

'Of course it is. You're using Glamour.'

'It's to do with my other face. If I must be so repellent in the daytime, I reserve the right to be beautiful beyond reason at night. It is only fair.'

'Repellent?'

'Yes.' Tyllanthine looked down her exquisite nose at Ilsevel. 'I was cursed. I'm a Korrigan, Ilse.'

Ilsevel nodded thoughtfully. 'We will mend that too, then.'

'You think I haven't tried?'

'Doubtless, but you did not have me. Nor Anthelaena. We will retrieve her, and both of us will fix you.'

'I have tried to recall Anthela, too.'

'We need Wodebean.'

'And you did not do this ten or twenty years ago because...?' Tyllanthine's glorious eyes were as cold as winter. 'Where *have* you been, little sister?'

'Keeping company with fish.'

'I beg your pardon?'

'At the bottom of this or that stream, eating insects for breakfast, lunch and dinner, and cold to my bones every moment.'

Tyllanthine's eyes widened. 'You were transformed?'

'Forcibly. A *frog*, Tylla. Given the choice I had far rather have been a cat. Just imagine the mischief Anthela and I would've got up to.' A chair sat vacant on the other side of the fire. Ilsevel fell into it with a sigh, and regarded her sister with a fraction of a smile. 'I am quite glad to see you, you know.'

Tylla eyed her with suspicion, but relented enough to roll her eyes, and say with a sigh: 'It is not wholly unpleasant to see you, either. I thought you... well, I do not know what I thought. Lost? In Torpor? Dead?' She said the words so coolly, without a trace of apparent distress at so terrible a sequence of prospects, and Ilsevel sighed inside. After so many years, could not Tylla find it somewhere in her glacial heart to care about *anything*?

'Thank you,' she said distantly, letting the rest of her sister's speech pass. 'What are you doing here?'

'Looking for Wodebean.'

'As am I. Do you imagine that this absurd parade will draw him to you?'

'He seems to be immune to my charms.' The perfect lips twisted with disgust.

Ilsevel smiled. 'How reassuring, for somebody ought to be.'

The sky-blue eyes glittered. 'Things are moving again, Ilse. People are waking up out of the Torpor— dangerous people. And now there is *you*. By what arts did you escape your frog-curse? No — never mind, there is not time. We need Anthelaena.'

'She is transformed. A cat.'

'I know. I have tried everything to return her to her rightful form, but to no avail.'

'Not quite everything, I presume, or you would have no need of Wodebean.'

Tyllanthine watched her in silence for a moment. 'The terms of that curse… it will not be easy to reverse it.'

'Oh?' Ilsevel studied her sister's countenance with interest — and suspicion. 'How do you know what the terms are?'

'How do *you* know what they are?'

'I do not, quite. I received information leading me to Wodebean, that is all. I know he was involved in the business somehow.'

Tyllanthine smiled. 'As did I.'

She was hiding something, Ilsevel could see it in the smug glitter of her eyes. But she knew better than to try to press her younger sister. The more she was asked, the more stubborn she would become — and the more she would enjoy the sense of power.

So Ilsevel said nothing.

Tyllanthine hated silence. It gave her nothing to work with. Her eyes narrowed in irritation, but she spoke. 'Someone must be restored to the throne-at-Mirramay as soon as possible, Ilse, and I am glad to see you, for you shall help me.'

Ilsevel straightened. 'Someone?'

'Anthelaena, by preference, since it's rightfully hers. If we cannot recall her, then it will have to be Lihyaen, if her spine can be stiffened enough for the purpose. And it had better be, because I'm sure you realise that in the continued absence of Edironal, the only other alternatives would be you or I. And we never did have much of a fancy to play queen, did we?'

'Lihyaen!' Ilsevel heard only about half of Tyllanthine's words, her mind caught and held by that one name.

'She is not dead.' Tyllanthine would typically rather die than show the smallest vulnerability, joy included; but even she displayed some small signs of pleasure at this news. A softening of her hard blue eyes, perhaps, and even the faintest hint of a genuine smile.

'How?' said Ilsevel faintly. 'I saw her body.' She thrust away the unwelcome memory: her beautiful, vibrant niece, a joyous child, turned white and cold and lifeless...

'Taken. A stock was substituted, a *very* good one. She is recently found.'

Much had been left out of this narrative; too much. 'Is she well?' said Ilsevel in trepidation. Had she suffered some permanent harm? Was she, too, cursed?

'Perfectly,' said Tyllanthine, to Ilsevel's relief. 'She is with some trusted friends, in Grenlowe.'

Ilsevel sat in silence for a time, her mind reeling. It was too much to take in; she would stupefy herself with the effort, if she did not take care. Grimly, she forced herself to focus on the most urgent points in Tyllanthine's narrative. 'A stock. Tylla, you know who's reputed to be the very best crafter of such things as that?'

'Wodebean, of course. Hence, I am in something of a hurry to speak to him.'

'Don't eviscerate him until I have finished with him,' said Ilsevel, ice-cold. 'He let her die, and he will pay for it.'

'Did he?' Tyllanthine tilted her beautiful head, her fathomless blue eyes unreadable. 'Are you so certain of that, sister?'

'He did not lift a finger to help, though I offered him every incentive to do so.'

'And yet, you say she is not dead after all.'

'I saw Anthelaena, Tylla. A great, purple cat, identical in appearance to that doll of hers, the one she *always* carried about — you will not remember, for she had outgrown it by the time you were born. But *I* know it was her. It must be. It cannot have been Wodebean's doing, for he is no witch, no sorcerer — how could he have contrived it? But she is not dead.' Ilsevel had repeated these words to herself so many times since her return to her own shape, hardly daring to hope. The queen had died; everyone knew that. Some said that heartbreak had killed her, for her husband was gone and her daughter dead. But Ilsevel remembered the truth: the terrible illness which had come upon her, so soon after Lihyaen's apparent death. She had faded fast; two days, and she had gone from vibrant (if grieving) good health to within a whisper of death. The Court physicians were powerless.

Do something, Ilsevel had begged of Wodebean, for she had feared that Anthelaena's was no natural illness, and there was no one at Court better versed in curses, enchantments and all manner of dark magic than Wodebean. It was a professional interest of his, for his livelihood consisted in large part of trade — not only of objects of great value and power, but also of the myriad components necessary to work such questionable magics.

I will try, he had said. But he had not tried, and Anthelaena had died...

...unless she had not.

'It must have been her,' said Ilsevel desperately. 'The coincidence is too great, otherwise. It *must* be her.'

Tyllanthine inclined her head with that faint, annoying smile of hers, and said: 'You are right: it was our sister, and she is not dead.' Ilsevel's heart leapt at this confirmation of her fervent hopes. 'But I have not been able to lift the enchantment that binds her,' continued Tyllanthine.

Weak with joy and relief, Ilsevel took a steadying breath. 'Why not?' she demanded. 'Have you not been at liberty all these years of my absence? What has prevented you?'

'I did not know where she was until a year past, and then I had not the materials,' said Tyllanthine sourly. 'They are grown scarce these past years.'

'Have you tried?'

'Of course I have,' snarled Tyllanthine. 'But not even the Goblin Market could furnish me with everything I have need of, and what then? What would *you* do, sister?'

'Consult Wodebean,' said Ilsevel at once. 'If there is anyone left who can lay his hands upon such articles as would be needed for powerful magics like that, it would be him.'

An unpleasant fellow, Ilsevel reflected. He had no hand in the laying of curses, typically, but he gladly supplied all the necessary accoutrements to those who did — for a price. Convincing stock-puppets was the least of it.

'Precisely,' said Tyllanthine. 'And that, dear sister, is what I am doing here.'

Ilsevel stood up. 'What were the results of your gambit with the flowers?'

'I irritated him excessively.' Tyllanthine smiled proudly. 'Enough so that he emerged, and suffered himself to be seen. And I have some one or two clues as to where it was that he subsequently vanished into.'

'Let us pursue them at once.'

Tyllanthine made no argument, and rose smoothly from her chair. 'Just one thing, Ilse,' she said.

Ilsevel, already on her way to the door, turned back. 'What is it?'

'Who was it that made a frog of you?'

'I would like to know the answer to that question myself,' Ilsevel replied. 'I was ambushed in the gardens at Mirramay, and I never knew by whom. All I saw was a figure in a white cloak.'

She was out, then, of the odd little house, back into the shadowy woods and the low boughs lit with starlight. 'Where was Wodebean last seen?' she said to Tyllanthine, who emerged from the tree behind her.

She did not hear her sister's response, for there came a sudden grip upon her ankle, as of icy fingers wrapped around her leg. Tightly, so tightly! It *hurt,* and she cried out with the pain, for her bones must break under the pressure of it—

—she fell, not merely a few feet onto the earthy ground but much, much farther than that. She fell and fell and landed at last in something soft yet icy, and a flurry of white powder flew up around her.

Snow.

She lay, shocked and trembling, her dazed eyes blinking up at a grey, cloud-laden sky. Snow drifted gently across her face and melted on her skin.

'Tyllanthine?' she whispered.

No reply came.

Carefully, painfully, she dragged herself to her feet. Her left ankle throbbed still with pain, but it held; it was not broken.

Turning in a slow, disbelieving circle, Ilsevel looked around. She had landed in the middle of a wood, not unlike the one she had left — except that daylight had replaced the night, and everywhere was deep snow. And how was this possible, when she had fallen and fallen through empty space? She certainly had not crashed through those snow-laden boughs now arcing over her head.

No sign could she detect of anything that might explain her sudden presence here. She had been snared like a fox and *pulled,* but by what?

Whatever it had been, it was gone.

CHAPTER EIGHT

'Father,' said Phineas some little time later. 'This is Mr. Balligumph. Mr. Balligumph, my father, Mr. Samuel Drake.'

The two men regarded one another.

Balligumph's request had been simple enough, on the face of it. *I want ye t' help me find a way back into the Hollows. Someone in these parts must know the way in, an' the way out. Use yer brain, young fellow, an' help me find it.*

Once the troll had explained what he meant by the Hollows, the matter became fractionally clearer to Phineas. What could he mean save the very place where he and Ilsevel had gone only the previous night? Well, he would take Mr. Balligumph there at once.

Only, the road that lay open during the revels would be closed, now. They would need help to get back in. They would need somebody who knew the secret of accessing it; someone, in short, with connections to the city's thieves.

Phineas did not know where to find Gabriel Winters, and that obliged him to approach his father, whom he had left tending the shop alone — and with a great, hulking denizen of Aylfenhame shambling along in his wake.

It was likely to be an interesting morning.

The troll, affable as always, tipped his hat to Phineas's father. 'Mornin',' he said agreeably. 'Pleased t' meet ye. Fine young chap ye have.'

Father, however, had not got over his surprise at the appearance of such a fellow as Balligumph; or perhaps it was merely the after-effects of the copious quantities of gin he had doubtless consumed the night before. He regarded the troll with a sour lack of cordiality, and grunted something that might have been a greeting.

Balligumph's gaze transferred to Phineas's face, asking a silent question.

Not one that Phineas could answer just then.

He cleared his throat. 'Er, father, Mr. Balligumph has asked my help and in turn I will need yours. Do you know where Gabriel Winters lodges?'

'He is not there.'

'I beg your pardon?'

'Cleared out of his lodges, night before last. No one knows where he's gone.'

Phineas's heart sank. He turned uncertainly to Balligumph. 'I am sorry, sir. I do not know who else might be able to help, if not Gabriel.'

The twinkle returned to the troll's eyes, and he grinned at Phineas's father. 'Unless I miss me guess, praps this gentleman can help me.'

Engaged in transferring a tray of unbaked bread into the oven, Samuel Drake did not reply.

'Yer familiar wi' the thieves' revels down by the water?' said Balligumph.

That elicited a flicker of a reaction. Drake paused for the barest instant, then continued unperturbed. 'I am a respectable baker, sir.'

'Men change,' said Balligumph.

Drake stopped, and regarded the troll with an unfriendly glare. 'Just what are you suggesting?'

'Nothin', my good sir,' said the troll amiably. 'I am only askin' fer a bit of aid. If you should happen t' know the way into that bit o' space in which they hold the thieves' market, I'd be grateful fer yer help.' To Phineas's surprise, a great, heavy-looking pouch of drab cloth had appeared in the troll's enormous hand. When Balligumph shook it, it clinked.

Father speedily revised his ideas. He looked from the pouch, to the troll, to Phineas, and gave a great sigh. Something like regret flitted across his wine-roughened features, and was gone. 'Phineas must watch the shop.'

'He cannot,' said Balligumph. 'He is comin' wi' me.'

Drake scowled. 'Then I can give you instructions. Whether or not they will work for you, I cannot say.'

Balligumph bowed his thanks. 'A fair compromise.'

Phineas heard all this with mild surprise. He knew that Gabriel Winters was not the only man of... questionable morals with whom his father was acquainted, to be sure, and had sometimes wondered about that. But that Samuel Drake should be in possession of such particular knowledge himself, as would win access to the thieves' market even when it was closed? Quite curious.

And it did appear that his father was avoiding his eye.

'There's a word,' said Drake. 'Changes once in a while. Just now it's: "Mirror-May."'

'Ahhh,' said Balligumph softly, as though the words meant something to him. 'An' what must we do wi' this phrase?'

'There is a door in a wall. Green-painted. Knock thrice upon it, and speak.'

'I know the way,' said Phineas.

His father looked oddly at him for that, but thankfully did not enquire.

Phineas found it convenient to study the window.

'Thank ye,' said Balligumph, and left the pouch on the edge of the nearest of the long tables of the Drakes' kitchen. Then, with a tip of his hat to Phineas's father, he ambled out into the shop, and thence into the street.

Phineas lingered a moment. 'Father?'

Drake glanced his way, but did not speak.

Hesitating, too many questions fighting for his attention, Phineas gave up with a sigh. He merely nodded a farewell to his father, and followed Balligumph outside.

'I am sorry,' he said to the troll, who was waiting just outside the door, drawing an enormous dark cloak around himself.

'Fer what, lad?' said Balligumph.

That, too, proved to be rather beyond Phineas's power to explain, and he felt vaguely disloyal for even attempting to apologise for his father's conduct. So he let that pass, too, and shrugged. 'To the waterfront?'

'Aye.'

The door was unassuming. Set into the side of a nondescript brick warehouse, its paint moss-coloured and peeling, it had no distinguishing features to set it apart, nothing to suggest that its purpose was in any way special. It was merely a door, with a great brass doorknob set into the centre.

Phineas found it by retracing his steps of the night before. He had passed down those streets without paying much attention, too intent upon the glowing waymarkers upon the floor. Now, though, he took a moment to examine the area more carefully.

'There,' he said, pointing to a spot on the floor directly before the portal. It did little to call attention to itself, but it was a slightly different colour than the stones paving the ground around it: more green than grey. 'Sagestone?'

'Aye!' said Balligumph in delight, and bent to scrutinise it. 'Ye've a fair eye fer detail, lad.'

Mild praise it may have been, but it was the first Phineas had received in some time. He tried not to let the extent of his pleasure show on his face, for fear of being thought altogether unreasonable, and turned his attention to the door.

'Yer father hasn't quite got the inflection right wi' the pass-phrase,' said Balligumph, as Phineas raised his hand to knock. 'You knock, an' I'll speak.'

'Very well, sir.' Phineas knocked thrice.

'Mirramay,' boomed Balligumph, so loudly as to alarm Phineas. He looked quickly around. There were some one or two people nearby, but perhaps they were too intent upon reaching the next place of warmth to pay heed to... to a gigantic blue-skinned troll bellowing strange words not ten feet away.

No, that could not be it. Phineas looked long at Balligumph, a little wild-eyed.

The troll winked. 'Never mind it, lad.'

The door creaked, and there came the sound of a latch falling back. Then it shuddered, spraying flakes of green paint, and... disappeared.

Darkness yawned.

Balligumph flicked his fingers, and a tiny ball of flickering white light materialised from somewhere. It threw out a surprisingly strong glow, illuminating an earthen floor and a passageway formed of tall, twisting hedges. The scene was reassuringly familiar to Phineas: he had trod this very road last night, though then it had been brightly lit and decked in streamers.

'I'll go first,' said Phineas. 'I know this place.'

Balligumph acquiesced with a nod, and onward Phineas went.

The air was hushed and still. Nothing moved, and there came no sounds at all as Phineas carefully stepped into the hedge-lined corridor and walked forward, the wisp-light bobbing before him. He could not even hear his own footsteps, or — more remarkably — Balligumph's; it was as though something shrouded the way in silence.

The effect was, if Phineas had been moved to admit it, slightly unnerving.

The hour was yet early, and one or two of last night's revellers still lay asleep under the hedges. They, too, seemed shrouded in an odd stasis; they breathed, but barely. He hesitated an instant, wondering if they ought to be helped. But they presented no signs of distress; if anything, they appeared sunk in a slumber of the utmost peace. He passed two humans in such a state, a rosy-cheeked woman in a red gown and a bearded young man smelling strongly of ale. There was a goblin, too, and a few other denizens of Aylfenhame whom Phineas could not identify.

Then, when the corridor promised to open out shortly into the wide expanse of the merry glade, Phineas saw someone he recognised.

His hat half-covering his face and his coat rumpled, Gabriel Winters lay in an inert heap. His open mouth proclaimed that he ought to be snoring, but no sound emerged.

Phineas knelt. 'Gabriel!'

The man did not move.

Gently shaking his shoulder, Phineas said his friend's name again, more loudly, but with no more response than before.

'Interestin',' mused Balligumph. 'It's like the Torpor, only not near so potent.'

'The what, sir?' said Phineas.

'A long an' deep slumber. The kind you don't always wake up from, though it ain't the same as dyin'.'

Phineas's concern grew. He shook Gabriel harder, and pinched him.

'Calm, lad,' said Balligumph, and knelt beside him. 'Yer friend is well. He's just sleepin' off the after effects of a fine night o' partyin', no?'

'I cannot wake him.'

'Ye can. Look, he's comin' awake.'

Gabriel had indeed stirred, and a hand went to his head. 'Nngh,' he said.

Phineas helped him to sit up. 'Gabriel. Are you well? It is Phineas.'

'So it is.' Gabriel peered blearily at Phineas, and shook his head in wonder, as though he might be imagining the slender, coat-shrouded figure kneeling before him. 'Strangest dream yet,' he remarked.

'It is no dream, Gabriel. You are in—'

'Thieves' Hollow,' said Gabriel in a stronger voice. 'I know. I've been stuck in here fer...' He looked around, blinking. 'Some time.' Then he surged to his feet, startling Phineas, and staggered off in the direction of the glade. 'That cursed wood!' he growled. 'It don't matter *which* direction you go in! Five steps, mebbe six, and yer back where you started.' Apparently intent upon demonstrating this point, he barrelled off into the trees, slightly unsteady on his feet but not at all deterred.

Phineas and Balligumph followed.

And he was right. Six steps or so beyond the edge of the clearing, as the great, shadow-wreathed trees loomed close and dark around them, another step carried them…

…back to the entrance of the glade, near where Gabriel had fallen asleep.

'I heard someone singing,' said Gabriel in disgust. 'I followed it, but I got nowhere near it. That wench, though,' and here he turned to look at Phineas, as though it was in some way *his* fault. 'That wench of yours, I saw nothing more of *her*. Off she went into the trees and never came back.'

'Ilsevel was here?'

'Aye. Not more'n a few hours ago, I saw her. But where she is now I can't say. The trees like her a deal more'n they like me, that's all I'm saying.'

'Or whoever was singin', mayhap,' said Balligumph.

Phineas looked sharply at him. 'Do you know what this means, sir?'

'I may have an inklin', at that, but I cannot say fer certain.' He frowned. 'Thieves' Hollow, ye called it?'

'Aye,' said Gabriel. 'It's been called such ever since I can remember.'

Balligumph grinned. 'A fittin' name. We are indeed in th' Hollows. A little nook someone has carved out fer their own amusement — someone of the name o' Wodebean, I am thinkin'. The question is: does it lead into th' rest?'

'The rest?' said Gabriel blankly.

Balligumph made a vague, sweeping gesture in no particular direction. 'The rest as is in that great hill yer city's built on.'

Gabriel blinked. 'I never heard there was more Hollows up there.'

'No. I am thinkin' as it's been closed off fer a while. But I'm also thinkin' as it's where Wodebean is t' be found.'

'The singing?' said Gabriel.

Balligumph chuckled. 'Woman's voice, was it?'

'Aye.'

'Unlikely t' be Wodebean, then, no? I heard as a lady, name of Hidenory, was lingerin' in these parts, an' it is much her style. The singin', anyway. Reckon as that's who ye heard.' His grin widened. 'An' I don't reckon as she quite had Wodebean's permission t' do it, neither. Interestin' times. Where was this singin' comin' from, do ye reckon?'

Gabriel, unimpressed, pointed one long arm into the trees.

'I thank ye.' Balligumph tipped his hat, and ambled off.

'You'll be all right, Gabriel?' said Phineas, eager to follow the troll but reluctant to leave his friend untended.

'Aye,' said Gabriel, and waved a hand in dismissal. 'After yonder troll, then, if you will.'

Balligumph's long legs had carried him rather far by the time Phineas caught up with him. He was already on the other side of the glade, and marching into the trees. Three of his long strides were all it took before he disappeared—

—and Phineas did too, back to the entrance.

'There you go,' said Gabriel wearily.

Balligumph chuckled, and began to pat the pockets of his coat and waistcoat. 'Clever, clever,' he murmured, and produced a gnarled pipe. He lit this, and stood for a moment in silence, smoking and thinking. 'Ilsevel went in, ye said?'

'Without a trace of trouble.'

The troll grinned widely. 'Aye. Well, no use wastin' our time tryin' t' assault Hidenory's singin' tree. Ilsevel's safe enough, if she is wi' her sister. As fer Wodebean...' He puffed at his pipe, and billows of smoke poured out, pale and ethereal. These coiled up into little knots of mist, which brightened until they shone with a mesmerising, starry light.

'Will-o-the-wykes?' gasped Phineas.

'Aye, but don't ye go worryin' yer head about them old tales. *These* little lot are the helpful sort o' wisp.' He waved a hand negligently and the wisps danced away, spreading out across the glade. Balligumph continued to puff at his pipe, sending more and more after them, until hundreds swarmed among the trees, sailing off into the shadows with a merry glitter.

Soon, they began to drift back.

'Nowt,' said Balligumph after a while, shaking his head. 'An' nowt. Still nowt.' With each pronouncement, another group of wisps popped one by one back into his pipe and disappeared. Eventually all of the bright, bobbing lights had dissipated back into smoke and vanished, leaving the wood dark once more. 'Nothin',' he sighed. 'Save Hidenory's singin' tree, o' course.'

'Sir?' said Phineas, puzzled.

'No way out but the way we came in. No sign of Ilsevel either, nor

Wodebean.' He tucked the pipe away into one of the pockets of his great coat, whereupon it apparently disappeared, to Phineas's fascination, for no tell-tale bulge suggested it remained therein. 'Tis an isolated pocket o' the Hollows, as I thought, wi' no way to get from here into the rest. An' so!' He patted Phineas's shoulder and went back into the corridor of hedgerows, moving purposefully.

Gabriel shrugged, and followed.

Phineas was about to follow suit, but a woman's voice halted him. 'Young man,' said someone in a low, dark tone. 'Stay a moment.'

Wide-eyed, Phineas stopped, and turned. He saw no one near. 'Yes?'

'What do you do here?'

'I seek Wodebean. And... and perhaps Ilsevel.'

'They are neither of them here.'

'So the wisps have just said. We are going.' He did not absolutely know that the speaker intended harm, but it was not a welcoming voice, and he was profoundly disturbed by its apparent lack of an owner.

'Tell the troll,' the voice said darkly. 'My sister is fallen through time. And Wodebean...' she paused. 'The Grim knows something. Tell him.'

'Fallen through time? You mean Ilsevel?'

'I do.'

Panic clutched at Phineas's heart. 'How is that— where is she— what can be done for her?'

'Nothing, by you. Tell the troll.'

'But please— I must help her. Tell me what to do!'

The voice sighed deeply. 'You are as bad as Balligumph,' she said tartly. 'I thought at least you could be relied upon not to take on. Tell the troll! The Grim!'

Phineas could not have said how, but felt that the voice was gone. 'No, please— wait!'

No answer came.

Balligumph, however, returned. 'You spoke,' he said gravely. 'An' I can see ye're upset. Somethin's amiss?'

'Hidenory was here,' said Phineas, a trifle shortly. He sighed. 'And gone again.' He relayed what she had said.

'Did not think t' tell me herself, hm?' said Balligumph. For the first time since he had arrived at the bakery, he looked displeased.

'I think she thought you might make a fuss,' said Phineas fairly, remembering her words.

'Or get in her way, belike.' The troll growled something. 'Tricksy creature, that Hidenory. But no matter. The Grim? Very well. The cathedral it is.' He laid a hand on Phineas's shoulder. 'Think carefully, lad. Fallen through time? Thas really what she said?'

'It was, I am sure of it.'

'Interestin'.' Balligumph squeezed Phineas's shoulder, and ushered him forward. 'I can see ye're troubled fer Ilsevel, lad, but try not t' be. *She* can take care of herself, make no mistake, an' wi' her sister on her tail, all will be well.'

Phineas did not doubt it. Nor could he have said what the likes of *him*, a mere baker's boy, could have done to help her when she had a powerful witch in pursuit.

But still. It went sorely against every principle he possessed to walk away from the glade, and from Ilsevel as well, and return to the city beyond the Hollows.

If Ilsevel were here, this is what she would be doing next, he reminded himself. Very well, then. If he could not help her, he and Balligumph could do the work she had been prevented from pursuing herself.

The air in the glade was warmer than it was outside; the biting chill came as a shock. Tucking his hands deeply into the pockets of his coat, Phineas was surprised to find something in the left-hand one — something with petals, and thorns.

Drawing it carefully out, he found it to be the very same rose he had returned into Ilsevel's possession not long before. She had been secreting things in his pockets again; but when?

Curious.

He tucked the rose back into his pocket — handling it carefully because *she* had entrusted him with it — and left the blossom sticking out of the top, this time. It seemed wrong to bury so much beauty out of sight.

Then, heavy at heart but resolved, he hurried in pursuit of Balligumph.

CHAPTER NINE

Time passed, and Ilsevel saw no one.

The wood seemed never to end, no matter how far she trudged. From time to time, a seeming curve in the pattern of the trees encouraged her to hope that she had stumbled upon a path, and that perhaps a meadow or a village or valley might lie just beyond her sight. But never did it prove to be true. Even the enchantments upon her clothes could not ward off the chill born of wet shoes and stockings and she grew miserable indeed.

She had retreated some way into her own thoughts, ignoring, as best she could, all that was comfortless in her surroundings, and thus it was that a new sound, however long hoped-for, took some little time to penetrate into her consciousness.

A slow, regular *thump thump*, attended by a soft, crisp sound as of snow crunching underfoot.

Someone walked nearby.

Ilsevel stopped at once, her heart thudding. Looking wildly around, she saw no one, and nothing moved. 'Hello?' she called. 'Is there someone?'

Nobody answered, but the footsteps grew louder, and nearer. At length, somebody came into view, bustling between the trees with a step far quicker than Ilsevel's own. She was immediately recognisable as a trow: short in stature and dark, she was wrapped in layers of silk and wool all in shades of blue, and a set of wooden pipes hung on a string around her neck.

'Good morning!' Ilsevel called, elated. 'Madam, may I request your aid?'

The trow stopped the moment Ilsevel's ringing voice broke the stillness of the leaden morning. She looked long at Ilsevel, confusion and wariness evident in her rigid posture and wide eyes. 'Who are you?' she said at length in a dry, scratchy voice.

'My name is— is Ilsevel,' she replied, settling once again for some semblance of an alias. She longed to announce herself under her own, true names once again, for it had been so long — so long! But caution won, and Ilsevel submitted to concealment. She began again. 'I am lost in these parts, and it is *quite* cold, and I wish you will tell me which way I must go to get out of this wood?'

The trow looked about, and a faint smile — almost a smirk — touched her lips. 'Going in circles, I'll be bound.'

'Why, perhaps I have been, at that.' Ilsevel looked around, uncertain. Truth be told, she had no means of telling whether she had passed these particular trees before. They were oaks, and ancient, and covered in snow; what more was there to consider?

'It is the way of this wood,' said the trow. 'It don't give up its tricks easy.'

'I only want to go somewhere warm,' pleaded Ilsevel. 'The wood may keep its tricks, and welcome.'

The trow woman was carrying something, Ilsevel now saw: a bundle lay in her arms, but it was wrapped in wool of the same colour as her cloak, and had not been apparent before. 'Carry this for me,' she said, holding out the bundle to Ilsevel, 'and you may come along with me.'

Ilsevel took it gladly, and instantly discovered it to be a child, for a dark, wizened little face peeped out at her from within the woollen folds. The creature was tiny, and weighed barely anything. 'Your child?' she hazarded.

'My Lallet,' said the trow, which Ilsevel took for confirmation. 'And you may call me Peech.'

'I thank you for your help, Peech,' said Ilsevel, and curtsied; not the way she had seen the women of England manage it, a mere graceless bob, and a dip of the bonnet. No, to Peech she made a reverence worthy of the court at Mirramay, for she felt rather as though the little trow woman might have saved her life. How much longer could she have lasted, alone in the snow, and going forever in circles?

Peech seemed tickled, and rewarded Ilsevel with a wry grin. 'Aye, well,' she said, and bustled off. Ilsevel hastened to follow.

They had not gone far before the woods came to an end. Ilsevel watched Peech closely, hoping to detect the trick or pattern that permitted the trow to find her way where Ilsevel could not. But she saw nothing out of the common way. Peech merely hurried on, moving at a fair clip, and within minutes the craggy oaks were behind them and they were passing instead through a snowy expanse of little hillocks. Trow knowes, Ilsevel realised, for Peech marched a winding path past several and then came to a stop at one particular one, a modest little hill liberally blanketed in snow, and with a neat round door set into the front. She took hold of a heavy brass door-knocker that hung upon it and clattered it wildly about, yelling, 'Peech and Lallet, and guest!'

The door was hastily flung open, and a second trow appeared there, a wizened, elderly fellow with wisps of white hair sparsely scattered across his scalp. His grass-coloured waistcoat was too big for him, and so were his apple-green shoes. 'Guest?' he said.

Peech pointed a long, sharp finger at Ilsevel. 'Lady there!' she announced. '*Fine* lady, I make no doubt.'

'Cold lady, too,' suggested Ilsevel hopefully, and was duly ushered inside. She suffered a moment's doubt upon approaching the door, that it should prove too small for her to fit. But as she drew near, it wriggled and coughed and surged suddenly to twice its former size, becoming more than capacious enough to suit her.

'Why, thank you!' said Ilsevel, and trailed her fingers across it as she passed, by way of gratitude.

The door shivered, and hurled itself shut again.

The knowe consisted of one wide, round room, with a low ceiling which proved not quite so accommodating as the door. Ilsevel could stand upright, but barely. On one side of the dwelling there were trow-sized beds, and a cradle for Lallet. On the other was a fireplace, flanked by a pair of soft but threadbare arm chairs. A fire was roaring in the hearth, and Ilsevel drifted insensibly towards it, wondering if it would be rude to remove her shoes. Ordinarily she would not hesitate, but you never knew with fae folk; some were funny like that.

'Get them wet things off you,' said Peech, and Ilsevel was happy to obey. Her skirts had survived mostly unwetted, thanks to her enchantments, but her stockings and shoes were all wet through, and these she stripped off with a grateful sigh. Peech bustled about, taking them from her and hanging them before the blaze. 'Now then, what's it to be?' she said. 'Roast pigeon I've got, or there's a pie if you prefer, with vegetables in it. And a junket of cream for afters.'

Ilsevel, who was very hungry, said: 'A little of everything, if I may.'

'Cold winds make for empty stomachs,' remarked the elderly trow wisely.

'That they do,' murmured Ilsevel.

There did not appear to be anywhere to cook anything in the house, which puzzled Ilsevel at first. But Peech went to a stout, if unlovely, chest of gnarled wood that stood behind one of the beds, and rapped sharply upon the lid — thrice. 'Pie!' she barked. 'Pigeon! And junket.'

Then she opened the lid, and out came all three. These she set before Ilsevel, who accepted them with gratitude — and eyed the chest with considerable interest.

Peech repeated this process, and delivered another set of comestibles to the elderly trow. 'Eat up, Pops!' she said, and Pops patted her head peaceably by way of reply.

She supplied herself next, and finished with: 'And sweet milk for Lallet,' which promptly appeared. That was that. The chest quietly locked itself and sat inert, looking by no means like the sort of powerful enchantment that had no business occupying so humble an abode.

For a little while, Ilsevel had no attention for anything but her food, and the pitcher of warm cider which Peech soon afterwards gave her (not from the chest, this time). But once she had somewhat satisfied her hunger, she had leisure to look about her, and take more careful note of Peech in particular. The trow had thrown off her enshrouding cloak, and for the first time Ilsevel noticed what she wore beneath: a neat, green-embroidered dress of thick cotton, with a shabby cream-coloured shawl tucked into the neck. The style was familiar to Ilsevel: wide skirts, long sleeves and a flat front, with buttons all in a row from neck to waist, and a deal of fabric behind. Only now did it strike her that she had seen no one wearing such garments since she had shaken off the transforming curse, and regained her human shape. Fashions had moved on, both in England and in Aylfenhame.

She must be very hard up, Ilsevel thought, if she is still wearing such outdated clothes. Her father, too, for Pops's long, embroidered waistcoat, knee-breeches and thigh-length coat were of an era to match his daughter's. The enchanted chest seemed even more incongruous in light of such conclusions as this, and Ilsevel began to feel that she was got into a very strange place indeed.

'The question may seem peculiar,' Ilsevel began, when a pause in Peech's almost ceaseless patter of conversation with her father permitted, 'But where is this place? Where is it I have come to?'

Peech gave her a measured look. 'How came you here, if you don't know where it is?'

'I was… brought, somehow,' said Ilsevel. 'By *someone*, I must suppose, but as to who it was or how it came about, I do not know.'

Pops had settled into one of the deep arm chairs and lit a pipe. This one did not produce smoke, to Ilsevel's interest: instead it emitted streams of tiny, fiery bubbles. They took a long time to dissipate, and soon the air over the fireplace was filled with drifting clouds of them. Ilsevel was fascinated to discover that they gave off a pleasant warmth of their own. Pops sat with the pipe's stem fixed most of the time in his mouth, but at length he took it out and said: 'Happens here and there, you know.'

'Aye,' said Peech. 'T'ain't the first time as we've had unexpected guests, though it has been a while. Last newcomer was nigh on ten year ago, now.'

Ilsevel blinked at that. 'You've had no new people here for a decade? Are you so isolated?'

Peech grinned. 'Aye, since my Gran's day at least. They call it Winter's Hollow, now. Always the snow, and there's no way in or out.'

Ilsevel knew not which of these dismaying and curious facts to respond to first. No way out? How was she ever to get home? She swallowed the mild panic she felt at that unwelcome piece of news, and focused her mind instead on the rest. 'Winter's Hollow,' she said, in a measured enough tone. 'Are there others, then, like it?'

'I heard tell as there's a Summer Hollow, someplace else,' offered Peech, rocking a drowsing Lallet in her arms. 'Cannot say as where, though.'

'There's all four,' said Pops. 'Spring and Autumn. Not as I've ever been to 'em.'

Intriguing, for Ilsevel had never heard of such places. It would take vast, powerful magics to hold even one such spot in a permanent state of winter, or summer, or spring, and there were four? Who had contrived such a thing, and why? And how was it that Ilsevel, knowledgeable as she was, and formerly resident at the very heart of the court of Aylfenhame, had never heard of it? The implication was that these Hollows were either of such great age that they had passed out of general knowledge; or alternatively, that they had been deliberately hidden from Mirramay because they were in no way sanctioned by authority.

Which was becoming a regular theme, of late.

'How is it that you are able to survive here?' she said aloud. 'If it is always winter, you must not be able to grow any food, and if you cannot get it from outside, then where?'

'The chests,' said Peech, and jerked her head in the direction of the one which had so obligingly furnished them with dinner. 'They gives out all the food we could need, and other things. Clothing and shoes. Curatives, and the like.'

Ilsevel regarded the chest again. 'Hm,' she said, somewhat nonplussed. 'Has your family always lived here?'

'Aye,' said Pops. 'Since my Gran's day at least.'

'Are there many families here?'

'Four-and-thirty,' said Peech promptly. 'Five-and-thirty soon enough, for Gladling's to wed with Tom Blossom's boy.'

That made for a larger community than Ilsevel had imagined, though still but a village. 'What do you all do?' she asked, her puzzlement growing. If they could not leave, could not grow food and had no need, in fact, to provide for themselves, what was their purpose? Why did they stay?

'Oh!' said Peech. 'Well, there is lots we've to do, to keep the chests dealing out. Me and Pops, we goes out collecting mushrooms in the woods — the same as you was lost in, lady. There is a type as thrives in the snow, though they can be hard to spot. Dizzy and Dapper, they's Vintners, they make ice wine. Messle, she gets silk from the snow spiders and spins yarn from it, and Melkin, that's her husband, he makes shawls and the like wi' the yarn.' Peech bustled around the house as she spoke, tidying and cleaning this or that, Lallet now returned to her cradle. Her patter ran on. 'There's Nax, he makes them pipes like the one Pap's so fond of. And Gloswise, she's a bit of an oddity. Her chest spits out all kinds of flowers, the kinds that don't bloom in winter. She winterfies 'em all, and puts them back in.'

Ilsevel's mind had begun to drift, lulled by the flow of Peech's chatter, but at that she sat up. 'Flowers?' she said. 'Like roses, for example? What do you mean by "winterfies"?'

'Aye, I saw a rose at her's once,' said Peech, flicking a duster over a windowsill. 'I don't know how she does it, but she makes 'em all frosted-like. Some kind of magic, she once told me, though I don't know as whether the magic's hers, rightly speaking, or something to do wi' the Hollow. Mebbe some of both.'

Several realisations came to Ilsevel all at once. Winterfied roses! *Here* was where Wodebean had got the one he'd dropped at the Stairs. Was he the mind behind this place — and the other Hollows? Was it he who kept them here, working away to create the magical goods and materials he later sold in Aylfenhame, and for nothing but food and outdated clothing in return? She would not put it past him. What a fine arrangement he had made for himself! She would make a point of disrupting it for him.

And as for her sister… those glamoured flowers she had made now appeared to Ilsevel in rather a different light. Had she merely been trying to get Wodebean's attention, or had she been indicating to him that she knew all about his Season's Hollows? Had they been more along the lines of a veiled threat?

And what did she intend to do, if she got hold of him? For though she loved Tyllanthine, Ilsevel knew full well that her sister's idea of appropriate behaviour did not always coincide with her own. Would she seek to rectify all that was wrong with Wodebean's little scheme, or would she prefer to join it? Either way, it was *so* like her to say nothing to Ilsevel about it!

But if Ilsevel was right, who had contrived that Ilsevel herself should be delivered here? It had happened when she was in Tyllanthine's own house, or directly outside of it. Her heart broke at the idea that her own sister might so betray her as to trap her in eternal winter, and she hastily shoved the thought far away from her.

Composure, she reminded herself. A member of the royal house of Mirramay does not lose her self-possession, no matter what the conditions.

She took a deep, slow breath, and made a resolution: she would find a way out of Winter's Hollow. That must be her first priority.

Then would come the matter of Wodebean, once again, and that of Tyllanthine also.

'Peech,' she said. 'Pops. It is not the first time you have received a new resident unexpectedly, you said. It happened ten years ago?'

'About that,' agreed Peech. 'Eleven year, perhaps.'

'Is that person still here?'

Peech grinned. 'Was Gloswise, and right enough she's still here.'

Ilsevel began to get a sense of terrible inevitability. There were too many coincidences occurring for there to be much real chance involved. 'If it is not too much trouble,' she said, 'May I ask that you take me to see her?'

CHAPTER TEN

Phineas had always found Cathedral Close an unsettling place to linger in during the night. Not that he was afraid, exactly, for there was nothing to fear. But there was a heavy stillness to the air, a blanketing silence, that could not but unnerve; and the great, looming shapes of the cathedral itself could do little to reassure. Tonight, a break in the clouds allowed a little moonlight through, and that soft light etched the vast bulk of the stone towers in deep shadow against the sky.

At least the sun would soon emerge, and dispel the unsettling effects.

Balligumph was serenely oblivious to atmosphere, and ambled along towards the cathedral's west front with sublime unconcern, whistling a faint ditty as he walked. He stopped before the huge entrance doors, shut and probably barricaded at this hour, and lifted his great betusked head. 'Hey!' he called softly. 'Tibs!'

Silence.

The troll whistled again, more loudly this time, and Phineas could only suppose that the tune was of some relevance. 'Tibs!' he called again.

Nothing happened — but then Phineas's sharp eyes detected a stirring among the shadows some way above the door, as though something very dark moved there. A dusty voice spoke. '*Mister* Tibs.'

Balligumph chuckled. 'Still jealous o' yer dignity, old friend? Very well. Mister Tibs it shall be, fer there's no doubt ye deserve the honour. Will ye come down?'

A shadow peeled itself away from the great, dark mass of the building, and fell headlong to the ground. 'Mister Balligumph,' it said, picking itself up. 'What an unexpected pleasure.'

'It has been a long time,' Balligumph agreed.

The creaky-voiced shadow proved to be a man rather shorter than Phineas, very dark of complexion, with a wizened face and a contorted posture. His hair and eyes were dark, too, and though his clothes were not actually black, the deep blue of his waistcoat and the dark purple of his breeches did nothing to lessen the general effect. He wore no hat and no coat, and no shoes either, and seemed superbly unaffected by the pervasive cold. He made Balligumph a stately bow, which seemed to Phineas in some indefinable way old-fashioned, and then those black eyes fixed upon Phineas himself.

'My new friend, from t' bakery,' said Balligumph. 'Mr. Drake.'

The title rung false to Phineas's ears, for only his father was ever called "Mr. Drake." He made no objection, however, for it seemed to be a custom between the two, and instead offered Mr. Tibs a bow. 'A pleasure, sir,' he said, some part of his mind marvelling that he could meet such a being without much alarm or surprise. Truly, he was growing used to the sudden incursion of Aylfenhame into his world. 'You must be the cathedral Grim?'

Mr. Tibs returned the bow, though without the reverence he had shown to Balligumph. 'That I am,' he said drily, and looked to the troll. 'Odd companions you keep nowadays, old friend.'

'He's a fine fellow,' said Balligumph comfortably. 'I've taken a liking to him.'

Tibs grunted. 'You did not disturb me only to introduce the baker's boy. What brings the two of you here?'

'Seen him afore, have ye?' said Balligumph.

'Passing this way and that with his boxes of good-smelling things. Of course I have.'

Phineas blinked. This person had been sitting up there on the walls, night after night, watching Phineas as he went about his morning deliveries? He did not seem as though he meant any harm, and he had certainly never offered Phineas any. But still, the notion of being so closely observed by an unknown being could not but be a trifle disturbing.

'Then ye may have seen someone else, a matter o' three or four days ago,' said Balligumph. 'A lady, Ayliri, an' in no way dressed fer t' weather. Passin' this way in somethin' of a hurry, and wi' Phineas in pursuit.' Balligumph winked at Phineas.

'I saw her,' said Mr. Tibs. 'Ilsevellian, was it not? I almost fell off the wall in surprise.'

'Just Ilsevel,' said Phineas uncertainly.

Mr. Tibs merely looked at him. 'Ah,' he said, though what it was he had drawn from Phineas's comment was unclear.

'Chasin' Wodebean?' put in Balligumph.

'I did see the Trader,' confirmed Tibs. 'But a glimpse, in truth, and I was no less surprised. I thought him long gone.'

'Tis long since he has shown his face,' Balligumph agreed. 'Somethin' has drawn him out, an' mayhap it was our Ilsevel. She's eager enough t' get hold of him, leastwise, an' me an' Phineas scarcely less so by now. T'other lady — Tyllanthine, you'd know her as — she says as you may know somethin'.'

Mr. Tibs's dark eyebrows sailed up at that, and he whistled. 'Both of them, is it? Well, now. I would like to know what she is after, getting involved.'

'Have ye no inkling?'

Silence for a time, as Mr. Tibs apparently thought that through. 'Perhaps,' he allowed. 'You know about Thieves' Hollow already?'

'Aye. 'Tis where we saw Tyllanthine.'

'Was it now?' That news was of interest to Mr. Tibs, too, for he fell silent again, with the air of a man mulling over a variety of reflections. 'I have seen Wodebean twice,' he said then. 'Once on the occasion you mentioned. And two weeks before that. And on *that* occasion, he was not alone. I saw them pass under the Arch on Newport.'

'Who was he with?' said Balligumph quickly.

Mr. Tibs shook his head. 'No one I recognised. A tall figure in a white cloak.'

The troll's head tilted, his great eyes narrowing. 'More an' more interestin'.'

Mr. Tibs put his gnarled hands into his pockets, and stared at the troll.

Balligumph shook his head. 'I have an inklin', thas all. And, there may be more than one fellow with a white cloak, after all.'

Mr. Tibs digested that. 'And why have you come asking questions of me, old friend?'

'The lady Tyllanthine says as you know somethin' about Wodebean.'

With a great, windy sigh, Mr. Tibs looked sourly up at the soaring building he had so long watched over. 'I tell you frankly, my friend, I would not wish to be drawn into any scheme of Wodebean's. And I would not like to see you so.'

'I think it's important,' said Balligumph seriously. 'I don't know yet what Wodebean may be up to, but Ilsevel's after a favour from him. Somethin' t' do with Anthelaena.'

Mr. Tibs's eyes widened. 'I see.'

'And Wodebean hisself, well. I find it mighty interestin' that he's been gone fer more'n twenty year an' then all on a sudden he's back. Thas happenin' to a lot of folk lately, an' I am makin' it my business t' keep tabs on 'em. Will ye help me?'

The sun was coming up, and in the wan, greying light of dawn Mr. Tibs's face resembled that of a gargoyle more than a little, especially when screwed up in thought. 'All I know about Wodebean, then,' he said with a sigh. 'He is almost as old as I am, though he's been known by several names over the years. He used to be attached to the Royal Court-at-Mirramay, many years ago. I do not know what were the circumstances surrounding his departure, but after that he… changed. He had been something of a procurer for the royal family — rare artefacts, lost heirlooms, unusual magical ingredients, that manner of thing. He took that expertise and began working for himself.

'He is said to have aided both sides during the recent conflicts. This, as you may imagine, made him unpopular, but he must have profited enormously. I do not know what became of him afterwards, but since his disappearance more or less coincided with that of the royal family, their opponent the Kostigern, and many of the supporters of both, it is widely supposed that someone punished his duplicity — either by killing him, or sending him into the Torpor.

'I first heard of his reappearance at the beginning of the autumn. It was rumoured that he was trading again, and indeed, a number of rareties long thought lost to the world began to appear in certain underground markets. Then came the opening of Thieves' Hollow and the gatherings there. If I had to guess, I would say he is cultivating a new circle of customers and suppliers, but for some reason he is no longer concentrating his efforts solely upon

Aylfenhame. He is expanding into England.

'Where he lives, I do not know, save that it cannot be far from here. Always I am hearing some whisper or other of him. And since he was able to throw open the Hollow now known as the Thieves' Court of Lincoln, I suspect him of having unprecedented access to the Hollow Hills beneath this city.'

'Thas my own conclusion,' Balligumph agreed. 'Tell me ye know how to get in, Tibs.'

'There was once an entrance part way down the Greestone Stairs,' said Mr. Tibs promptly. 'Which Wodebean has clearly been using, but the key is lost to all but him. There was another under the Arch at Newport, which he also appears to have revived.' He thought a moment. 'I know of no more, and no way to utilise those two without the knowledge only Wodebean seems to have. But… there is one more thing I can tell you.'

'Anythin' could be of use,' said Balligumph.

Mr. Tibs nodded. 'Missing persons,' he said incomprehensibly. 'I hear tell, now and then, of a human woman or child vanishing without trace, for the most part never to be seen again. Five times it has happened in the past ten years, that I know of, and always they were last seen in the same part of the city — out near the castle. It may be nothing, Balligumph, or it may be mere human shenanigans.'

'You said "for the most part",' put in Phineas.

Tibs's black gaze rested upon Phineas. 'I did, at that,' he said with a faint smile. 'Most were never heard from again, but there was one who came back. She reappeared as suddenly as she had vanished, wearing clothes of a fashion dating to some twenty or thirty years ago, and talking wildly of a place where it is always summer. She had not aged a day, Balligumph. As you may imagine, these circumstances proved alarming to her bereaved loved ones, and she was not much attended to.'

'What became of her?'

Mr. Tibs shrugged. 'I do not know. She ceased to wander the streets after a day or two, and I have not heard her spoken of since. But her name, in case you would like to find her, was Eleanor Phelps. She lived on Drury Lane.' With this, Mr. Tibs nodded to Balligumph and to Phineas and swarmed up the cathedral wall, like a darting shadow. Phineas thought he saw the Grim's withered face looking down upon them from far overhead, now merely one of many grotesque carvings adorning the ancient stonework.

'Phelps,' mused Balligumph. 'Ye know that family, Phineas?'

Phineas had already indulged in his own reflections upon that point. 'No, I never heard the name. But I know someone who will certainly be able to tell us more.'

Mrs. Batts was at home, together with her daughter and two of that damsel's closest cronies. Their snug house was crammed full of holly and evergreen, and so liberally decked with colourful ribbons that Phineas's eyes were quite dazzled upon entry. He smelled roasting meat, probably left over from last night's repast, and the more promising aromas of chocolate and new bread, heralding breakfast.

'Why, Phineas!' said Mrs. Batts. Her face lit up at sight of him, which caused him some guilt. He had never taken up her kind invitation to partake of her family's festivities, and had not come to do so now.

'Er, good morning, Mrs. Batts,' he said awkwardly, and nodded his head to Miss Batts. 'Lizzie.'

'Come in, come in,' said Mrs. Batts. 'Is your father with you?'

'I'm afraid not, though I... er, I have brought another visitor with me, if I may introduce you.'

'Any friend of yours, my dear,' said she, and Phineas's heart sank a little, for when she saw Mr. Balligumph she could only—

—screech in surprise, if not horror, which was exactly what she did upon her first glimpse of the troll's great blue face, his tusks twitching as he smiled. 'Mornin', Mrs. Batts!' he said jovially, ignoring her reaction with admirable grace. 'Apologies fer breakin' in upon yer breakfast. My name's Balligumph, an' yer young friend here's kind enough t' be helpin' me wi' a small problem I have on me hands just now. Ye don't mind givin' us yer assistance fer a minute or two, I hope?'

Mrs. Batts, white-faced, only stared. Lizzie and her companions had rushed up at sound of her scream, and now all four of them stood crowded around the door, goggling at poor Balligumph.

'He is a good fellow,' said Phineas. 'You need not be afraid.'

Mrs. Batts gazed next upon *him*, and with an expression of such flabbergasted wonder that he knew not what to say. 'Does your father know of this?' she said at last, in strident tones.

'He does. Mr. Balligumph made his acquaintance earlier this

morning.'

Mrs. Batts threw up her hands, and retreated to the relative safety of her parlour. 'As you will, then,' she said. 'Come along, girls.'

Phineas entered the house, and found himself obliged to duck his head to avoid tangling his hat in the profusion of evergreens wreathed around the door. The troll fared rather worse, and arrived in the parlour at last with a new, if haphazard, garland of festive shrubbery around his hat.

'Tea?' said Mrs. Batts weakly.

'Oh, no, thank you,' Balligumph smiled. 'We won't intrude on yer peace fer very long.'

Phineas did not decline. He was shivering with cold, and knowing that he must soon venture back out into the chilly streets he was not loath to avail himself of anything warming that might be going. Mrs. Batts' hand shook only slightly as she poured out a cup for him, and she contrived not to spill a drop.

'Thank you,' he said with real gratitude, and wrapped his hands around the cup.

'*Phineas*,' hissed Lizzie. Her round, pretty face was dead white. 'What are you *doing*?'

'I will explain,' he replied wearily. 'Someday.'

Balligumph removed his hat, and set it upon the table-top. 'Thing is, we are lookin' fer someone.'

Phineas waited for him to continue, but realised after a moment that Balligumph had quietly passed the conversation to him, for the troll sat looking at him expectantly, and with an encouraging smile. 'Oh,' said Phineas. Yes, after all they *were* his friends. 'Um, there was a story about a girl called Eleanor Phelps that we heard from… well, from somebody just now, and we were wondering if you might know anything about her.'

Mrs. Batts dropped her tea cup. The sudden shattering sound rent the air, making Phineas jump. She took up a handkerchief and began mopping hastily at the spilled mess, casting one brief, fierce glance at Phineas. 'What do you want to go stirrin' all that up for?' she demanded.

Phineas blinked. 'I, um, apologise if it causes you any pain, Mrs. Batts.'

She poured herself tea into a fresh cup, the tremor in her hands more pronounced. 'Eleanor Phelps,' she said heavily. 'Maud's girl.

Went off to market nigh on eleven years ago, an' never came back. Broke Maud's heart, an' mine too, if you must know. We thought she was dead.

'Then, ten years later, when at last Maud had finished grievin', back she came. Mad as anythin', she was, kitted out in them dresses my mother used to wear when I was but a child, and sayin' the strangest things... broke Maud's heart all over again.' She shook her head sadly, and fell into a maudlin reverie over her new cup.

'Er,' said Phineas. 'What became of her after that, Mrs. Batts?'

Mrs. Batts blinked at him, her brows going up. 'Oh, she was sent off to live with a cousin in the country. What else do you do wi' mad relatives? Maud visits her every week, but she says as there's no change. She's still ramblin' on about them friends she says she made under the ground someplace, *where*, if you please, the sun is always shinin' and the roses are always in bloom.' She pursed her lips, then, and looked consideringly at Balligumph. 'Don't think it never occurred to us that she might ha' strayed into Aylfenhame, Mr. Baldigot, for it did. She swears as that isn't what happened to her, and besides, she ain't aged one bit. Nearin' thirty, an' still looks like a girl o' eighteen. How do you explain *that*?'

'I cannot, indeed,' Balligumph said thoughtfully. ''Tis quite the mystery, an' one I would like t' get t' the bottom of right away. If'n ye could give us the girl's address in the country, we'll be on our way, an' thank ye very much.'

Mrs. Batts sighed, and set down her cup. 'I shan't tell Maud,' she decided. 'The poor lady's had enough to worry her. But if you can find out what really happened wi' Eleanor, and somehow mend whatever it was, I shall be grateful to *you*.'

'We will do our best,' promised Phineas earnestly, for his heart was much moved by the tale.

Mrs. Batts smiled at him. 'You're a good lad, Phineas. She's livin' on the edge of some town o' no consequence up in the Wolds, cousin's name is Marjorie Bamber.' She frowned fiercely in thought, and finally pronounced: 'Tilby! That's the name o' the town.'

Balligumph went still. 'Are ye quite sure, ma'am?'

'Yes,' she said with unanswerable certainty. 'That's the place.'

They were out on the street again moments later, Phineas having gulped what was left of his tea in a hurry, for the troll seemed suddenly in great haste to leave. 'What is the matter, sir?' said

Phineas, quickly donning his hat.

'Tilby,' said the troll grimly, 'is where *I* live, an' I ain't never heard o' no Eleanor Phelps livin' there.'

CHAPTER ELEVEN

Well, what a turn up fer the books! Mysteries upon mysteries, an' a maddenin' mess it were becomin'. Eleanor Phelps, o' Tilby? Marjorie Bamber? I knew no such folk.

Thas not t' say they weren't there, mind. I make it me business t' learn as much as I can about the folk o' Tilby, but I can't know everythin' — especially if someone's going' t' some trouble t' pass unnoticed. An' mayhap they had good enough reason t' do that.

Well, I took Phineas wi' me an' off we went t' catch a coach, straightaway-like. In the meanwhile, unbeknownst t' us at the time, poor Ilsevel were still lost in Winter's Hollow — an' learnin' a deal of interestin' things, herself.

Gloswise, to Ilsevel's amazement, turned out to be human, or perhaps half human. She was a small woman with faded red hair and an attitude of weariness, though there hung about her the unmistakeable sparkle of magic. She lived in a wood-framed cottage on the edge of the trows' knowes, a place fancifully decked about inside with flowers beyond counting — all real, and all blooming, despite the harsh winter's chill. Peech walked in without knocking, a comfortable action proclaiming her close friendship with the inhabitant.

'Glos!' she called. 'Got you a visitor.'

Gloswise sat in the window with a pile of roses and violets in her lap. She did not appear to be much engaged by them, for she stared listlessly out at the snowy trees beyond the glass. But her head turned swiftly at Peech's words, and when she saw Ilsevel she leapt to her feet. 'But... but you are a stranger!' she cried.

'I am but just arrived,' Ilsevel agreed, and added drily, 'Somehow.'

Gloswise crossed the room and took hold of Ilsevel's hands. Her grip was tight, rather desperate. 'Then you are no voluntary traveller either!'

''Tis a lady of eminence, Glos,' Peech warned.

Ilsevel looked upon the trow with interest. 'How did you contrive to find that out?'

Peech made a derisive noise. ''Tis all over you. I've need only to use me eyes.'

'You are perceptive.'

'I flatter meself I am.'

Gloswise released Ilsevel's hands and stepped back. 'Forgive me,' she murmured, subjecting Ilsevel to a keener scrutiny. 'A lady of eminence? And yet, I feel that I have seen you before.' She looked particularly at Ilsevel's silvery eyes, and her own widened. 'I was once at the Court of Mirramay, and I could almost swear that I saw—'

Ilsevel sighed. 'You may call me My Lady Silver, if you wish.'

Gloswise took hold of the back of a chair, and gripped it tightly. 'You were dead!'

'Is that what they said of me?'

'The... the palace never said so for sure, but rumour had it—'

'Rumour tends to be notoriously ill-informed,' Ilsevel said tartly.

Gloswise dipped her head. 'Forgive me.'

'I was trapped,' said Ilsevel.

'How came you to be released?'

'A good lady found me, and knew me for enchanted.'

The mind of Gloswise was busy with all manner of reflections, for she scarcely attended to this speech. 'Does that mean— what of— My Lady Gold?'

'The queen is not dead either.' Ilsevel spoke firmly. 'Merely... hidden. I am trying to retrieve her, or at least I was until I found myself marooned in this place of wretched cold.'

'Someone is trying to prevent you?' said Gloswise. She had recovered her composure, and spoke with more self-possession. In her keen gaze, Ilsevel detected a clever mind.

'Perhaps,' she allowed. 'I do not know.' She certainly preferred the notion to the possibility that Tyllanthine had dispensed with her. But if Gloswise was right, who could Ilsevel have encountered recently who might have recognised her, sought to do away with her, and found such peculiar means of doing so?

Unless Wodebean had heard of her pursuit of him. That hobgoblin really had a very great deal to answer for.

Which brought her purpose in seeking Gloswise back to her mind. 'You know the name Wodebean?' she asked.

'No.'

That took Ilsevel aback, for she had confidently expected a yes. 'Oh. Then— then how came you to be here? Who brought you?'

'I do not know. I fell through the road one night, and awoke in a snow drift. This cottage was vacant, and Peech and her family made it habitable for me. Then came the flowers in the chest. I kept them at first, to brighten the house, for by then I knew it would always be winter here. But one that I touched turned all to frost, and I sent it back with the chest, as ruined. The next day, I found thirteen more in there exactly like the original: pink roses. I frosted them all, and...' she shrugged. 'That is what I do here.'

Ilsevel looked meaningfully at her clothes. 'Have you always worn garments like that?'

Gloswise frowned down at her dress — a blue cotton caraco jacket and a wide skirt to match, both printed with sprigs — as though she did not understand the question. 'Why, yes, always.'

She had been stranded in Winter's Hollow for some years, then. Ilsevel's feeble hopes sank. If Gloswise had not found a way out in so long a time, what chance did Ilsevel have of escape?

Her thoughts flew to the chest in a sudden flash of inspiration. Gloswise's was prominently placed beneath a large window, a gnarled oaken box of considerable size. Ilsevel strode over to it and lifted the lid, examining the interior.

It was empty.

'What happens when you put something inside?' she asked.

'It is taken,' said Gloswise, exchanging a puzzled look with Peech.

'By what? How?'

'By what, we do not know. It simply goes.'

'Vanishes,' prompted Ilsevel.

'Aye,' said Peech, watching Ilsevel suspiciously. 'What is in yer head, Lady Silver?'

Ilsevel rested the lid against the windowsill, and smiled at Peech and Gloswise. 'Has anybody ever got in?'

'Got into the chest?' repeated Peech in horror. 'Why, and whatever would we do that for? There is no knowing what would happen!'

'You might go somewhere else,' said Ilsevel. 'Somewhere you would rather be.' She set one foot on the edge of the chest, preparing to climb in.

'My Lady Silver!' said Gloswise, and darted to catch at her arm. 'Pray, do not. I do not know that the flowers I put in there actually go somewhere else. They might simply be destroyed, and what if such were to happen to you?'

'It would make no sense for them to be destroyed. What would be the use of these chests, if that were the case? And I fancy I have some idea as to where they are going.'

Gloswise cast an agonised look at the chest. 'Then let someone else go,' she pleaded. 'Aylfenhame has too much need of you. You cannot gamble like that with your life.'

'Clearly no one else is prepared to make the attempt,' retorted Ilsevel. Without awaiting further interference, she stepped into the chest and planted both feet firmly on the bottom.

Nothing happened.

Several seconds passed, then Gloswise and Peech grabbed an arm each and hauled Ilsevel out of the chest again. 'Thank goodness,' said Gloswise.

'Reckless,' scolded Peech.

Ilsevel extracted herself from their grip, and smoothed her gown. 'Nothing untoward occurred, however, so I trust I may be forgiven.' She was disappointed.

Puzzled, she sat down before the chest and stared at it. Something was tickling at the back of her mind, some feeling that this was not the first time she had encountered an enchantment of this approximate sort. Oh, the spells themselves were none too difficult, nor too rare; it was not unusual for a skilled practitioner of those arts to arrange ways to move articles quickly from one place to another. But these chests were an unusually potent example of them, and that there existed an entire network of such things in so odd, and apparently isolated, a place intrigued Ilsevel considerably.

The primary question in her mind was: where were those articles placed in the chests being delivered to? And whence came those things that appeared within? It occurred to her that the two places in question were not necessarily the same.

'You do not, I suppose, happen to possess some scrap or other of paper, and an article to write with?' said Ilsevel at length to Gloswise.

Gloswise began to fuss about in search of such tools, and Ilsevel returned to her examination of the chest. This one was different from the one at Peech's house: it looked more ancient, its hoary old wood contorted with age. Despite this, it also seemed more ornate, and more skilfully constructed: Peech's was a mere plain affair, but Gloswise's had handsome bronze hinges and, more interestingly, a stout, engraved lock. It was also lined inside with grass-green silk.

'And was this chest already here when you took this house?' Ilsevel said to Gloswise.

'That it was,' said Gloswise. 'All of the furniture was already here.' She put a ragged-edged piece of parchment into Ilsevel's hands, and a marvellous golden plume of a quill.

Using the chest's top as a desk, Ilsevel began to write.

Lady Silver, Ilsevellian, of the Royal House-at-Mirramay, has been involuntarily transported to the place known as Winter's Hollow and demands immediate release. Her confinement is unlawful and improper and the consequences of its prolonged continuance shall be dire indeed.

She signed it with her name in a flourish of ink, and looked up. 'You do not happen to have sealing wax as well?'

Gloswise shook her head.

Ilsevel glanced with regret at the ring she wore on her right little finger, the royal seal that would prove her status. 'Ah, well,' she said. 'This will have to do.' She folded up the note. 'May I now have one of your winterfied roses?' Upon being given one, she secured the note to the rose's stem and opened the chest.

When she herself had stepped in, nothing whatsoever had happened. But when she dropped the rose, it did not even hit the bottom of the chest before it vanished.

That rather confirmed one suspicion of hers: that the chests would transport only those things they recognised as required. That, too, interested her greatly, for it was a sophisticated refinement, one she had never before encountered. Most such articles gaily whisked away anything that happened to find its way inside, including, in one vividly remembered instance, a live kitten. Tyllanthine had been inconsolable until the creature had been retrieved.

She sat waiting in hope for a few minutes, but nothing happened, so she turned back to the other two women. 'Peech,' she said thoughtfully. 'It was you who arranged for this house to be made over to Gloswise, did you not? How came it to be empty in the first place? Who used to live here?' For if there was already an enchanted chest and a houseful of furniture here when Gloswise arrived, it stood to reason that the cottage had once had another occupant. And probably not a trow, either, since they preferred their semi-underground knowes.

Peech returned Ilsevel's inquisitive look with a dubious stare. 'Twas a feller,' she said. 'Name of Pandigorth. Used to make poisons from things as grows out in the woods — berries an' the like. Nasty stuff, but he were high-favoured. Got all kinds of good things out of that there chest, fer his venoms.'

'He was human?' Ilsevel prompted. 'Aylfish?'

'Aylir. Handsome sort, not too old. Disappeared one day.' Peech shrugged.

Ilsevel sat up, excited. 'Vanished! How came he to do that?'

'No one knows. Day came an' he weren't here no more. Some said he had finally got hisself lost in them woods and froze to death. Some say he found a way out of the Hollow. Others say he got to be so high-favoured he were taken out, somehow. No way of knowing now.'

This lack of information was disappointing, but Ilsevel was nonetheless encouraged. Did she dare hope that this Pandigorth had, one way or another, effected his own release? She did. She had seen the nonchalant way with which Peech navigated those maze-like woods; surely Pandigorth, accustomed as he must have been to traversing the woodlands, must have known them just as well, and walked them just as confidently. Why would he suddenly lose himself somewhere within, and die? And how could he have done that without someone like Peech eventually discovering his remains?

She sat taller, feeling somewhat reassured. There was a way out, somehow, and she would find it — even if it meant having to work her way into a position of "high favour" with the mysterious operators of the chests.

Which gave her an idea. There having been no response yet to her note, she requested another page of Gloswise, and bent to pen a second missive.

Lady Silver, Ilsevellian of the Royal House-at-Mirramay, offers the following bargain, which may be of interest to the recipient of this note.
She is in possession of information regarding the whereabouts of a large number of royal heirlooms, artefacts and jewels, and will consider sharing some portion of these with the recipient if her demands are met.

That would do. The word consider committed her to nothing, but the note would indicate that she was a person worth bargaining with. She fixed it to another rose, dropped the whole lot into the chest, and sat down to wait again.

Some time passed.

'Perhaps some tea?' said Gloswise at last. She glanced at a handsome silver clock upon the wall and said: 'Supper is usually delivered in about one hour from now. Perhaps you shall receive your reply then, Lady Silver.'

The light had faded, and the cottage grown dim. Ilsevel had scarcely noticed, but Gloswise had lit lamps and candles, and Peech had placed herself in charge of boiling water for tea. Soon all three women were seated around Gloswise's pretty little tea-table, partaking of a fragrant brew. Conversation between Gloswise and Peech was desultory, and Ilsevel hardly participated at all. Her attention shifted between the chest and the clock, and the minutes dragged slowly by.

At last the clock chimed the hour, and Gloswise got up directly from the table. The chest had filled itself nicely. Ilsevel helped to remove a hearty array of pies, tartlets, roast meats, vegetables fricasseed and stewed, candied fruits, sweet puddings and a jug of wine. That this was far beyond Gloswise's usual allotment was evident from her wide-eyed amazement as she conveyed dish after dish to table.

Ilsevel noticed with interest that the pies, puddings and tarts came in exactly three portions of each. She also recalled that Peech had seemingly found no difficulty in providing extra food for Ilsevel earlier in the day. Her presence here was being accounted for — but how came it to be known who she had first fallen in with, or to whom she had gone later? They were, she was persuaded, somehow under observation, and she began to look around at the articles in the cottage with a new interest. She did not immediately notice any mirrors, but it did not have to be that. It might be anything.

She began to despair of there being any answer to her notes, when dish after dish was unpacked from the chest without any sign of a reply. But there at last, at the very bottom, was a silver salver upon which a letter sat in solitary splendour. It was a beautiful, delicate thing, made from sugar-paper and wrapped up in a purple bow.

Ilsevel unfastened the ribbon with trembling fingers, and smoothed out the paper.

Welcome, Lady Silver, it said.

And that was all.

Ilsevel screwed up the pretty thing, and hurled it away. Welcome, Lady Silver? Was that it?

Those three words were unusually communicative for so abbreviated a letter. They told her unequivocally that she had not been conveyed here by mistake; her captors knew exactly who she was, and had deliberately sought to imprison her. Nor were they inclined to bargain with her, or to offer any information whatsoever as to the reasons for her capture. She was not, then, to expect release.

Was it her determined pursuit of Wodebean that had brought her such calamity? But why? He had shown ample skill at evading her, and need only continue to do so, if he did not wish to speak with her. She was not aware of having uncovered anything to his detriment that was not already widely known about. And what else had she done, or threatened to do, of late?

Save for retrieving Anthelaena. She had made no secret of that resolution, though she had not communicated it to many. Tyllanthine? It could not be Tyllanthine. Surely it could not. What reason could she have for obstructing Ilsevellian's attempts to extract their sister, the Queen-at-Mirramay, from her own form of imprisonment? Why would she lie to Ilsevel, and pretend to help her, only to betray her?

But if it was not Tyllanthine's doing, and it did not especially make sense for it to be Wodebean's, who had buried My Lady Silver in the heart of Winter?

CHAPTER TWELVE

Ah, Tyllanthine — or Hidenory, as she is most often called nowadays. Tricksy woman. Tricksiest woman I ever encountered, no word of a lie. There's never any tellin' whas really goin' on in her head. Changin' her face, changin' her name, changin' her plans! She is one big secret, an' she likes it that way.

She ain't above tellin' a bit of a lie, if it suits her purposes. That I know. But she ain't in a hurry to deceive them as she cares for, neither, an' if I know one thing about Tyllanthine it's this: she cares about her family, whatever else appearances might suggest. I didn't believe she'd ha' harmed Ilsevel, nor Anthelaena neither. But what, then, was she doin'? Sendin' me to Mr. Tibs, rather than just tellin' me what she knows. Keepin' secrets from her sister, too.

She's got somethin' t' hide, thas clear enough, but I ain't sure as to whether it's anythin' nefarious. More'n likely her years of bein' six people all at once have landed her in such a tangle, she don't know which way she's goin' anymore.

Well, there was nowt to be done about it just then. Me an' Phineas had no choice but t' follow the trail Tibs set us on, an' thas what we did.

Phineas got down from the coach with a feeling of having strayed so far out of the pattern of his regular life that he had no idea how to get back again. He could not remember ever having left Lincoln before, for one thing; now here he was on the edge of a quiet little town somewhere out in the Wolds, accompanied by an enormous troll, and on the trail of a faded old mystery which had nothing whatsoever to do with anything he was qualified for.

He had mixed feelings about the whole business. Part of him felt out of his depth, and pined to be back in the kitchens he knew, baking the familiar breads and cakes, and chatting with Mrs. Batts about the progress of the new pastry-shop. However troubling a topic the latter was, he was got into far deeper waters now.

But some part of him was beginning to enjoy this new existence. *This* part remembered the drudgery of his job, the poor relationship he suffered with his father, and his general poverty, and found the change highly agreeable. He tried to suppress those feelings, knowing full well that the interlude would come to an end soon enough, and back to the kitchen he would go. But it refused to be entirely done away with.

He greeted the town of Tilby with bright attention, noting with eager interest its jumble of houses in all manner of fashions and styles, the sleepy air of tranquillity it possessed beneath its blanket of deep snow, the rolling landscape of hills in the midst of which it was tucked like an egg in a nest.

He soon noted a fair number of differences between Tilby and Lincoln. For one thing, Mr. Balligumph attracted every bit as much attention here as he had in the city, but it was of a different character. Fewer responded to him with amazement or alarm; instead he was greeted with great cordiality by those few they passed in the quiet streets, and they expressed surprise only at seeing him away from his customary bridge.

The town possessed rather more than its share of fae residents, at that. Walking down what seemed to be the town's central street, Phineas and Mr. Balligumph passed no less than three household brownies bustling along upon some errand or another, clad in the same fashions which their taller human counterparts wore. He saw others, too, creatures to whom he could put no name, wandering the streets as comfortably as though this were Aylfenhame.

'This *is* in Lincolnshire, is it not?' Phineas said after a time. 'We have not travelled out of England?'

Balligumph chuckled. 'Aye, 'tis England right enough. 'Tis a popular spot for those choosin' t' move out of Aylfenhame, though, and becomin' more so all the time.'

'Why is that, sir?'

The troll shrugged his great shoulders. 'There's always been somethin' about Tilby which speaks t' them as was born and raised in Aylfenhame, though 'tis hard t' say what it is. Now we have Mr. and Mrs. Aylfendeane livin' not far away, too — Miss Ellerby as was, an' her Ayliri husband out o' Aylfenhame. They've made it their business t' serve as somethin' of a sanctuary t' those with real pressin' reasons to leave their old lives behind, an' that alone has increased the population o' fae here quite a bit.'

'Is that why Miss Phelps was sent here?' Phineas guessed. 'You think she is not mad, don't you sir? She had somehow got into Aylfenhame, and her family did not believe her.'

Mr. Balligumph did not immediately reply. He seemed to be thinking. 'Mayhap,' he allowed. 'But while the existence of Aylfenhame ain't such common knowledge in the city as it is here, it's not unknown. Folk don't take against it so much as to label a woman mad fer claimin' t' have had anythin' t' do with it. An' there's some other things that don't make sense about it, like them clothes. No, I think it's the Hollows she went into, an' no doubt a mighty strange tale she came back with.' He paused to give a great, windy sigh, and added: 'Now if only I knew how t' find her. It's puzzlin' me a great deal. How can two such ladies have been livin' here a while, an' me knowin' nothin' about it? Best I can think of is t' ask around, an' thas what we're goin' t' do.'

'Are you so well-acquainted with everyone here as to know all the residents' names?' asked Phineas.

'Aye. I've made it me business to know.'

'Then perhaps they are not known by the names we were given?'

Balligumph sucked upon a tooth. 'To take a false name, now, thas the kind of thing ye only do if ye're hidin'. An' I dunnot know why two such ladies as we are lookin' fer would hide theirselves like that. But yer right. T'would be an explanation.'

'Two ladies, one of whom must be somewhat Mrs. Batts's junior, by the descriptions she gave. The other could be of any age, but in all likelihood is somewhat older, if she has her own establishment, and was in a position to take in a cousin in trouble. The Phelps family is unlikely to be gentry, if they are friends with Mrs. Batts, but if they live in Drury Lane then they are not poor either.' Phineas considered a moment. 'It is my guess, sir, that Marjorie Bamber is a woman of middle age, either unmarried or a widow, and of modest but not straitened means. If she is using a name that is not her own, then perhaps she moved to Tilby *with* Miss Phelps, both ladies being wishful of concealment, or perhaps just privacy, if Miss Phelps' circumstances were so troubled. Miss Phelps herself must also be a spinster, since Mrs. Batts mentioned no husband, though she may be posing as a widow.'

Mr. Balligumph stopped, and regarded Phineas with some surprise — and approval. 'Ye're good at this, lad,' he said.

'And Mrs. Batts mentioned that the cousin, Marjorie Bamber, lives on the edge of Tilby,' added Phineas.

Balligumph spent two minutes more in deep rumination, and then his face lit up. 'Edge o' the town!' he proclaimed. 'Two ladies livin' quiet-like, in a smallish way, wi' no husbands or children, and some distance in age between the two. Why, Phineas me lad, I think ye've cracked it. If them two ain't Mrs. Willis an' Miss Walker, then I'll be blowed.' He grinned. 'Moved here nigh on a year ago, but ye don't hear much of the two of 'em. They don't hardly set foot out o' their house, an' keep theirselves to theirselves. I seen Miss Walker only once or twice, an' I'll tell ye: she don't *seem* mad t' me.' He looked around, getting his bearings. 'This way,' he announced, and set off at a great, rolling stride which Phineas struggled to keep pace with. 'T'ain't a large town, Tilby,' he said over his shoulder. 'Won't take long t' reach the Willis an' Walker place.'

Phineas pulled down the brim of his hat against the icy wind, shoved his hands into the deep pockets of his coat, and hurried after the troll.

Mrs. Willis's cottage stood by itself at a little distance from the rest of the town, with nothing but dark, frosty fields spreading behind it. It was as Phineas had imagined: neither a mean dwelling nor a handsome one, but unassumingly respectable, with pale stuccoed walls and large Georgian windows.

'Ye should knock,' Balligumph instructed. 'Ye'll cause a deal less consternation when they open the door.'

The residents of Tilby seemed little concerned by Balligumph's size or unusual appearance, but Phineas yielded to the request without complaint, and stepped up to the door. He rapped the plain iron knocker three times, and waited.

It was swiftly opened by a maid-of-all-work, younger than Phineas, a girl with a timid demeanour. 'Aye?' she whispered.

'Is this the home of Mrs. Willis?' Phineas asked, Balligumph having stepped away out of immediate sight.

'Aye,' said the maid again.

'Are either of your mistresses at home? My name is Ph— Mr. Drake, and I would be glad to speak with them.'

The maid glanced behind herself into the dark hallway, clearly uncertain. 'Step in, Mr. Drake,' she said, and held the door for him. 'I will ask.'

Phineas was not left to wait long in the hall. A dark-haired lady about the age his mother would now have been came out of a snug parlour to greet him, though her manner was not welcoming. She eyed him with a touch of wariness, and looked him over carefully before she spoke. His apparel announcing his lack of status clearly enough, she did not curtsey. 'Yes?' she said. 'I am Mrs. Willis. What may I do for you, Mr. Drake?'

Phineas hesitated, and decided to abandon caution. He could think of no way to make his enquiries that would not alarm her, so he simply said: 'Good morning, Mrs. Willis, I am sorry to interrupt. I am looking for Miss Eleanor Phelps. Do you know anyone of that name?'

'No,' she said at once, though she noticeably stiffened. 'There is no one of that name here.'

'Are you certain?' said Phineas. 'Please think carefully, Mrs. Willis. We are not here to cause the least harm or distress to Miss Phelps. Rather, we are in need of her help.'

'You are, are you?' The words were spoken pugnaciously, but Mrs. Willis could not conceal a degree of curiosity.

'We are trying to get into the Hollows,' said Phineas. 'It's urgent.'

Mrs. Willis took a step back towards the parlour. 'I think you had better go,' she said coldly.

The front door opened, revealing Mr. Balligumph. He tipped his hat to Mrs. Willis. 'Ma'am,' he said affably. 'Ye may know o' me, I hope? I'm Mr. Balligumph, keeper o' the Tilby toll bridge. Are ye sure we can't persuade you t' help us?'

Mrs. Willis looked upon Balligumph with decided distrust, bordering upon alarm, and backed away another step. 'We have nothing to—' she began.

But then a younger woman appeared behind her, and gently clasped her shoulders, cutting her off mid-sentence. 'Marjorie,' she said softly. 'It is all right. If they were here to create trouble for us, they have had ample opportunity to do so.'

Mrs. Willis, or Marjorie Bamber, gave a great sigh, and visibly capitulated. 'Very well,' she said ungraciously. 'Will you come into the parlour?'

They went gratefully, for a fire made the parlour toasty warm, and the walk from Tilby's main street had left Phineas with a chill in his face. He was happy enough to sit near the blaze, accept a cup of tea from Miss Phelps, and let Balligumph take over the conversation.

Miss Phelps appeared to be approximately of an age with Phineas himself, perhaps two or three-and-twenty. But he remembered what Mrs. Batts had said about her long absence, and her failure to age. What was she truly, then? Three-and-thirty? She wore her pale brown hair neatly coiled up, and had on a plain dress: no display or vanity about her at all. She seemed composed enough, but Phineas thought he saw signs of a troubled mind in her dark eyes, which were not at all as tranquil as her outward demeanour. She poured tea and sat down, giving her attention primarily to Mr. Balligumph. Unlike her cousin, she seemed in no way disquieted by having the troll tollkeeper appear in her parlour for tea, which rather bore out her story of having spent some years in a place very different from England.

'The Hollows are not like England, Mr. Balligumph,' she began. 'Nor are they like Aylfenhame, I understand. I met denizens of both countries Beneath. Time moves differently there. You may imagine my dismay when I returned to find I had been gone for more than a decade, and was long since given up for dead.'

'Tis not a fixed characteristic of all the Hollows,' said Balligumph. 'Ye were unlucky indeed, Miss Phelps, if that was the way of it. An' it weren't random. Someone must've done that on purpose.'

'To me personally, or to the place I was in?' said she.

Balligumph shrugged. 'I cannot yet say as t' which it was. Tell me, though. How did ye end up Hollows-side?'

'I had gone out for a walk that evening,' answered Miss Phelps. 'It was a daily habit. I used to walk around the castle walls, it was pleasant at that hour. Nothing untoward had ever happened to me there before, but on that day I saw something unusual. I was passing the gates, and I thought I heard a creature crying for help, or perhaps a child. Something was certainly in distress, so I went nearer. But there was nothing there that could explain the sound. Instead I saw a dancing light, like a will-o-the-wyke, and an odd, stooped man in a red cloak. He did not seem to see me. He spoke a strange word, and to my amazement he disappeared. Well, Mr. Balligumph, I had been hastening towards him, convinced that he was somehow responsible for tormenting a creature, and intent upon putting a stop to it. Perhaps I came too near to the spot in which he'd been standing, for I fell somehow, and never hit the ground until some time later. And then I was not in the city anymore.'

'Unlucky,' murmured Balligumph. 'He had just opened a gate through, an' ye got caught in it. I cannot say as to how ye heard them sounds, but wi' Wodebean one never knows. I will ask, though,' and here he sat forward, intent upon Miss Phelps. 'What was the word that ye heard the stooped man speak?'

'It is difficult to remember,' she said apologetically. 'It was a long time ago, and it was certainly spoken in no language I know.'

'Twasn't "Mirramay", by chance?'

'No, that was not it.' She sipped tea, thinking, while Phineas sat unable to help holding his breath. Mr. Balligumph sat likewise, frozen with his tea cup halfway to his mouth, waiting in hope.

'I cannot remember the whole word,' she said finally. 'It was a long word. But it began with something like *anthem*.'

Balligumph stiffened. 'Anthelaena? Might that ha' been it?'

'Yes!' said Miss Phelps. 'That must be the very word, sir, I am quite persuaded. But how did you know of it?'

Balligumph did not directly answer her. 'Interestin',' he murmured. 'Very interestin'. Whas a fellow known fer playin' both sides doin' usin' Her Majesty's name fer a password? An' the royal city, too, fer Thieves' Hollow!' He shook himself, apparently recalling his company, and smiled at Miss Phelps. 'Ye've been a vast help, Miss. Our thanks.'

She smiled equally upon Phineas and Balligumph, and said to the latter: 'If I had known you were such a charming fellow, I would have called upon you before now, Mr. Balligumph.'

The troll winked. 'Yer always welcome t' visit my bridge, Miss Phelps. An' you, Mrs Bamber.'

Marjorie smiled faintly. 'It is Miss Bamber.'

Balligumph rose from his chair and made her a deep bow, and then another to Miss Phelps. 'Ye're both grand ladies in my book. If'n ye'll excuse us now, we have a deal t' do.'

Phineas, though, was not quite ready to leave. 'Um, a moment,' he said diffidently. 'If it is not too much to ask, Miss Phelps, may I enquire what you did during your month in the Hollows? We heard something of its always being summer there?'

She nodded, frowning. 'Perhaps that does not seem remarkable, since to my understanding I was not there long. But the conditions were peculiarly unvarying; to one used to England's changeable weather, it could not but strike me as unusual. I asked those I met if it was always thus, and they said it was.'

'Did it never rain?' Phineas could not imagine such a place. How could anything survive long without rain? And there had been talk of flowers.

Miss Phelps gave a wry quirk of a smile. 'Oh, it did, but only ever at night. Almost everyone there was primarily employed in growing flowers, you know. Every imaginable kind, but most especially roses. And there were many kinds of folk there, too. One or two humans like me, and others who looked nearly like me but with odd curls to their ears, and a way about them like... like they were something other. Brownies, goblins... many others I could not put a name to.'

'A populous place, then? Was it large?'

'Oh, no. Scarcely larger than Tilby, I would say, and if there were as many as a hundred people there I should say I was surprised.'

Phineas did not immediately know what to do with this information, but he committed it carefully to memory nonetheless.

'One last thing,' he said, as another thought struck him. 'How was it that you came to get out again?'

'It was that same fellow,' said Miss Phelps. 'The one I followed, that evening. He came on purpose to fetch me away, he said, though he would not explain why. And I do not know how he contrived it, either, for there were no words spoken that time. He bid me step into a great chest, and I almost refused, for how absurd it seemed! But then I was back in England.'

Wodebean had made a point of rescuing Miss Phelps? Phineas exchanged a puzzled look with Balligumph, and saw in the troll's face that he had no more explanation for this development than did Phineas. A brief mental review of everything they knew about Wodebean revealed no clear pattern of behaviour whatsoever; the fellow was a muddle from start to finish.

He wondered, not for the first time, why Ilsevel was so angry with him. He had cheated her, she'd said. How?

Phineas made his bow, with a murmured thanks, and he and Balligumph shortly afterwards took their leave.

'What line o' questioning were ye on, lad?' said Balligumph as they regained the street.

'Oh, I do not know,' answered Phineas. 'Not precisely. But this is all quite the puzzle, and I fear we will have to unravel it piece by piece. I thought it best, then, to secure a few more pieces, while I had the opportunity.'

Mr. Balligumph doffed his hat to Phineas, and said with a rumbling chuckle, 'Like I said, lad. Ye're good at this.'

Phineas blushed, and hoped the troll would not notice.

He did not seem to, for he had transferred his attention to the sky, grown night-dark while they were drinking tea with the two ladies. 'I would like nothin' better than t' go back to Lincoln right away, an' see if My Lady Gold's name works fer gettin' into that Hollows spot. But it's late, an' I fancy ye are tired. No?'

'I can go on, sir,' said Phineas, trying to look like a man who was game for anything, and not like a very young man who was indeed growing weary, besides being hungry and cold as well.

'I dare say ye can, but *I* would rather not. If we are to hazard them Hollows, best t' do it on a full stomach an' a night's rest, would ye not agree?'

Phineas agreed.

'Well, then,' said the troll cheerfully. 'Permit me t' extend to ye the hospitality of my home. It ain't much, an' it is stuffed under a bridge an' all, but it has all the things a feller needs.'

And so Phineas Drake, baker's boy, found himself entertained for the night in surprisingly commodious accommodation beneath the Tilby toll-bridge. The troll had somehow contrived to stuff an entire house under there, as he put it: a smallish house, to be sure, with only four rooms, but they were airy and spacious and very comfortable. Whitewashed walls and sturdy oak furniture he had, with a snug kitchen in one room and an equally cosy parlour in the other. The third room was the troll's bedchamber, and the fourth... well, when he first opened the door it appeared to be some kind of studio, for three easels dominated the space and there were pots of paints littered everywhere. He had apparently been painting landscapes, though the third contained a sketch of a lady.

'Ahem,' said the troll, and quickly closed the door. 'No, that won't do. Here.' He rapped thrice upon the door and said clearly: 'The second bedchamber, please.'

When he opened the door again, the studio was gone, and the room instead held a bed sized perfectly for Phineas, liberally supplied with blankets and pillows; a closet; a chest-of-drawers, with a ceramic washbasin set atop; and a window seat piled with cushions. In the darkness, Phineas could not see the view out of those improbable windows.

'Will that do?' said the troll — with, to Phineas's befuddlement, a discernible trace of anxiety.

'Oh, goodness,' said Phineas. 'Of *course*, sir. It is the nicest room I ever was offered.'

Mr. Balligumph gave him an odd look. 'Is it, now? 'Tis a shame, lad. 'Tis nothin' much.'

Phineas shrugged, unwilling to try to explain. The room was filled with comforts, that was what made the difference. Pillows and soft things and a fireplace, *with a fire in it*. He could not remember the last time such an array had been placed at his disposal, and some part of him felt that he did not merit such luxury. But he squashed that part, thanked his host most sincerely, and retired to his unexpectedly wonderful bedchamber at once.

In the end, it was some time before he went to sleep. He sat a long time in the deep armchair before the fire, toasting his toes in the blazing warmth and thinking very deeply indeed. He saw nothing of the flames, for Ilsevel's face hovered in his mind's eye, her hazy silver eyes bright and lively, her pale hair tossing in the chill winter wind. Where was she?

CHAPTER THIRTEEN

Whatever the manoeuvrings of her captors, Ilsevel had not the smallest intention of waiting quietly for them to consent to release her. If there was a way *in*, she reasoned, there must be a way *out*, and nothing would prevent her from finding it.

But she was destined to endure a deal of disappointment, for her determination was not much shared by her fellow residents of Winter's Hollow. Gloswise talked as though she wished for nothing more than to be liberated from the place, but Ilsevel could not find out that she had ever made much effort to secure her own release. A very little exploration upon her first arrival had apparently satisfied her that there was no way out, and she had settled down to a life of comfortable captivity ever since. Ilsevel could not but suspect that Gloswise was much more pleased with her life than she was disposed to admit to, and she could not altogether blame the other woman for it. She lacked for nothing but summer weather, after all, and lived an unusually carefree existence, supposing she could overlook the lack of choice she had been given in the matter — and it seemed that she could. Her response to Ilsevel's questions was largely useless. 'It is of no use tramping about in the snow,' she said more than once. 'There is only this valley, walled in with snow all around, and no way of going beyond.'

Very well, then: she would abandon all thought of walking to freedom. But what of magical means? She and Gloswise had both been transported to the Hollow by some magical force, and it stood to reason that some magical force might take them out of it again. But here, Gloswise proved wholly incurious. 'I do not know,' she said, when Ilsevel enquired as to the mode of her arrival. 'I fell through the road.'

'Did you perhaps endure the sensation of something — or some*one* — clutching at your ankle?' said Ilsevel.

Gloswise thought. 'Now I think of the matter, yes. There was that.'

'As though you had been dragged through?'

'Something of that sort. But it ought only to have thrown me off balance, no particularly great pressure being exerted. How did I come to fall? And how did the road fall away beneath me?'

Ilsevel began to form a theory. There was a person somewhere, perhaps tucked away in the Hollow itself, who had the means of wresting open a door between England and the Hollow Hills, and of hauling people through it. Apparently upon command or instruction, for Ilsevel's own capture had certainly not been by chance, and Gloswise's was most likely not either.

'Is there any part of the valley which is particularly difficult to get into?' Ilsevel enquired. 'Or better yet, impossible?'

'No,' answered Gloswise. 'Every inch of it is accounted for.'

Of course it was; those obliged to live in such a confined world would certainly make the most of it. But where, then, might such an odd creature find to hide itself? Underground, perhaps — but then, the trows' knowes were all partially dug below, and they were everywhere about. Would not some one or other of them have run across the creature by now, if it were down in the earth?

But there was also that maze of a wood — the place where Ilsevel had herself arrived, and also, she surmised, the place where Pandigorth the poison-maker had disappeared. Judging from Peech's words, few ventured to enter those woods without good reason. 'Gloswise,' she said. 'Think a little more, if you please. You said you woke up in a snowdrift, when you first came here. Where was that snowdrift?'

'In the woods,' said Gloswise promptly. 'I almost died of exposure before Peech found me.'

Peech again. Ilsevel retreated to the window seat, thinking. She had been staying with Gloswise for two days now, the cottage being better suited to accommodate her than Peech's more cramped dwelling. Peech had not returned since that first day, so if Ilsevel wished to question her, she would have to venture out into what promised to become a blizzard before long, and find the trow woman's knowe. She was beginning to feel that the expedition would be worth it. Did anybody but Peech ever wander those woods? How came Peech to do so with such equanimity? For it seemed more than probable that something among those dizzying trees was responsible for the presence of both Gloswise and Ilsevel at Winter's Hollow, and possibly others besides. If she wanted to go in search of it, she would need a guide.

Ilsevel cast a brief, dismayed glance at the outside world, what little she could see of it through the driving snow, and stood up. 'I need to find Peech,' she told Gloswise.

Gloswise, too, looked to the window. 'Can it not wait until the snow stops?'

'It is quite urgent. I do not ask you to take me there, if you would rather not, but do, pray, furnish me with directions.'

Gloswise put down her embroidery with a sigh. 'No, you will never find it in those conditions. I will come with you.' She rose from her seat beside the fire and put a thick coat on over her outdated gown, and donned stout boots and a wide-brimmed hat to match. 'You may borrow that one,' she said to Ilsevel, pointing at a second coat which hung near the door.

But Ilsevel declined. 'These garments keep me warm enough, though they do not look capable of it.' Only her feet were in any danger, but no boots of Gloswise's could serve better than Ilsevel's own. Ignoring Gloswise's sceptical look, she threw open the door and marched out into the wind. She shivered mightily, more because one normally *would* than because she felt much of the cold. The snow was so thick as almost to blind her; her enchanted gown could do nothing whatsoever about *that*.

No matter. Onward she must go, and so onward she *would* go. She waited only long enough for Gloswise to catch up with her before venturing off into the inclement weather, thankful at least that it was not yet dark.

Pops opened the door, and stared at them with the air of a man seeing visions. 'What! And in all this snow? Come in, come in.'

'I need Peech,' said Ilsevel, politely but firmly declining the invitation. The trows' little parlour radiated warmth, and looked dangerously snug from outside; she would not permit herself to be too tempted to linger.

Peech appeared at the door a few moments later, shooing Pops out of her way. 'Wist! What is this?'

'I am going into the woods,' said Ilsevel. 'And I would be grateful for a guide, Peech.'

The trow looked Ilsevel over from head to toe, her expression one of frank disapproval. ''Tis madness, that's what,' she pronounced. 'And I thought you of sound mind, My Lady Silver.'

'My Lady Silver chafes rather under captivity, and being in possession of some small theory as to a mode of escape, is anxious to explore the possibility without delay.'

'Oh, aye?' answered Peech. 'That tired of the snow, are you? And here not more'n two days, at that.' She tsked and tutted, but she went to fetch her coat and shawl regardless, and came out into the cold. 'Quickly, then. Me dinner's here soon.'

She suited action to words, setting off through the snow at such a rapid pace that she was almost lost to sight before Ilsevel had quite realised she had gone. She hurried to catch up, and only belatedly realised that Gloswise was not at her heels.

'We have lost Gloswise!' she called.

'Gloswise is a woman of sound sense,' called back Peech. 'And has doubtless thought it wiser to stay by my nice, warm hearth wi' Pops.'

The implication, of course, was that Ilsevel was *not* a woman of sense. Well, so be it then! If only madness could secure her release from this strange place, then madness she would gladly embrace.

She was hard pressed to keep pace with Peech, for though the trow was much shorter than Ilsevel she contrived to move at a startlingly rapid trot. There was no further time, breath or opportunity for conversation; all her efforts were bent upon keeping Peech within sight, and not falling too far behind. They soon passed from the expanse of the valley, dotted here and there with the trows' dwellings, and into the dark, knotted trees of the snow-drowned woods. Try though she might, Ilsevel could discern no pattern to Peech's movements, and soon felt hopelessly lost among those craggy old trees. Peech, though, never hesitated.

At last, the trow stopped. 'This is the middle,' she announced.

Ilsevel, looking around, discerned nothing to differentiate this spot from any other in the wood. 'Is there something significant about the middle?'

'Tis the oldest bit,' explained Peech. She stood, arms folded around herself and beginning to shiver with the cold.

'Thank you,' murmured Ilsevel, momentarily stymied. What now? She thought rapidly. 'This may seem an odd question,' she began.

'Belike,' said Peech. 'You are an odd woman.'

Ilsevel smiled briefly. 'But,' she persevered, 'have you ever seen anything out in these woods that resembled a chest?'

Peech frowned. 'A chest? Like the one in me house?'

'Well, perhaps not exactly resembling that. But some form of container, which might be enchanted in similar fashion to your own, or Gloswise's.' She had visited the residences of some few of the denizens of Winter's Hollow by now, and had noticed that they were all equipped with some form or other of the magical chests — and all of the residents performed some useful task or another, usually the crafting of saleable objects or the gathering of rare materials. Well, then. Supposing there was someone here whose appointed task was to import residents from time to time, it stood to reason that it would be cared for, and effectively paid, in similar fashion.

Peech was thinking. 'Odd question, aye,' she finally pronounced. 'What would a chest be doing out here?'

'Satisfying the requirements of a creature who might be living out here,' said Ilsevel.

'Nobody lives out here. Ain't never seen a house, or anything like that.'

'It might not be the sort of being who would choose to live in a house. Or if it was, the house might not be visible.' She stamped once in the snow, illustrating her point.

'I'd have seen somethin' of a creature like that, or somebody would.'

'Perhaps not.'

Peech sighed. 'I think yer mad, My Lady Silver, but if you're quite set on it, come wi' me.' And off she went again, darting hither and thither through the trees like a sparrow. As near as Ilsevel could tell, they proceeded to walk in a more or less perfect circle, but when Peech stopped again they had arrived at a quite different spot. The boughs hung lower, and there was an unusual, heavy stillness to the air.

Lifting her stoutly-booted foot, Peech kicked at something which gave a hollow *thud*. 'Here. I noticed this a time or two, and wondered what it might be. Cannot say as it looks like a chest, though.'

Ilsevel went nearer. The object in question was an odd bank of earth protruding from the base of a vast tree-trunk, though so drenched in snow that Ilsevel could discern nothing further about it. She set to, scooping snow away with her hands, until more detail emerged: it was a mess of gnarly roots all twisted up together, and though the arrangement was by no means box-shaped she could well imagine that it might function as some form of container.

There was, however, no sign of anything that might function as a lid, or a lock, or any means of entrance at all.

'Excellent,' she murmured. 'I think this is the very thing, Peech.'

'Good. And what now are you fixin' to do with it?'

Ilsevel had not the smallest idea, but she was in no way disposed to admit it. So she sat on it. 'Wait,' she said, with a brilliant smile for Peech.

'Wait? You will die of the cold.'

'Unlikely.'

'Not impossible.'

'But unlikely.' Ilsevel smoothed the front of her enchanted gown, striving to look as unconcerned as possible. She *was* a touch worried about the long-term effects of the weather, but it would not to do be deterred by it.

'I cannot wait wi' you,' said Peech. 'You may be cold-proof, but I am not.'

Ilsevel's heart sank, but it was the response she had expected. 'I understand.'

'Right.' Peech hesitated, eyeing Ilsevel uncertainly. 'You cannot find your way out of this wood alone. You do know that?'

'Peech. If you would be so good as to pass this way again tomorrow, I would be much obliged to you. If you should find me here, half-frozen but breathing, pray take me home. If I am dead, dispose of my remains. But I think and I hope that you will find me gone.'

Peech's face soured. 'Yer a mighty cool one, ain't you?'

'Not much ruffles me.' And when it did, Ilsevel would rather die than make a display of herself.

'Good luck to you,' said Peech shortly, and marched off into the driving snow, futilely tugging her shawl tighter about her shoulders.

Ilsevel watched her go, and flatly refused to feel forlorn.

'Right,' she murmured, and settled herself more comfortably atop the mound of roots.

Gradually, the light faded. Evening drew in, bringing with it a lessening of the snow but an increase of the biting wind. Even shrouded in enchantments as she was, Ilsevel began to feel its effects, for the wind howled through the close-crowding trees like a wild creature, making merry with her hair, and sending sprays of snow into her face. 'Stop that!' she said, sharply.

Chastened, the wind slunk sulkily away.

That interested Ilsevel. The elements had not responded to her commands since Anthelaena's fall, and they still did not in Aylfenhame. What manner of place *was* this, that the wind recognised the faded authority of My Lady Silver?

She sat mulling this over, ignoring the way the darkness grew denser and more oppressive as night crept in. If there was a moon, it was hidden away behind the thick, unfriendly clouds, and not a glimmer of its light filtered through to the woods where Ilsevel sat alone. She could see nothing, not even the shape of her own hand.

But the darkness and the intense silence seemed to amplify her hearing, for she *heard* a great deal. The swaying of the boughs in the somewhat gentled breeze, and the occasional *thud* of snow falling from the branches to the ground. A scritching and a scratching somewhere: a tiny wild thing sought, probably futilely, for its dinner. That smote Ilsevel's heart, to her dismay, and struck her equally as a means of experiment.

'Food for the animal,' she said crisply. 'And a light.'

There came light, a sudden blossoming of clear starlight and silvery moonglow: a pair of wisps had leapt to answer her summons. 'Thank you,' she told them with a smile, and they bobbed and brightened.

By their combined light, she could see that the branches all about were bristling with berries, bright red and glossy black. These dropped to the floor in a steady rain of fruit, and the animals she had heard darted forth to claim them: mice, and shrews. Tenacious little beings, to survive the endless Winter.

But… need it be endless? For if she held sway over this place then might she not alter such punishing conditions?

Hmm.

'Enough of winter!' she proclaimed. 'Let the seasons be restored.'

The snow stopped, but she had not time to observe whether her will was carried out in all its particulars, for there came a groaning and a creaking beneath her: the roots were come loose, and writhing madly about. Speedily, she hopped off the mound and stood a little way apart, watching by wisp-light as the great pile of roots unwound itself to reveal a gaping, dark hole.

Abruptly, she understood. 'There is no creature!' she declared, and her hand darted out to catch one of the snaking roots.

It fought her grip, but she held it fast. 'It is a *tree*,' she hissed. 'You are responsible for bringing me here, are you not? One of your wretched roots reached up, and caught me down! But who told you to do it?'

The tree, or at least its roots, flew into a frenzy of distress, but Ilsevel stood firm. 'You begin to comprehend the extent of your error, I perceive,' she said coolly. 'But your master, whoever that may be, does not. You will take me to him.' With that, she released the root and let it fall, and stepped smartly into the dark space that yawned in the tree's trunk.

All lights winked out, leaving Ilsevel in darkness. And then, as before, she fell.

She emerged somewhere so blazing with bright, golden lights that her eyes were quite blinded, and for some moments she could only clench them tightly shut against the assault. At length, cautiously, she peeped with one eye.

Nothing that she saw made the slightest sense.

A comfortable couch upholstered in bright green silk was beneath her, and she lounged upon it as though she had arranged herself there. But there was an end to idle luxury, for all about her was thriving industry and furious effort. She sat in a rather large hall, wood-panelled and crowded with tables. A goblin sat at each one, surrounded by heaped piles of cloth in every possible colour, and frantically engaged in sewing. A great chest, taller than any goblin, dominated the far wall, its lid open; perched on a shelf above it was yet another goblin, a huge pile of completed garments waiting on his other side. As she watched, this goblin snatched up a gown — a pretty printed cotton creation, made after the same fashions as Peech and Gloswise wore — and hurled it carelessly into the chest. 'Family Snowdrop,' said the goblin in a bored tone. Another dress followed. 'The Borage household.' And so on, garment after garment, breeches and shirts and jackets and shawls, every one of them far outdated in style.

So mesmerised was she by this curious factory that she failed at first to notice another figure, not a goblin but a hobgoblin, who stood against one wall, silently observing the proceedings. He wore a dark red mantle swathed around his stooped shoulders, its hood hiding his face in deep shadow.

She would know him anywhere.

'Wodebean!' she gasped, momentarily stunned beyond words. So long and frustrating a search and then t*here* he suddenly was, standing there as calm as you please, just as though he had not been leading her a merry dance all these many weeks long!

Then, recovering from her surprise, she launched herself off the gorgeous couch and descended upon him, blazing fury. 'How dare you imprison me!' she intoned. 'How dare you evade me! We had a *deal*, Wodebean!'

Not even the vision of My Lady Silver descending upon him in a mood of flaming wrath could disconcert Wodebean. His head turned her way; a pair of eyes glinted at her from within the depths of his hood; and he made her a deep, deep bow. It was not ironical, not even to her unamused eye. 'Welcome, My Lady Silver,' he said in his dry way, and Ilsevel was flabbergasted. For unlike the insult of a note she had received, this was no mockery. She heard the ring of truth in the hobgoblin's voice: he meant it, every word.

CHAPTER FOURTEEN

Goblin tailors, eh? Odd lot, them. Last I heard they was workin' fer Grunewald, the Goblin King — or he was sponsorin' the rabble. Somethin' along them lines. There's nothin' they love better'n to sew, an' they'll do it all day an' night. Perfect fer the likes o' Wodebean, no? How they came t' pass into his employ is somethin' I will ask His Majesty, next time I get the chance.

Meantime, clever of My Lady Silver t' find his elusive self! I don't mind admittin', though — I weren't any nearer t'understandin' his conduct than Her Ladyship. I had been gettin' an inklin' meself that sommat were not makin' sense wi' him. Consider them passwords. Mirramay? The royal city. Anthelaena? Her Majesty's name, afore she were gone. Lookin' remarkably like a loyal supporter o' the Crown of Aylfenhame, no? But he were certainly no such thing back when it mattered. Change of heart, mayhap? We'll find out.

'Anthelaena,' intoned Balligumph.

Phineas stood beneath the great gate of the castle at Lincoln, unconsciously holding his breath as he waited for something to happen.

Nothing did. No whirl of uncanny energy, no whisking away of Phineas and Balligumph to places distant and strange, not even a sparkling light or an odd, inexplicable sound. The wind softly blew, cold rain fell upon Phineas's nose, and they remained exactly where they were.

'Hm,' said the troll. 'I suppose it were too much to hope that the password would be the same as it were ten year ago.'

'Try some others,' said Phineas. 'Did you not say there was some manner of pattern emerging?'

'Aye!' And Balligumph rattled off a string of strange words, only a few of which Phineas recognised. "Tyllanthine," he had heard that one before. And again, "Ilsevellian", as the Grim, Mr. Tibs, had called the woman Phineas knew as Ilsevel.

He wanted to enquire about this discrepancy with her name, but did not quite dare, for what business was it of his? And Balligumph was busy. "Edironal", he said, and "Hidenory", and "Grunewald", and several other things that whisked by too fast for Phineas to catch.

At length, he ran out of new words to try, and stopped. The atmosphere remained prosaically inert, and the troll's face fell in disappointment. 'Well, dash it,' he muttered.

Phineas thought.

'Did Miss Phelps ever specify which gate she meant?' he asked after a while.

Balligumph just looked at him. 'What?'

'There are two gates to the castle. This is the main gate, so I assumed it was this one that she meant. But thinking about it, if she lived on Drury Lane and she was out for a stroll, it is probably the rear gate she walked past that evening.'

'What a treasure ye are.' Balligumph's face split wide in a grin, and he made an ushering motion. 'Lead on, my fine guide! I'd be all at sea without yer help.'

Phineas made haste, for the rain was soaking through his hat. Half-melted snow slushed unpleasantly underfoot as he splashed his way around the castle walls and at last reached its second, smaller gate, which was closed tight against the weather and the world. Perhaps it would not matter that it was.

'Let's try again,' said Balligumph, and off he went, rattling through the same long list of words which, presumably, held some form of connection with the two passwords Wodebean had been known to use. But he began at the end first, and went backwards through, to Phineas's confusion.

'Anthelaena,' said Phineas, when the troll was not more than halfway finished with his list.

Then came the lights, and the sounds, and the swirl of energy all in one go. Wisp-lights like the ones Balligumph had summoned at Thieves' Hollow danced at the edges of his vision; the mellow, haunting tones of distant bells sounded in his ears; and some force he could not name picked him up like a warm summer breeze and swept him off.

He landed hard upon dry, solid ground. When he opened his eyes, all was golden sunlight, and his chilled, rain-drenched body insensibly relaxed a fraction in the sudden rush of warmth.

'Well,' he said reflectively. 'This looks like Summer.'

'Oh my!' said a light voice from somewhere nearby. 'Are you quite well, my lord? You should not lie in the road like that, you will be trampled! Do let me help you up.'

Phineas twisted his head, blinking against the strong light. A short, slight creature bent over him: a pixie, or something of that kind? The features gracing that tiny face were neither feminine nor masculine; Phineas judged the pixie to be a she by virtue of the clothing she wore, a dress that looked woven from thistledown and hung about with flower petals. She wore a hat, too, perched atop her shock of dandelion-yellow hair, though a moment's scrutiny revealed that it was not a hat so much as an attractively curled ash leaf. 'Hello,' Phineas croaked, his throat unaccountably dry. 'I did not mean to lie down in the road, and will get up in a moment.' His limbs felt weak and he hurt in a number of places. With a groan, he gritted his teeth and levered himself to a sitting position, and then upright.

Standing, he towered over his solicitous new friend. This did not appear to trouble her in the slightest, for she smiled cheerily up at him and made a gesture of approval, her small hands weaving in the air. 'And where do you come from, my lord?' she enquired, examining his attire with interest.

'I am no lord,' said Phineas. 'My name is Drake, and I am a baker. I come from England, but I think that is far away from here.'

To his surprise, she clapped her hands at that, her face lighting up. 'A new traveller! It is too long since we had any! And a baker, how perfect. Lantring left us some time ago, and since then I have not had any cake at all.'

'I do not mean to stay,' Phineas said, as gently as he could, for he felt obscurely guilty at the prospect of disappointing so cheerful a soul. 'I am here to look for…' He could not finish the sentence, for two things struck him at once. One, that he did not precisely know what he was here to look for, only that he and Balligumph had resolved upon investigating the truth of Miss Phelps's story. Was this, too, part of the endless hunt for the elusive Wodebean?

The other thing was that Balligumph himself was nowhere in evidence. Phineas turned slowly in a full circle to make sure. He saw that he had been deposited in a fine, flourishing meadow of low grass dotted with poppies and cowslip and dandelions; that there was a long, dry dirt road running through it, quite wide, into the middle of which he had fallen; that there were some tall cedar trees on the horizon in one direction, and the glitter of water somewhere upon the other; and that there was no one in sight at all save for himself and the pixie.

He did not much welcome the prospect of being stranded in this place without Balligumph, especially considering that time appeared so much disordered out here. Would he emerge after a few hours, or a few days, to find a decade gone in England? Or a century? That prospect prompted a strong shudder, and for a moment he could not breathe.

He could not imagine why Balligumph would be unable to follow him here, nor why the affable troll might choose not to, but that problem being the least pressing of those that now faced him, he put it out of his mind.

'Oh, but no one leaves!' the pixie was saying cheerily. 'Leastwise, not many. Will you please make me a cake?'

'You said Lantring left you,' Phineas reminded her.

'Oh yes, but I meant that he died.'

Oh. Phineas frowned, disheartened. 'But there was another who left in more ordinary fashion, for I have met her. Her name is Eleanor Phelps. I think you must know her?'

The pixie shook her head.

'A human, like me? Not very old, her hair like—'

'We have not had any humans in a long time,' said the pixie, and seemed to dismiss the subject, for she rattled on. 'My name is Bix! You must have a name, and you will tell me what it is, won't you? And then I will take you to Lantring's old house. It still has the stove and the tables and the rolling-pins and everything! You will be very comfortable there and make us lots of cakes.'

'I have told you my name,' Phineas reminded her. 'It is Phineas Drake.'

'You shall be Mister Drake,' decided Bix. 'That is the way humans do it, is it not? And it sounds well! Come, Mister! I *really* want a cake.'

'Bix,' said Phineas, slightly desperate. 'If you can help me with something, I will bake you twelve cakes.'

'My favourite ones?' said Bix instantly, her eyes narrowing.

Phineas blinked. 'Er, yes. What are your favourite ones?'

'Sun cakes, with a honey core, and plumberries.'

'I do not know that recipe.'

'Lantring has it. Come *on*.' Bix grabbed him by the arm and hauled.

Phineas trailed helplessly after her. 'Do not you want to know what you are to help me with?'

'I am sure whatever it is will be easy!' she said gaily, and set off at a trot.

'I need to find a chest!' Phineas persevered. 'One large enough for a human like me to get into.'

Bix fell to laughing. 'I *told* you it would be easy!' she crowed. 'Why, there are chests like that everywhere!'

There was one in Lantring's house, Phineas soon discovered, and as Bix had promised it was plenty large enough for him to get into if he wanted. It was a heavy pine wood contraption, as long as he was tall, and about four feet high. He hauled up the lid at once and stepped in, discreetly crossing his fingers.

Nothing happened.

With a sigh, he replaced the lid. Would he have to search every house for the one Miss Phelps had vanished into? Would it help, if he did? For she had not been unaided; perhaps it had been some action of Wodebean's that had made a simple chest into a means of escape, and he could dance in and out of wooden boxes all day long if he chose, without securing anything like the same result.

He had relied too much on Balligumph, he now saw. Assuming that the troll would go wherever he went, and that he would be carrying some solution to every conceivable problem in one or another of his deep pockets, Phineas had not carefully enough considered the trouble he might be in were he to succeed in following in Miss Phelps' footsteps. Now he was in trouble indeed, for if time swirled about oddly in this endless summer, he could discern nothing that would indicate the fact, or serve to warn him how much of it was passing elsewhere. The place — Summer's Hollow, Bix called it — had an air of sleepy timelessness about it, as though it were too lazy to move through time the way everything else did and simply lay comfortably inert.

All he had to help him was Bix, a flighty pixie who was fixated upon cake and who forgot half of the things he said the moment the words left his lips.

So be it, then.

'Bix,' he said, as they explored Lantring's house. 'Let's play a game.' The house could have been situated anywhere in England, for it was a timber-framed building with whitewashed walls, low ceilings, crooked doorways, uneven floors and every other feature of a cottage a few hundred years old. It was equipped as a bakery, with every convenience Phineas might require to produce a fine batch of cakes — save that the stove was, perhaps, a few decades out of date. No matter. It would serve. 'I will make you one cake for every chest you find and explore for me,' he offered. 'I am looking for one that will serve as a way out of Summer's Hollow.'

'But they are *all* ways out of the Hollow,' said she plaintively.

Phineas, bent over the stove in the neat, cool kitchen, straightened to look at her. 'I beg your pardon?'

'We put flowers in them,' she explained. 'And they go away somewhere.'

'Flowers?' His thoughts rushed at once to the inexplicably fresh rose that Wodebean had dropped. He had wondered as to its source. Where was it? He had left it in the pocket of his coat, which (being too warm in this climate) now hung on a peg by the door. He hurried to retrieve it, and showed it to Bix. 'Like this one?'

The pixie examined it doubtfully. 'It looks like one of ours, though it did not look like *that* when it was sent away.'

'No,' agreed Phineas, tucking it into the pocket of his waistcoat. 'It has been a bit altered.' He thought. 'Does nothing else go away, when you put it in the chest?'

'The cakes did.' Bix pointed a finger at Lantring's pine chest. 'He piled them all into there — or not *all*, because some were for us! — and they went. And other times things appear, like food. Not cake, though I wish it would. And clothes, though not this dress because I made it.' She plucked at the wispy skirt of her little gown. 'I put others like it in the chests and they go, too, but when I put in a stone

I found near the lake it just sat there.'

Phineas thought fast. The chests, then, were obviously enchanted to take or deliver, but only specific things. 'Where do the flowers go to?' he tried.

Bix shrugged. 'Nobody knows.'

To wherever Wodebean was, perhaps? The notion did not seem so very far-fetched. And according to the testimony of Miss Phelps, Wodebean could occasionally be counted on to assist a person wrongly stranded in the Hollows. Did not he, Phineas, count as such? He had not been brought there by design.

Then of course, there was the theory he had been developing with Balligumph: that Wodebean, unlikely as it may seem, was a staunch supporter of the deposed royals of Aylfenhame. Phineas could not count himself among their number, being largely unacquainted with the whole affair; but he *was* a staunch ally to Ilsevel, or Ilsevellian, or My Lady Silver, or whatever she was pleased to call herself. His mind shied away from connecting her too closely with the concept of royalty; what *had* she been doing wasting her time on him, if she were a woman of such dizzyingly high status? But none of that mattered. If he considered himself her friend, and he did, then he and Wodebean might just have something in common.

He must get Wodebean's attention.

'Those cakes of yours, Bix,' he said. 'Your favourites. What were they again?'

'Jellied cakes!' she answered promptly, her eyes shining. 'Chocolate pond cakes! And the ones with the sugared bells!'

'Sun cakes, was it not?' prompted Phineas.

'Oh yes, I like those too.'

'With honey cores, and... berries?'

Bix's whole face suffused with ecstasy. 'Plumberries,' she said in tones of hushed reverence.

'Is that not what Lantring used to make?'

'His Speciality.' Bix nodded solemnly.

'Good.' Phineas found a plain cotton apron hanging on a hook near the stove, and put it on. 'Find me the recipe, Bix,' he instructed. 'And some plumberries, and you shall have your cakes.'

'How many?' Her small face had gone business-like again, all traces of rapture gone from her suddenly steely voice.

Phineas eyed her. 'How many do you want?'

'As many as I can eat.'

'Oh? In how many minutes?'

She crossed her arms huffily. 'In an hour.'

'I do not have an hour. Five minutes.'

'Five! An outrage, Mister Drake! Half of an hour.'

Phineas began ostentatiously measuring flour into a bowl, out of the stoneware bins he found lined up beneath the main table. 'Seven minutes,' he said calmly.

'Fifteen!'

'Eight.'

Bix stamped her foot. 'I do not like you at all, and I will not help you!'

'Then you will not get any cake.'

She whimpered, a sound of pure agony, and wilted like a flower. 'Nine?' she said hopefully.

Phineas smiled down at her. 'Nine it shall be. Are you a very fast eater?'

'Extremely,' she said stoutly, and the look of determination on her pale features convinced Phineas that she meant it.

He doubled the quantity of flour.

Never had he baked so peculiar a recipe, Phineas thought an hour or so later, when the cakes were almost ready to remove from the stove. When Bix had spoken of "sun cakes", he had thought she was using a figure of speech, or that perhaps it was a whimsical name she had come up with all by herself. He expected bright, sunny-looking cakes, turned yellow by some clever ingredient, or an excess of butter. Instead, he had mixed honey into the batter by the ladleful, and then — to his astonishment — she had instructed him to set the bowls of batter in the window, directly in the strongest shafts of sunlight.

And they had soaked up the sunshine, like a dry cloth absorbing water. Under Phineas's amazed eyes, the cake mix had turned steadily brighter and more golden, until the batter itself began to emit a faint, sunny glow.

'Done!' Bix had then announced, reigning over the departed Lantring's recipe book like a tiny tyrant, and Phineas had then to dollop the cake-dough into his predecessor's tins as quickly as he could, adding a generous spoonful of honey to the centre of each. The plumberries proved to be aptly named: they looked like miniature plums, though when Phineas ate a few he found them to be somehow sweeter and also tarter than any plum he had ever eaten.

When he, hands wrapped thickly in cotton, extracted the cakes from the heat and laid the trays on the table, Bix actually climbed the table-leg in her haste to get at them, and had to be bodily held back. 'They are very hot!' Phineas warned her.

'I do not care!' panted Bix, and did her best to swarm out of his grip.

'You will when your mouth is burned,' said Phineas, not in the least bit discomposed by the wildly writhing pixie he barely managed to restrain.

'My nine minutes hasn't started yet, has it?' Bix looked up at him with huge, anxious eyes.

He shook his head. 'It begins when you eat your first mouthful.'

Bix sat down heavily, and laid her head against Phineas's leg. 'Shall I have to wait long?'

'No. Only a few minutes. How long has Lantring been gone, Bix?'

'Oh, ages and ages!' she said, surprising Phineas not at all considering her extreme fervour for the cakes.

If Eleanor Phelps had spent a month here and returned to find more than ten years had passed in England, how long might "ages and ages" seem like to the outside world? Even making allowances for the natural exaggeration (and imperfect grasp of details) of a being like Bix, Lantring must have been gone for rather more than a month of Hollows-time. He hoped, then, that the sudden appearance of anything at all in Lantring's long-abandoned chest would attract the notice of Wodebean; the more so if it were Lantring's own speciality.

He curbed his impatience for a little while longer, for he would not see Bix harmed, however great his need for escape. When he judged the cakes cool enough to touch, he carefully extracted a few.

Bix's eyes lit up.

'These are not for you,' he said mildly, and carried them over to the chest. He dropped one in, half expecting that it would hit the solid wooden panel at the bottom with an unlovely *splat,* and disintegrate.

Instead, to his delight, it vanished almost as soon as it left his fingers.

He dropped three more, and stepped back. If that would not get

Wodebean's attention, no amount of cake ever would.

'Right,' he said, turning back to Bix. 'Are you ready?'

She bared sharp teeth at him in a feral grin. 'I am *ready*,' she growled.

Phineas began to transfer cakes from the trays to the large plate he had already set before Bix. 'Then I charge you to... begin!'

Bix fell upon the cakes like a woman starved, and all but disappeared in a hail of flying morsels of sweet, sticky crumbs. Many more went into her mouth than onto the table or the floor, but still she contrived to create an astonishing mess as she gobbled and gnawed her way through cake after cake after cake.

Phineas, nursing a fluttering feeling of anxiety somewhere in his belly, had no appetite for cake at all. He kept an eye on Bix and he watched the clock, but most of all he watched the chest.

'Please,' he said involuntarily, when a few minutes uneventfully passed. 'Please be an appreciator of cake, Wodebean.'

CHAPTER FIFTEEN

'You were safer there, you know,' said Wodebean, his voice as dry and dusty as the wind in the height of summer.

Ilsevel glared. 'In Winter's Hollow? Absurd!'

'It is in no way absurd. Or were you hoping to spend another few years as a frog?'

'You knew about that?' Ilsevel felt rage boiling up in her, and for a moment could scarcely breathe for fury.

'Yes, but—' Wodebean held up a hand. 'It was not I who cursed you with that shape.'

'Then who was it?'

Wodebean hesitated, watching her carefully. 'That is a more complicated question than you know.'

Ilsevel took a deep, short breath, and swallowed her ire. 'This is no time for prevarication, Wodebean. It is time for the truth. You have cheated me, and you *will* answer to me for that!'

His head tilted, a mere slight inclination. 'Oh? How have I done so?'

'My sister. Anthelaena! Your reigning queen! You made not the smallest effort to cure the disease which ravaged her, though you *promised* me you would help!'

'That is true,' said Wodebean calmly. 'Indeed I did not.'

Ilsevel gasped. 'Oh! So you do not deny it!'

Wodebean gave a slight, wry smile, the expression barely

perceptible beneath the shadow of his hood. He said nothing.

'She was *ill*,' said Ilsevel venomously, and advanced slowly upon Wodebean, every part of her alive with the need to tear him to pieces. 'You promised to find the means to heal her, and you did nothing! You will pay for it now, Wodebean. She is trapped in the form of an animal, and without the proper assistance she will remain so forever. You *will* help me find the means to restore her.'

Wodebean merely watched her approach, unmoved. 'Consider,' he said softly. 'Your sister was not ill, My Lady Silver.'

'Oh, cursed with some foul disease, some wasting enchantment — I know it was no natural thing, no mere happenstance. It could not have been.'

'In fact, she was poisoned.'

Ilsevel stopped, momentarily taken aback. 'Poisoned? How can you know that?'

Wodebean gave a great sigh, and pushed back the hood of his deep red mantle. His face was lean and bony, all sharp angles, his olive skin stretched tightly over prominent cheekbones. He had deep-sunk eyes whose colour was almost as much red as brown, and smudged beneath with shadow. Gold hoops glinting with rubies adorned his narrow nose and the tip of one ear. He had more hair than was usual for a hobgoblin, a dark thatch of it curling over the collar of his cloak. He returned Ilsevel's gaze calmly, and said: 'Because I am the one who poisoned her.'

Ilsevel, conscious of a depth of rage she had never known before, knew not how to answer him. She could only stare, bereft of words, as a hot fury boiled up so fast she thought, distantly, that she might explode with it.

But the hobgoblin read the look in her eyes easily enough, and held up a hand. 'Hear me,' he said. 'Consider. What were the conditions at the time?'

He did not expect her to *speak,* did he? She could only spit her fury like a cat, and she would not so demean herself; not before an audience, even if they did not seem disposed to pay the smallest attention to what was passing before them.

Wodebean smiled, very faintly. 'You never did learn the identity of your enemy, did you? No, before you ask, I do not know it either. Your sister Tyllanthine is not the only Glamourist of remarkable ability in Aylfenhame, is she? A different name, a different face, for every one of his enemies and supporters alike. That was the Kostigern. How, then, do you defeat such a foe?

'You do not. You cannot overpower an enemy you cannot find, cannot see, cannot put a name to. You can only trick him, out manoeuvre him, foil his schemes by playing his own games against him — and winning. That is what I did, My Lady Silver. I made of myself a willing servant of the Kostigern's at the Court-at-Mirramay

— or so I made him believe. Think, then. What would have happened, had I been able to do as you asked, and cured your sister?'

Ilsevel felt numb. 'She... she would have recovered. The royal city would never have fallen.'

'She would have recovered. The Kostigern would have destroyed me for my failure, my disobedience, and sent another after Her Majesty in my place. And another, and another, until she was dead, and then every last one of you would have shared her fate thereafter.' Wodebean gazed at Ilsevel with cold, flat eyes and never blinked. 'I poisoned Her Majesty, My Lady Gold, because if I had not, someone else would have done it for me. I chose a poison which was deadly to an Aylir and without a cure — thus fulfilling my obligations to the enemy. But I chose a venom that was harmless to animals. I poisoned her, and I engineered her transformation into the form she currently wears. And thus, she still lives.' He smiled slightly. 'As do you, and your sister Tyllanthine, and the princess Lihyaen. How do you think any of this was contrived?'

'Lihyaen?' Ilsevel repeated, blinking stupidly. Her fury was gone, sliced neatly to pieces by Wodebean's coolly logical words; all she was left with was confusion. 'But she— she was killed, or thought killed—'

'Thought dead,' Wodebean agreed. 'Like her mother. Tyllanthine and I arranged between us for her removal from the royal city. She was as much in the way as Anthelaena, you see, and had we not taken upon ourselves the task of her murder, that, too, would have been given to another — and carried out to the letter.'

'The stock,' Ilsevel whispered. 'It could only have been your work.'

Wodebean had the effrontery to appear pleased by this praise. 'Thank you, My Lady,' he murmured. 'It was one of my best, I admit.'

'Tylla said— she said— she *colluded* with you? With the Kostigern?'

Words failed, leaving Ilsevel with nothing but bewildered silence.

'She played the same dangerous game as I, though with the kind of complexity I could never have accomplished. How many parts she played at Court! The queen's disaffected and disloyal sister; the princess Lihyaen's eminently corruptible nurse; oh, she found myriad ways of seeming to aid him, while at the same time foiling every one of his plots that she could. She is an admirable woman.' His brow darkened, and he added: 'She has paid dearly for it. More so than I.'

Ilsevel was recovering from her shock, and the tumult of emotions that had succeeded it, and now her thoughts were turning and turning, slotting pieces together. 'Edironal?' she whispered. 'And... and me?'

'There I have no information for you. The king's disappearance was no work of mine, nor of Tyllanthine's; we do not know what became of him. And I had nothing to do with your transformation, either.'

A figure in a white cloak; that was all Ilsevel had seen. It could not have been Wodebean indeed; she had not suspected it of him. That white-shrouded figure had been far too tall, and besides, the hobgoblin before her did not possess the necessary arts to work such magic. But had it been Tyllanthine? Oh, Tylla! They had spoken of Wodebean so recently, and not a word of this had she spoken to Ilsevel. But did that mean Wodebean lied? No. How like Tylla it was, to keep information to herself unless it was forced from her — however important it may be.

Another, treacherous little hope flared up in spite of her anger: the hope that Wodebean spoke the truth. Oh, Wodebean! So long a trusted member of the royal court; never a courtier, but a colleague. Never a friend, but an associate. His departure from the royal city, his descent into thievery and trickery and contraband — these tales Ilsevel had heard told, since her return to her rightful shape, and they had puzzled almost as much as they had hurt her. But had it all been a ploy? Was he not, after all, the traitor he had seemed to be?

And Tyllanthine...

'I could wish,' she said, in a surprisingly measured voice, 'that you and Tylla were not so cursed secretive, my good sir! If all that you say is true, *why* could not one of you have told us — at least about Lihyaen? The pain you caused! Anthela's face—' She broke off, unable to put words to the memories she held. Anthelaena's face, when Lihyaen had died. Fury rose again; even if he had acted in good faith, he had *much* to answer for, and she dearly wished to make him pay for every agony he had inflicted upon others.

Wodebean had looked upon the queen's suffering, too. As had Tyllanthine. And neither of them had said a word to alleviate her pain. Appalled at the ruthless resolve that could render any such course of action possible, Ilsevel felt a fresh desire to rend the hobgoblin apart with her bare hands.

Wodebean still had not moved. He might have been a statue, save for the way that his black eyes glittered as he looked at her. Even his lips barely moved when he spoke. 'Tyllanthine and I made vassals of ourselves,' he said quietly. 'We could not merely pretend to support so wily and ruthless an enemy as the Kostigern; he had ways of knowing, you see. We had to do everything he asked of us. That meant that *your* reactions had to be sincere — yours, and Anthelaena's — or the masquerade would shortly have been discovered, and all our hopes of success depended upon our duplicity never being exposed. And further, consider. If you had been captured, rather than killed: what might you have revealed about us, if you had known the whole truth?'

Ilsevel gritted her teeth around the torrent of abuse she longed to hurl at him. She could not fault his logic, curse him again and again, but did it truly justify his behaviour? Did it exonerate Tyllanthine?

Could any of it even be relied upon as the truth? It was a clever story, one she would dearly love to accept in its entirety, for then she would never again have to doubt her sister's loyalty, nor hold Wodebean in contempt. But that alone made it suspect. He was cunning enough to spin just the right tale to pacify her, to calm all the worries of her anxious heart, knowing how desperately she would want it to be true.

'What, then, became of the Kostigern?' she said, when she had regained control of herself. 'If you and Tyllanthine were so clever, did you succeed? His disappearance: was that, too, your work?'

'No,' said Wodebean, and the syllable contained a world of regret. 'It was not our doing. He simply... disappeared. We thought it some new ploy of his, a scheme he had not seen fit to impart to us — and we worried, that he had found us out. But weeks and months passed, and he did not come back. I have never discovered what became of him.'

Ilsevel considered this in taut silence. 'I do not trust you,' she said flatly.

Wodebean inclined his head. 'Nor should you.'

She blinked at that. 'What, then, is all this tale for, if not to win back my trust?'

'It is an explanation. You were owed one.'

She advanced upon him at last, unsure whether she would prefer to claw out his eyes with her fingernails or catch him in an embrace. Secretive, duplicitous and ruthless he may have been — but if his account were the truth, he had also saved the lives of her sister and niece. 'And why now?' she said, recalling her attention with some difficulty. 'If it was so important to tell me none of these things before, why now?'

'The Kostigern is no longer among us, and the threat to your family is no longer immediate. But, My Lady, there are whispers that he shall be found. His followers of old are waking again; attempts have been made, and more will follow. If he is brought back to an empty Mirramay, who is to prevent him from attempting a claim upon the sovereignty at once? And what if he should succeed? Princess Lihyaen is liberated, and you have been restored to your natural form. It is time to bring back Her Majesty, My Lady Gold.'

Ilsevel stared hard at Wodebean, scrutinising his odd, bony face as though it might somehow reveal to her the sincerity of his clever words. 'You have so many answers,' she said. 'But never the ones that matter the most. What became of the Kostigern? Or His Majesty the King? Why is Tyllanthine burdened with the Korrigan's curse — is that your doing, too?'

'I do not know the answers to any of those questions save the last,' said Wodebean. 'My Lady Tyllanthine's curse is not my doing. She will not admit to me the truth, but I fear that curse is the Kostigern's work. It was laid upon her shortly before the traitor's disappearance.' His mouth twisted. 'When I said that she paid dearly for the games she played, it is that to which I referred. I fear she displeased him.'

'My poor sister.'

'It will be dealt with.'

'And you?' she said, watching him closely. 'Where have you been all this time, Wodebean?'

'In Torpor.' He smiled briefly. 'After the fall of Mirramay, those of the court who survived were not lenient towards those who had aided the enemy. In their haste to escape punishment, those known to have been among the Kostigern's supporters eagerly betrayed the rest, and my name was mentioned by several.'

'Why should they have been lenient?'

'Indeed.' Wodebean shrugged, the first real movement she had witnessed from him.

'Without you and Tyllanthine, Mirramay might never have fallen.'

Wodebean smiled faintly. 'Without Tyllanthine and me, Aylfenhame might have had a different ruler these past few decades. You cannot know how many schemes we destroyed.'

Ilsevel could only sigh, for who could argue with him? There were too many might-have-beens, too many possibilities, and none of them could now be weighed and deemed superior to the rest. She abandoned the topic, forcibly returning her mind to what was important now, to the reason she had so long sought for Wodebean: Anthelaena. 'You will help me restore My Lady Gold,' she said in a voice of steel.

'I will. I have made preparations, though there is more yet to be done. When all is prepared, I shall approach Tyllanthine — and you.'

An enquiry as to the nature of these preparations hovered upon Ilsevel's lips, but before she could utter the words there came a commotion among the goblins. Curiously intent upon their work, they had ignored Ilsevel's conversation with Wodebean entirely, and continued sewing furiously away. But now the little cross-legged goblin that fed clothes into the chest had hopped down off his shelf and was dashing towards Wodebean, waving something in his hand. 'Master!' he cried.

'That reminds me,' murmured Ilsevel as the goblin approached. 'The Hollows? What are they for?'

'They are some of the preparations I mentioned,' replied he briefly. 'I set them in motion long ago.' He turned his attention to the goblin, who deposited a sticky and rather mauled-looking cake into his hands. 'Passed through from Comestibles,' he panted. 'Came through the Summers chest.'

Wodebean examined the ruined cake with more interest than its sorry appearance seemed to warrant, and then looked keenly at the messenger. 'Was this the only one?'

'No, Master! There are more.'

Wodebean nodded once, and set off in the direction of a tall archway that led into another large, well-lit hallway, Ilsevel trailing along at his heels. The second room echoed the first, except that there was a mixture of different people here — goblins, Ayliri, brownies and even a troll — and they were making food, not clothes. Ilsevel smelled such a medley of aromas that she could discern no particular scents, though around her she saw everything from salmagundy to syllabubs being made; stewed ragout of meat, jugged hare, an array of pies, and even a floating pond pudding. Wodebean passed straight through without pausing, nimbly weaving his way through the many trestle-tables set up to support the labours of the cooks.

An antechamber lay behind, a bright room full of windows looking out over a wide meadow. It was spring out there, somehow, and it occurred to Ilsevel for the first time to wonder where she was.

Four vast chests were lined up along the centre of the room. One was stout pine wound about with holly and evergreen and mistletoe; one was gnarled rowan decked in bright berries; the third was white oak wreathed in flowers; and the fourth was some honey-coloured wood Ilsevel did not recognise, which appeared to be sprouting a flourishing carpet of flowers. It was to this last chest that Wodebean stepped, and threw open the lid.

Inside lay three more cakes, these in rather better shape than their unfortunate sibling. Wodebean looked at them in silence.

'Curious,' he said after a while, and tapped one long finger against his chin. He snapped his fingers, and a goblin in a red hat and jerkin appeared almost immediately at his elbow. 'Did Lantring of Summer's Hollow not depart some time ago?' he said crisply.

The goblin had brought a ledger with him, so large a book that he had trouble carrying it. He dumped it onto the floor, where it landed with a terrific *thud,* and bent to leaf furiously through it. 'Aye, Master!' he declared after a few moments, and pointed a thin finger at a scrawled entry on a particular page.

'Then how is it that his signature dish is coming through the chest? Is it a time discrepancy again?'

The goblin shook his head, emphatic. 'No, Master! All four chests have been checked and serviced recently, sir, and they are *functional!*'

Wodebean picked up one of the cakes and took a bite. He chewed thoughtfully, and to Ilsevel's surprise his face briefly lit up. Had she ever seen him smile before? 'Perhaps the records were in error,' he mused, and to her surprise he got directly into the chest — taking care not to stamp on the remaining cakes — and promptly vanished.

She made a belated attempt to catch hold of his cloak as he went, but her fingers found nothing but air.

Glowering down at the overly enthusiastic goblin, she said acidly: 'Wretched fellow, your master.'

'Oh, no, no, no!' said the goblin, beaming at her. 'He is not at all wretched, my lady, not at all!'

She sighed and gave up the point, wondering vaguely what Wodebean was feeding this absurd creature. Before she had had more than two minutes to ponder the hobgoblin's absence, however, and to wonder if he was coming back, he reappeared — and he was not alone.

Phineas Drake, coatless but with his ever-present cap stuck into a pocket of his waistcoat, appeared in the chest beside Wodebean, his arm clamped in a firm grip. 'I have found a sneak,' said Wodebean, shaking him. 'A sneak with remarkable skill in a kitchen, but a sneak nonetheless.'

Ilsevel folded her arms, and took a moment to survey the picture they made: Wodebean, eyes fiercely alight, no doubt plotting what terrible things he would do to the intruder he had intercepted; and Phineas looking simultaneously elated and hang-dog, the former expression coming to the fore when he set eyes upon her. 'Ilsevel!' he said exultantly, though his eyes shifted guiltily to Wodebean as he spoke. Then, to her surprise and annoyance, he appeared to recollect something and made a hasty, awkward bow in her direction.

'Oh, dear,' she sighed. 'Who have you been talking to?'

Wodebean looked from Phineas to Ilsevel, his brows lifting. 'I see you are not unacquainted,' he surmised.

Ilsevel waved a hand, indicating that Phineas should be released. 'Congratulations, Wodebean,' she said drily. 'You have captured my favourite baker.'

CHAPTER SIXTEEN

Phineas offered the lady a cake.

He had been toying idly with a leftover one (astonishing that there had been any left uneaten at all, for Bix was voracious in the extreme). Though it was undoubtedly a fine cake, as well as an intriguing one, he had been too nervous to eat even a morsel of it, and had merely been passing it from hand to hand as he waited. And then had come Wodebean, in a whirl of unexpected and unaccountable wrath; he had scarcely paused to question Phineas but had got hold of him by the arm, and snatched him away.

Disappearing from one chest and reappearing in another had been much as Phineas had supposed would happen. But finding Ilsevellian waiting on the other side — My Lady Silver, She of Disconcertingly Towering Eminence and Woefully Satirical Eye — had taken him entirely by surprise. Delighted to see her but uncertain as well, afeared of Wodebean and confused as to his destination, Phineas was temporarily bereft of words. All he could find to do to express his relief at finding her safe was to extend the hand in which he held that one, uneaten cake. Only belatedly did he realise that he had fidgeted with it to the point that it was no longer quite presentable.

Ilsevel raised one, speaking brow.

'I should accept it, if I were you,' said Wodebean gravely. 'It is very good.'

Heartened by these words, Phineas risked a glance at the

hobgoblin. Wodebean did not appear any less displeased. 'I was looking for Ilse— for My Lady Silver,' he explained. 'She vanished abruptly from Thieves' Hollow, and we were concerned—'

'We?' interposed Ilsevel.

'Mr. Balligumph as well as me.'

'Of course she vanished,' said Wodebean coldly. 'I arranged that she should.'

'You,' said Ilsevel, levelling a finger at Wodebean, 'are altogether too interfering!'

He appeared faintly amused by that, and made Ilsevel a tiny bow. 'Perhaps,' he allowed. 'Tyllanthine asked it of me.'

'But...' said Phineas, frowning. 'But Tyllanthine said nothing about it.'

'Of course she did not.'

Ilsevel was looking wrathful, all white about the mouth. 'Am I to know why I was so ruthlessly hustled out of the way?'

Wodebean sighed. 'That she did not tell me.' He retrieved a slightly squashed example of Phineas's sun cakes from a pocket somewhere in his mantle, and took a big bite. 'I did remonstrate with her,' he said thickly. 'For what it is worth. She does not listen to me.'

'But you do all her bidding.'

He looked faintly abashed at that. 'We have been... assisting one another for a long time.'

'No more of it as it applies to me, if you please,' said Ilsevel.

'It appears to be quite useless, anyway,' Wodebean agreed. 'We ought to have anticipated that the Hollows would obey you.'

That interested Ilsevel enough to dispel her anger, for though she maintained her arms-folded posture of displeasure she said with considerable curiosity: 'Oh? And why ought you?'

'They are in Torpor,' said Wodebean, with a grin that struck Phineas as faintly mischievous. 'Nothing changes there. To the lands of the Hollow Hills, My Lady Gold still reigns at Mirramay, and all her family are to be obeyed without question.' He paused in momentary thought, and added: 'This may not have occurred to me, but I suspect that Tyllanthine knew it.'

This made little sense to Phineas, but Ilsevel appreciated it. She let the reference to her sister pass — though the flicker of annoyance that crossed her face suggested she was not untouched by it. 'A clever use of the Torpor,' she commended him. 'Yours is a mind I would not like to cross swords with, Wodebean.'

'Despite all appearances to the contrary, you never have, My Lady.' He bowed and added, 'Nor shall you ever.'

Ilsevel returned his bow with a slight curtsey of her own, and in her eyes was grudging respect. 'That said,' she murmured, 'if you ever *dispose* of me again, I shall not rest until I have ruined you, heart and soul.'

He smiled, a genuine smile, and nodded. But instead of answering directly, he said, incomprehensibly to Phineas's ear: 'There are velvet queen parasols at Autumn's Hollow.'

And she laughed, throwing up her hands. 'Of course there are. How convenient.'

'Carefully planned, Lady Silver,' he corrected. 'Not convenient.'

Phineas, silenced, directed a questioning look at Ilsevel.

'Velvet queen parasols,' she repeated. 'It is a type of mushroom, vital to a variety of potent enchantments, concoctions and spells. They grow only where the Queen-at-Mirramay has lately stepped, which is difficult just at present since she has been absent from her throne for a long time.'

'I did hope that the effect would hold in spite of her alteration in shape,' said Wodebean. 'But no.'

'Since when may a cat hold the throne of Aylfenhame?' said Ilsevel.

'When the cat in question is the reigning monarch in an altered shape, I thought it not absolutely impossible. But I made other arrangements, just in case. And the roses of Summer's Hollow are kin to those that used to wreathe the throne-at-Mirramay.'

'These mushrooms are needed for turning the queen back into a person?' Phineas ventured, wondering at the words that were coming out of his mouth. 'And the roses?'

'Indeed,' said Ilsevel, but she was staring at him, narrow-eyed.

Phineas flushed. 'What is it?'

'You were looking for me?' she said abruptly.

He nodded warily.

'You went into Summer's Hollow to find *me*?'

His flush darkened, until his cheeks felt warm. 'I did not then know that you were in Winter's Hollow. Mr. Balligumph had a notion there were other Hollows, you see, and it did not seem unlikely that you had gone from one to another. So we went looking for a way into one or another of them, and—' He stopped, because her narrowed eyes had melted into a soft smile, and she was staring at him with an altogether different demeanour.

'Thank you,' she said.

Phineas, disconcerted, fell to stammering. 'Um, y-you're welcome. My Lady.'

She blinked, and stopped smiling. 'I did not *need* to be retrieved, as must be perfectly apparent, and you put yourself in sad danger of becoming a permanent resident of Summer. Which could be termed foolhardy, Mr. Drake. But I am nonetheless grateful for your efforts on my behalf.' All this was said in a much colder tone, an alteration in manner which puzzled Phineas. But he remembered the smile, and was content.

'You are welcome,' he said again, this time without stammering.

Wodebean watched this exchange with a faint, wintry smile. 'Mr. Drake has proved quite capable of manipulating me. It is an unusual achievement.'

Phineas had ceased to find the hobgoblin alarming, but he could by no means follow the trader's train of thought, so he merely waited.

'I should like to talk to you about it sometime,' added Wodebean. 'It is a long time since I have been beaten at my own tricks.' He looked Phineas over, and his eye alighted upon the glittering rose still sticking out of Phineas's pocket. Before Phineas could react, he put out a hand and snatched it up.

'Interesting,' he said, looking intently at each of its frosted petals. 'Sugar?'

'Yes,' said Phineas, and sighed. Was he now to catch trouble over the rose as well?

But Wodebean merely handed back the rose. 'A natural-born counterfeiter,' he pronounced. 'When you grow tired of baking, Mr. Drake, apply to me.'

'I-I beg your pardon?'

'I should like to employ you.'

'As a *counterfeiter*?'

Wodebean's black eyes twinkled. 'Among other things.'

'Stop that,' said Ilsevel crossly. 'That is *my* favourite baker, as I have already told you, and I shall not permit you to turn him into a crook.'

Wodebean inclined his head, gracious in defeat — but the twinkle never left his eyes. 'As you say, My Lady Silver.'

A counterfeiter. Phineas, thinking confusedly of his father, of the Thieves' Markets and of Gabriel Winters, felt numb. Counterfeit-work! What he had done to the rose had been intended to enhance, not to deceive. But did that matter?

He had lost the thread of the conversation for a little while, in his dismay. But Ilsevel's voice recalled him from his unhappy thoughts, when she said, loud and incredulous: 'Her *belt buckle?*'

'It does not have to be a belt buckle,' said Wodebean. 'Any personal items will suffice, provided they were hers for some time, and often used or worn when she was in her natural shape.'

'Belt buckles,' said Ilsevel with a long sigh. 'Ear-jewels, shoes, books, brooches, hair ornaments, rings, pens, the royal crown—'

'Not the crown,' interjected Wodebean. 'Too many others have worn it before her.'

Ilsevel conceded this point with a nod. 'Her gowns, perhaps. The Queen-at-Mirramay's pocket watch — Anthelaena began that tradition, you know, so the thing is hers entirely. My Lady Gold's Lyre. That band of stars she used to wear around her arm. The shoe-roses she wore to the last Court Festival, the ones with the butterflies. Would any of those be of use?'

'All of them,' said Wodebean.

'*All?* I am not sure I could find half!'

'All,' said Wodebean again. 'She has been a cat for many years, Lady Silver. It will take a great deal to remind her of who she used to be.'

Ilsevel gave him a flat stare. 'Have you been to Mirramay lately, Wodebean?'

'Ah... no. I have not been welcome there in some time.'

'It is empty.'

He blinked. 'Empty?'

'It is the royal city, and the Court was its heart. Take all of that away, and what is left? Those who once lived there have drifted away, the place is now swarming with Grunewald's folk, and the city has been looted so thoroughly that scarcely a trinket remains.'

'But your gowns were still there?'

'I had a large wardrobe of garments, Wodebean, and I found only three gowns remaining. And those I was able to retrieve only because I had sent them out for mending. I found them under the bed in one of the maids' rooms. Apparently no one thought it worth their while to ransack the servants' quarters.'

Wodebean looked nonplussed. 'Then what has become of Lady Gold's personal things?'

'I imagine my sister's jewellery is now adorning some looter.'

'The Thieves' Market,' interjected Phineas.

Ilsevel blinked at him.

'Do you remember what we found there? Lady— Lady Somebody's shoe-rose, and a Herald's Harp.'

'Lady Galdrin's shoe ornaments! Yes, she was a devotee of the Court, and the Harp was from the palace itself. He is right, Wodebean. Some of these things are surfacing in the shadow markets, and *you* are the king of all unsanctioned trade, are you not?'

'Ah...' For the first time since Phineas had arrived, Wodebean looked uncomfortable.

'They must be found,' said Ilsevel relentlessly. 'And quickly.'

'It will not be easy.'

'And the velvet queen parasols must be brought from Autumn's Hollow. What else is required? You did not happen to bring any of those roses with you from Summer, Phineas?'

Phineas shook his head.

'I need your sister,' said Wodebean. 'The enchantment was of her devising, and we must create its cure together. Where is she?'

'If you do not know where she is, you cannot think I have better information.' There was a trace of bitterness in Ilsevel's voice.

My sister is fallen through time. The words echoed in Phineas's mind. 'Your sister is Hidenory?' he asked Ilsevel.

'That is one of the many names she has used,' she said. 'Tyllanthine is her true name.'

'She went looking for you,' he told her.

Ilsevel blinked at him. 'But she cannot have, for it is through *her* machinations that I fell into Winter's Hollow to begin with.'

'I...' Phineas was silenced, for she had sounded so sincere. 'I thought that she would search for you. If not, then I do not know where she can have gone to.'

'She will not be found until she wishes to be. In the meantime! The parasols, Wodebean, and the jewellery.'

'I will need help,' said the hobgoblin.

'Any assistance I may render is yours.'

Phineas said, before he had time to reflect, 'And mine, too. If… if I can be of use.'

Wodebean only looked at him in silence, impassive and unreadable. But Ilsevel rewarded him with a smile — even if it was a scheming, somewhat gloatful one. 'Oh, yes,' she said with great satisfaction. 'You shall be very useful indeed, dear Phineas.'

Phineas tried not to feel too badly out of his depth, and failed.

CHAPTER SEVENTEEN

Them gates! Whisked Phineas off, an' me right behind him — but it weren't Summer's Hollow I got into! Don't rightly know where it was. Some other path o' the Hollows, most like, but long abandoned. Empty patch o' forest. I wandered around in there fer some time before I realised Phineas weren't wi' me, and then my wisps got me out. But Phineas! It were a while before I learned what had become o' him.

Tyllanthine, now. I did a hear word o' her. Dancin' about in the city, she was, always askin' and askin' — but not fer Wodebean, this time. Fer a gown made o' gold tissue, or some such. Fer shoe-buckles an' a hair-comb all covered in jewels, an' above all fer a doll. Shabby thing, this doll, or so she said, wi' all its fur long since gone, an' in the shape of a cat.

This puzzled me right enough, 'til I learned the details o' the curse. Do ye know much about curses? There's ways to rid yerself of one, but either ye must trick it, as the Goblin King did wi' the Teapot Society, or ye must meet the conditions laid down by the one who set the curse in the first place.

Well, Wodebean an' Tyllanthine wanted nobody takin' that curse off Lady Gold who wasn't equipped t' deal wi' the consequences. The poison, see? No one knew if it would still affect her, once she was her normal self again. Would the passage o' time wear away its effects, or would she be changed back t' her usual self only to snuff it on the spot? Risky business. An' nobody wanted Her Majesty fallin' into the wrong hands altogether, if someone on the side o' the Traitor were t' discover their ruse. So they built in a lot o' conditions. No one's turnin' My Lady Gold back into herself unless they's got hold of plenty o' the bits an' pieces she used t' call her own — *reminders, like, o' the person she once was. But many years have passed, and time has scattered them far an' wide...*

'Butterflies?' repeated Gabriel Winters, with a look of blank incomprehension. 'Shoe-roses with butterflies?'

'They are not just shoe-roses,' said Ilsevel, with as much patience as she could muster. 'They *are* roses, which my sister was wont to wear upon her shoes. And alighted atop these roses are butterflies, of the miniature variety, with wings of star-dusted gossamer. I believe they are white.'

'The roses?' said Gabriel, with a curl to his lips that she did not know how to interpret. 'Or the star-dusted gossamer butterflies?'

'The roses. The butterflies have wings of gold.'

'Of course.' Gabriel looked at Phineas. 'Is she altogether well, yer friend here?'

Phineas sighed. 'I told you, these are things out of the common way. From Aylfenhame.'

'Even things out of Aylfenhame ain't that improbable.'

'Yes, but these belonged to the queen!' said Ilsevel, stifling with difficulty an impulse to beat him about the head with one of her shoes.

They had gone to Gabriel out of mild desperation, for Wodebean had said: *I used to be the king of unlicensed trade, but do please recall that I have been in Torpor these many years.* He denied having ever seen such articles as Ilsevel described pass through any Thieves' Market he had ever called, nor had he or his agents been offered anything nearly so interesting.

Ilsevel, alas, could well believe it. Whatever had become of those trinkets, it had probably happened some time ago, while Wodebean lay aslumber. Indeed, most of the folk of Aylfenhame who might be able to claim any connection with the Court of Mirramay had either fallen into the Torpor likewise, or died in the conflict, or had vanished without trace. Where, then, could they expect to find help?

Perhaps in England, Phineas had said. *Where in Aylfenhame could you expect to sell anything known to belong to the queen?*

He was right again, his good sense making light work of the problem.

Supposing you wanted to sell them, he had added, rather more worryingly. *Were it me, I might prefer to keep them.*

Indeed. The notion that Anthelaena's personal effects were scattered all over Aylfenhame, hoarded away in the collections of unknown and unidentifiable denizens, was a chilling one, for how could they ever hope to discover them? Horrified, she had only been able to stare at Phineas.

Some of them were probably sold, Phineas had hastily said.

She hoped so.

They had found Gabriel Winters lingering at the waterfront, not far from the door that led into Thieves' Hollow. There was a public house there, and Gabriel had been monopolising a table all the long morning through, by the looks of him. It had been Phineas's idea to seek his help, of course. The man was of an age with Phineas's father, if not rather older, and had been deeply engaged in the thieves' community ever since his youth. *It is a place to start,* Phineas had said.

But not a good place to start, perhaps, for Winters was of no use whatsoever. 'The queen,' he repeated, and took a long drink from a tankard of something foul-smelling. He set the vessel down with a thud, and shook his head. 'I've heard of no such fancy.'

'A lyre, made from snowleaf wood, and with strings of coloured waters?' said Ilsevel.

Gabriel shook his head.

'A gown of gold silk-tissue, with ribbons of mist? A band of starlight, to be worn around the arm? A pocket-watch made of pearls, which tells the time in six or eight places at once?'

Gabriel shook his head again and again, his frown growing deeper and darker with each new item upon Ilsevel's list. '*Lady,*' he interjected at last. 'Believe me, if I had seen anything like that in these parts, I would have wasted less time scrubbin' about in the dirt after the miserable rubbish as usually passes through my hands. Maybe in London such marvels could pass wi' no comment, but not here. And not even there, I'm persuaded.'

'But,' said Phineas. 'Some articles from the royal court in Aylfenhame lately passed through the Thieves' Market.'

Gabriel looked sharply at Phineas. 'Certain of that?'

'My Lady Silver is quite certain of it.'

Ilsevel added her corroboration of this. 'We are not far from Mirramay, here. It is not so far-fetched.'

'Not far from where?'

'Mirramay, the royal city. Not in literal terms, for this city and mine are in different lands. But if I step through a gate in these parts, and enter into Aylfenhame, I am not more than half a day's ride from the palace.'

'So,' put in Phineas. 'Anyone fleeing Mirramay with their pockets full of royal loot might well find this a convenient place to rid themselves of it.'

'All that's as may be,' said Gabriel grimly, 'But I ain't seen anythin' like you describe. But then, such fine wares is not fer the likes o' me. You would need to talk to someone higher up.'

'Higher up in what?' said Phineas.

Gabriel smirked. 'Thieves has a pecking order, same as everyone else. Some of us are more powerful than others, and I ain't nearly powerful enough for your purposes. And if it's twenty years ago yer interested in, or more, well…'

'Well?' prompted Phineas, when he did not finish the sentence.

Gabriel drained his tankard in one long swallow, and wiped his mouth on the sleeve of his coat. He appeared to be on the point of saying something, then stopped, shook his head, and began again. 'The Thieves' Market. Who was selling them things from the Court?'

'His name we did not ask,' answered Phineas. 'But he was short, with a lot of pale hair, and he wore a bright cloak.'

'Dark hat? Shape of yer own?' said Gabriel, indicating Phineas's cap with a jerk of his chin.

'That was him.'

Gabriel nodded once. 'I know him. Oleander Whiteboots is his name, but they call him Magpie. Not because he cannot resist something shiny — in this trade, who can? They call him Magpie 'cause whenever something especially good comes up, he's the first to snag it. No one knows how.'

'Small wonder, then, that he had Lady Galdrin's shoe-buckle,' said Phineas.

'We need to talk to him,' said Ilsevel firmly.

But the man just shrugged. 'He comes fer the Market, most times. Never see him otherwise.'

'And when is the next Market?'

'Twelfth Night.'

This made no sense to Ilsevel, but Phineas sighed as though it made more sense to him than he liked. 'That is still ten days away!'

'I cannot help that, Phineas.'

'You must know something more,' Phineas pleaded. 'Please, think.'

Gabriel sighed, and gestured to the barkeep to top up his tankard. He sagged over the table-top, his hat laid down upon the bench beside him, his greying dark hair all twisted about by wind, or perhaps agitated fingers. He struck Ilsevel as the very embodiment of weariness, were such a quality to take human form. He had great, dark pouches of skin under his eyes, and those eyes were faintly bloodshot to boot. 'I don't know, Phineas,' he said roughly. 'I'll tell you truly, I am far more concerned about yer father than about any tissue gowns from some far-off court of nobility.'

'Why?' said Phineas quickly. 'What is amiss with Father?'

'When was the last time you saw him?'

'The day before last.'

'I ain't seen him since then, neither. Nobody has. The shop's shut up, ain't been opened for two days in a row.'

Ilsevel saw worry and guilt written clearly across Phineas's face, and impulsively reached out to grasp his hand. 'It is the season for celebrating, is it not?' she reminded him. 'He has gone for a holiday, depend upon it.'

'My father never celebrates,' said Phineas shortly, and Gabriel, too, was looking at her as though she were mad. 'And he would never shut the shop for two days together, especially not at this season.' He stood up abruptly, jamming his cap back over his curls, and said curtly: 'I must find him.'

He was gone before Ilsevel could reply.

'I rather need him,' Ilsevel said to the old thief.

Gabriel raised an eyebrow at her. 'Why? Lady like you can fix yer own problems, I'll wager.'

'All the better with the right help.'

'Ain't that the way with us all.' He stared moodily into his tankard, now brimming once again with the abominable substance he apparently termed *drink*, but did not take a swallow. 'Old man Drake's in a bad way,' he said suddenly. 'Has been since Phineas's mother died. It was *she* made him go straight, or leastwise, he did it for her — and for Phineas, as was a babe-in-arms then. But he never took to it, and I fear as he has gone back to his old trade.'

'Which is?'

'Highway robbery.' Gabriel smiled faintly at Ilsevel. 'Phineas won't find him now.'

Ilsevel stood up swiftly. 'Oleander Whiteboots,' she said, looking down upon the crumpled man before her. 'Quickly. There is more you could tell me, I am sure.'

Gabriel screwed up his face, whether in thought or protest Ilsevel could not tell. 'Forget him,' he said. 'Said to be a counterfeiter of unusual skill. Has a way of makin' a thing look like *just* what you were wantin', when it ain't at all. That harp you said you saw? Probably no such thing.'

'It was assuredly a harp,' said Ilsevel, disquieted.

'No doubt, but unlikely to be the one you had in mind.'

'So you do not think that this Whiteboots has any genuine Court articles, after all?'

'He may. He may not.'

Ilsevel nodded once. 'I thank you,' she said, remembered belatedly to smile, and left the tavern at a brisk, purposeful walk. But she had not gone much beyond the threshold when the thief called her back. '*Lady!*' he bellowed.

She returned to the table.

'There is one other thing,' he said. I hardly like to tell it to you; it is most likely moonshine.'

'Tell me anyway.'

'Aye.' He glanced about, as though to be sure there was no one near enough to overhear him, and leaned his grizzled head a little nearer to Ilsevel. 'There is an old tale in these parts. I cannot say how old it is, but I first heard it when I was about Phineas's age, or near enough. The Queen's Hoard.'

'What?' Ilsevel sat quickly upon the bench, her attention fixed. 'Go on.'

He gave a small, wry smile. 'Treasure tales are common as muck, you must know that. But this one tells of a hoard of jewels that once belonged to a great queen. Marvels beyond imagining, naturally, and they're said to lie "under the hill" — not that anyone has made sense of that.'

'The hill,' echoed Ilsevel thoughtfully. 'There is only one hill hereabouts, is there not?'

Gabriel nodded. 'Aye. You can see it from here. It's the one with the city built on it.'

'Has anyone tried to find this hoard?'

The thief grinned. 'I know of one or two who wasted a deal of time digging about up there, as though it were like to be buried in some obvious spot. Needless to say, nothing was found.'

Ilsevel felt a surge of excitement, and an almost painful hope. Gabriel Winters was right: tales of treasure hoards were by no means unusual, and most were — as he had put it — nothing but moonshine. But the details of this one agreed so perfectly with the very articles she was looking for; was that like to be a coincidence?

Furthermore, while she could well imagine that the folk of England would not find the sense of the words "under the hill", *she* very well could. There were Hollows under there, and somewhere there would be a way in; one that a simple Englishman was unlikely to guess at.

She beamed her delight, and stood up from the bench so fast that she almost became entangled in her skirts, and toppled down again. 'I thank you!' she said. 'I bless the day that I met you!'

And away she went, leaving Gabriel Winters to blink after her in befuddlement.

Phineas, of course, was long gone by the time she regained the street, but she could guess where it was he had gone. Clutching her bonnet against the strong, chill wind, she turned her steps towards the very hill which might, if she was lucky, contain the answers to all her beleaguered sister's problems, and hastened up the slope to Phineas's family shop.

She found him standing outside of the bakery, hands tucked deep into his pockets, his coat collar turned up to keep the wind off his neck. So absorbed was he by his thoughts that he did not immediately notice her approach; and she soon saw why, for the great front window, so recently ablaze with festive colour, was boarded up. A sign hung there, saying simply: CLOSED.

Uncertain what to say, Ilsevel waited for Phineas to speak first.

At length, he did. 'I went inside. He has taken all his clothes, and left no word for me.'

Was this the right moment to repeat Gabriel Winters's opinion as to the fate of the elder Mr. Drake? She could hardly suppose that Phineas would welcome the news. Honest Phineas, who had reacted with such horror to Wodebean's half-joking designation of him as a counterfeiter. How much had he ever known of his father's past life?

Some — his friendship with Winters was proof enough of that. But all? It was, in all probability, no accident that Winters had shared that particular confidence with Ilsevel only after Phineas had left. She was to tell him of it, but... perhaps not yet.

'He will come back for you?' Ilsevel suggested.

But Phineas, his mouth set in a grim line, shook his head.

'Did you love the bakery so much?' Ilsevel said.

His mouth quirked, a smile more bitter than mirthful. 'I ask myself: Shall I take it on? I know that I could, and it is my home. And yet... I do not know that I want to.'

'It is a difficult decision.' Ilsevel, still unsure what to say, felt that her words were inadequate to the occasion. Did he feel as she had, upon returning to Mirramay? Did his heart plummet as hers had, when she entered the empty, deserted palace that had once been her home? She had hardened her heart, then, for all that was dear to her seemed lost.

Not quite all, as it had subsequently turned out. Her sisters may be in trouble, but they were not gone; and, against all odds, her niece yet lived. Did just such a mitigation lie in store for Phineas? Would his father come back? She could not know, and did not wish to falsely raise his hopes. So she said nothing, only waited with him in silence.

Company was more than she had had, anyway.

After a while, Phineas gave a soft sigh, and turned his back upon the boarded-up window. He had a smile for Ilsevel even then, and being Phineas, his next words were an apology. 'I am sorry, My Lady Silver. Where were we, before I ran away and left you?'

She smiled back. 'I need not impose upon you further, if you had rather go in search of your father.'

'I do not know where to look,' he admitted. 'And you need me more than he does, for now.' He said no more, but his eyes clearly said: *I hope?*

She did not, in all truth, need him. Not really. Some other local person could just as well answer her questions, and guide her about the town, as Phineas could. Perhaps even better. But she had grown accustomed to his presence. That calm good sense he had in such abundance had more than once prevented her from haring wildly down the wrong path; his clever brain had seen answers where she had found only confusion; and it was long — so, *so* long — since anyone had treated her with such care. He was kind in an unassuming way, as though it were so natural for him that he did not even have to think about it. Probably he did not.

She could manage without Phineas, but she did not want to.

So she said: 'I do indeed, for what do you think? Your excellent friend gave me a clue, just after you left, and it is a fine clue! I have high hopes for it.'

'Gabriel did?' Phineas gave her his blank stare — the same look he had greeted her with when she had first encountered him in his shop. But she was learning that his mind was by no means as empty as his expression had then suggested. Somewhere behind those green eyes lurked a thousand thoughts and ideas; his clever brain was collecting and sorting everything he saw and heard and discovered, fitting together the pieces, finding a way through any difficulty.

'An old legend,' she supplied. 'The Queen's Hoard. Said to be hidden under the Hill.'

Phineas's eyes narrowed. 'Which hill?'

By way of answer, Ilsevel lifted one booted foot and stamped upon the pavement. The Drakes' bakery — or what was left of it — was situated some halfway up.

Understanding dawned. He was silent for a moment. Then, 'The Greestone Stairs. There is a way into the Hollows from there, but it is Wodebean's way, and leads, no doubt, into the very same spaces we have but lately left.'

'Yes,' Ilsevel agreed.

'But there are more. The gates around the castle, that go into Summer's Hollow.'

'Possibly the others, too,' Ilsevel added. 'Winter and Autumn and Spring. But Winter's Hollow, at least, is a small, confined space, with no roads leading out of it. The residents could give me no hint of a way through into any other place — not into England, not into Aylfenhame, and not into any other Hollow.'

'So they are pockets of land, sealed, and with only a gate into England by way of entry or exit?' Phineas mused. 'Except, there are the chests.'

'And Wodebean always seems to contrive some way in or out.'

Phineas nodded. 'I would like to know whether Wodebean created these Hollows, or whether he merely turned them to his own purpose. How long have they been dedicated to the seasons?'

'Long,' said Ilsevel. 'So I surmise from those of Winter's Hollow.

If he created them, he did it long before Anthelaena's demise.'

'Anthelaena,' repeated Phineas. 'Your sister.'

'Yes.'

'Queen of Aylfenhame.'

'She was, once.'

Ilsevel expected more questions, but Phineas was silent. His face filled with a weary melancholy as he looked at her, and he seemed to shrink, turning in upon himself as though in defeat.

A blink, and the impression was gone. 'You had better tell me the whole story, I think,' said Phineas.

Ilsevel sighed, and linked her arm through his. They had lingered long enough outside of the boarded-up shop; she began, gently, to lead him back up the hill. 'It began more than thirty years ago,' she said. 'Anthelaena and I were not so very old, then, and our sister Tyllanthine rather younger still. There had been peace in Aylfenhame for generations, but trouble came upon us… we became aware, by degrees, of a traitor somewhere at Court. One who sought to overthrow our family, but who would not do so by direct means. He would not oppose us openly; he brought no armies to our gates. Instead, he remained in the shadows; making deals behind our backs, coaxing and bribing our supporters away from us, countering every good we sought to do with trickery and lies. So clever an enemy was he, that to this day we do not know his identity.

'It seems Tyllanthine found a way to reach him. She pretended to disaffection, made a turncoat of herself…' *Pretended?* Whispered Ilsevel's heart. *Did she?* 'And Wodebean also. Then, all at once, everything went so wrong. My sister's husband, the king, went hunting one morn and never returned. Their child, Lihyaen, died in her bed one night — or so it seemed. And then Anthela…' Ilsevel's grip tightened on Phineas's arm, her thoughts awhirl. 'Died. Poisoned by Wodebean, it appears, in a plot formed with Tyllanthine… and saved. By a curse. Trapped into a cat's shape, in which form — I am to understand — the poison cannot destroy her.'

'You seek to reverse this curse?' Phineas said.

'I do. Tyllanthine also. But a curse is an intricate thing, Phineas, and this more so than most.'

'What became of the traitor?'

Ilsevel shrugged. 'The Kostigern, as we called him? I do not know. He disappeared, I am told, soon after Anthelaena's apparent death.

But this happened after I, too, was cursed. I was turned into… into a frog, and only recently liberated.' Saying the words out loud sparked off a stream of questions and thoughts, the most prominent among them being: why had she been only transformed, and not killed? This hardly seemed to correspond with the rest of the Kostigern's behaviour. Just *who* had it been, shrouded so completely within that white cloak?

Phineas was frowning. 'Every claimant to the throne so neatly removed. Dead, as far as he knew, for was that not the intention behind Wodebean and Tyllanthine's plans? With king, queen and princesses dead or otherwise disposed of — all save Tyllanthine, who he thought to be his own creature — *then* was the moment to reveal himself, to make an attempt upon the throne. Yet, he did not.'

'I wonder,' mused Ilsevel. 'Did he suspect such a trap? Had he reason to imagine himself tricked?'

'Perhaps. Or perhaps something befell him.'

'They say he is coming back,' said Ilsevel. 'Wodebean believes it to be so. His supporters, long lost in the Torpor, are waking up again. They are looking for him.'

'Hence the hurry to revive the queen.'

'Yes.'

'Why… how are they coming out of this Torpor?'

'That is not known. But it is not just our enemies. Many of our friends chose the Long Sleep, too, or were forced into it, and they are also returning. They do not know what has drawn them to wakefulness.'

Phineas stood in silent thought. They had paused on the edge of Castle Square; a drizzle of rain came down, beading Phineas's cap in drops of clear water and settling upon his nose. He paid it no heed. His eyes were far away, and Ilsevel wondered where his quick mind had taken him.

At last he said: 'Where is Wodebean?'

'Gone after his traders, he said. He seeks traces of Anthelaena's wardrobe, and her jewels.'

Phineas merely nodded. 'We need Mr. Balligumph,' he decided. 'And your sister Tyllanthine.'

'Balligumph?' said Ilsevel in surprise. 'Is he, too, awakened?'

'I do not think he was ever asleep. He talks as though he has been guarding the Tilby toll-bridge these many years, and he knows a great deal.'

'To Tilby, then? I cannot imagine where my sister is got to.'

Phineas began to walk again, but in an altered direction. He paced now towards the soaring shape of the cathedral, shrouded in rain and looming against the cloud-darkened sky. 'Let us put that aside for the moment,' he recommended. 'Tyllanthine will return when she's ready, perhaps bringing something useful. Just now, I want to talk to Balligumph.'

'Then I do not know why you are going that way,' said Ilsevel, quick to follow in spite of her words. 'Did you not place him at Tilby?'

'Usually, but he has been in the city a great deal, and that is where I last saw him.' He passed under the cathedral gate and approached the west front, his chin tilted up as he scanned the golden limestone walls. 'Mr. Tibs?' he called.

A grotesque shape detached itself from an alcove above the door, and flowed to the ground in a ripple of shadow. 'What is it?' hissed a dark little voice.

'Have you seen Mr. Balligumph today? I've need of him.'

'He went in the direction of the Stairs, not two hours ago.'

Phineas smiled, and touched his hat. 'Thank you.'

The knot of shadow gathered itself, and began to flow away.

'One other question,' said Phineas, and the shadows roiled to a stop. 'The Queen's Hoard. Have you ever heard any such report?'

'Why, yes,' said the voice of Mr. Tibs, with a dry chuckle. 'Certainly I have.'

CHAPTER EIGHTEEN

Phineas found Mr. Balligumph seated comfortably upon somebody's doorstep, part way down the slope of the Greestone Stairs. He sat with his elbows upon his knees and his hat in his lap, intent upon the spot where Wodebean had contrived to vanish. A vast smile split his face when he saw Phineas and Ilsevel on the approach, and he got up to make a deep bow — to Ilsevel, Phineas reminded himself, though the troll seemed to include the baker's boy in the gesture. 'Phineas-me-lad!' he said delightedly. 'An' Me Lady Silver! What a joy. I thought at least one o' ye gone for good.'

'For shame, sir,' said Ilsevel, a smile in her voice. 'There is not a man or woman alive, I am persuaded, who can match Mr. Drake for wit.'

'Nor a hobgoblin, neither?' answered Balligumph with a twinkle.

'It appears not.'

Phineas, conscious of a flush creeping up his cheeks, thought it wisest to make no reply. Instead he said: 'I had hoped to find you still in the city, sir. You did not come to any harm on account of that passage into the Hollows?'

'Psh! No. What could harm a great lumberin' fellow like me?' His amiable grin flashed. 'Though it did set me t' thinkin'. Ye made it into Summer's Hollow, did ye?'

'I did, sir.'

'And out again, by his wiles,' put in Ilsevel.

'Well, an' I did not. Pesky thing landed me somewhere else altogether, and nowhere nearly so interestin'.'

'Some other part of the Hollows?' said Phineas, intent.

'Aye, but wi' no sight or sound of another soul. If it were ever much visited, it ain't now. Nowt to see but trees.'

Phineas thought. 'How was it that you came to escape, sir?'

'I've me ways. Wodebean, now. Did the pair o' ye get hold of him?'

Phineas gave the troll a quick account of his meeting with Wodebean, upon no part of which Balligumph chose to comment. He merely listened in silence, nodding thoughtfully.

Ilsevel added, when he had finished, 'And do you want to know what happened to Anthelaena? *Wodebean happened!* And Tyllanthine. They poisoned her, and turned her into—'

'A cat?' interjected Balligumph. 'Purple, and somewhat oversized? Aye. Ye're not the only one t' guess the identity o' the one they call Felebre.'

Ilsevel, silenced, blinked. 'That cannot be good,' she said.

'Not in the least. They are not wrong, yer sister an' Wodebean, t' feel it's time sommat was done.'

'We've need of much,' said Ilsevel, grimly. 'Anything and everything connected to Anthelaena as the queen, Balligumph. Velvet queen parasols, roses from her throne, every personal article of hers that's still in existence—'

'Aye.'

'They are scattered across England, Aylfenhame and the Hollows.'

Balligumph nodded his great head, then set his hat back upon it with a purposeful air. 'Ye aren't minded t' despair, now, I trust?'

'Never,' said Ilsevel. 'But a vast task lies before us, and I hardly know where to begin.'

'Yer sister Tyllanthine has made a beginnin',' Balligumph offered. 'She's off t' the Goblin Markets.'

Ilsevel stared. 'What?'

'Ye saw fer yerself what's become of Mirramay, no? Grunewald's folk have quite taken it over, an' if anybody's had chance to pick over the palace, it's them lot. Wodebean can try t' catch 'em if he likes, but he's been gone too long. His people as was, they answer to Grunewald now, an' Grunewald… well, even the Goblin King is no match fer Tyllanthine.' Balligumph chuckled.

'I wouldn't be so sure,' said Ilsevel. Phineas, shocked by the coldness of her tone, glanced at her: her face was set, her lips a thin, tight line.

'She'll deal wi' him. Anywho, if yer thinkin' he's a traitor, too, yer mistaken. Never had a thought t' overthrowin' Anthelaena, Grunewald. He had a treacherous sister wi' some mighty fine skill at Glamour an' a penchant fer pretendin' t' be him. Thas all.'

Ilsevel, silent, swayed a little in the wind, as though her knees declined to hold her. Phineas suppressed an urge to prop her up; she would not welcome the gesture. 'Is no one as I thought them to be?' she whispered.

'Likely not, ma'am. But ye've staunch enough allies in Phineas an' me. Thas enough t' be goin' on with, no?' He smiled kindly at her, prompting a long sigh from the princess.

'It is more than I had hoped for,' she said.

'Anyroad,' continued Balligumph. 'If Grunewald's folk found anythin' o' Anthelaena's still lingerin' at Mirramay, I'll wager His Majesty has it somewhere safe, an' Tyllanthine will get hold of it. Things that were carried off an' not given into His Majesty's hands, well, they may turn up at the Market, an' Tyllanthine will squirrel 'em out. The two o' ye an' me, now, we must try another source.'

Ilsevel was frowning. 'I wonder if it is a coincidence that Tylla chose Winter's Hollow for me.'

'Since it's Tyllanthine, most likely not.' Balligumph grinned. 'What did ye learn from the trip?'

'A great deal,' said Ilsevel slowly. 'I am not sure how it applies, yet, but perhaps it will.'

Balligumph looked at Phineas. 'An' Summer's Hollow?'

'Roses,' said Phineas. 'Wodebean's been growing the Queen's Roses down there.'

'Ah! Good fellow!' Balligumph clapped his great hands.

'There are velvet queen parasols at Autumn's Hollow,' said Ilsevel. 'And, Balligumph, those Hollows obey me. The way Mirramay used to.'

'Better an' better. Well then, what now?'

'The Queen's Hoard,' said Phineas. 'The thieves talk of it, and Mr. Tibs has heard tell of it. Somewhere under the Hill, they say, but how to get there?'

'Wi' gates takin' us every which way,' said Balligumph. 'An' wi' no measure o' reason?'

Phineas, his thoughts awash with disparate pieces of information, strove to make sense of them. There was a pattern somewhere within, of that he was convinced; some latent sense to the whole mess that would give him the answers he needed, if only he could find them.

For the present, he could not.

'Mr. Tibs had a name,' offered Phineas. 'The thieves of England do not know it, but the fae-folk do. They call him Gilligold.'

Balligumph went still. 'Gilligold?' he echoed. 'Tibs is certain of it?'

'He claims so.' Phineas did not add that Mr. Tibs had offered the name in a half-whisper, as though afeared of being overheard.

The troll took off his hat again, and twirled it between his hands. Then, to Phineas's surprise, he uttered an oath, and jammed the hat back over his curls. 'Ye're right, milady,' he said to Ilsevel. 'We've some hard work ahead.'

'I do not know that name,' said Ilsevel. 'Who or what is Gilligold?'

'A myth,' said Balligumph. 'I ain't heard tell o' him for nigh on a hundred years. The richest fellow in all of Aylfenhame an' England combined, or so they used t' say. He lived deep in the Hollows, wi' doors to everywhere an' nowhere, and everythin' that's desirable could be found somewhere in his lands. If some household item went missin' an' was not t' be found, folk used to say that Gilligold had got it.'

'But he is real,' said Phineas. 'Is he not?'

'If Tibs thinks it's so, then I wouldn't gainsay him.' Balligumph heaved a great sigh, and straightened his shoulders. 'He won't be easy t' find, an' then there's the little matter o' gettin' in. It's said he has a pair of giants t' guard the doors of his palace, an' many a fiendish trick t' keep folk away from his treasures.'

'Giants,' mused Ilsevel. 'That's as may be. But we have a princess, a baker and a bridge-keeper. How can we fail?'

It took Phineas a moment to understand that Lady Silver had spoken in jest. 'I shall bake them into submission, shall I?' he offered. 'Like the plums in Jack Horner's pie.'

Balligumph chuckled. 'Not forgettin' our church-Grim. Mr. Tibs is a knowin' feller. Did he say owt about where Gilligold lives, Phineas?'

'He believes it to be somewhere in the Hollows, sir, but could not say more than that. He, too, has heard nothing of him in many years. But…'

'Yes, lad?' Balligumph prompted.

Phineas pulled the brim of his cap lower over his eyes, for the chill rain was growing insistent. 'If this Gilligold has been out of sight or hearing for so long as to be largely forgotten, how did he come by any of the queen's possessions? And how came Mr. Tibs to hear of it? If Gilligold has not stepped out of his Hollows himself, then someone has stepped *in*.'

'Someone who had access to the palace at Mirramay, in the months following Anthelaena's apparent death,' put in Ilsevel. 'Or with contacts who did.'

'There must be a way in,' said Phineas. 'And out again. And if only the fae-folk know the name of Gilligold, then it is someone of Aylfenhame who's done it.'

'I'd be inclined t' say Wodebean,' growled Balligumph. 'Or someone like him. Except as he's mentioned nothin' of it t' ye, an' I cannot see why he would hide it, considerin' his stated goals.'

'Do we believe him?' said Ilsevel coolly.

Balligumph made a back-and-forth motion with his hand. 'There's no sayin', with such a fellow. But if he does know, he ain't tellin'.'

'I do not deal with Gilligold,' came Wodebean's dry, dark voice, and Phineas jumped. The hobgoblin had emerged from the Hollows again, and done it so soundlessly and so stealthily that none had noticed. 'He cheats,' added Wodebean.

'So he is real?' said Balligumph.

'As real as I am. We were rivals, once.' Wodebean's habitual cloak shrouded his face; as ever, Phineas could detect nothing of his expression. 'I won.'

'And what became of him after?' demanded the troll.

Wodebean did not precisely answer this question. 'I would not be surprised if he does have some lackey chasing after trinkets on his behalf.'

Phineas gave a slight, diffident cough. 'Forgive me, sir, but if he has succeeded in stealing most of the queen's possessions out from under everyone's noses, I would say this is the work of no mere lackey.'

The shadowy hood was turned in Phineas's direction; the boy was studied, perhaps with little approval. 'My absence must have been of service to him,' said the hobgoblin.

'Or *her*,' put in Ilsevel.

Phineas frowned. 'You are thinking of Tyllanthine again?'

'Perhaps. What better way to keep Anthela's things — and therefore, her life — safe but to arrange for them to pass into the hands of someone like Gilligold? Or,' she amended, with a grimace, 'to prevent Lady Gold's ever being restored to life and limb, if that were her true goal.'

'I doubt it,' mused Balligumph. 'It is easy t' credit Tyllanthine wi' too much, is it not? I have had word of her across half the city, lookin' fer just such articles as we are interested in. It does not seem t' me as she knows where they are gone to. An' now she is at the Goblin Court... Wodebean. Who at the Court o' Grunewald is capable of such feats?'

'Me,' said Wodebean.

Balligumph blinked at him. 'Ye were never His Majesty's subject.'

The dry voice turned faintly amused. 'Was I not? I am of his people.'

'True enough. Well — an' did ye take the Queen's Hoard t' Gilligold?'

'No.'

'Then ye aren't much use t' us, are ye?'

'But I could have. Do not waste your time at the Court; if there is aught to be learned there, Tyllanthine and I will find it out. Seek instead... the old ways.'

'The *old* ways—' Balligumph, spluttering in irritation, did not trouble to finish the sentence, for Wodebean had vanished as silently as he had arrived. '*Hobgoblins,*' muttered the troll in disgust.

An idea formed in Phineas's mind, but Ilsevel forestalled him. 'The Hollows,' she said. 'They are suspended in time, are they not? Some of them?'

'Tyllanthine said you had fallen through time,' put in Phineas.

'I was gone back some few decades,' Ilsevel agreed. 'More, belike, for the landscape knew me and did my bidding. It was as though Anthelaena and Edironal had never died.'

'Nor have they,' put in Balligumph. 'Well — no sayin' as t' Edironal, t' be fair.'

'It was as though the King and Queen of old reigned still at Mirramay, and I, as the Queen's second, were still afforded all my old authority. Ah, how I missed it!'

'Perhaps the denizens of the Seasons' Hollows know more of Gilligold,' suggested Phineas.

'Mr. Balligumph,' said Ilsevel, turning to the troll. 'You said, did you not, that the gate which took Phineas into Summer's Hollow deposited you elsewhere?'

'Aye.'

'Then they are not fixed passageways; they are changeable. They can be changed.'

Balligumph gave her a quizzical look. 'Perhaps, but by what arts?'

'Why, by mine! Let us see if they will obey me.'

A hope flared in Phineas's heart, though not unbalanced by doubt. 'But you do not know where it is we must go,' he pointed out. 'How can you order yourself conveyed to an unnameable place?'

'Somewhere in those Hollows is someone — or some*thing* — that knows of Gilligold. Be it Aylir or human, goblin or pixie, or, curse it, leaf, flower or tree, I will find it out, and it will answer to me.'

Ilsevel was a little terrifying in this mood, Phineas thought, eyeing her uneasily. But then, she was also magnificent. Her silver eyes shone with resolve, and the very wind seemed to collude to render her more splendid still, sending her pale hair tossing around her face as though with a power all its own.

Then again, considering the substance of My Lady Silver's words, perhaps it was no mere seeming. Did even the winds of England recognise the faded power of the Court-at-Mirramay?

'To Summer's Hollow, then?' Phineas croaked.

'Yes,' said Ilsevel decisively. 'We must gather roses as we go, and the velvet queen parasols, and — oh, everything! Take me to the gate, Phineas.'

Suppressing a traitorous sensation of unease, Phineas offered the lady his arm, as though he were a gentleman himself. She took it with a nod, and not quite a smile.

Balligumph heaved himself to his feet, whistling an airy tune. 'Will ye be requirin' company, me lady? Elsewise I shall make enquiries among some other folk.'

'Pray do,' said Ilsevel. 'Though take care, Mr. Balligumph, as to who you ask. We would not like Gilligold to be forewarned.'

Balligumph tipped his hat, smiled congenially, and ambled off, whistling and singing. 'Little Jack Horner sat in a corner, eating his

Christmas pie…' But he stopped, breaking off his song mid-melody, and threw some small object over his shoulder. Phineas barely caught it. 'If ye should happen t' get yerselves lost in them Hollows, that there will get ye out again. Take care not t' lose it, now.'

It was a glass sphere, only an inch in width, and perfectly clear — or so it seemed at first. But as Phineas gazed upon its glossy surface, intrigued, a mote of colour sparked in its depths and grew, shifting through all the hues of the rainbow.

He put the pretty thing carefully into his pocket.

Ilsevel had scarcely paid heed to this exchange; probably such wonders were commonplace to her. Impatient to begin, she strode off ahead of Phineas, marching up the hill towards the castle with her hair streaming behind her, the folds of her velvet gown whipping about her frame. 'It is not far, is it?' she called back, the wind snatching her words away almost as soon as they were uttered.

Phineas gathered his courage, and hastened after her.

CHAPTER NINETEEN

When I said I was plannin' t' enquire with some other folks, I meant, in particular, Oleander Whiteboots. See, Gabriel Winters was right about him — a counterfeiter, an' a talented one at that. No trace o' shame about him, either. Happy enough t' pass off his wares as the genuine article.

But ye cannot make a convincin' copy of sommat ye've never seen, right? If the wily fellow produced a Herald's Harp that could deceive even My Lady Silver as t' its provenance, then Whiteboots has seen a real one. An' there is that shoe-buckle, too. That chap has been pokin' about at Mirramay, an' no mistake. I reckon as that's what took Tyllanthine off t' the Goblin Court. If Whiteboots is sellin' counterfeits, what has he done wi' the real articles? Mayhap he still has 'em, someplace.

Or mayhap he's the fellow as has been channellin' all manner o' valuables t' Gilligold, in which case... he must know where the rogue is t' be found.

Either way, I had a powerful wish t' talk to him without delay, an' a sneakin' suspicion that he weren't hidin' at the Court at all...

I also had a notion that Tyllanthine's ideas an' mine may be runnin' along similar lines. Who would find Whiteboots first, she or me?

Bix took one look at Ilsevel, and fell upon her face.

It appeared to be with reverence rather than shock, for she contrived to land in an approximate semblance of courtly obeisance, and she was distantly heard to be gabbling flattering things as she lay there, her tiny face planted in the vibrant grass of Summer's Hollow. 'Great Lady of the Court, Princess of all that is Cake — I mean, Good — our humble Hollow is unworthy of your presence but we will be nice to you, *I swear*, and—' There was more, but it was too muffled and garbled for Ilsevel to discern any actual words.

'Princess of cake?' Ilsevel echoed, mystified.

'She is fond of it.' Phineas, meanwhile, was staring at Ilsevel as though he had never seen her before. 'I wanted to ask how she recognises you, but you are... different.'

Ilsevel raised a brow in silent question.

Phineas said, with a cough, 'You are... shining. Well — not precisely *shining*, there is no actual light coming off you, but you have some manner of — of glow about you that I cannot quite...'

He really could not, quite, for worlds failed him and he returned to gazing in silence.

Ilsevel considered. The circumstance was promising, all told; it suggested to her that she was, indeed, restored to some semblance of her former power — for a little while, at least.

Bix looked up, and her bright eyes travelled from Ilsevel's face to Phineas's, and back. 'You travel in high company,' she said.

Phineas flushed. 'I... I do.'

'Oh, no! I meant Milady.' The look she directed at Phineas held an alarming mixture of hunger, adulation and greed, and Phineas took an involuntary step back.

Ilsevel did not trouble to suppress her smile. 'Do I take it you have been baking for her, Phineas?'

'Just once!'

'If I am Princess of all that is Cake, what does that make my friend here?' said Ilsevel to Bix.

'The High King — the Emperor! Is there higher than an emperor?' Bix scrambled to her feet, and drifted — perhaps involuntarily — nearer to Phineas.

'Almighty God of Cake,' said Ilsevel. 'That is you, Phineas. I am far out-ranked.'

Phineas, the fool boy, looked more mortified than gratified, and Ilsevel sighed. There would be no making a courtier of him.

'I have need of your aid, Bix,' said Ilsevel.

'Yes?' Bix breathed, her eyes still fixed on Phineas's face.

'*We* need your help,' Ilsevel amended. 'We need a rose, one of those that grows here. The very finest there is.'

'Oh!' said Bix. 'Then you will not want one of the *ordinary* ones. You will want one of the *special* ones.'

'What is the difference?' said Ilsevel politely.

'You will know, when you see them.' She smiled hopefully at Phineas. 'The special ones are *very* special.'

'I am sure they are,' said he.

'You aren't supposed to take them. The Warders will dislike it.'

'My Lady Silver may have anything she chooses, no?' said Phineas.

'The Warders won't be *pleased*,' Bix repeated, with emphasis.

Phineas sighed. 'Very well. What will it be, and how many?'

'Cloudy starcakes, with jelly pearls,' said Bix promptly. 'Six dozen.'

'*Six*? For shame! Shall you be so greedy before My Lady Silver? When she is in such need of you!'

Bix lifted her chin. 'A fair wage for labour! Shall it be five, then?'

There followed a deal of wrangling back and forth, while Ilsevel wondered, bemused, what a cloudy starcake might be. Phineas, she saw, was not in the least cowed by the pixie's strident manner, and handled her very cleverly. They settled at last on three dozen cakes, and a triumphant Bix swept Phineas and Ilsevel alike off to a neat, pretty house, of human or Ayliri proportions — a place with which Phineas was clearly familiar, for he went at once into the kitchen and fell to work.

Ilsevel kept herself out of the way.

Some little time later, an enormous batch of delicate little cakes was bringing out of the oven, to the obvious enchantment of Bix. No less to Ilsevel's delight, were the truth told, for she had derived no small degree of pleasure from watching Phineas work. He moved with a confidence not often displayed, and with an obvious joy in the endeavour; Ilsevel could not remember ever enjoying any labour half so much.

And the results of his efforts were... remarkable. Pale little things, the cakes contrived somehow to appear translucent, cloudy indeed, as though whirled up out of the morning mist. Something twinkled atop, like stars, and what Bix had called jelly pearls resembled real pearls most closely, save that they melted between the teeth. Ilsevel devoured a specimen with almost as much gusto as Bix, and looked upon Phineas with something akin to wonder.

'I've seen nothing like this since Mirramay,' she said. 'It reminds me...' *Of happy times,* she had been going to say: of the days when Anthelaena and Edironal had reigned upon their joint thrones; when she herself and Tyllanthine had held places at Court; when their family had been united and happy, and all the realm of Aylfenhame united and happy likewise... but a swift pain stole her words, and she did not attempt to finish the sentence. Were those days lost for always?

Phineas had taken Bix's praise as his due, with a swift nod and the satisfied smile of man who knows he has done his work well. But at Ilsevel's words, a flush of strong colour suffused his cheeks, and he could not meet her eye. He mumbled some acknowledgement, too softly to be understood, and busied himself with the tidying of the kitchen.

Ilsevel removed a tray of the cakes.

'But—!' Bix, halted mid-gobble, gazed upon Ilsevel in utter woe. 'But they are mine!'

'So they are, and you shall have them when you have taken us to the roses. Time presses, Miss Bix! We cannot linger here forever.'

She received the benefit of Phineas's support, and under their joint admonitions, Bix consented to guide them. But she kept a suspicious eye on the tray in Ilsevel's hands, with the effect that she scarcely watched where she was going, and had thrice to be rescued from an unhappy tumble by Phineas's quick hands.

The neat house with the kitchen was part of a knot of similar buildings, all of them inhabited, for the windows filled with the faces of curious residents as Phineas, Ilsevel and Bix appeared in the square. Some of them recognised Ilsevel's eminence, for their eyes widened, and they dipped their heads in belated deference. But none of them came out of their houses, and the winding little street was almost deserted.

Remembering the chill and the rain of England, Ilsevel turned her face up to the sun as she followed in Bix's train, grateful for its warmth, and the brightness that lifted her spirits. It was easier to believe, in so flourishing and well-lit a Hollow, that some good lay in her future; that all was not destined to be forever lost. Phineas, too, felt its effects, for though he watched both Bix and their environs as carefully as ever, he began to whistle a tune as he walked.

Bix led them out of the cluster of houses and into a stretch of green-and-golden meadow beyond. A yellow-paved road wound its way through, along which Bix trotted in happy anticipation of her reward. Wild roses and sweetpeas tangled through the hedgerows flanking each side of the road, and cowslips and bluebells and honeysuckle; a mass of summer beauties all flowering at once, filling the air with a hazy perfume and the song of contented bees. The place was intoxicating; Ilsevel, lulled by the sunny peace of the Hollow, felt a lurking sense of regret that she could not stay.

The merry little road went on for some way, offering several turnings into places unknowable; Bix ignored all of these. At length the pathway flowed like a river into the yellow-paved courtyard of a handsome estate, walled on three sides. A tall house dominated the space, its white stone walls gleaming in the sun. It had oddly coloured windows, a thicket of turrets like an array of hats, and a great pair of doors at the front.

The gate was flanked by a pair of bronze-wrought statues. Each took the tall, slender shape of a hare seated upon its haunches, ears raised to the sky. The hares wore jackets with braided toggles, and feathered hats.

As Ilsevel's little party approached, the statues shimmered like heat on the water, and came alive. 'Names!' barked the hare on the left, his bronze hide now white and soft-furred.

'And purpose!' roared the other, its nose twitching furiously as it inhaled the scents of its visitors.

'They want a rose,' announced Bix. 'A special one.'

'Unthinkable!' barked the first hare.

'Insupportable!' shouted the other.

'Our names are Phineas Drake,' said Ilsevel demurely. 'And Lady Silver.'

The first hare blinked, and refocused its gaze upon Ilsevel's face. The dark eyes narrowed. 'Aye, looks likely,' said he.

'Seems possible,' said the other hare.

'My Lady Silver,' said both hares at once, and bowed.

'I need some of my sister's roses,' she said, with a gracious smile. 'And quickly, please.'

'At once!' said both, and dashed away.

They were back in the blink of an eye. Both carried a rose between their lips, though the flowers were not quite the same. One was pure white, absurdly oversized and alight with moonglow. The other was bright gold, similarly enormous, and shining like the sun. The hares bowed low, and laid both blossoms at Ilsevel's feet.

Ilsevel stared at the plucked roses, momentarily overcome. Oh, these were they indeed. Well she recalled how they had twined about her sister's throne in glorious profusion, moonlit and sunlit both… 'I thank you,' she managed to say, though the lump in her throat all but stole her words.

Phineas came a little nearer. She felt his warmth at her side, a surprisingly comforting presence. 'A question for the Warders,' he said.

The hares straightened. 'Speak!'

'Do either of you know the one called Gilligold?'

'He is dead,' said one of the hares.

'No, he's quite alive,' said the other.

'Are you certain?'

'Certainly.'

Phineas interjected with a polite cough. 'If he is indeed alive, where might we find him?'

Both hares were silent for some time. 'Not here,' said one at last.

The other slowly shook his head. 'Not here at all. But not far, either.'

'Where, then?' said Phineas, with admirable patience.

'Follow the road,' said the hares. 'The Lady will know.'

Shielded by Phineas's opportune questioning, Ilsevel had enjoyed a few moments of peace in which to collect up the roses, unobserved. The tray she had passed off to Bix, and the pixie, oblivious to anything but her repast, was happily engaged in its dispatch. But these words of the hares broke in upon her reflections, for she realised that the Lady in question was meant to be herself.

She looked up. 'Shall I, indeed?'

The white hare thumped upon the road in question with one long foot. 'Old roads,' he said. 'Old ways.'

Seek the old ways, Wodebean had said. Ilsevel regarded the road with fresh interest.

'Gilligold,' said the other hare. 'The oldest.'

'Be careful, Lady Silver,' said both the hares together.

'Thank you,' she murmured.

The hares nodded, and in the blink of an eye they were bronze again.

Ilsevel bent, and laid a hand upon the stones. 'Take us, then,' she commanded. 'Farther back.'

She was obeyed. The world shimmered around her and ran like water; she had time only to grab for Phineas before the road gathered itself in a wave of magic, and obligingly swept her away.

She emerged in spring. The heat of Summer's Hollow lessened, and became balmy; a light breeze tugged playfully at Ilsevel's hair, redolent with the scents of fresh earth and fresh air. The road lay still beneath her feet, but its stones were green and moss-grown. Budding willows arched gracefully over the pathway ahead, and a wide, clear pool of still waters lay behind, its surface scattered with lily-pad leaves.

Casting about for Phineas, Ilsevel found him a-wander in the grass several feet away, screened from view behind a spray of willow branches. She paused long enough to ensure that he was unharmed by the crossing, then took his arm and swept him relentlessly along the winding green road. 'In spring,' said she as she strode along, 'The throne stood in a carpet of snowdrops, and it bore a mantle of dewberry-roses and blue moonflowers. Somewhere in this Hollow there must be some specimen of these, if Wodebean has done his work well.'

Phineas fell into step beside her, his ever-present cap restored to his head. He had, it seemed, no comment to offer, and they proceeded in companionable silence for a time. The willow-grove gave way to a grassy valley, and the road dipped smoothly downwards.

Ilsevel discerned somebody coming towards them from the far side of the valley, a figure shrouded in shapeless, dark-coloured robes. A glimpse of an ancient face revealed the stranger to be an elderly woman, her straw-like grey hair protruding untidily from within her deep cowl. Ilsevel would have contented herself with a polite nod to this unpromising-looking passerby, but as the woman drew near them she stopped, and surveyed Ilsevel with an intent, searching look. Her eyes alighted upon the twin roses tucked into Ilsevel's sash, and lingered.

'You have them all, I trust?' she said.

'I beg your pardon?' said Ilsevel.

'You *did* retrieve the hellebore?' The voice, exasperated in tone, struck Ilsevel as familiar; the more so when the woman cast a look of withering frustration skywards, and folded her arms with a sigh. '*Must* you be so unreliable?'

The word *korrigan* flitted through Ilsevel's mind. 'Tylla?'

'The same.'

Ilsevel felt an obscure flash of irritation. 'I understand that this particular transformation was not of your own choosing, but really! You term *me* unreliable? Why will you never consent to be yourself? I have forgotten the face of my own *sister*.'

'So have I,' said Tyllanthine.

Ilsevel blinked. 'What?'

The crone, Tyllanthine, waved this away. 'The hellebore. They were in Winter's Hollow. You did contrive to collect some?'

'Is that why you sent me there?'

'That, and to keep you out of trouble. You have been causing quite the stir. It was inconvenient.'

'Some instruction would have been useful. Then, you would not have had to dispose of me.' An ocean of words hovered upon Ilsevel's lips: questions, as to Tyllanthine's failure to take Ilsevel into her confidence. Reproaches, for the pain she had inflicted upon both Ilsevel and Anthelaena. Despair, for the endless secretiveness with which Tyllanthine approached *everything*.

She uttered none of it.

'Must you have me spell everything out for you?' said Tyllanthine waspishly.

Ilsevel could only glower her displeasure.

Phineas said, in his mild way, 'An oversight, Highness. We are on our way to find some now.'

'You do know this is not Winter?' said Tyllanthine tartly.

'Not yet,' said Phineas.

Tyllanthine's eyes narrowed. 'This is no task to trifle with, baker's boy.'

'Nor are we,' said Phineas, unruffled.

'What did you find at the Court?' asked Ilsevel.

'Grunewald denies all knowledge. According to him, the palace was stripped bare of valuables by the time he and his people arrived.'

'Do you think he spoke the truth?'

'Yes,' said Tyllanthine.

'You are certain.'

'Yes. He has mobilised the Court to the search, and will call a Goblin Market. If anything of Anthelaena's is still circulating among the folk of the Goblin Lands, some example of it should turn up.'

'Splendid. And what are you doing in Spring's Hollow?'

'Something else,' snapped Tyllanthine.

'If you are after the moonflowers, pray do not trouble to say so,' said Ilsevel with deceptive politeness. 'It is not as though Phineas and I have more pressing errands to attend to, after all.'

This sally received only an irritated sideways look. 'Quickly, now,' said Tyllanthine, and moved off.

'Where are we to find you?' Phineas called after her.

Not at all to Ilsevel's surprise, this query went unanswered.

Phineas looked nonplussed.

'Anthelaena and I were twins,' Ilsevel sighed. 'Tyllanthine is much younger. She has always hated that.'

'Ah,' said Phineas.

Vaguely ashamed of the display she and Tyllanthine had made, and unsure why she should care for the possible disdain of someone so far removed from her life and her station as Phineas, Ilsevel knew not what more to say. So she began walking again, and Phineas once again fell in silently beside her.

The road stretched on and on.

'This takes too long,' Ilsevel decided after some ten minutes of walking. She stamped lightly upon the green-paved road and commanded, 'Pray convey us to Wodebean's garden.' That was a safe enough request, surely; what else of the horticultural might the hobgoblin be supposed to have busied himself with at Spring's Hollow?

The road shivered and shone, and Ilsevel's steps sped to an impossible pace. The grassy plains either side blurred to a morass of green; trees shot past in a haze, or perhaps Ilsevel shot hazily past the trees; and then they were come to another high-walled enclosure guarded by another pair of statues, this time twin oversized stoats. Their long bodies were coiled into a resting posture, but at Ilsevel's greeting the bronze shapes became flesh and fur, and straightened.

'I am Lady Silver,' said Ilsevel, keen to reach the point as quickly as possible. 'I am here to retrieve my sister's flowers.'

'Lady Silver for Lady Gold!' barked one of the stoats.

The ornate wrought-iron gates opened, and Ilsevel stepped through.

'And who are *you*?' said the other stoat, staring hard at Phineas.

'No one,' he said.

The gates began to creak closed again.

'Oh, stop that,' said Ilsevel crossly. 'He is my boon companion and he is coming with me.'

'*Yes*, Milady!' said the stoats together, and sat as straight and tall as their counterparts, the hares.

With a suspicious glance at them both, Phineas followed in Ilsevel's wake. 'Boon companion?' said he, when they were both fairly past the stoats.

'Creatures of ceremony,' she said dismissively. 'Wodebean took them from the palace gardens, I imagine. They are impressed by grandeur.'

'I suppose "friend" has less of a ring to it,' Phineas agreed.

Perhaps the stoats might not have prized the term, but Ilsevel found that she did. Shades and shadows, when had she last had a friend? Tucking her arm through Phineas's, Ilsevel kept him near as she made her way through Wodebean's garden, and found herself comforted.

The garden was enough to wring her heart, for it, too, bore all the familiarity of a home she had not seen in too many years to count.

Here was the carpet of starry-white snowdrops which burst joyously forth at the dawning of spring, in honour of the Queen; and there, just yonder, clambering with bright glee over a tangled trellis, the dewberry-roses and moonflowers, gleaming mauve and white and cerulean in the soft sunshine. Half expecting to see Anthelaena herself appear, Ilsevel swallowed down another lump in her throat.

Goodness, but it was growing difficult to maintain her composure.

When she felt certain of her capacity to speak sensibly, she said: 'Pray you collect me a snowdrop or two, Phineas, and I shall gather the rest.' Phineas bent to the task with as much reverence and care as she could wish, and it was the work of a moment to pluck a mauve dew-rose and a velvety moonflower herself. These three blossoms she tucked carefully into her sash with the roses of Summer, and they returned to the road.

A stamp of her foot and a clear cry of, 'Onward, and farther back!' and they were away.

CHAPTER TWENTY

Winter bit, fierce and relentless, and Phineas bitterly regretted the loss of his coat. He and it had parted ways somewhere between Summer's Hollow and Wodebean's odd abode, and he had never got it back. His shirt-sleeves could offer no defence against the chill wind, and his woollen waistcoat was too worn, and too brief, to be much more use. He wrapped his arms around himself and tried his best not to shiver; Lady Silver needed no complaining, ill-equipped baker in her train, and whose fault was it that he was cold?

Ilsevel stood hesitating, looking about with palpable confusion. Her beautiful brow was creased with doubt, and she bit absently upon her perfect lip.

Phineas had never seen her at a loss before.

'It appears I do not know where we are,' she confessed. 'And I ought to, for have I not spent some days in Winter's Hollow? But then—' and with these words the tension cleared from her brow '—if I have not arrived by the same means, why should I appear in the same spot? We will follow the road, Phineas.'

The landscape looked featureless to Phineas's eye, and he did not wonder at her puzzlement. The road had not gone, but it was hard to see, for in this place it was translucent and ice-white and looked made from crystal — or perhaps, from ice itself. Much of it was so liberally dusted with snow that it had all but vanished from sight altogether.

Everything else was deep snow, a rather undulating terrain, and a profusion of dark, gnarly trees devoid of leaf or berry.

Ilsevel made her usual gesture of request: a stamp of one foot upon the road. It would, Phineas supposed, get the attention of any road in possession of ordinary good sense. 'To—' she began, but Phineas held up a hand, and pointed.

A little way ahead, but barely discernible around the curve of a corner, was a low, oakwood fence displaying a hand-painted sign.

Phineas went nearer.

Dizzy & Dapper's, read the sign. *Vintners to Her Majesty the Queen.*

It was these latter words that had caught Phineas's attention, and Ilsevel appeared no less arrested. They pushed open the little gate and went through together, finding themselves before a tall house built of red and brown brick, with a steep-sloping roof, a profusion of chimneys and a door painted cheerily crimson. Pine trees crowded closely around it, their branches laden with snow, but behind them Phineas caught a glimpse of low buildings of sturdy, wooden plank construction.

When Ilsevel approached the bright red door, it opened of its own accord and a merry melody split the air. *Mr. Dizzy and Mr. Dapper bid you welcome!* sang a sprightly voice.

An elegant hob stood waiting on the other side of this lively portal. He was half Phineas's height, but what he lacked in inches he made up for in character. He wore a velvet jerkin as red as his front door, with matching britches, striped stockings and polished black shoes with enormous silver buckles. A kerchief of snowy white linen encircled his throat, a profuse black beard adorned his chin, and his feathery black locks sported a baggy red velvet cap. He smiled broadly at Phineas and Ilsevel, revealing three golden teeth. 'Welcome,' he said expansively. 'What is it to be? The finest we have? Why, yes! Only the best for such delightful customers!' He bowed low, mostly to Ilsevel, whose fine attire seemed to warrant the distinction.

'You must be Mr. Dapper,' said Phineas.

'That I am. Mr. Dizzy is in the workshop, applying the finishing touches to what *may well be* our best brew yet. Ice-wine of the most delicious, my lady, the most dulcet, the most delightful! Flavoured with dewberry and rosy-fingered dawn, is that not marvellous? Is that not *genius*? I am persuaded you will agree! A taste, for the lady?'

'Rosy-fingered *dawn*?' echoed Phineas.

'Homer,' said the hob briefly, with a look of marked distaste at Phineas's threadbare waistcoat. Clearly he considered the shortcomings of the garments as reflective of the shortcomings of the wearer. 'Eos, goddess of the dawn, with her slender golden arms and rose-touched fingers! Positively *hauling* in the light every morning, and let me tell you, that is no easy task, for there is no arguing with a winter's night, you know. Some little glimmer of that unearthly radiance we have contrived to capture, and imbue into our most excellent beverage — and there is even,' and here he lowered his voice, and leaned nearer to Ilsevel, 'a touch of dew. *Spring* dew, my lady, borrowed from our sister Hollow at *very great expense.*' He winked at Ilsevel and stood back, hands resting upon his splendid paunch as he beamed his satisfaction upon them both.

'You say you are vintners to the queen?' said Ilsevel, wisely declining to be drawn upon the topic of ice-wine, or rosy fingers either.

'That we are, my lady! Suppliers to Her Majesty's table, by special royal charter.' He appeared to expand a full inch as he uttered these sacred words, puffing up with a pride Phineas found repellent. A proprietor ought not have to work so hard to sell his wares. If they were as superior as Mr. Dapper claimed, they would sell themselves.

'I see,' said Ilsevel blandly. 'And when was the last time you heard from Her Majesty?'

'*Heard* from Her Majesty!' repeated Mr. Dapper. 'I assure you, my lady — though *indeed* Her Majesty's banquets could hardly proceed without our diligent efforts, we do not at all affect so high a degree of importance as to — that is, we should never *aspire* to—'

'Let me see that charter,' said Ilsevel crisply.

So involved was he with himself and his ice-wine, Mr. Dapper clearly had not made any close inspection of the lady standing before him. He did so now, or some quality of hers finally penetrated his cloak of self-absorption, for he looked full into her face, and words visibly died upon his lips. He swallowed, and bowed, and said something that sounded like, 'At once, my lady,' and then he scurried away.

'You see,' said Ilsevel, 'I remember ice-wine. My sister was especially fond of it, and if this is indeed the court supplier, then I should like to procure some of it.'

'She may remember it, too,' Phineas concurred.

Ilsevel nodded. They had not to wait long, for Mr. Dapper was soon back, all in a flurry, and laying an exquisite document into Ilsevel's hands. Ilsevel unrolled it rather carelessly, to the evident chagrin of Mr. Dapper, who made helpless swiping motions with his hands as though he might prefer to take it back from her, but did not dare.

'I will take some,' she announced, having read it through, and handed it back to its grateful owner. 'The last wine that you sent to my sister's table, if you please.'

'Your— y-your *sister*,' gulped Mr. Dapper.

'My sister, the queen,' Ilsevel confirmed, and fixed Mr. Dapper with a resolute eye.

The hob began positively to quake, and scuttled away again with so low a bow as almost to lose his cap.

'I will also be needing a coat,' Ilsevel said to his retreating back. 'A warm one.'

Mr. Dapper questioned neither request. He was gone for some few minutes, and when he returned it was with a frosty glass jug in one hand and a dark woollen coat in the other. He offered both to Lady Silver, who took them with grave thanks and immediately passed the coat on to Phineas.

Oh.

Words rose to his lips, too jumbled a mixture of gratitude and objection to form a sentence. A coat of Mr. Dapper's could only be too small? But no — it twitched in his hands and began to grow, and before long it was long enough to reach to his ankles, and broad enough at the back to comfortably match the breadth of his shoulders. Heavy in his hands, it was of thick, fine-woven wool and well lined; better by far than any coat he had ever owned before. He donned it with shivering gratitude.

Lady Silver was not finished. She took a length of fabric from her own velvet gown — he did not understand how — and draped it around Phineas's neck. Buttoned in wool, his throat wrapped in enchanted velvet, Phineas went from half-frozen to warmer and more comfortable than he ever remembered feeling before.

Lady Silver, in that moment rather close, met his eyes briefly, and there was a smile in her own. Phineas had not the words to express his feelings at being cared for — at being *remembered* — but perhaps she understood, for the smile reached her lips before she moved away again.

'Thank you, Mr. Dapper,' she said, with a stately nod for the vintner. 'One more question, if I may. You continue to supply Her Majesty's table?'

'Most faithfully, Highness!' said Mr. Dapper, his spine very straight and his chin high. 'Every drop of our best goes to Her Majesty's Court.'

'Well,' said Ilsevel, when they had regained the road. 'That is one way to ensure a steady supply. Wodebean's wiles.'

Phineas, however, had been thinking. 'Perhaps not, milady,' he offered diffidently, loath to contradict a princess.

Receiving, however, the encouragement of a raised brow and a heartening lack of chastisement, he went on. 'If these Hollows are indeed a way back in time, as Mr. Balligumph's and your sister Tyllanthine's words seem to suggest — and there is the matter of their clothes, being very old-fashioned as they are, and Wodebean has gone to a lot of trouble to keep them in the same kinds of garments — well, is it not possible that Mr. Dapper is not ignorant? It isn't that he knows nothing about Her Majesty's fate. It is that Her Majesty has not yet died, or appeared to, because in Winter's Hollow the date is no later than about, say, 1786.'

Ilsevel digested that in thoughtful silence. 'But time *must* pass,' she said. 'How else are they able to produce anything? There are flowers growing in Summer.'

'Do you think it possible that time is not stopped, only... slowed? And circular, somehow. They are not moving forward, because they are living the same season over and over again. The season of the year before your sister's death, perhaps.'

'There seems a terrible cruelty to that.'

'Perhaps,' said Phineas with a small smile. 'Many might choose it, if it meant never growing any older.'

'But never to grow older is never to grow at all!'

'I would not choose it myself,' Phineas conceded.

'Nor I.'

'But,' said Phineas, and hesitated. 'You do not appear to grow old anyway, Highness.'

'I do,' she said, with a swift smile. 'Just... slowly. Pray do not take to calling me "Highness," Phineas, and if you should begin to consider the obsequiousness of a Mr. Dapper as any model for your behaviour then I shall be forced to do something unspeakable to you.'

A grin escaped Phineas's self-control. 'But, milady,' he objected. 'Mr. Dapper was very helpful.' He had tucked his frozen hands into the deep pockets of his purloined coat, and they were, at last, beginning to warm.

'It was his duty to be so,' she said sternly, but then relented. 'Not that I am ungrateful. It is obscurely comforting to meet with those for whom my family has never been gone.'

Phineas thought, wistfully, of his mother. What would it be like, to find a way to go back to the years before her death? It struck him that he *had*, in effect, for if it was 1786 or thereabouts in Winter's Hollow, then his mother would still be a young woman, perhaps of his own age. But that was in here, and she had been out *there*, and there could be nobody in the Season's Hollows who had ever known her.

He dismissed the thought.

Ilsevel linked her arm with his. 'Road!' she said imperiously, with that little stamp of her foot. 'Convey us to my sister's hellebores.'

The rushing and swooping happened again, and then they were

standing before another walled garden, this one blanketed under snow. A pair of snow-draped stags stood guarding the gate, but these did not speak; they merely made slow reverence to Ilsevel, their elegant heads dipping low, and remained that way as she passed.

The garden was a carpet of simple, five-petalled winter's roses, growing proudly from the snow as though untouched by it. They were the velvet-blue of midnight, and each bore a sparkling coat of starry frost limning its petals. Ilsevel gathered three.

'That is the way Wodebean's rose looked,' Phineas pointed out. 'The frost.'

'Gloswise has, by some trickery, learned to mimic the effect,' Ilsevel agreed. 'But only these are True.' She carefully tucked the delicate flowers away. The jug she had hung from a length of ribbon over one shoulder; noticing this, Phineas quietly took it from her and hefted the burden himself, winning a nod of thanks from Lady Silver. 'One more, Phineas, and then we will find out where Gilligold hides himself.'

'Lead on, ma'am,' he invited. 'I follow.'

Upon Ilsevel's command, the icy road rippled beneath their feet and turned to tawny brown. The dark, bare trees faded, the snow went away, and the air perceptibly warmed. Colour bloomed all around Phineas: oak and ash and elm trees decked in cinnamon-coloured leaves, and orange, and berry-red, and bright gold. The smell of wet earth and mulch met his nose, and a low mist clung close to the ground.

Something, however, was amiss. Phineas could not have said what alerted him: some quality to the shadows that ought not to be there; some detail out of place that he could not define; a twist in the air, a crack in the sky.

Ilsevel felt it, too. She stiffened, and drew Phineas nearer to herself. 'I do not—' she began, and then stopped, frowning. 'The road. Where is it?'

That was it, or part of it: they stood with their feet securely upon brown-paved stones, but the road proceeded only so far before it faded, as though the rest had been swept away. And beyond the ending of the road, the landscape was palpably different: the shadows were deeper, the mist thicker, and dark shapes flitted among the gnarled trunks of ancient trees.

'Perhaps we need not go that way,' offered Phineas with faint hope.

'The parasols are there,' said Ilsevel.

There was, indeed, a cluster of delicate mushrooms poised at the edge of the shadows. They clambered up the trees in airy profusion, and Phineas could well imagine that they spread over the ground beneath the mist as well. They were velvet indeed, mossy-furred in bejewelled shades of purple and blue, and their spreading caps resembled a profusion of diminutive ladies' parasols opened up against the sun.

Permitting himself a small sigh, Phineas drew himself up in readiness. 'Of course they are,' he said. 'Where else would they be?'

Nothing about the misty copse struck Phineas as obviously dangerous; he could not have said why the sight of it made his heart quicken its pace, or sent a stab of unease lancing through his guts. That Ilsevel felt it too was evident in the way she drew herself up, tossed back her hair, and strode forward with the purposeful walk of a woman determined, at any cost, *not* to appear afraid.

Phineas hastened to keep pace with her.

When they had got within three steps of the velvet queen parasols, a voice spoke. It was a darkly glittering voice, a slithering voice, a voice of velvet and wine laced with thorns. 'My lady,' it said.

Ilsevel froze.

'Why, you have brought me a gift,' continued the voice, with a deep chuckle. Shadows unfurled in coiling tendrils and reached for Phineas's feet; with a thrill of horror he realised that, in speaking of a gift, the voice had been referring to *him*.

CHAPTER TWENTY-ONE

'He is no such thing,' said Ilsevel, charging herself to speak clearly, and without fear, for to show herself afraid would be a grave mistake.

'Then you come to offer yourself?' said the voice, and shadows flowed over Ilsevel's feet. They were cold and damp, like old pondwater, and she suppressed a strong desire to back away. 'Better and better.'

'Of course not,' she snapped. 'You forget yourself. You forget your place.'

'And what,' whispered the voice, 'is my place now, Lady Silver?'

Phineas drew nearer, though whether he sought to offer or seek protection she could not have said. 'You *know* this — this — creature?' he hissed.

She did. There was no mistaking that voice. 'It has been many years,' she said, hoping Phineas would be satisfied with so brief an answer.

He was not. 'Who is it? *What* is it?'

Something chuckled darkly, and the mist thickened and rose. 'They used to call me Blight. Darksworn. Shadow's End.'

'A host of absurd names,' Ilsevel agreed.

'But fitting,' said the voice. 'I served your family well, My Lady Silver. Do I not deserve a reward?'

'Your life is your reward,' she said crisply. 'Such as it is.'

The fog retreated a little, taking the shadows with it. They left in their wake an expanse of parched grass, dried to a husk, as though the life had been sucked out of it. A cluster of parasol mushrooms lay limply among them, withered and dead. 'You are ungenerous, princess,' chided the voice.

'How did *this* serve your family?' Phineas said, staring wide-eyed at the destruction.

'It was long ago,' Ilsevel sighed. 'Hundreds of years, Phineas. Those were... different days, and some of my ancestors were not so gentle as my sister, nor so wise. They used the Shadow's End as — as a form of punishment.'

'Justice,' whispered the voice.

Ilsevel ignored that. 'It was kept at Court, beneath the palace-at-Mirramay, and those who... displeased the king, or the queen, were sent as...'

'Gifts,' said the voice silkily.

Ilsevel sighed. 'It was still there when Anthelaena ascended the throne. Starved and weakened and resentful, but alive — after a fashion. She disposed of it, though I never did gather how, or where it was dispatched to.'

The wreathing fog developed a greenish tinge. 'She imprisoned me, but I... escaped.'

That interested Ilsevel. 'I am persuaded you could not. Evade the power of the seated monarch? How, pray?'

'All things are possible,' hissed the voice, 'with the right help.'

'Who helped you?' Ilsevel spoke sharply, alarmed, for the prospect boded very ill indeed.

But the voice was silent.

Phineas said, 'What are you doing here, Blight?'

'Guarding,' whispered Darksworn.

'Guarding what?'

Again, there was no answer — not in words. But the fog and the shadows retreated a little more, exposing a pair of trees, dead at the roots, their trunks covered in rotting parasol mushrooms.

'Whoever freed it is no friend to your family,' Phineas said softly.

'Then it is none too difficult to guess at the identity of its preserver.' The Kostigern would find the Darksworn, in all its resentment and hunger, a natural ally.

But did that mean that their enemy had known that Anthelaena had not died? Had the Kostigern discovered Wodebean's ploy, and

Tyllanthine's, and sought to block the queen's return?

Had that been why Tyllanthine had been cursed?

Her thoughts roiled with speculation and possibility, not untinged with fear. Resolutely, she called them to order; now was not the time. 'Friend or not,' she said, a note of steel creeping in to her voice, 'it must still obey me.'

'I must not,' said the Blight, and a foul, grating laugh shivered through the fog. 'The Pact between your family and mine is broken, princess.'

'Then we shall bargain,' said Ilsevel, betraying none of her dismay. 'Whatever your preserver offered to you, I shall better it.'

'You cannot.'

'What were you promised?'

'My old position restored,' whispered the Blight. 'My condition bettered. My hunger sated. More *gifts*, princess, from your world and beyond. A kingdom all my own…'

'This is to be your kingdom, is it?' said Ilsevel with scorn, indicating the confines of Autumn's Hollow with a sweep of her arm. 'It is a prison.'

'It is a beginning,' said the Blight. 'I await his ascension, for the rest.'

'To the throne? You will wait forever, for your faithless preserver is gone.'

The shadows shifted; the fog roiled. 'That is a lie.'

'It is not. You are tricked, Blight. This place is in Torpor. Time has passed you by, and you do not even know it. The worlds beyond have moved on. Decades have passed, and he who sought the throne is vanished.'

'And what became of him?' The words emerged as a faint whisper, so faint she had to strain her ears to catch them.

'That is not known.'

A chuckle again, long and low. 'Then it is you who are tricked, princess. He is not gone. He waits, and he will return.'

'And you will wait forever, will you, on the mere chance of it?'

'I am more ancient than you can imagine. What are years, to one such as me?'

Phineas moved, all at once. She had received no warning of his intent; he had given no sign of his plans. He was gone from her side and into the fog, moving at speed, the scarf she had herself wound around his neck now pulled up to half-cover his face.

Shadows swallowed him.

'Phineas!' she cried — too late, too late. She heard a cry.

'Fool boy,' chuckled the Blight. 'Delicious boy.'

Her stunned wits recovering, Ilsevel gathered herself and went after him. But here he was already stumbling out again, coming towards her with the shambling gait of an old, old man. He extended a hand; she reached for it, but instead of clasping her fingers he dropped into her grasp something soft and delicate. A velvet queen parasol — no, two. Sound and whole and plump, their colours untouched, they glittered faintly in the light.

'Phineas,' she gasped, barely pausing to store the precious mushrooms before she caught him up. 'What have you *done?*'

'The Blight is here to guard, not to destroy,' he said, and she did not like the weakness in his voice. 'They are most of them intact.'

Shadowy tendrils reached for Phineas, grown darker, angrier; Ilsevel hastily drew him farther away. 'And at what price have you gathered these?'

It was the Darksworn who answered her. 'Not enough,' it growled. 'Slippery boy, come closer again! *You* are the price I claim for My Lady Silver's treasures!'

Phineas was shaking all over. He staggered on, farther away from the shadowed copse, and Ilsevel supported him as best she could. 'What has it done to you?' she demanded.

'I do not know,' gasped Phineas, though she could see for herself some part of the cost of his actions, for the hand that had held the mushrooms was no longer young and strong. The fingers, clasped so firmly and tenderly within her own, were thin and frail; his skin was parchment, wrinkled and time-stained. Had he lingered much longer, he must have lost the whole.

'It has taken some of your life,' she said grimly. 'It shall be made to return it, my Phineas!' So saying, she turned back, and would have marched at once to wrangle with the Darksworn.

But Phineas caught at her dress with his undamaged hand, and his grip was still strong. 'No,' he said, breathless but firm. 'You cannot defeat it, Lady Silver. Not yet. You must let it go.'

'It ought to have been me,' she said coldly, and tore herself from his grasp. 'You shall not pay this price, Phineas. This debt is not yours to settle.'

He spoke only one word, but it was enough to slow her, enough to cease her reckless march. 'Please,' he said.

She sighed, and turned. He had not the strength to stand unaided, and had sunk down into the road. He made a sorry figure, his young face white and drawn. There were wrinkles around his eyes that had not been there before. 'I must,' she said, but there was a pleading note to her words that could only undermine them.

'No,' said Phineas. 'It is done, and for the best. I don't regret it.'

Ilsevel went back to him, and helped him to his feet. 'You need help.'

He swayed, and almost fell again. 'Please.'

They had regained the road by this time, or what was left of it. Ilsevel said, her arms full of Phineas, 'Good road, if there are kind souls left in this cursed place, pray take us to them.'

The vivid trees shimmered around them, and rushed away. When the world slowed again, they stood before a timber-framed cottage, a barrow full of freshly-dug vegetables standing ready beside its front door. The proprietor, an Aylir woman of some age, looked up in surprise. She had an embroidered scarf over her wispy grey hair, and her frame was bundled up in coats and shawls against the frosty chill in the air.

'I beg you,' said Ilsevel without preamble, for Phineas was growing heavier in her arms, his legs less and less able to support him. 'If you have food to spare, and a bed for my friend, I shall be everything that is grateful.'

The woman looked Phineas over, and nodded. 'The fog?'

'It was that, yes.'

'Ought not to have gone in.' The woman shook her head, but she was already moving towards her cottage door. 'I've a stew on the simmer, it will be ready now. And bread in the oven.' Ilsevel's nose had already alerted her to these details, the moment the door opened, and her stomach duly informed her that it had been hungry for some time.

Within a few minutes, she was seated in a whitewashed chamber at the back of the little cottage, Phineas prone in the narrow bed beside her, and both busy upon the bowls of steaming stew the good woman had put into their hands. She had even found a nightgown for Phineas, and had heaped the bed with extra blankets.

Phineas ate like a man who had not seen food for a week. This heartened Ilsevel, for she could well believe that the Blight had taken the nourishment from Phineas's limbs; food was what he needed.

When he had eaten everything he had been given, and half of her portion as well (freely donated by Ilsevel), she said: 'You were a fool.'

Phineas only smiled. As worn and strained as he looked, there was an air of happiness about him that Ilsevel could not understand — an air, even, of serenity. His eyes closed, and he slept.

Quietly, Ilsevel stole away.

She found their hostess in the kitchen, hard at work upon a bucketful of potatoes. She was giving them a sound scrubbing, but she looked up when Ilsevel came in. 'And how is the young man?'

'Very grateful for your care, as am I. He's eaten the lot, and I am sure it will do him good. He's sleeping now.'

'You look in need of a kip yourself.' She turned back to her work, brisk and cheerful, the thick bristles of her scrubbing-brush *swish-swishing* loudly in the stillness.

Ilsevel wondered when she had last slept a night through, and could not remember. 'May I know your name?' she said, passing the point over.

'I am Eleri.'

'Ilsevel. Are there... are there others here?'

'To be sure there are,' said Eleri briskly. 'Not so many as once there were, perhaps, but enough.'

'Enough for?'

'To work the fields. To keep the sun rising every morning. Here.' She filled Ilsevel's hands with potatoes, pointed her to the table, and set a small knife down there.

Ilsevel dutifully began to peel, albeit clumsily. 'Where do they go, the ones who have left?'

'Haven't left, precisely. Folk pass on, sometimes.'

And Wodebean, apparently, was bringing no one new in. Was that because of the Darksworn? Did he even know that the Blight was there?

Ilsevel wanted to ask if Eleri was happy, but she was forestalled by a question from the Aylir woman. 'What was it you and yonder young fellow were doing, wandering those roads?'

'Passing through,' said Ilsevel vaguely.

No reply. When Ilsevel glanced up, she found herself fixed with an uncompromising stare.

'It is the truth,' she protested. 'We are looking for Gilligold.'

'*Him?*' said Eleri. 'What manner of fools are you?'

'Our need is urgent, I assure you, or we should gladly abandon this quest.'

'What need have you for gold, or jewels, as could justify the journey?'

'It is a matter of some very particular jewels, which he has purloined from a… friend of mine, and which are urgently required.'

'You'll not find him.' Eleri went back to her scrubbing, *swish, swish*.

'We are determined.'

Eleri shook her head. 'Old as the Hollows, that one, and twice as wily. He's hidden the door so well, none now remember where it was.'

'It is said that all the Hollows in these parts are connected to one another, or at least that one may go from one to another with ease enough, if one has the means. I have found this to be true.'

'Bypass the door?' That gave Eleri pause. 'What manner of power have you, to need no doors?'

It was Ilsevel's turn to hold her silence. After a moment, Eleri turned, and subjected Ilsevel's calm countenance to a close scrutiny.

She had not, perhaps, paid close attention to Ilsevel before, distracted by Phineas's pitiable state, and then by her own labours. Now she saw Ilsevel clearly.

A potato fell back into the bucket with a *plop*.

'Perhaps you've a chance,' she said.

'I am hoping so.'

Eleri shook herself, and turned back to her bucket. Questions hovered palpably about her, but she had resolution enough to voice none of them. 'I believe I've a message for you,' was all that she said.

'For *me?*'

'If you are Lady Silver, aye.'

'Then I will claim the message. What is it?'

'Seek the rose, ware the thorn.'

Turning it over in her mind, Ilsevel could not wring any particular sense from it. But she committed it carefully to memory nonetheless. 'And who has left it for me?'

'A man in a pale cloak. I never saw his face, nor learned his name.'

A disquieting answer; nonplussed, Ilsevel put aside the many questions it conjured for another time. 'I thank you,' she said, formally acknowledging receipt. 'And I thank you, again, for your care of me, and of my friend.'

Eleri merely nodded. 'Shall you sleep a little?'

Ilsevel gladly put down the knife, and her half-peeled potato. 'Thank you. I believe I shall.'

CHAPTER TWENTY-TWO

'I seek a grub,' called Hidenory, or as she was truly named, Tyllanthine. 'A worm. A maggot. The filth that crawls in the dark, the dirt-eating wretch, the miserable specimen of fae-kind that calls himself Oleander Whiteboots.'

She had asked this question time and time again, though the query itself had become increasingly embroidered with unflattering epithets as the days had passed. Unbelievably, she had got nowhere. She had crossed Gadrahst from east to west, gone into the very heart of the Goblin King's Court itself, enlisted His Majesty's aid — even begged assistance from the absurd human-girl he had the temerity to name consort, though she was as low-born as it was possible to *be* — and for what! Few claimed any acquaintance with the fellow, and those who did denied having seen or heard from him. Circulating his description proved of little benefit either, for Redcaps were not so rare as all that, and what was particularly distinctive about a Redcap in a bright cloak? He was proving as elusive as Wodebean, and Tyllanthine had long since lost patience with *that*.

Perhaps the troll was right. If Whiteboots had ceased to consider himself a denizen of Aylfenhame and gone into England, then she was on a fine goose chase indeed. Were that the case, Balligumph would find him.

But Tyllanthine was not so sure. Where would a weasel like Whiteboots go? If he was not to be found in Aylfenhame, then he would do as Wodebean had done, and many another before them both: he would disappear into the Hollows. Those Hills were the cracks between the worlds, the lawless wilds where anything might be permitted to pass. In the absence of the monarch, Aylfenhame itself was increasingly sliding into a similar chaos — but a king still ruled in Gadrahst, and the land remembered Anthelaena, however long she had been gone.

What was England? A mere faded, insignificant place, where trickles and dabs of magic might but briefly gain a hold, and only in sparse, scattered pockets, like Tilby. No, the place for a maggot like Oleander Whiteboots was somewhere deep in the Hollows.

Tyllanthine, abandoning Aylfenhame, sought him there. She found no trace of him at Thieves' Hollow, nor in Summer, Winter, Autumn or Spring. But whispers reached her ears: a glimpse here or there, a rumour, an echo. Traces of his passage there were, and Tyllanthine clung to the scent like the finest foxhound.

In a distant, dusty Hollow, reached by a winding path out of the heart of Winter, Tyllanthine at last caught strong scent of her quarry. There was a tavern there, and an odd place for a tavern it was, to be sure. A grey sky hung glowering over a low, rickety building made from hammered planks of some contorted wood; water surrounded it, a shallow, greenish-tinged pond that smelled oddly of mint and pondweed and fresh grass. The place had too many chimneys, every one of which poured white smoke into the air, and there were too many doors in the walls.

Tyllanthine had walked, very carefully, over the crude little bridge and gone through the nearest of the doors: bright green, though its paint was peeling.

The interior of the tavern was much as one would expect of such a place: well supplied with tables and chairs and drinkers, and smelling strongly of wood-smoke and mead. A suffocatingly hot taproom she had been prepared for, considering the chimneys; but there turned out to be only one fireplace.

Every single person in the tavern looked up as she came in. They were a varied crowd: Tyllanthine's glance took in several brownies, hobs and goblins, hobgoblins, pixies, one or two Ayliri, a lone human (elderly) and even a troll slumped in a far corner.

She had taken immediate advantage of the sudden silence to outline her request.

'He is a Redcap,' she went on, when still nobody spoke. 'A known trader at the markets at Thieves' Hollow. A notorious counterfeiter, a thief and a scoundrel to boot. Give him to me and I shall reward you splendidly.'

'Oh?' said a rotund gnome in a feathered cap. 'What reward?'

Tyllanthine displayed a pouch full of gold, and fended off one immediate attempt to relieve her of it the quick way. 'You know not who you are dealing with,' she said pleasantly to the culprit, a boggart who slunk, scowling, back into the shadows.

To her disappointment, even her handsome reward did not appear to be productive of much. People were turning away, returning to their beverages, dismissing her from their notice. Nobody spoke up.

But as she hobbled slowly to the door, defeated and angry, she felt a slight tug upon the loose sleeve of her tattered robe.

A gnome stood there, unusually short even for one of her diminutive race, and oddly dressed in a haphazard patchwork of fabrics. She had positioned herself in a nook beside the door, where she could not be seen by the occupants of the tavern.

Tyllanthine hastily stooped, as though to adjust her shoe. 'What have you to say?' she whispered.

'He's here, madam,' said the gnome.

'*Here?*'

The gnome nodded. 'Them as drinks here, they are all his friends. Bad as he is, every last one, and they protect each other.'

'Why, then, are you different?' Tyllanthine had learned to take a suspicious view of everything — learned it the very hard, very painful way. She never forgot it, not now.

'He is cruel,' whispered the gnome. 'And he cheats us. *They* do not know it.'

Largely, Tyllanthine accepted this. Resentment over double dealing often led to betrayal in turn. 'I do not see him,' she pointed out.

But the gnome shook her head. 'You came in by the wrong door. Go out, and come back in again by the red, but you must first knock thrice and say, "Shadow's End," or it won't open.' With which words she melted away, and was gone.

Tyllanthine straightened her aching back, sparing a resentful thought of her own for the aged and aching muscles she was cursed with, and made her painful way back out of the door again. She went slowly around the rickety building until she came to a red-painted door, this one kept in better repair than the others: the paint was shining and new.

She knocked three times, stifling a sigh at the dreary mundanity of the ritual, and said: 'Shadow's End.'

She did this warily, and from a little distance, in case the gnome's instructions had been some manner of trap. But nothing happened. The tavern did not swallow her, and nobody appeared. So she grasped the big brass knocker in the middle of the door and turned it.

Bolts flew smoothly back, and the door swung open.

On the other side of *this* door was a quite different room. It was spacious, with a large fireplace at either end — both lit, and roaring with cheerful flames — and a handsome canopied bed in the centre hung with tapestries. Soft couches and chairs occupied other parts of the room, and there was a large dining-table, too, flanked by ten or twelve chairs. It was a castle in miniature, a chamber fit for a lord's residence. And it glittered and twinkled and shone, for the furniture and the floor were heaped with treasure.

It was the dull, predictable kind, for the most part: an abundance of gold (coins, goblets, necklaces and crowns); precious jewels (rubies, diamonds, emeralds, sapphires — all the usual sort); silks and velvets (doublets and soft caps, gowns, tapestries, table-cloths, headdresses, and so on). Tyllanthine's nose also informed her that the occupant possessed considerable riches of other kinds: spices from afar, fragrances, fruits and confectionery.

'Not a bad lot,' she said, for however uninteresting it might be it was certainly a valuable hoard.

'Not bad at *all*,' said the lord of all these riches. He was sitting in a chair that more nearly resembled a throne, a stupendous construction positioned in the centre of the room. He did not make an especially convincing vision of a great lord, for though his cloak was brightly coloured it was of no especially fine make, and only of plain woollen cloth; the dark cap he wore might be good velvet, but it bore signs of having been haphazardly dyed, according to the ways of the Redcaps; and he wore not a single jewel anywhere about his person. His boots were ancient, dusty and cracked. He looked a drab little sparrow amid the splendour of his treasure-hoard, but his eyes glittered in a way Tyllanthine did not at all like, and she would not make the mistake of underestimating him.

'Oleander Whiteboots,' she purred, shutting the door behind herself. 'I have been looking for you.'

'I had heard.' He said nothing else, nor did he move; he only watched, more like a cat than a sparrow, and a vicious creature at that.

Tyllanthine being too tired and far too *old* to waste time on such games, she ignored this predatory look and got briskly to the point. 'I am here to arrange a trade with you. You will give me all of her late Majesty's possessions, and I will give you any price you care to name.'

Oleander Whiteboots sat up a little at that. '*Any* price? That is a dangerous offer to make, my good lady.'

'I know it.'

The Redcap looked her over, taking in the ragged robes she wore, none too clean; the boils upon her creased, prematurely ancient face; the frizzled mess of her grey-white hair, sticking out from beneath her hood. 'And what could a mere hag do for me?'

'You have lived too long to be much taken in by appearance,' said Tyllanthine with disapproval.

A glance down at Oleander's filthy boots served to remind him of his own unprepossessing appearance, and he inclined his head in acknowledgement of the point. 'Still,' he said, watching her closely. 'What can you offer?'

'I am a witch of great power. There is no Glamour beyond my skill to weave.'

'That could come in useful,' conceded the Redcap.

'And I will give you some treasures in trade,' she continued. 'Items from the Court. Jewels and silks that once belonged to the princesses Ilsevellian and Tyllanthine and Lihyaen.'

Oleander's eyebrows rose, and his eyes glittered with avarice. 'How came you by such articles as that?' he breathed.

Tyllanthine merely returned him a look. It said, *are you such a fool as to expect an answer?*

His mouth quirked into a bitter smile, and he inclined his head. 'I would be tempted by such a bargain, had I any power to fulfil it.'

This took Tyllanthine aback. She had been prepared to meet with some manner of ploy — an attempt to pass off counterfeit objects as the true treasures, in the most likely case. She was ready to counter such an attack as that. But plain honesty disconcerted her. 'Why cannot you?' she said, after a moment's hesitation.

'I have already sold them,' said Oleander Whiteboots with a silky smile. 'For a better price than yours, and to one who will never release them. You will never get the Queen's Hoard, my good hag.'

Tyllanthine drew herself up, knowing that her face darkened with a foreboding anger like a storm-cloud obscuring the sun. She gave herself an illusory aura, a mantle of dark power. Her eyes — her own eyes, the only part of herself the curse did not alter — bore into Oleander's, dark with a terrible purpose. 'Let me be understood,' she said softly. 'I will find these articles, no matter whom I must destroy in the attempt — even if that prove to include myself. You will tell me to whom you sold Her Majesty's possessions, Oleander Whiteboots. You will tell me where to find your buyer. You will tell me anything else I require as well, or you will never leave this room again.'

Oleander Whiteboots merely smiled. 'I find that I like it in here,' was all that he said.

A perfect answer. Frustration and anger, fear and foreboding, sadness and pain and rage and despair — all these roiled within Tyllanthine's mind and heart and oh, how she longed for somebody upon whom she might fairly give vent to her fury! And this miserable specimen, with his self-satisfied air and his risible failure to understand whom he had offended — oh, he would do nicely.

With a small, vicious smile, Tyllanthine went to work.

The old roads, Ilsevel soon found, spanned a very great distance indeed.

If she had entertained any fond imaginings that she might, with a single step, go from Autumn's Hollow into the lair of Gilligold, she was soon obliged to abandon such fancies.

Phineas's recovery was speedier than she had at first hoped, and the two were soon venturing forth from Eleri's comfortable cottage and finding their way back to the road again. Perhaps it was because some part of the road had been lost, or perhaps it was some other trouble; but when Ilsevel, with Phineas's arm clasped through hers, issued her orders to the road: 'On to the place where Gilligold hides, and quickly!' — they were indeed swept away into somewhere else, but it was nowhere of any use at all.

They emerged in a different Hollow, and an odd place it was, for it appeared to consist of a wide meadow ringed in hedgerows, and with a single house planted in the centre of it. The house was of a bygone fashion, though it nonetheless appeared quite new. A grand place, built from great blocks of pristine, pale-yellow limestone, it had casement windows, a columned portico and a handsome pediment to its roof. An Ayliri woman was in the process of descending the steps that led up to the double front doors: a noblewoman, clearly, for her bearing and attire equally proclaimed it so. Ilsevel regarded the stiff, embroidered silks of her gown, the voluminous skirts, the tall, elaborately curled style of her hair, and wondered whence this woman could possibly hail.

Undaunted, Ilsevel strode up to the foot of the stairs, aware that Phineas was trailing some way behind her. A great coach with oversized wheels and far too much gilding stood waiting nearby, with four hobgoblin footmen perfectly matched in height poised to assist their mistress on her travels. Considering the confines of the Hollow, Ilsevel wondered where the lady could possibly be going to.

'I bid you good morning!' she greeted as she drew near the lady. 'My companion and I seek the one known as Gilligold. He does not, by chance, live here?'

The lady tilted her head at Ilsevel — carefully, so as not to dislodge the lace-and-pearl headdress perched atop her heaped curls. 'He does not,' she said.

'But you know of him? Do you know where I may find him?'

The lady had not yet paused in her slow descent, but she did so now, two steps from the bottom, and regarded Ilsevel. She took in Phineas, too, with a flickering glance which soon found him unworthy of scrutiny. 'Who asks for him?'

'My Lady Silver,' said Ilsevel.

But the lady frowned. 'Impossible. The Lady Ilsevellian is but a child.'

That silenced Ilsevel. Before she could decipher the meaning behind so unexpected a speech, Phineas had drawn near. 'We are gone back some years, I think,' he whispered. 'No one has seen Gilligold for a hundred years, remember.'

Of course. The garments, and the house — Gilligold's name had faded from use because he had hidden himself away in some Torpored Hollow, where time had ceased to hold any sway. In effect, he had ceased to exist — except in the past. Thus, that was precisely where the roads had taken her.

Ilsevel let the question of her identity pass unanswered. 'It is a matter of the gravest urgency,' she said. 'I must find him.'

The lady made her stately way down the remaining steps and stood considering Ilsevel. She took in the majesty of her gown, and, perhaps, the glitter of enchantment upon it; the brooch upon her shoulder and the jewels in her hair; the peculiarity of her silver eyes, and the depth of power and authority that lay there. 'The coach goes into Deepmantle shortly. You may travel with me, and hail another coach from there.'

Ilsevel curtseyed her thanks, though the lady's manner was in no way conciliating. She did not receive the compliment of a curtsey in return; the lady merely nodded coldly and got into the coach, her footmen clustering around her.

Ilsevel stepped in after, drawing Phineas with her. The poor boy was more impressed by the fine lady's repelling manner than he ought to be. Truly, he thought too lowly of himself.

The moment the coach doors closed behind Phineas, the equipage began to move. It occurred to Ilsevel that she had seen no horses, nor any sign of some other, load-bearing animal; the coach, it seemed, moved under its own power. It travelled along the winding road almost to the edge of the meadow, and then, in a blur of grass and hedgerow, it made the leap from Hollow to Hollow and they were in Deepmantle.

It proved to be a glade, overhung with the heavy boughs of velvety-green trees. The coach brought them into what appeared to be a regular coach-station, for there were oaken signposts driven into the earthen floor at regular intervals. Their coach drew up before one that read: "Downdew" — the name, presumably, of the Hollow from which they had just come. The lady descended from the coach without so much as glancing at Ilsevel, let alone Phineas. Her footmen ushered her in the direction of a sign saying "Mossdale."

Ilsevel surveyed the others. Shadowridge and Moonblight; Sagewood and The Seaward Peak; Wisewinds and The Wildbarrow; Willowhaven, The Rains, Threewoods and Fivewoods and Sevenwoods — on and on went the signs, and none of the names engraved upon them were in the least bit familiar to Ilsevel.

Ilsevel tried the road. 'Onward to Gilligold, if you please,' she whispered, but nothing happened. She was not surprised. Gilligold lay farther back, beyond the power of My Lady Silver.

'Phineas,' said she. 'I fear we are undone. I have not the smallest idea where to go.'

Phineas, practical soul that he was, began to wander, approaching some few of the various travellers who were bustling from coach to coach. Ilsevel heard the word 'Gilligold' repeatedly pass his lips, only to be greeted with shakes of the head, and, on occasion, a positive recoil. She took up the endeavour herself and went from stranger to stranger — and what an array they made! Some were dressed like the lady of Downdew, but many more sported garments of the most outlandish, recognisable, in some cases, as fashions from ages long past; in others, reminiscent of nothing Ilsevel knew.

But the former gave her an idea. She began to approach those whose clothing betrayed their origins as of an earlier age; those with embroidered, wide-skirted coats and long, curling wigs; with doublets and velvet caps, with great ruffs around their necks and stockings upon their legs. And, at last, she began to meet with some success; for instead of blank looks she perceived glimmers of recognition. The eyes of these more knowledgeable souls, however, slid away from hers, unwilling to meet her gaze. Their lips tightened, they looked at the floor, they shook their heads and slid away from her.

Gilligold, she judged, was somewhat feared.

At length, Ilsevel lost her patience. She took up a station in the centre of the chaos, and spun upon the spot until she began to rise. When she had gone up some ten or twelve feet and hovered nicely above the heads of all those below (or most of them; there was an occasional troll or giant to be glimpsed among the mass of travellers); she clapped her hands thrice. The sound emerged much amplified, and split the air of Deepmantle sharply, cutting through the hubbub of chattering voices. 'Which coach,' called she, when she had their attention, 'goes farther back?'

It was a giant who answered her, his face not far off level with her own. He smiled amiably, touched the brim of his shabby straw hat, and said: 'That'd be Derrydock, lady, or Crowsfoot.'

Ilsevel thanked him prettily, and descended.

Phineas stood gazing at her in awe.

'Come, now, you have seen me do that before,' said she, with a roguish smile.

Phineas, surprisingly, grinned. 'So I ought rightly to be used to the sight of a princess of Aylfenhame hovering over my head like a butterfly?'

'There are greater marvels, you know.'

'Doubtless, but how many of those do you think Phineas the Baker's Boy has seen?'

'True,' she murmured. 'I begin to forget where you come from, my Phineas.'

That prompted a flush, whether of pleasure or of mortification she could not tell, for his smile faded and he dipped his head.

'Crowsfoot,' she said briskly. 'Or Derrydock, Phineas, and quickly.'

The Crowsfoot coach was the sooner discovered, and in they climbed. Ilsevel could have blessed the amiable giant, for when the coach ejected them again at the end of a short, bumpy journey, but three new signs greeted them.

Redguard, said one.

Grove Ashbloom, said the second.

And the third said, *Warethorn Rose*.

Ilsevel clutched Phineas. 'Look! That must be it.'

Phineas stared at the third sign with unconcealed scepticism. 'Warethorn Rose? Why?'

'Because Eleri gave me a message.' Quickly, she related what their erstwhile hostess had said. 'Don't you see? Seek the rose, ware the thorn! Warethorn Rose!'

'Why not just leave the name of the Hollow, then?' Phineas objected. 'Did it have to be a riddle?'

'Of course it did,' she said impatiently. 'Have you never set foot in fae-country before?'

'No.'

Ilsevel blinked. 'Well then, yes: we love a riddle. They are...safe. Interesting. Diverting, clever, admirable — it is the more remarkable that we have not encountered more.'

The look Phineas directed at her remained sceptical. 'And who was it that left this message for you?'

'A man in a pale cloak.'

'And how was it known to this cloaked figure that you would someday need this information — and seek it at Autumn's Hollow?'

'I do not precisely know, Phineas, but we have not the time to consider the matter now. Warethorn Rose may not be Gilligold's own Hollow, but that there is something of interest to be found there seems indubitable. We go on.'

Phineas bowed. 'Lead on, then, My Lady Silver.'

Some minutes later, the coach rolled slowly away with Ilsevel and Phineas inside it. The equipage was shaped rather like a gigantic pumpkin wearing a peaked cap, which delighted Ilsevel but puzzled Phineas. 'It probably was a pumpkin, once,' she told him. 'Where do you think coaches come from?'

'A coach-builder,' said Phineas promptly.

'How tiresomely mundane.'

Phineas produced that grin again. 'Why, have you never set foot in England before?'

Ilsevel rolled her eyes at him, and settled into her coach-seat with a tiny yawn. 'Coach-builders,' she muttered in disgust, which made Phineas laugh so hard he could barely keep his seat. 'And what is so funny?' she demanded.

'Princesses,' he said, unhelpfully.

Ilsevel raised both her eyebrows.

'Bet you anything you like there's a coach-builder in Aylfenhame. At least one.'

'For what purpose?'

'Building vehicles for those as don't have enchanters of impossible ability at their beck and call.'

Ilsevel considered that. 'I know of no such thing,' she said loftily.

'Exactly my point.'

'I am not following your point.'

Phineas's grin widened. 'I begin to wonder how you survived at Mrs. Yardley's boarding-house at all.'

'With great difficulty. But,' she added nobly, 'one is sometimes called upon to make sacrifices.' She shuddered at the recollection. 'Not even a fire in the morning! I have never been so cold.'

Phineas's smile faded. 'Have you really never gone without a fire before?'

'Discounting my regrettable years as an amphibian, no.'

The look on Phineas's face turned wistful, and he abruptly turned away to look out of the window. The countryside was flying by at such speed, Ilsevel could not determine whether they travelled through fields, meadows or woods — there was only a blur of green. 'I never saw any coach go so fast,' Phineas said, in a transparent attempt at changing the subject.

Ilsevel permitted it. 'Enchanters of impossible ability. How much we have to thank them for.'

The coach, if possible, sped up still more, until Ilsevel could almost have sworn that its wheels had left the ground altogether.

In fact, they had.

'We are *rising*,' gasped Phineas, clutching his seat.

The haze of green dropped from sight, replaced by a darkening sky. Ilsevel drew nearer the window, and risked a look out. The ground was some way below them, and rapidly dwindling. 'So we are,' she said thoughtfully.

'How does it *fly*?'

'It is enchanted to do so. You are not afraid, my Phineas?'

His grip upon the seat was white-knuckled, but he said stoutly: 'No.'

'The coach will not drop us.'

'How do you know?'

'It is not permitted to do so.'

She received in response only a wild-eyed stare, and felt moved to pat his knee in an attempt at comfort. But this merely transferred the stare from her face to the hand resting upon his leg, and since he did not appear pleased she withdrew it.

Before she could speak again, a great, wracking shudder rocked the coach, followed by a *bump*, and then stillness.

'I believe we have arrived,' she said cheerfully, and threw open the door. Their carriage had alighted upon a charming silver bridge, and at the other end of the bridge there proved to be a grassy pathway winding up to the top of a tall peak. 'We are come to the pinnacle, I observe,' she commented, and stepped out onto the bridge. A brisk wind tugged immediately at her gown, powerfully enough that she was obliged to steady herself against the side of the pumpkin-coach. 'Take some care, Phineas, when you step out,' she called. 'The wind is in a playful humour.'

For a moment she wondered whether Phineas would follow her at all, but he was a brave soul, and soon joined her upon the bridge. The wild look had not left his eyes. 'The pinnacle?' he echoed. 'But it is not so tall a hill as all that.'

'Is it not?' Ilsevel gazed upon the evidence before her eyes: the heavy cloak of mist clinging to the high peak, and the glimpse of a dark landscape some way below.

'In England, it doesn't look half so tall. Nor even half *that*.'

'Ah,' said Ilsevel with a faint smile. 'England.'

'Tiresomely mundane,' said Phineas with a small sigh. 'I was forgetting.'

'It has its merits,' said Ilsevel, as, with a thankful pat for the coach, she set off across the bridge.

'Such as?'

'One Phineas Drake, Baker. I find him a congenial fellow.'

Phineas, it appeared, did not know what to say to that, for he vouchsafed no reply. He kept pace with Ilsevel as she crossed the bridge, even tucking his arm through hers, which was not at all a poor idea in all the wind. They soon alighted upon the grassy rock peak of the hill itself, a vibrant array of mandrakes and hemlock, heather and thistledown strewn among the grasses. A glance back revealed the pale coach darting away ground-wards again, starlight clinging to its wheels.

'Now then, what—' began Ilsevel, but she was prevented from completing the sentence, for two dark shapes loomed abruptly out of the mist and the shadows and words left her.

They were very tall, very *large* dark shapes, and their demeanour was not in the least bit conciliating. 'Trolls,' she uttered intelligently, and stopped. Not giants after all, then, though they might as well be, for they were rather larger even than Mr. Balligumph, and nowhere near as friendly. They were oddly clad: one wore an ochre-yellow velvet doublet and matching hose, both rather grubby, and his hat was crowned with an extravagantly tall, bedraggled plume. The other wore a long, skirted coat of black cloth frogged in silver, with breeches and stockings and buckled shoes. He was missing the curls that would have matched such attire, but he had a wide-brimmed hat with a plume to rival his companion's.

'How the ages fly,' Ilsevel commented. 'And in quite the wrong direction! I believe nobody has worn such a coat since at least my grandmother's day.'

'What's wrong with my coat?' demanded the troll with the silver braid and the wide brim. His tusks, she was pleased to note, were not half so handsome as Balligumph's.

'Nothing at all,' said Ilsevel with a conciliating smile. 'In fact, it is a particularly fine specimen. May I know the name of your tailor?'

'You may not. Why came you to Warethorn Rose?'

The other troll had, apparently, been fast asleep, for he awoke with a loud snort and blinked in astonishment at Ilsevel and Phineas. 'What, is it visitors again? Gollumpus! Behold!'

'I see them, Nigmenog.'

Nigmenog was more amiable than Gollumpus, for he advanced to shake hands with Phineas and Ilsevel, crushing their hands in his mighty grip. 'Welcome, welcome!' he said affably. 'Tis a long way you've come. Nobody comes up this far anymore, nobody at all.'

'You must be very lonely,' said Ilsevel sympathetically.

'Not at all,' said Gollumpus repressively.

'Oh, shockingly!' said Nigmenog. 'Shall you be staying long? You must tell us all about yourselves!'

'I do not know precisely how long we shall remain,' said Ilsevel. 'That must depend upon the conclusion of our business. We are here to see Gilligold.'

'You cannot,' said Gollumpus.

'*Well*,' corrected Nigmenog. 'You can, but only if you can pass the Door.'

'Which door?'

As though alerted by the sound of its name, a great set of double doors appeared in luminous outline, shining through the thick mist. Night was fast falling, and in the gathering gloom Ilsevel had not been able to see very far. She now realised that a tall, craggy rock wall stood a little way behind Nigmenog and Gollumpus, by its appearance absolutely impassable, save by the grand doors the troll-giants flanked between them.

'It couldn't have been easy, I suppose?' sighed Phineas at her elbow.

Ilsevel smiled her best smile at Nigmenog, judging him an easier target than his brother. Were they brothers? 'Shall you kindly open it for us?'

'If you pass the trials.' Nigmenog said this with a huge, exuberant smile.

'Nobody ever passes the trials,' offered Gollumpus.

'It is long since anyone even tried,' agreed Nigmenog, his smile unwavering.

'I do not suppose,' said Ilsevel with deceptive diffidence, 'you might consent to open the Door for My Lady Silver?' And she let her lofty status, her absolute right to power, gather palpably about her. It shone especially from her strange silver eyes, and these she directed at Nigmenog with just a *hint* of pleading.

'No,' said Gollumpus.

Nigmenog regarded her thoughtfully. 'Clearly you're a lady of eminence, and full fair to look upon besides, if I may be so bold! But, good lady, nobody passes the Door without first passing the trials.'

Ilsevel sighed. 'Very well. And what must we do?'

'You must answer some questions correctly.'

'And what are they?'

Nigmenog looked intently at her. 'I will give you the questions, but first we must be clear between us. Is it your stated intention to attempt the Door?'

'It is.'

The question and its answer was of greater importance than she had imagined, for the clear, ringing toll of a bell echoed from somewhere, and the light limning the Door glittered.

Nigmenog went on. 'If you should fail to answer correctly, do you agree to pay the price?'

Ilsevel's eyes narrowed. 'What price are we agreeing to?'

Nigmenog did not precisely answer. He gestured to himself and Gollumpus, and that toothy smile flashed once more.

'I do not understand you,' she said.

But Phineas's quick mind had put it together. 'We will become the new guardians of the Door.'

'You will forgive us, I know, if we should wish for your failure,' said Nigmenog genially. 'How many years has it been, Gollumpus?'

'Many.'

'Most turn away at this juncture,' Nigmenog confided. 'Call back the carriage and sail away, leaving us to our fate…'

'How wretched of them,' said Ilsevel.

'The cheek of such people,' agreed Phineas.

'The very heights of selfishness.'

'Nothing can excuse such conduct.'

Nigmenog nodded along with this exchange, the picture of indignation. 'But you will not abandon us so. I knew the moment I set eyes upon you both! You are made of better stuff.'

'We shall not be half so selfish, I assure you,' said Ilsevel.

Nigmenog beamed upon her. 'Then you'll attempt the trials?'

'*I* shall, certainly, and I shall pay the price if I should fail. Phineas must answer for himself.'

Phineas did so, without hesitation. She had left him the option of leaving, should he wish it, for what was Anthelaena's fate to him? But he said in his strong, young voice, 'I, too, will try.'

'And pay the price?' prompted Nigmenog.

'If I fail, I will pay the price.'

Nigmenog clapped his hands together. 'Excellent. Well then, shall we get on?'

'Please,' said Ilsevel. 'It grows dark.'

Nigmenog stood tall, and straightened the hem of his doublet. He intoned: 'How many snowberries grow in the sea?'

'Why, that is easy!' said Ilsevel. 'The answer is—'

But Phineas pinched her arm, turning the word she had been going to utter into a surprised and indignant *ouch!*

'It can never be easy,' he reminded her.

'But the answer is perfectly obvious.' She would not speak it aloud yet, if Phineas insisted, but everyone knew that the snowberry grew among the Merribourne Peaks in the far south-west of Aylfenhame, and *not* in the sea! So the answer could only be none.

But Phineas said, 'Remember what you said about riddles.'

Does it have to be a riddle? Phineas had asked.

Of course it does, she had replied. *This is fae-country.*

'You have misrepresented the case, sir!' she said to Nigmenog. 'These are not questions at all, but riddles!'

'What is a riddle but a question?' he countered.

'Is that a riddle as well?' said she in disgust.

'It is a question.'

Had he not been so tall or so broad, Ilsevel would have been strongly tempted to offer him violence.

'What is the next question, sir?' put in Phineas, before she could act upon this blameless inclination.

'How many stars are there in the sky?' said Nigmenog.

An impossible question! Ilsevel's indignation grew, but Phineas merely nodded. 'And the third?' said he.

'What is the difference between a dragon?'

Ilsevel waited, but nothing more was forthcoming. 'A dragon and what?' she prompted.

Nigmenog merely smiled.

'A dragon and *what?* Come now, that is not even a whole question!

It is but half a one!'

'It is a riddle,' said Phineas wearily.

'Are these the same riddles you ask of everyone?' Ilsevel demanded.

'The same *questions*,' said Nigmenog. 'No, lady, they are brand new! Just for you, and your fine companion.'

'What an honour.'

'We could not be more pleased,' Phineas put in earnestly.

'Delighted beyond words,' added Ilsevel.

'Positively bursting with joy,' said Phineas.

Nigmenog nodded as though this fulsome praise were no more than his due. 'Well, well, time passes. What shall you answer?'

'May we have time to confer?' Ilsevel said.

'You may!' answered Nigmenog grandly, as though unveiling some glittering prize. He made a go-forth gesture with one great, velvet-clad arm.

Gollumpus, silent throughout, merely stood.

Phineas, though, did not immediately consent to follow Ilsevel a little way apart. 'I have a question of my own,' he said to Nigmenog. 'Only a small one.'

'You may ask,' said Nigmenog graciously.

'Earlier, you said: visitors *again*. Has anyone else been here recently?'

'A horrid old woman. She was most impolite.'

'Insulted my hat,' put in Gollumpus unexpectedly.

'Insulted mine, too! And she said she spurned our riddles. *Spurned.*'

Phineas looked at Ilsevel. 'I wonder what your sister was doing up here?'

Nigmenog blinked, incredulous. 'Nay, she cannot be your sister, so fair as you are!'

Ilsevel ignored this. 'It does not appear that she was here to make an attempt upon the Door,' she said to Phineas.

'What did the horrid old woman do while she was here?' said Phineas.

Nigmenog shrugged his gigantic shoulders. 'She insulted us, as I have told you. And then she walked about, talking to herself all the while, until Golly and I thought her quite mad. Then she went away.'

'Where did she walk?' said Phineas.

Nigmenog gestured. 'That way.'

That way was so shrouded in shadow as to be wholly obscured.

'Thank you,' said Phineas politely. Taking Ilsevel's arm, he guided her gently *that way*, directly into the darkness. Ilsevel soon missed the lambent glow of the Door; the light had not been strong, but it had been vastly better than nothing.

But shortly, a mote of light sprung to life in the air near her ear, and swiftly grew in strength and brilliance until it shone like a star. It bobbed cheerfully upon the breeze, far more upbeat (Ilsevel thought in exasperation) than it had any right to be, under the circumstances.

'Most interesting,' she said. 'Where did you get a wisp-light from, my Phineas?'

'Mr. Balligumph gave it me.'

'What a useful fellow he is.'

The wisp, however, did not seem inclined to do very much of anything. It hovered there, bobbing up and down, merrily sprinkling light all about (for which Ilsevel was grateful); but the light illuminated nothing more than heathery grass beneath their feet, flanked on one side by a thicket of harebell, dog-roses and thorns growing at the base of the wall, and on the other by an alarming drop into thin air.

'If it please you,' said Phineas with his diffident charm, 'we should like to know where the Princess Tyllanthine went when she came here.'

This question puzzled the wisp, perhaps, for it dithered about a while, swaying back and forth as though in deep thought — or, perhaps, dancing. 'It is not dancing?' said Ilsevel in concern. 'It does not imagine itself summoned in order to perform for us a quadrille?'

'And all by itself,' said Phineas. 'That would be a feat. But no, I don't think so. Look.'

The wisp had, indeed, pulled itself together, and begun to wander away. So listless, so seemingly aimless, was its progress that Ilsevel continued to suffer grave doubts as to its understanding. But then it stopped, mere inches from the rock wall, and brightened, gleaming like a cheery wisp-smile.

'Thank you,' said Phineas, and collected something pale that lay, pinned beneath a chunk of rock, upon a jagged outcropping. 'It is a note,' he said, and passed it to Ilsevel.

The note said only, *He is fond of treasures. Ware the Thorn, Ilse.*

'If she means Gilligold, I *know* he is fond of treasures,' said Ilsevel in exasperation. 'Is that not precisely why we are here? And what can she mean by the Thorn?'

'We will shortly find out,' said Phineas. 'I hope.'

Indeed, if the alternative was to spend the next century or two at the Door. Ilsevel folded the note, smothering her feelings of frustration as best she could, and tucked it inside her bodice.

'These were with it,' he said, and put something else clothish into her hands. It was a cotton bundle; the contents proved to be a wisp of dried grass, and a withered piece of dried fruit. 'I do not at all understand what they are for,' he complained.

The grass, dead though it was, had its beauties, for it was ethereally pale and shone silvery in the wisp-light. The fruit was a mouthful of apple, desiccated but edible. 'Treasures,' she said, somewhat enlightened, and wrapped them carefully back up in the cotton. This bundle, too, went into her bodice.

In answer to Phineas's questioning look, she said only, 'We will shortly discover their use. It is more pressing to come up with an answer to those three questions.'

'I can answer them,' said Phineas.

'Can you indeed?'

'Most certainly.' He spoke stoutly, but his abundant confidence could not quite instil Ilsevel with very much to match it.

But her own mind being perfectly blank of possible answers, she was obliged to trust him. And it was not so very difficult to do so, after all, for had he not repeatedly proved that he possessed remarkable quickness of thought? Ilsevel had known few to match him.

So she said, 'Let us go back, then,' and they followed Phineas's wisp back to the two trolls at the Door. Phineas carefully gathered up his wisp once they were back within the Door's fulgent glow, and restored it to his pocket.

'I am ready to answer,' he told Nigmenog.

'Excellent!' said the troll, with the smile of a creature that knows himself within minutes of freedom. 'Say on, then!'

'The first question: how many snowberries grow in the sea? The answer is: as many as red herrings swim in the wood.'

Nigmenog's smile faded a little, and he scratched his head. 'I think it a fair answer, Golly, do not you?'

'It is,' growled Gollumpus.

Phineas, almost imperceptibly, relaxed a fraction. His hand found Ilsevel's and clutched it tightly. 'The second question,' he continued, his voice gaining in strength. 'How many stars are there in the sky? Why, as many as there are grains of sand in the sea.'

Nigmenog squinted at him. 'You are sure of that, are you?'

'I am,' said Phineas. 'You may count them to make certain, if you wish.'

Nigmenog cast a quick glance up into a sky littered with a vast number of stars. 'Some other time, perhaps,' he muttered.

Ilsevel, heartened, gave Phineas's hand an approving squeeze.

'And the third question?' said Nigmenog. 'Have you an answer for that, too, you clever young wretch?'

'I have a great many answers to it,' said Phineas, and Ilsevel heard in his voice that his mischievous grin was back. 'What is the difference between a dragon? Why, a foxglove, because it never rains on Tuesdays.'

Nigmenog blinked. 'Is that so?'

'Yes. Or an apple, because a hat has no feet.'

Nigmenog grunted.

'And a chicken, because a cat cannot fly.'

'Is that all?' said Nigmenog.

'No! The difference between a dragon is a crayfish, because strawberries are red and blueberries are blue, and also—'

'Aye,' said Nigmenog wearily, holding up one large hand. 'That'll do, lad.' He spoke with the defeated tone of a man resigning himself to an inevitable fate, and hope flared to life in Ilsevel's breast. 'You can pass,' said Nigmenog.

'You remarkable boy!' Ilsevel crowed. 'My Phineas, I could kiss you.'

Phineas flushed, but Ilsevel was not given time either to act upon this statement or to retract it, for Gollumpus said, 'Wait,' and her heart sank again. 'Can we not keep one of them?'

'Why, no,' said Nigmenog, but he looked appraisingly at Phineas and Ilsevel in turn. 'We did have an agreement, Golly.'

'But they need not both pass,' said Gollumpus, far too reasonably for Ilsevel's liking. 'Let one of them take *my* place, and the other may go.'

'Why cannot one of them take *my* place?' said Nigmenog, drawing himself up. 'It is I who has done all the work! I made up all the questions, Golly!'

'I have been here longer,' said Gollumpus.

'That is a lie! It has been far longer for me!'

The Door, meanwhile, had decided the issue independently of either Nigmenog or Gollumpus, for the light around it grew as it slowly creaked open. 'Come on,' said Ilsevel, and tugged Phineas after her as she darted nimbly through the Door. They ran, at least until they had got beyond the circle of luminous light, and the sounds of the trolls' disagreement began to fade behind them.

Ilsevel found herself laughing. 'Oh, my Phineas, where did you learn to do that?' she gasped.

Phineas blinked at her. 'What?'

'Such perfect answers! And yet, they made no sense whatsoever to me.'

'They are not meant to,' he said. 'Nobody could make sense of such questions, not even the asker. So the answer to them all, really, is 'I don't know, and neither do you,' but it would be sadly flat to say so in so many words, would it not?'

'Except the snowberries,' said Ilsevel. 'I am perfectly certain that the answer to that question is: none.'

'Are you?' countered Phineas. 'Have you been into the sea to check?'

'No,' Ilsevel had to concede.

'So the answer is, *I don't know, but probably none,* or in other words exactly as many as fish you might expect to find swimming about in Sherwood Forest.'

'You,' said Ilsevel, 'are quite wasted on bread, my Phineas.'

'Bread is good,' he answered earnestly. 'People thrive upon bread. It is a useful thing to do.'

'It is. But it is a fitter profession for someone else.'

'Someone like who?'

Ilsevel shrugged. 'Someone less dazzling.'

That silenced him. After a few moments, when he did not speak, Ilsevel said: 'Well then, where to? Shall your wisp help us again?'

Phineas retrieved it from his pocket and set it afloat once more, whereupon it obligingly brightened. 'To Gilligold, good wisp,' he said hopefully. 'And speedily, if you please.'

'But carefully,' Ilsevel added. 'For I am not comfortable about this mysterious *Thorn* we are constantly being told of.'

'Carefully,' agreed Phineas.

The wisp sailed happily away, and Ilsevel and Phineas fell into step behind it.

CHAPTER TWENTY-THREE

Beyond the wall, the darkness proved not nearly so fathomless as it had been outside the Door. It seemed somehow that the silver stars shone more brightly here, bathing the heather and the harebell in a soft, pale light more than sufficient to navigate by. Lights, also, danced among the shadowed trees, fairy-lights to Phineas's eyes. A path lay spread before their feet, quartz flagstones embedded into the grass; scented hedges rambled along either side, and from within those verdant bushes glittered the ethereal shapes of flowers, glinting with their own soft-shaded lights. Never before had Phineas witnessed such unearthly beauty. He walked along at Lady Silver's side with his hands deep in the pockets of his coat, eyes everywhere as he delightedly devoured every glimpse of colour and light.

Some of his happy feelings faded a little when Ilsevel abruptly snapped, 'Stop staring.'

He swallowed. 'I am sorry.'

She relented enough to say: 'Such beauty is deceptive, do you not see? Dangerously dulcet. Do not forget that we have twice been warned.'

The Thorn. Phineas had indeed forgotten, lulled by the perfumed air, the starry flowers, the gentle lights of the night garden. He made himself take in the glory with but half an eye, alert for signs of approach. But there came none. The night was still; barely a creature stirred, only an occasional bird heard winging its way into the night from somewhere overhead.

Then Ilsevel stopped.

'What?' whispered Phineas, fully alert in an instant, and braced for trouble.

Ilsevel pointed.

A rose lay in the path.

It was no ordinary rose, either, for it was snow-white and glimmered with a light like the stars. It looked familiar.

Ilsevel thought so too, for she made a hasty check of the sash in which she had been carrying their gathered flowers from the Seasons' Hollows. The gathered knot she had made around their collected stems was empty; the flowers were all gone.

'Who took them?' she hissed in a low voice. 'Did you see anyone, Phineas?'

'Not a soul.' He stooped to pick up the rose, but Ilsevel's hand darted out and fastened, vice-like, around his wrist. 'Wait.'

He paused.

'Seek the rose, ware the thorn. Is this some kind of trap?'

Phineas quietly withdrew his wrist from her grip, and straightened. 'Let us leave it there for now, then.'

Ilsevel's agreement to this plan was signalled in her moving forward, stepping carefully over the beautiful rose in the path.

The other rose, the sunlit one, lay a little farther ahead — and there was something else there. A soft light shone in the ground, and when Phineas approached he saw what appeared to be a pane of crystal-clear quartz set into the grass. Behind it, a lyre was imprisoned. Carved from a moon-pale wood, it was an instrument of breath-taking grace and delicacy; its strings rippled like water, and glittered in an impossible array of colours.

'That is my sister's,' Ilsevel gasped, coming up beside him. 'She used to play ancient airs upon it, after the Summer feasts.'

'Then an important question is answered,' said Phineas calmly. 'Gilligold indeed has some of your sister's lost treasures.'

'Yes, but...' Ilsevel knelt in the dew-damp grass and touched the quartz, then rapped upon it. 'But how may they be released?'

'We will find a way, I promise.'

Ilsevel looked up at him, uncertain, but she nodded after a moment and rose to her feet. 'I wonder what more there are?' she said, more briskly, and set off anew.

They covered some distance upon the path over the next half-hour, as it wound its way slowly up to the very top of the peak. At intervals they found more of Ilsevel's stolen flowers, together with the jug of ice-wine Mr. Dapper had given them, all strewn temptingly in their way. They also discovered more of the quartz-bound caches, containing: an ethereal gown of whisper-thin golden silk, wreathed in misted ribbons; an armband of clear jewels, glittering with captured starlight; a bejewelled hair comb, from which a velvety orchid-blossom grew; the lost shoe-roses, with their star-dusted butterflies; a pearlescent pocket-watch, clear waters swirling beneath its glassy face, its hands telling the time in many places at once; and a shabby little doll in the shape of a cat, its hide stitched from much-worn purple velvet.

'All her things,' choked Ilsevel, and for the first time since Phineas had met her, her composure hung in tatters. He heard tears behind the words, and it cost her a visible effort to restore herself to her usual serenity.

Phineas made bold enough to take her hand, as she had earlier taken his. 'We will soon restore them to her,' he said gently.

'We must, Phineas,' she said, her old fierceness creeping back into her voice. 'We *must*. It is wrong that they should be here! What *is* this place? By what right are Her Majesty's personal wonders held prisoner here? Gilligold shall answer for this!'

Phineas preferred her anger to her tears, for while the former brought with it a useful energy, the latter could only break the heart. So he encouraged this happier flow of thoughts, though his mind turned busily upon the problem even as he comforted her. What was this place, indeed? Who made of it a shrine to a lost queen? And how, indeed, were they to retrieve even one of Anthelaena's possessions?

'I believe we must spring the trap,' he said softly.

Ilsevel's head came up, and she directed at him a swift, keen look. 'What are you thinking, my Phineas?'

'That we might wander here for hours without learning anything of use, and we are not so well-supplied with time as all that. If the Thorn lies waiting for us, very well: let us announce ourselves.'

'Your wisp,' she said.

He had forgotten. 'What of it?'

'Can it lead us to Gilligold?'

Phineas did not trouble to answer, merely taking the wisp from his pocket and casting it up anew. There it hung like a tiny, giggling moon, and Phineas felt insensibly heartened by its presence. 'Wisp, take us to Gilligold?' he asked.

But the wisp, so helpful before, did not seem able to assist him now. It bobbed and flowed in circles, spiralling far up into the sky before coming down again in a flourish of starlight. If it were not for the absolute lack of results its antics produced, Phineas might have said that it looked triumphant.

'You celebrate too early,' he told it. 'You have not yet taken us to Gilligold.'

The wisp flashed, then darkened. He had irritated it.

Ilsevel was looking about, as though she might see Gilligold at any moment. But nobody was to be seen save for themselves; and when Ilsevel called Gilligold's name, no one answered.

With a sigh, Phineas reclaimed his wisp.

'The trap it is, then,' said Ilsevel ruefully, and straightened her shoulders. She began to stoop, but it was Phineas's turn to halt her in the attempt.

'Let me,' he said.

'Why?'

He smiled, as best he could. 'The world will not miss a baker's boy so very much as it will miss My Lady Silver.'

'Maudlin words, my Phineas! Surely nothing so terrible as all that is like to come of it?'

'I hope not,' he said. 'But if only one of us is to survive, it must be you, for who else is to take these things away from here, and revive your sister? It is not a task I can perform.'

'It is not a task I can perform either, without you.'

He hid the warmth at heart that these words prompted, and set aside the confusion also. 'Then you had better look after me,' he said with an attempt at a grin. 'If I am dead in five minutes I'll be vexed with you.'

Ilsevel levelled a finger at him. 'Stop joking, start doing,' she commanded, but a smile lurked in her eyes.

Phineas nodded — and hesitated. What was he to expect, indeed?

Well, boy. You put on these shoes yourself; best walk in them.

He bent, and collected the delicate object that lay near his feet: one of the velvet queen parasols.

Nothing very much happened; he was certainly not attacked. It was only that, when he straightened, he discovered himself to be somewhere else — and there was no sign of Ilsevel.

He was underground, as though he had noiselessly dropped into the earth. The darkness there was alleviated only by a dim lantern hanging from the packed mud of the ceiling. This lantern, an ethereal, silvery thing, swung slightly back and forth, though no breeze existed to set it into motion. The chamber was barely as wide as Phineas was tall, and contained nothing else.

'Hello?' he called uncertainly.

No answer came.

Light glittered, making him blink. The air grew colder, and dank.

Then, at last, a voice spoke. It rumbled through the earth beneath his feet, and shivered up the walls. 'Why are you here, Phineas Drake?'

Phineas carefully stored the delicate mushroom in a pocket of his long coat. 'I am here to help Ilsevel,' he said, as calmly as he could.

'My Lady Silver,' said the voice, and laughed. 'Princess of Aylfenhame. Enchantress. She is far older than you, Phineas Drake, far wiser, and infinitely more powerful. And you are here to… help.'

Phineas swallowed. 'I…' he began, and his words dried up. 'I… she — she is not familiar with England, the way I am. She asked for my aid.'

'You are not in England anymore. This is her world. *Our* world.'

And Phineas had no place whatsoever within it. He understood the implication clearly enough, and could find no way of refuting it. What *was* he doing out here?

The riddles. He had answered those; Ilsevel had praised him for it. He said this.

'True,' conceded the voice. 'That was a worthy service. But do you really think she could not have managed without you?'

Of course she could. She was a princess of Aylfenhame. She would have found her way through, with or without Phineas. 'But,' he said, rallying, 'why then does she keep me with her?'

'Perhaps,' whispered the voice, 'she finds you… amusing.'

Perhaps she did. That look in her eyes sometimes, when she looked at Phineas — he took it for a smile of approval, but did it not seem more likely that it was a smile of amusement? Tinged, on occasion, with derision, and that was fair as well, for he was only

Phineas Drake.

'Are you the Thorn?' said Phineas softly.

'I am sometimes called so.'

And no wonder, for every word bit and scratched like a thicket of thorns, inflicting a hundred tiny wounds.

'And what do they call you, Phineas Drake?' continued the Thorn. 'The baker's boy, wasn't it?'

'It is what I am.'

'A fit companion for a princess,' hissed the Thorn, with withering sarcasm.

Then it began to seem as though the voice was his father's, and at his most disappointed. 'And you are not even a very good baker's boy, are you?' said the Thorn. 'You should be in England, tending your family's shop in your father's absence. But you have abandoned it.'

'The... the Lady Silver's need was the greater,' faltered Phineas.

'She took you along out of pity,' said the Thorn cruelly, and since the words echoed the doubts Phineas had been harbouring in his own heart, they cut like knives. 'Forlorn little baker's boy, lost and confused! Poor Phineas Drake. She could no more leave you alone there than she could have left a puppy to starve in the snow. But make no mistake, baker's boy. There is a limit to her patience and her pity. When she is finished with you, she will cast you from her presence without a moment's hesitation.'

'She would not,' whispered Phineas, trying desperately to believe it.

The Thorn chuckled. 'Will she not? You are a menial. You are nothing to her but a fleeting interest, a passing convenience — how could you ever be more than that?'

Phineas shut his eyes, as though by doing so he could shut out the voice as well. He tried to remember the Ilsevel he knew: the warm look she sometimes directed at him; the way she spoke of him, and to him. *My Phineas.*

But the visions slipped away. He saw a great lady instead, terrible and proud, beautiful beyond belief and so very far above him...

Go, said this Ilsevel, cold as winter. *I have no further need of you.*

Something precious shrivelled inside him, and died without a sound.

'You should leave,' whispered the voice. 'Go home. Save her the trouble of tending to you; save yourself the pain of a dismissal.'

'How?' whispered Phineas. Never in his life had he felt smaller or more pitiful; if he could have erased himself with a thought, he would not have hesitated.

'I can help you there. Only tell me that it is what you wish, and it shall be done.'

Phineas saw, in his mind's eye, My Lady Silver walking steadily away from him, back turned, not an ounce of warmth or welcome left in her. *It is what must be*, he thought in despair.

'It… it is what I wish,' he said painfully, and every word hurt as he forced it from his lips.

There came the sensation of a vast satisfaction. It radiated from the walls, wrapped Phineas like a suffocating cocoon. 'Good little baker's boy,' said the Thorn.

Defeated, Phineas awaited his fate.

The moment Phineas's fingers touched the fallen mushroom, he was gone.

That was it. No flurry of darkness to sweep him away, no sudden attack, not even a whisper of sound; he was simply gone.

'Phineas!' she called, her heart pounding wildly.

No answer came.

'Right,' she muttered, and retraced her steps along the path until she came to another of her soundlessly stolen flowers: a frosty, velvet-blue hellebore. She took a steadying breath, braced herself, and bent to collect it.

And then she, too, was somewhere else, as soundlessly as Phineas had disappeared. She did not even experience any sensation of movement. The cool, clear night air simply faded, replaced by the dank-smelling air of some underground spot. A single, silver-wrought lantern hung from the earthen ceiling of some uninspiring underground chamber, and that was all. The room did not have the courtesy to provide her with a chair, let alone a way out.

Ilsevel drew herself up. 'Where is Phineas?' she snapped.

'The baker's boy,' said a dark, low voice. 'Does it matter?'

To Ilsevel's alarm and dismay, these words echoed in her heart, sinking deeper with each repetition until she almost began to believe them. *Does it matter? Does it matter?* Did it matter, indeed? Why should the fate of a tradesman in any way concern her?

'Yes,' she hissed, pushing these thoughts away. 'It matters a great deal.'

'Why?' whispered the voice, and that, too, resounded in her mind, growing bigger and more penetrating, more difficult to dismiss. Why indeed? *Why?*

She took another slow, deep breath, sternly steadying herself. 'Because he is my friend,' she said firmly. 'And full worthy of being so.'

'And you, My Lady Silver,' said the voice softly. 'Are you a worthy friend to him?'

Ilsevel wanted at once to answer, without the smallest doubt, *yes*. But to her own surprise, she hesitated. Was she? What had she ever done for him? She had shamelessly ripped him out of his own life, his own world, because it had suited her to do so. She had needed — nay, *wanted* — his help and his company, and so she had simply taken both, recognising in Phineas a person who would gladly let her do it.

What had she given back?

Nothing.

Unable to defend herself, she was silent.

The voice laughed. 'Quite so. And it is not your first failure, princess, is it?'

Visions drifted through Ilsevel's mind. Her sisters: Anthelaena, who had died. *No*, she was not dead, but she was in exile, cursed and broken, and had remained so for years. Where, in all this time, had Ilsevel been? Why, transformed, for like the weak, pitiful excuse for a princess that she was, when the enemy had come for her she had fallen in an instant. She'd had to be rescued.

And Tyllanthine? Poor Tylla, her youngest sister, forever excluded and marginalised... she and Anthelaena had both failed Tyllanthine, had been failing her from the moment of her birth. She remembered, with distant pain, the gentle chiding of her own mother, so long ago. *Do not forget Tyllanthine. Take Tyllanthine with you.* Wrapped up in each other, she and Anthelaena had so often failed to heed their mother's advice. If Tylla had grown up into a bitter, hard, untrustworthy woman, whose fault was it that she had?

The list went on. Her niece, Lihyaen, whom she had failed to protect — it had fallen to others to do that. Edironal, Anthelaena's husband. Dead? Missing? She did not even *know*. She had failed everything, everyone, she had ever professed to care for — even the throne at Mirramay itself. And what was she now doing but casting desperately about, trying — too late, too *late* — to correct the terrible consequences of her own inadequacy?

Distantly, some part of her recognised that these thoughts were not hers, and not the truth, and that part briefly rallied. 'These things,' she forced out, 'were not my fault.'

'No, no!' said the voice soothingly. 'Of course they were not your fault, princess.' Ilsevel felt, for an instant, a little eased — but the voice went on. 'They were, however, your responsibility. Were they not?'

Of course they were.

'But,' she said, her hands going to her face. 'But…' She could not think clearly; doubt, regret and misery shrouded her thoughts like an impenetrable fog, and fight though she might to hack through them to the clarity she *knew* must lie somewhere beyond, she could not maintain her grip on any more reasonable thought. They slipped through her fingers like bright, glittering fish, and swam heedlessly away.

Phineas. That thought flashed into her mind, cutting through the darkness, and she grabbed hold of it like a drowning woman offered a rope. His face was, for one searing instant, vivid in her mind: that grin he had when something pleased or amused him; the look of tender concern he sometimes wore when he thought she was not paying him any attention; the vulnerability of him, which he strove so hard to hide; the absurd, painful youthfulness of the clever baker's boy. The hopefulness he had, whatever happened to harm or disconcert him. His diligence, his quickness of mind, his staunch reliability. The way he *cared*.

'What,' she said, mustering herself, 'have you done with Phineas?'

'What, are we back to that? The little baker's boy?'

'Yes, we are back to that. Is *this* what you have done to him?' The thought horrified her. She, My Lady Silver, Princess Ilsevellian of Aylfenhame, replete with a self-confidence to which she had been born, raised with an unshakeable sense of her own power — indeed, her own *right* to power — why, if even she could be damaged by the insidious whispers of the Thorn, what effect might the wretch have upon poor Phineas? What defences could he possibly have against it? He had no high station to protect him, no sense of grand purpose, no power of any kind. Even his own father had been disappointed in him, though Ilsevel could not in the smallest degree understand why, and his mother had been dead too long to be anything to him now but a regret. For all his brilliances, Phineas would crumple like wet paper under this kind of treatment.

He'd need her.

She had no right to be defeated by such paltry attacks. Would she let mere words vanquish them both? She would not.

'How dare you,' she uttered fiercely, and her fractured confidence grew with every word. '*What* are you, that you should attack me so? I am, as you have kindly reminded me, a princess of Aylfenhame and I will not be so spoken to!'

'You are presently at my mercy, princess, and as such you will be spoken to in any fashion I so choose.'

This was better. Insidious, poisonous whispers Ilsevel could not so well withstand, not when they were saying the same things she sometimes said to herself. But direct opposition was another matter entirely — particularly when she was so absolutely in the right.

She drew herself up. 'And who are you, then, that you take such a right to yourself?'

'They call me the Thorn.'

'An absurd name.'

Silence, for an instant. Had she disconcerted the creature? Good.

But not for long. 'What will they call you, in ages to come?' continued the Thorn. 'The third princess? The weak princess, powerless in her own defence, who needed everyone else to save her?'

But the spell was broken; these insidious words could no longer harm her. 'Oh, do stop,' she said impatiently. 'There is no shame in sometimes needing the help of others, and I am far from powerless.'

Silence.

'Tell me who you are,' she commanded. 'Who you *really* are.'

'I will not.'

'Are you Gilligold?'

'No.' The word was uttered with scorn.

'Then who? Someone I have known? You appear to know a great deal about me.'

'I will not answer your questions, Lady Silver.'

'Very well. I am not so interested as to be overpowered with curiosity. You will instead release me, and restore Phineas to me.'

'Is that what you wish?' whispered the voice.

'It is!'

And then the underground cavern was gone, and Ilsevel stood once more under the starlight. A cool breeze ruffled her hair, there was grass at her feet, and to her intense relief there was Phineas at her elbow. She clutched him. 'Listen,' she said fiercely. 'You must put that creature's words out of your mind. There is not a particle of truth to anything that he said.'

Phineas sighed, and leaned against her. 'If there were not a particle of truth to it, then it would not be nearly so persuasive.'

He was right. The Thorn had a talent for finding the weaknesses in one's own character, or position, or history, and exaggerating them until one could see nothing else. 'Still,' she insisted, 'what truth there might be is twisted out of all sense or recognition and you must not let him overpower you.'

'Oh, I did,' said Phineas softly. 'I was quite overpowered.'

'But you are here now, with me. Cast him from your mind, my Phineas. Do not let his poisonous words linger in your heart, for I declare them *false*.'

She spoke with all the authority she could muster, and for an instant the very air rang with it.

Phineas did not seem much affected. 'I will try,' he said wearily.

Ilsevel was forced to content herself with that.

So intent was she upon the matter of Phineas's state of mind that she had not taken careful note of her surroundings. It occurred to her at last that they had not been returned to the same place from which they had been taken. They stood some way farther up the peak, near the pinnacle. The stolen flowers hung once again from her sash, and the jug of ice-wine had been restored to Phineas's possession.

And there was something odd about the terrain up there. The greenish stuff at her feet that she had, at a glance, taken for grass — or perhaps for moss, or something of that sort — was nothing of the kind.

She bent down, and touched her fingers to it. 'Phineas,' she said thoughtfully. 'This is velvet.'

Phineas stooped, and applied his hand to the ground. 'It... it appears so,' he said doubtfully. 'How can that be?'

How indeed? What manner of madman would array the earth in velvet? It was rumpled and creased and... was that a *pocket* stitched into the surface?

Ilsevel stuck in her hand to check. It was. 'This is somebody's velvet doublet.'

'But it is enormous.'

So it was, but that was clearly no impediment to its existing. Moreover, it did not appear to be an improbably gigantic doublet spread upon the ground; it had too much shape for that, too much in the way of bulges and swells, and, well...

'Somebody is wearing it,' said Ilsevel.

Phineas took a step back, and cast a long look over the gentle slope of the hill they were presently standing upon. 'Nobody could be so vast,' he said.

Ilsevel saw his point, for the distance in question was improbably huge considering that, if she was correct, they must be standing upon the doublet-wearer's belly. And a fine, swollen paunch he had at that. 'It used to be said of Gilligold,' she began, 'that as his hoard of treasures grew, so did he. I am not sure anybody has ever taken it as the literal truth; more as a figure of speech, in some obscure way. But it was also said of him that he was the richest person in Aylfenhame, and by a *long way*, Phineas, so if it should happen to be the literal truth after all then he must indeed be the size of a mountain!' She picked up her skirts and ran lightly up the slope, for on the far side it dipped downwards again and she was almost *sure* there must be a head up there somewhere.

'Phineas!' she cried soon afterwards. 'I have found an eye!'

Phineas, incredulous, joined her, and looked at the spot her pointing finger indicated. 'I see nothing of the sort.'

Ilsevel prodded the eye in question with her foot. The ground here was bare — if ground it was — and though the light was too low to be certain, it did have something of the appearance of weathered skin. 'I think it is an eye,' she insisted, 'closed at present. Have you anything sharp about you?'

She received a suspicious stare, and good Phineas took a step back from her. 'You are not going to put out the eye?'

'Gracious, no! I am only going to stab the sleeper a bit, to see if he wakes up.'

'We are standing on his face,' Phineas reminded her.

'So you do believe me!'

'Whether I do or not,' said Phineas steadily, 'if you are right, we are standing on his *face*. Are you sure you want him to wake up?'

'I am persuaded we will not much rouse him. He has practically taken root here.'

Phineas raised a disapproving brow, but he did produce a short knife from one of his pockets, and handed it to her. 'Stab away.'

Ilsevel immediately sank the point of the knife into the maybe-face, not too far from the possible-eye.

Perhaps she had not *truly* believed in her own surmise, for when the eye snapped open, revealing a pale-blue eyeball the size of a four-horse carriage, she squeaked and took a great jump backwards — almost toppling Phineas in the process.

'Steady,' he said, catching her fast, and setting her back upon her feet.

'Thank you,' said Ilsevel quietly, and then, in ringing tones, uttered, 'We bid you good day, sir!'

A second eye opened, and the pair blinked sleepily.

'We are here to bargain with you, sir!' proclaimed Ilsevel, and took up a station atop the sloping ridge that could only be a nose. 'You *are* Gilligold, I suppose?' she said, suddenly anxious, lest they had stumbled into quite the wrong mountain-sized man.

A rumbling began in the great giant's chest, followed by a tearing cough; the ground jerked and shuddered, and Ilsevel almost fell off her perch. 'Who calls my name?' said a booming, earthy voice, and the hill echoed with the sound.

'Lady Silver,' said Ilsevel proudly. 'I am a princess of Aylfenhame, sir, and I am here to retrieve the articles you have most disgracefully stolen from the Court-at-Mirramay!'

Phineas gave a slight cough. 'Perhaps a more conciliating approach?' he said in an undertone.

'Nonsense!' she said firmly. 'A villain must answer for his crimes!'

'My good lady,' rumbled Gilligold. 'How very small you are.'

Ilsevel stamped her foot upon his nose. 'In fact, sir, it is you who has grown vast.'

The eyeballs swivelled as Gilligold looked about himself. 'How did there come to be so much sky?' he complained. 'And so little of anything else?'

'You have stolen too much, and grown too big. It is, therefore, quite your own doing.'

Gilligold accepted this placidly. His eyes began to drift shut. 'At least I am comfortable,' he said drowsily.

'I am inclined to think that you are not,' said Ilsevel, and stamped again upon his nose. 'There is naught beneath you but solid rock, sir, and you have not even a blanket against this chill night air! Should you not like to be a little smaller?'

The eyes opened again. 'Perhaps I might, at that.'

'Then you will give back to me the articles you stole from Her Majesty's Court.'

'I?' said Gilligold in an injured tone. 'I do not steal.'

'Then you have acquired all these things from somebody who does, which amounts to the same thing,' said Ilsevel, beginning to grow impatient. 'Come now, will you not give them to me? You could hardly miss them, so well-supplied with treasures as you are.'

'Am I?' said Gilligold sleepily, and shut his eyes again.

Ilsevel brandished the knife, and would have driven it into his nose without compunction, save that Phineas caught at her arm. 'My lady,' he said. 'Don't forget your sister's note.'

He is fond of treasures, it had said. Well, yes. Of course he was.

But it had also contained two objects.

Ilsevel retrieved the bundle of cloth from her bodice.

'Perhaps you might consider a trade,' she said, and pricked the tip of his nose with her knife.

The eyes flew open. 'Have you brought treasures?'

Ilsevel held her two prizes before his eyes: the withered grass, and the shrivelled piece of apple.

A blink. 'And what are these pitiful things, that they should equal the Queen's Hoard in worth?'

'This,' said Ilsevel, holding up the silvery grass, 'was gathered from the throne of my noble grandmother, the queen Titania, when she ruled over all of Aylfenhame. And this—' she held up the apple '— is an apple gathered from the Goblin King's own enchanted orchard, in the days before it was lost. Artefacts of vast power, and much more useful to *you* than my sister's old ball gown.'

'Done!' said Gilligold.

This took Ilsevel aback, for she had expected some argument, or at least a little bargaining. Were they so very valuable as all that? Ought she to have offered only one? She felt a sense of foreboding, for perhaps she ought not to put *two* such articles of power into the hands of one such as Gilligold.

It was too late, however, for the grass and the apple were gone from her hands; Gilligold had taken them already. She felt the ground buckle under her feet as he, rather horribly, smiled — and seemed to go back to sleep.

'Wait!' she called. 'My sister's treasures!'

'Just knock upon the caches,' rumbled Gilligold, without opening his eyes. 'They will answer to you.'

He spoke and moved no more.

'If this is what Torpor looks like,' said Ilsevel, peering at his great, slumbering face with a perverse fascination, 'I do not at all want to try it.'

Phineas took her hand, and pulled her away. 'Come, before he changes his mind.'

He ran, and Ilsevel followed.

'Why did that work?' Phineas said, as they traversed the rumpled swell of Gilligold's gigantic belly. 'He traded all the Queen's Hoard for a handful of grass!'

'Grass that once grew upon the throne of the most powerful — and, I may as well add, most famous — faerie queen there ever was,' Ilsevel reminded him. 'And those apples were true marvels, every one of them. The Kings of Gadrahst — the Goblinlands, that is — once possessed an enchanted orchard, and every fruit that grew upon every tree held some magical property that might be harnessed only by eating some part of its flesh. I cannot tell you how many desirable enchantments might be wrought with such articles. Gilligold has more jewels and gold than he could ever need or use, and appears to be so bored by them that he has drifted off altogether.'

'And what will he do with the grass, and the apple?'

Ilsevel tried to appear unconcerned, though the same concern gnawed at her. 'At present he appears content to sleep on the matter.'

They had reached the path by this time, and increased their pace, the ground being reassuringly solid under their feet. Soon they came upon the quartz-bound caches again. Ilsevel fell upon the nearest, the one containing Anthelaena's hair-comb, and rapped smartly upon it.

The quartz melted away at her touch, and she seized the comb.

'Quickly,' she said, possessed by an inexplicable urgency. Perhaps it was the sense of near completion, the fact that her sister's restoration might be imminently achievable; whatever it was, she was suddenly unwilling to lose so much as a single unnecessary instant.

She tore from cache to cache, wresting free their contents, until at last her own hands and Phineas's were filled with Anthelaena's glittering treasures.

Back to the Door they ran, the roses and hellebores and moonflowers bobbing at Ilsevel's waist, and the jug of ice-wine swaying from Phineas's shoulder. The Door still stood open; they burst through it and kept on running, to the indignation of Nigmenog and Gollumpus. 'Now, now!' called Nigmenog as they tore past him. 'Is that polite? I should think not! Come back here!'

They did not pause, not until they had reached the shining silver bridge. There they stopped, all at once, because the bridge was no longer empty: the dark shape of an unknown person stood there.

Surprised into silence, and alarmed lest someone should have come to take the Queen's Hoard away again, Ilsevel could only clutch Anthelaena's harp and doll and shoe-roses to her chest, panting for breath. 'Who—' she began.

'Don't stop *there*,' said the figure with Tyllanthine's voice. 'The coach will be here any moment.'

The figure was indeed robed, and the shape of the hood was familiar. Ilsevel let out a sigh of relief. 'We have got everything,' she told her sister, holding out her hands to show off the proof.

But Phineas hung back. 'I have heard much about Glamours lately,' he said. 'Are you sure this is Tyllanthine?'

'Oh, for *goodness'* sake,' snapped Tyllanthine. 'Are you still carting this mushroom about?'

'No doubt about it,' said Ilsevel acidly, though she felt an unaccountable surge of affection for her irascible sister as she spoke. 'There was never anyone to match her for venom.'

Eloquent in silence, Tyllanthine turned her back upon her sister.

And then came the carriage speeding up to the bridge, bright with promise and starlight. It drew up near to Ilsevel, and the doors opened invitingly.

'Get in!' said Tyllanthine. 'No time to lose! All has been made ready, but if we do not make haste we will be honoured with some *most* undesirable guests and I should not like to have to kill anybody today.'

'Where are we going?' said Ilsevel as she dashed for the carriage, clutching Anthelaena's precious treasures to her chest.

'Why, to Mirramay, of course! They are waiting for us.'

CHAPTER TWENTY-FOUR

If Ilsevel had been disposed to resent Tyllanthine for leaving her sister and Phineas to encounter all the risks of Warethorn Rose, she was shortly obliged to reconsider, for Tyllanthine certainly had not been idle. A succession of coaches brought the victorious party to the gates of Mirramay, and hastening through them shortly afterwards, Ilsevel found a city transformed.

When last she had stepped through those vast, majestic gates, she had discovered her erstwhile home to be abandoned, save for rag-tag bands of darkling fae wandering hither and thither. Her heart had ached sorely at the sight of its once-grand houses tumbling down, its wide, airy streets soiled with litter and debris. The palace had been worse, far worse, for it was stripped of its treasures; what remained of its furniture was broken and worn, its upholstery hanging in tatters. Her solitary footsteps had echoed sadly through the abandoned halls, and she had not encountered a soul.

The city that now met her gaze was the Mirramay of her memory, the home of her youth, and her heart soared. The derelict buildings were, by some miraculous art (or, more likely, Glamour) restored to their former beauty; the low winter sunlight glinted off walls clad all in white, or in ice-blue and rose and pale gold, lit with great, bright, crystal-clear windows. Pearly gilding glittered here and there, and silver carving, and statuary, and the triple fountains that had marched along The Queen's Way for so many ages past were pristine and perfect, pouring streams of water into the frigid winter air. Ilsevel's hopes and spirits rose with every step, and she hastened towards the Palace, eager to discover what more marvels of restoration awaited her at her former home.

But Phineas, who had kept pace with her most of the way down The Queen's Way, had somewhere dropped back, and Ilsevel became abruptly aware of his absence. She paused, too, leaving Tyllanthine to sail on ahead, and turned back.

Phineas stood in the centre of the crossroads fifty feet back, the wide boulevard with its glittering fountains behind him. He stood agape, staring ahead at the great golden palace with an expression of... awe? No, it was not awe. As Ilsevel drew nearer, she discovered it to be something more akin to woe.

'Why so cast down, my Phineas?' she said. 'It is no great punishment to look upon such beauty, surely?'

Phineas transferred his woeful gaze from the palace to Ilsevel's face. He appeared to be trying to speak, but the words would not come. Instead, he silently held out the armful of Anthelaena's treasures which he had been so carefully guarding, gold silk-tissue trailing from his fingers.

'I cannot take them,' she said, confused, for she was too burdened herself to manage Phineas's as well. 'Why should you wish me to?'

'I... I cannot,' whispered Phineas.

'Whyever not?'

He looked about, from the honey-gold palace to the graceful spires topping the manor-houses to his right and left, and finally to the white-paved road beneath his feet. 'It is too much. I am not... this is no place for me.'

Ilsevel understood. Where she saw the familiar streets of her home city, and the beauty and grace to which she had been accustomed ever since her birth, Phineas saw an intimidating magnificence, the likes of which he had never experienced in his life.

'It is only splendour,' she said, with an encouraging smile. 'Why should you be unworthy of beauty, my Phineas?'

In answer, Phineas merely looked down at the coat he wore — splendid only because it was borrowed — and past it to the shabby trousers he wore underneath, and the muddy, cracked leather of his boots.

'Mere apparel,' she said. 'Easily resolved.'

'You'd as well dress a sparrow in jewels,' said Phineas bluntly.

'You are no mere sparrow. You are the equal of anything and anyone, Phineas, and let no one persuade you otherwise.'

'It is not my place.'

'Your *place*?' Ilsevel stared, dumbfounded, and stifled an urge to shake him. 'Your place is wherever you wish it to be, and *if* you should wish it, that place is by my side.'

He looked up, directing a searching stare at Ilsevel. 'Why?'

'Because I have declared it to be so.'

This did not much impress him, for he said nothing.

'Phineas...' said Ilsevel, more gently. 'I... I do not want to do this without you.'

He visibly wavered, then with a sigh, he took a step towards her. 'Do not forget about me,' he said, and she judged that it cost him to say it.

'I could not. Come, now, or Tyllanthine will have both our heads.'

'Do you think she needs an excuse?'

Ilsevel laughed. 'I concede the point.'

The palace was another wonder all its own, for the ancient snowleaf trees grew still in the courtyard, their trunks still clad in golden bark, though their white leaves had fallen for the winter. The twin pools were full and clear, though their blue-green and rose-lavender waters were coated in ice. Inside, many surprises awaited.

The first was that the interior had been, somehow, restored, and looked almost as it had on the day of Anthelaena's death. A fire roared in the hearth of the Great Hall, and the tapestries — from Queen Titania's day — hung once more upon the walls, their colours jewel-bright and new. The moss-and-silver carpets ran once more down the corridors, the mirrors and paintings in their iridescent frames hung once more upon the walls, and even Ilsevel's favourite chaise-longue was back in the alcove in the library, the one under the window, where she had so often retreated with a book. Going from room to room with tears in her eyes, Ilsevel could not find the words either to thank Tyllanthine, or to ask her how she had accomplished it — *where* she had found all these lost things.

Tyllanthine, uncharacteristically forthcoming, answered the unspoken question anyway. 'The Goblin Market,' she said, pointing at a pair of tall amethyst vases filled with clear water and silver fish. 'Together with most of the paintings, and some of the furniture. And then Grunewald had some, you know — for safekeeping, he swears, and that may even be the truth. Wodebean recovered some other things from the Thieves' Hollow, and from other traders of his acquaintance, and then I had reserved a few articles myself. And I divested the wretched Oleander Whiteboots of fully half of his hoard.'

Ilsevel could not speak. She could almost begin to lament Tyllanthine's thoroughness, for it began to seem that she had stepped back many years in time, to the heart-breaking days before Edironal's disappearance; before the deaths of her sister and her niece; when she had been happy, and had not known what waited in her future.

She swallowed these feelings, mustering every shred of cool composure at her disposal, and managed to say, 'You have worked wonders, Tylla.'

Tyllanthine said, 'I know. Quickly now, for we are late.'

Belatedly, Ilsevel remembered Tyllanthine's earlier words: *They are waiting for us.* 'Who awaits?' she asked, but Tyllanthine did not seem disposed to speak further, and only hastened on, leaving Ilsevel and Phineas to trail after her.

Ilsevel, recognising the passage her sister took through the winding corridors, realised that they were on their way to the throne room. So it soon proved, for Tyllanthine turned a corner, hurried up the wide, ivy-wreathed steps of the grand staircase, and unceremoniously threw open the pearl-tinted doors to the throne room.

And Ilsevel was briefly taken aback, for a great many people were gathered therein.

There was Grunewald, the Goblin King, wearing the human face he so much preferred to his own. He wore full Court regalia, and shone with power and jewels. Next to him stood a human girl with dark hair and bright black eyes, clad in similarly splendid attire; she looked quite at home there. A young Ayliri woman stood on the other side of the room, dressed in the enchanted attire of a princess; puzzled at first, Ilsevel realised, with a shock, that this was Lihyaen, for she had her mother's clear golden eyes. She was grown now, no longer the child Ilsevel had known; she looked hale and well, but tense, and Ilsevel longed to go to her. But she was flanked by a motley band of humans, half-humans and Ayliri, and even an unusually well-dressed brownie; Ilsevel recognised none of them, and they were too thickly crowded around the princess to admit of Ilsevel's approach.

There were others in the crowd that she knew: Mr. Balligumph, for one. That tall figure rising so far above the heads of the rest could only be the tree-giant, Sir Guntifer Winlowe, a favoured courtier and Palace Guard of her grandmother's. Wodebean had taken up a position in a shadowed corner, recognisable only by the characteristic red of his mantle, and the hunch of his shoulders. She saw Iseult and Valiel, two of her sister's ladies-in-waiting; her own friend Lady Galdrin, statuesque in an emerald gown and white, bejewelled wig; the pixies Wyn and Hedwig, once the haunts of the gardens; and almost every household brownie that had ever attended upon the palace.

A full company of the Palace Guard surrounded the great, glass throne, each resplendent in the mulberry-velvet coats and silver braid of their ceremonial uniform — though the swords belted at their waists were not at all for show, nor were the bright spears each guard held in their left hand.

Upon the throne itself, in the centre of the wide, plush cushion of silvery velvet, was the purple-furred cat. The creature was far larger than a cat had any right to be, and was curled up comfortably there, apparently fast asleep.

Distantly, Ilsevel discovered a new memory of this cat: the recollection burst upon her all at once. She had glimpsed the creature as a frog, when she had yet to be freed from her own transforming curse; the cat had seemed far larger, then. She had sniffed at Ilsevel's frog-face, and stuck out her tongue; licked Ilsevel from head to tail-stub; and then darted away. It had not been many days later when the hob-woman had arrived, with her potions and her cures, and restored Ilsevel to her natural shape.

No mere chance after all, then. Ilsevel's recovery had been Anthelaena's doing.

Tyllanthine bustled up to the throne, oblivious of her ragged robes among all the Queen's splendour. In a gesture of unusual tenderness, she laid a withered hand briefly along the cat's head as she passed. Anthelaena awoke — and began, with deliberate care, to wash one of her paws with her long, rough tongue.

Ilsevel began to see the trouble. For though Anthelaena obviously recollected some part of her past — she had found Ilsevel, after all, and known her in some, vague way — she did not in the least resemble a Queen of Aylfenhame anymore. She looked all cat, as comfortable in the shape as any feline born to it, and though her throne-room was crowded with her own friends and family, lords and ladies, handmaidens and servants and guards, she paid as little heed to any of them as might a cat born and bred.

It would take a great deal to remind her of who she really was.

'Ilse!' snapped Tyllanthine. 'Hurry.'

Hurry. Yes, because though the palace appeared filled with friends, that did not preclude the possibility of there being enemies abroad, too. The sooner Anthelaena was restored to herself, the better. Ilsevel wrested herself free of her tangled thoughts, and stepped smartly up to the throne.

Tyllanthine had acquired her own armful of treasures, gleaned, perhaps, from the Markets and the Hollows and from Grunewald. She held up a glove of cloud-like lace and it rose obediently to hover above the throne. A necklace of rainwater-pearls followed it, and that was all; Tyllanthine, empty-handed, advanced upon Phineas.

That would not do.

Ilsevel intercepted her, and thrust Anthelaena's harp and shoe-roses and pocket-watch into her sister's arms, and then the cat-shaped doll. She turned to Phineas herself, and divested him of the starlit armband, the orchid comb and the mist-beribboned gown more gently than Tyllanthine would have done. He looked ready to vanish straight into the crowd, but she held him with a look. 'The jug,' she said. 'We will need it shortly.'

'I will leave it here.'

'I will need *you* shortly.'

He blinked at that, more consternated than pleased, but she did not have time to explain or to argue. She returned to Tyllanthine, and set the rest of the Queen's Hoard into airy orbit around Anthelaena's recumbent person.

Then came the flowers. The velvet queen parasols she put into Tyllanthine's hands; the blooms she carried to the throne itself. They required no coaxing whatsoever. When she took up the sunlit rose and held it to the glass, a stem sprouted at once; leaves burst forth, and silver thorns, and within moments a rose-vine was snaking its way around the throne's clear-glass frame, putting forth golden buds. The moonglow-rose performed the same feat; hellebores twined about the legs and carpeted the ground; the dewberries and moonflowers blanketed the arms and the seat; and soon little of the throne could be seen beneath its viridian mantle.

Through all of this, Anthelaena continued to bathe herself, oblivious.

Ilsevel retrieved the jug from Phineas, and poured ice-wine out into the air. It emerged in a glittering, frosty stream and began to whirl, making of itself an icy goblet brim-full of wine. To this Tyllanthine added powders and plants: another wisp of faerie-grass went in, along with the parasol-mushrooms; a fresh, white snowleaf; a dewdrop of water from each of the pools in the palace courtyard; a golden hair, which could only be one of Anthelaena's own; a sparkling tear, probably Lihyaen's; and, incongruously, a tiny cake, cloud-like and frosted. Anthelaena's favourite.

As each item left Tyllanthine's fingers it vanished into the icy goblet without trace, as though it had never been. But each added its potency to the brew, for a light grew steadily from the depths of the wine and overflowed, lambent with every colour. 'It is ready,' whispered Tyllanthine, but when Ilsevel would have turned at once and delivered the goblet to the sleeping queen, Tyllanthine bid her pause. She raised a hand, and gestured, and Wodebean came forward from his shadowed corner. He had an Aylir man with him: Ilsevel recognised the fellow as Indalon, the Court Physician. Part doctor, part enchanter, he'd had the care of Anthelaena and Tyllanthine and Ilsevel since they were children. When Ilsevel had last seen him, he had been haggard and distraught, unable to cure the poison that ravaged the queen.

He was serene now, but he had aged more than he ought. His hair, once a lively chestnut-brown, was white through-and-through, and he had the stooped shoulders of a man who had lived long and borne much. He met Ilsevel's eye as he approached the throne, and dipped his head.

Not before she had seen a trace of anxiety there.

That sobered her. When Anthelaena had taken the cat's shape, she had been near-dead with disease — or, as Ilsevel now knew, with the effects of the poison administered by Wodebean. So many years as a cat, a creature immune to the venom, ought to have cured her; certainly she displayed no signs of illness. But what if it had not?

'My Lady Silver,' said Wodebean in a low voice — prompted,

perhaps, by the darkling look Ilsevel had not been able to help directing at him. 'Indalon has worked year after year upon the matter of the Queen's ailment. Upon receiving information from me, he has developed... a possible cure.'

Possible. Ilsevel's heart froze at the word. If the transformation had only suspended the progress of the poison, not eradicated it entirely, what were they all about to do to Anthelaena? Would she return to her rightful shape, only to sicken and die? Would Indalon's cure, if it were such, be enough to save her?

Courage, she told herself sternly. Would they leave Anthelaena forever a cat, for fear of the consequences of restoring her? No. Unthinkable. It was impossible to do otherwise than to proceed.

But it was Phineas's face that steadied her, for he had not gone. He stood, silent and staunch, at the front of the crowd surrounding the throne, and he looked back at her with the kind of calm, steady faith that she needed. What would Phineas do, in her shoes? Why, he would go steadily on, and so must she.

Lihyaen came forward, and Grunewald. That the Goblin King made so prominent a display of his presence seemed to Ilsevel highly significant; what greater show of loyalty to his fellow monarch could he make? And he was not merely showing his face. With him came all the power of the Goblin Court, and he willingly lent it to Anthelaena now. Proud, wild Grunewald knelt in symbolic fealty before the queen's throne, and his power wreathed Anthelaena in a mantle of dark fire.

Lihyaen knelt before her mother — and so, incredibly, did Tyllanthine. There came a rustling and swishing throughout the throne-room as all those gathered went to their knees before their lost queen.

It fell to Ilsevel to set the goblet of ice before her beleaguered sister, and to coax her to drink. Indalon and Wodebean hovered at her elbow; the physician held three crystal phials in his hands, each filled with a differently coloured liquid. One of them bubbled and frothed.

Ilsevel wished, desperately and devoutly, that he would not be called upon to use them.

For a moment it appeared as though Anthelaena would continue in a state of obliviousness, for she barely glanced at the cup set before her. She began, with studious gravity, to wash her left ear.

'Felebre,' said Tyllanthine, sharply.

This was a name the cat-that-was-once-Anthelaena recognised as her own, for she looked at Tyllanthine, ears forward, alert.

'Drink,' ordered Tyllanthine.

The cat lowered her nose to the goblet, took a cautious sniff, and to Ilsevel's relief she began to lap at the cold, intoxicating, enchanted wine contained therein. She did not like the flavour; heartily, she sneezed.

But she continued to drink.

It began as a low, silvered mist, creeping with catlike stealth over the floor of the throne room. Tendrils of it wound their way up the slender glass legs of Anthelaena's throne, growing thicker and brighter with light and magic and hope, until it reached the cat's great paws.

No one breathed.

Anthelaena had finished the contents of the goblet and now sat, tall and serene. Did she know what was occurring in that moment? Was she Anthelaena in her mind, or Felebre still? There was no telling; her clear golden eyes were hazy, whether with sleep or enchantment Ilsevel could not have said. She blinked, thrice.

A heady fragrance enveloped the throne, and it was not just the mingled aromas of the roses and hellebores. Taking a long, slow breath, Ilsevel detected the familiar scent of those cakes Anthelaena so much liked; of the fragrance her sister had so often chosen to wear; the smell of fresh dew on the grass outside the breakfast-parlour window, where she and Ilsevel had so often eaten together; even the achingly familiar scent of her hair.

Anthelaena recognised these scents, too, for her nose lifted to the air and she inhaled deeply. Her tail began to lash, and she sneezed, three times, so hard as to set her whole body a-shake.

And then, at last, she began to change. Her body lengthened and grew; the silky purple fur faded and became skin, pale and clear; her tail vanished, her ears shrank and disappeared beneath tousled, pale golden hair. Only the colour of her eyes remained the same: rich, liquid gold, like a summer afternoon.

She was beloved Anthelaena again, and Ilsevel could barely see her for the tears that blurred her vision and poured down her cheeks.

'Anthela,' she gasped, and all but hurled herself upon her sister.

She was not alone in doing so, for Lihyaen had been of the same mind. Even Tyllanthine, losing some part of her customary aloofness, was disposed to embrace her.

'*Please*,' came an unfamiliar, male voice, cutting through the growing clamour sweeping across the throne-room. 'Let me reach Her Majesty.'

It belonged to Indalon, and Ilsevel felt shamed, for in her joy and relief she had not thought. Of *course* the physician must see the queen, and at once. But Anthelaena knew her! She had reached for Ilsevel, even as Ilsevel was reaching for her; their hands had touched; and Ilsevel had looked into those golden eyes and seen, at last, clear recognition, and all the love she had so long missed. Painful it was, to tear herself away, and cede her place to Indalon and Wodebean. But she must. She stepped back, and felt Lihyaen's hand creeping into her own instead. This she gripped, for mutual comfort, and waited.

Anthelaena looked hale. Nothing about her seemed wasted or faded. Her skin held the glow of good health, her pale hair was shining and thick, and her eyes were rapidly losing their cloud of confusion. Nonetheless, Ilsevel held her breath as Indalon made a close examination of the queen, conferring in a low voice with Wodebean all the while.

Anthelaena bore this patiently, and answered those questions put to her with all the serenity she had always used to display. But the physician lingered rather long, and a glint of mischief crept into her face.

'Gentlemen,' she said, in her low, measured voice. 'Be assured I shall *not* die. I do not feel particularly in the mood, just at present.'

'Your Majesty,' faltered the physician, and exchanged an uncertain glance with Wodebean.

But the hobgoblin was smiling. 'When does Your Majesty expect to feel in the mood?' he enquired.

'Not for a great while!' pronounced Anthelaena, and got to her feet. Unused to her two legs after so long with four, she was observed to wobble; but being Anthelaena, even this she did with grace. She was splendidly unclad, but this inconvenienced her not one whit, for the dreamy mists which had effected her transformation clung to her still. She stood tall, wreathed in the power of her kingdom and Grunewald's, her eyes alight with joy and sunshine and her hair anointed with stars.

Then she laughed, and spun, and rose smoothly into the air.

'Come, come!' she called, and with a flick of her fingers sent moonflowers bursting up the walls. 'Have we not suffered enough? No more a long face! I bid you all be merry, for I am returned, and I shall *live!*'

The throne-room erupted into cheers, and mirth, and well-wishes, and the chatter of excited speculation. Ilsevel was no less vocal among them, for she could have sung her heart out with joy.

Then Anthelaena descended in a whirling rush, and in another moment she was in Ilsevel's arms, fair squeezing the breath out of her sister's body with the force of her embrace. 'I missed you *so much,*' she gasped, and Ilsevel, wordless, could only hold her and weep all over again.

Few sought their beds in Mirramay that night. Tyllanthine and Grunewald's preparations had not been limited to the transformation of the palace, the preparation of the throne-room, and the gathering of the Court. They had also, with fine optimism, given orders for a grand feast to be held in the great dining-hall. Lyrriant the Piper was in attendance, flanked by fiddlers and drummers and singers and many more. The hall rang with music and merriment; there was feasting and dancing all the night long; and through it all the restored queen scarcely sat still for three minutes together. Her feet would carry her this way and that, and she went darting from sister to daughter to courtier to friend and all around again, delighted by her reunion with them all. Everywhere she trod, pale hellebores sprouted in the wake of her passage.

She more often returned to Ilsevel than to any other. The bond between them had always been boundless, and it was there still, as strong as ever, as though it had never been severed at all. It felt as though Ilsevel had lost an arm, but had grown so used to its absence that she had ceased to notice it at all — until it was abruptly restored. Now, she could not imagine how she had ever contrived to manage without it.

Tyllanthine was not forgotten. With the falling of night, Tylla's hag-visage had dropped away, leaving her in all the glory of her beauteous glamour, and in that guise she took the greatest pride in sitting with her sisters at the head of the Queen's Table. Between them, there was so much to be said that some hours passed away in conversation.

It was only much later, when half the Court was dancing waltzes to the tune of Lyrriant's pipes and the other half engaged in dispatching the ice-wines and honey-meads and other fine beverages afforded by the palace's pantries (or, more likely, from the stores of the Goblin Court), that Tyllanthine looked about her and said: 'I see you have shaken off that boy.'

Ilsevel froze, horror turning her limbs to water. 'Phineas,' she muttered, and leapt out of her seat. 'Where is he? He cannot be gone!'

'He has been gone these two hours at least,' said Tyllanthine, with splendid indifference. 'I thought you must have sent him away.' She expressed the idea with obvious approval, which only heightened Ilsevel's dismay.

Of course she had not dismissed Phineas, but what she had done was almost as bad. *Do not forget me,* he had pleaded, afraid that he would drown in all the splendour and chaos of the Court. And, for a little while, she had.

'My dear Ilsevellian,' said Anthelaena, concern underlying the playful mirth of her words. 'Who, pray, is Phineas? A boy! Is he handsome? I should like to meet him.'

'He is my friend,' said Ilsevel, and had not time for more, for she had gathered up her skirts and set off at a run. He was nowhere in the banquet-hall, and he was not outside; he was not among the maze of corridors, nor had he lingered in the throne-room. He could not be found in the kitchens or out in the courtyard or, in short, anywhere at all. He was gone.

'Are you looking for Mr. Drake?' came Wodebean's voice from somewhere near at hand.

Ilsevel whirled, and found him concealed, as ever, in a shadowy corner. 'For Phin— yes, for Mr. Drake. Have you seen him?'

He had found her in the courtyard, pacing restlessly back and forth between the two frozen pools, consumed with confused self-reproach. How could she have forgotten Phineas? Deplorable. But how could she so soon leave Anthelaena? Impossible.

'He has gone back into England,' said Wodebean. 'Mr. Balligumph called the ferry for him.'

'The ferry?' echoed Ilsevel. 'Do the ferries fly again?'

'Only one, yet, I believe. But with Her Majesty returned, perhaps others will be commissioned.'

'Very good. I shall go to the bell.' The bell in question hung by the city gates. Wrought from crystal and wreathed in enchantment, its clear tones pealed across the skies when rung, summoning the nearest ferry-boat.

'The bell has not yet been restored,' said Wodebean, halting Ilsevel in the process of striding away.

'Oh,' said she, dismayed. For she *must* go after Phineas; that fact did not long admit of any doubt. But how was she to get into England? It was not the Solstice, nor any of the Feasting Days, so the gates would all be closed. And if the ferry could not be summoned either, then what was she to do?

Wodebean regarded her in silence. At length he said: 'It may not be wise to leave Her Majesty, Lady Silver. She has not yet taken up all her scattered power, and is in a vulnerable state. And news of this night's work will spread. Enemies will gather about the Court, as they have before.'

Ilsevel bit her lip. 'I know,' she said. 'But I cannot neglect Phineas. Anthelaena is presently surrounded by every possible ally, and she is well-guarded. And I will not be away long! She will scarcely have time to notice my absence.' Ilsevel meant every word, for she would not consent to be long parted from Anthelaena now.

'Shall you not?' said Wodebean tonelessly. 'What do you mean to do?'

'I mean only to retrieve Phineas, and come straight back.'

That these words did not quite find favour with Wodebean was evident from his silence. But he did not choose to argue with her, nor to explain what fault he had to find with her plan. Instead he simply held out his hand. In his palm there rested a delicate whistle, made from the same iridescent crystal as the bell that had once hung at the gates. 'I will need this back, My Lady Silver.'

'You shall have it.' Ilsevel snatched up the whistle, paused only to express the depths of her gratitude to Wodebean, and blew a sharp blast upon it.

Something roiled among the moonlit clouds at once; great billows of air came spiralling down; and then a ship appeared, its single sail flying proudly, and swept airily down to land not far from Ilsevel.

A gangplank dropped, with a smooth *swish*, from the boat, and the captain came smartly down it: an Aylir woman clad in trousers and a blue coat, her dark hair bound in braids. 'Where to?' she said cheerfully, and only belatedly realised to whom she was talking; then she made Ilsevel a crisp bow. 'Lady Silver!'

'To England, please!' said Ilsevel. She strode without hesitation up the gangway, and took up a station near the front of the boat. The captain whistled, the winds gathered and whirled, and the ferry sailed off once more into the skies.

CHAPTER TWENTY-FIVE

I need hardly tell ye wi' what joy I witnessed Anthelaena's return. The realm has sorely felt her absence! Nowt can thrive in Aylfenhame wi' no Majesty upon the throne, an' t' watch it dwindle an' wither — well, it's been breakin' this old troll's heart fer many a year. Not t' mention that Anthelaena herself could never have warranted such a fate. Good folk deserve better.

Speakin' of good folk, I took Mr. Phineas home right enow. He weren't happy. Wrung my heart, it did, t' leave him, wi' no one t' welcome him home, an' no one t' care fer him. But I had a notion tha' Her Ladyship Silver was in need of a little thinkin' time — and mayhap a bit of a kick, so to speak. There's no worthier heart than that of young Mr. Drake, an' I thought — I hoped — that she knew it.

Well, and so. While Aylfenhame rejoiced at the return o' the Queen, an' the land itself unfurled t' welcome her back, My Lady Silver was wingin' her way back t' England...

In the chaos and excitement of his journey through the Hollows, and the Queen's restoration to Mirramay, Phineas had almost forgotten the fate of his father's bakery. Brought face-to-face with its boarded-up frontage upon his return, he felt all the impact of its closure anew. Perhaps some part of him had hoped he might find his father waiting for him; that the elder Mr. Drake might have reconsidered, and come back for Phineas after all.

He had not.

Dawn was breaking as he stood there, staring in renewed dismay at the remains of his home. He could not, now he thought about it, remember when he had last slept, and his limbs were so heavy he had to exert an extraordinary effort to drag himself around to the back, up the stairs, and in at the back door. He struggled to think.

Not thinking about Ilsevel — that must be his priority. As he opened the shutters in the kitchens and the pantry, laboriously pulled off his borrowed coat (could it ever be returned to Mr. Dapper?), pulled on his apron, and began to mix dough, he was careful not to think of her at all. He did not think of her as he reflected upon how, without Lady Silver's help, he might contrive to restore the coat to its rightful owner. He did not think of her as he remembered the cloudy cakes her sister so much enjoyed, which he had sampled at the banquet and might contrive to recreate. He absolutely did not picture her face as he added sugar and spices to his dough, and only belatedly recalled that his ovens were cold and dark and he could not bake it; that the shop had been closed for some days, and would have no customers even if he could; and that, by now, the new pastry-shop must be open only a few doors up the hill, and his labours were no longer required.

These successive realisations were enough to finish him.

Some hours later, he was seated still on a stool in the stone-cold kitchen, head upon the table, exhausted but unable to sleep, when there came an insistent knocking upon the window. The sound roused him enough to sit up, but not enough to drive him from his stool. He remained there, shivering and befuddled, until the street-door opened and Ilsevel appeared.

'Phineas!' she said, and went to him directly. He found his hands taken and pressed, and her beautiful eyes filled with concern and remorse as she looked into his face. 'Phineas, how can I possibly express how sorry I am? I did *not* forget you, or I did not mean to, only there was so much to think of — so much to concern me — no, I should not try to explain. Nothing can excuse it.'

Phineas studied the table. Its roughened surface briefly entranced him, and he occupied himself in tracing its convoluted whorls with his eyes; it was easier, and safer, than having to look at Ilsevel. 'Do not regard it,' he said. 'You had much to occupy you, and I had no claim on your attention.'

'But you *did*, Phineas,' said Ilsevel. 'You do. Come, the ferry is waiting for us.'

He looked up at that, his brow clouding. 'The ferry?'

'It will take us immediately back into Mirramay. Is there anything in particular you wish to take with you? Shall I help you to pack it up?'

'My Lady Silver,' said Phineas slowly. 'What can have put it into your mind that I would go back to Mirramay with you?'

She faltered. 'You... shall not you?'

He withdrew his hands from hers, gestured around at the drab, cold kitchen in which he sat. 'This is my world. Yours could not be more different, could it?'

'But there is a place for you there, my Phineas. With me.' She looked ready to take his hands again, but Phineas kept them out of her reach.

'There is not,' he said quietly. 'Not with you. I might take up a place in your kitchen, perhaps, and bake your favourite sweets, but that is not — that — I would rather—' He paused, and swallowed down the terrible words that had hovered on the edge of being spoken. 'I thank you, your highness,' he said, more calmly, 'but I cannot go with you.'

'I would not send you to the kitchen,' she answered, aghast.

'That is where I belong.'

He risked a look at her, for it would be the last time he would ever do so. My Lady Silver stood very close; tall and silent, impossibly beautiful as she ever was — and impossibly far beyond him. Exhausted as he was, unwashed, hungry and cold and without hope... he had never felt more unworthy.

No, that was not quite true. Watching her step up to her sister's side in the throne-room at Mirramay; seeing her wreathed in all the magic and glory of Aylfenhame, all but a queen in her own right; she had *shone*, the moon to Anthelaena's sun. He had known, then, that the Ilsevel that he had briefly known was a trick of the light, an illusion he could keep only for a little while. She was Ilsevellian, My Lady Silver, and he was only Phineas Drake.

'Must I beg you?' she said softly.

'*Please*,' he said, driven off his stool at last; he backed away from her, creating as much distance as he could before his back hit the wall. 'Please, do not torment me.' Her very presence was enough, and he prayed that he would not be obliged to see her again — even as he desperately hated the prospect of her eternal absence.

She bowed her head. 'Of course,' she said, and retreated towards the door. 'Accept my apologies, Phineas.'

The door blew in the wind, and she was gone; gone before Phineas could muster a reply.

Something twinkled upon the table where he had sat. A rose lay there: the very same one he had picked up off the street, after his first glimpse of her. How long ago it seemed.

He collected the rose, handling it with reverence, and laid it tenderly upon the window-sill.

Then he went upstairs to his dark, half-frozen bedchamber, and put himself to bed.

Some days later, an altered Mr. Drake stood in a different kitchen, scrubbed and attired in a fresh, new apron. He was no longer alone, for two apprentices rather younger than he worked under his supervision, and he himself was overseen by Mr. Waller, the proprietor. The new pastry-shop had indeed opened, and upon application Phineas had been quickly taken up as an employee.

It had cost him sorely to do so, for it had meant giving up: on his father's bakery, where he had lived and worked his whole life through, and on his father also. Not a word of the elder Mr. Drake's whereabouts had he been able to discover, and not a word from him had he received. He had disappeared without trace — leaving, to Phineas's horror, a debt-burdened property behind him. The Drake Bakery was gone, given into new hands.

For a few days, Phineas had welcomed the change in his circumstances, for it had always soothed him to engage in productive labour. To mix and knead and shape and bake; these were things he could do. These were simple things, but useful. They brought him peace.

But as he grew accustomed to the new pattern of his days, that hard-won feeling of peace left him. His wayward mind *would* stray, whisking him away from the settled course of his day and landing him back in all the glorious madness, the shining unpredictability, of the Hollows, and of Aylfenhame. He tried to talk of his experiences, and found himself branded a liar, or a fool; he soon learned to hold his tongue, to revisit those days only in the privacy of his own mind.

He tried not to. To think of magic and mystery and beauty could only hurt him, for no more marked a contrast could there be between that whirl of enchantment and the simpler life that lay before him. No farther removed could he feel from the strange beauty of the Hollows, and the majesty of Mirramay; from the joviality of Mr. Balligumph, and Wodebean's intrigue; Mr. Dapper's natty pomposity, the staunch loyalty of the Garden Warders; the infuriating mystery of Tyllanthine, and the utter glory of Lady Silver.

And if he was severed from it forever, it was his own doing.

There had not been a doubt in his mind or heart, when he had sent Ilsevel away. He had looked at her and seen only an impossible dream, but he had not looked closely enough. Wrapped up in his own misery, too shattered to reflect clearly, it had not occurred to him — not until it was far too late — that she had not asked him out of guilt, or pity. She had looked upon him with a genuine concern, which owed nothing to remorse. She had pleaded — might have done more so, if he had let her. She had looked on him with… with love. Had he imagined it? No.

And he had sent her away.

Perhaps he had not known his place, once removed from the familiar patterns of English life; but, perhaps he had not needed one. Perhaps he could make a space for himself, somewhere in between the kitchens and the palace. What might not be possible, in Aylfenhame?

But it was too late. He had closed those doors forever, too consumed with his own inferiority to give it a chance. And for what? His shop was lost, his family destroyed, and the few prospects left to him brought him no joy.

He suffered under these mortifying realisations for some four or five days, and then he made up his mind. That evening, when Mr. Waller's pastry-shop closed up for the night and its employees scattered to the winds, Phineas packed up his few possessions, donned Mr. Dapper's delicious coat (which he had not dared to do since his return from Mirramay), and set out for the coaching-inn upon the hill. He waited all night for the stage to leave, and when at last it did he was on it.

By the middle of the following morning, he arrived in Tilby; on foot, weary, cold and terribly hungry, but alive with anticipation and hope — and fear.

The bridge was as he remembered, arching over the icy river on the outskirts of the town. He walked into the centre of it, cleared his chilled throat, and called tentatively: 'Mr. Balligumph?'

'Aye!' came the troll's deep voice at once, and the toll-keeper himself immediately appeared. He grinned cheerfully at sight of Phineas, which had a heartening effect upon his spirits. Phineas smiled back.

'Good morning, sir,' he said. 'I, um, came in hopes that you might… help me.'

'Is it My Lady Silver?' said the troll.

Uncomfortably aware of the flush that spread over his cheeks, Phineas nodded. 'She — she came back for me, you see, but — well, she had forgotten me, before that, and I was — that is — I sent her away,' he finished miserably.

If he had feared to receive an uncongenial response from Mr. Balligumph, he need not have wasted his cares, for the troll nodded sympathetically and fell into a brief rumination. 'It is difficult, when ye first visit Aylfenhame,' he said, seating himself comfortably upon the bridge. 'An' ye have had the fortune an' misfortune t' find yerself in mighty high company! I don't wonder that it knocked ye fer six.'

'That's it, sir, indeed,' said Phineas.

'Is it that ye want t' go after Her Ladyship?'

Though he had journeyed to Tilby with no other purpose, Phineas felt consumed with shyness, and studiously eyed the floor. 'Would it be so absurd?'

'She invited ye, did she not?'

'Y-yes, she did, but what if she…' He paused, and thought. 'Can she *truly* want me?'

'Why should she not? Now—' Mr. Balligumph held up a great, blue hand to forestall Phineas's immediate response. 'Give me no guff about yer status an' hers. There may be fine lords aplenty at the Court, an' there'll be more t' come — but she didn't ask any of *them*, did she? An' she never has. Did ye know that My Lady Silver's unassailability was once legend at Mirramay?'

Dumbfounded, Phineas could only shake his head.

Balligumph chuckled. 'Oh, aye. Courted time and again, she was, an' never so much as a flicker of interest did she show. I've a sense she has no taste fer grandeur, Mr. Drake, an' the high an' mighty ideas tha' so often come with it. What she wants is a fellow wi' a good heart on 'im, and thas you.'

'I'm a baker's boy,' said Phineas softly.

'No. Ye're Mr. Drake, a fine young man as happens t' have a talent fer confectionery. What else ye may choose t' be in Aylfenhame, well, thas up to you.'

These words filled Phineas with such hope, he could almost have embraced the troll. But the happy feelings were gone again almost at once, for had he not destroyed his chances with Ilsevel? Nothing could have been colder than his manner of parting with her! He had not even said goodbye.

He said some of this.

But Mr. Balligumph waved it away. 'Here,' he said, and pulled something glittering from a pocket in his brown woollen waistcoat. It was a whistle. He held it out to Phineas, who took it in wonder and surprise. 'Lady Silver — *Ilsevel*, as we shall call her, fer it's a less imposin' name — well, she left that wi' me. She said as how she hoped ye might change yer mind, an' she wanted you t' have a way back.'

Phineas clutched the whistle in a hand that shook, unable, for a moment, to speak. 'She left this for *me*?'

'Aye, an' mighty cast down she was by yer rejection, I can tell you.' The kindly troll's tusks spread wide as he smiled upon Phineas, a twinkle in his eyes. 'Go on wi' ye, now. She's waitin'.'

Phineas, a stream of disjointed thanks pouring from his lips, embraced the troll after all, and ran out into the bare earthen field beyond the bridge. Raising the whistle to his lips, he blew hard, and a fierce wind at once blew up to swirl around his feet.

'Mind ye come back t' visit now an' then!' called the bridge-keeper, and Phineas turned to wave his assent.

Then he lifted his face to the skies, and awaited the arrival of the ferry to Aylfenhame, bringing his future with it.

There, now! A fine, happy endin' after all, which is as I like. I can tell ye tha' My Lady Silver and her Mr. Drake had some trouble at first, fer no doubt there's a gulf between them. But thas as may be. They're happy as can be, last I heard. Phineas has got a house in Mirramay, somethin' less splendid than the palace — though far finer than the shabby place as he was used to. Her Ladyship spends half her time there wi' him, and the rest at the palace wi' her sisters. It's a fine arrangement. An' if Phineas is sometimes called in t' share his expertise wi' the bakers at the palace kitchens, well, no one minds that at all — least of all Phineas. I'm persuaded nothin' will ever convince that young man t' give up bakin' altogether.

As fer Anthelaena, she's goin' on splendidly — fer now. There's rumblin's of trouble on the horizon — but then, when ever is there not? It's certain there was some as witnessed her return that weren't so happy about it as you or I. His Majesty Grunewald has given her half his guard, until she should set her own Court fully to rights, an' ye may imagine that Ilsevel an' Tyllanthine is keepin' a close watch over her.

As fer the identity of Ilsevel's tormentor, well. Thas another question. Who was it that removed My Lady Silver from the Court? After all, anybody may wear a white cloak…

I'm minded t' think, though, tha' mayhap it ain't always the hand of the enemy at work. This white-mantled fellow might ha' done a deal o' harm — but *ultimately a deal o' good, also. A tricky business, ain't it? We shall see. I'll be keepin' a close watch on things, as I always do.*

Watch yerself on yer way out o' town, now. There's snow comin' in. If ye should fancy another tale, why, come back! Any day! Though mayhap in better weather, no?

Books By Charlotte E. English:

Tales of Aylfenhame:

Miss Landon and Aubranael
Miss Ellerby and the Ferryman
Bessie Bell and the Goblin King
Mr. Drake and My Lady Silver

The Wonder Tales:

Faerie Fruit
Gloaming

The Draykon Series:

Draykon
Lokant
Orlind
Llandry
Evastany

The Drifting Isle Chronicles:

Black Mercury

Made in the USA
Coppell, TX
06 May 2020